THE
FIRE
SEEKERS

FIRE
SEEKERS

The Babel Trilogy
BOOK ONE

RICHARD FARR

SKYSCAPE

SKYSCAPE

Published by Skyscape, New York
www.apub.com

Amazon, the Amazon logo, and Skyscape are trademarks of Amazon.com Inc. or its affiliates.

ISBN-13 (hardcover): 9781477847732
ISBN-10 (hardcover): 1477847731
ISBN-13 (paperback): 9781477825662
ISBN-10 (paperback): 1477825665

Library of Congress Control Number: 2014907841

Cover design by Will Staehle
Book design by Paul Barrett

Printed in the United States of America

For Aidan and Declan

A father may be forgiven, perhaps,
for wishing upon his sons the richest, most dazzling,
most extravagant success of all—
a life well lived.

So, like, no pressure or anything.

"Then the Architects put forth their hands, and touched our mouths, and said to us, behold, we have put our words in your mouths."
—From the so-called Akkadian Version, circa 2500 BCE.
(Compare Jeremiah 1:9)

"If this is real, then everything we thought we knew about human civilization—the origin of cities, religion, language itself—it's just frost on the windowpane."
—Morag Chen

"Nearly all crazy theories are false. That's the easy part. The hard part is that there are no interesting theories except the crazy ones that turn out to be true."
—Professor Derek Partridge

The Eastern Mediterranean and Mesopotamia

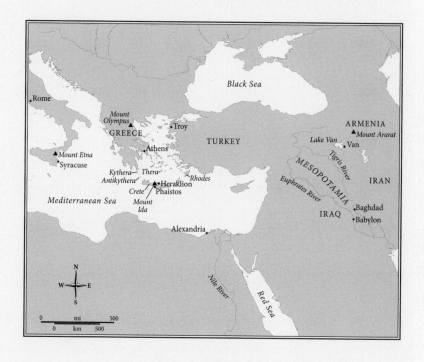

PROLOGUE
DISK MEMORY

I'm conscious of the light.

Conscious of the strong, pale-yellow sunlight that's flooding down through high windows into the big white room. Conscious also of the rare artifacts that surround me on every side: pitchers and bowls, a fresco of vaulting acrobats, a bronze bull's head so real it makes my skin crawl, a statue of a bare-breasted goddess holding snakes.

Conscious also of my father, arms crossed, watching me.

One of the world's leading experts on ancient languages: I say that, you'll know what to expect, won't you—gray beard, jacket and tie, thick glasses, plenty of dithering and muttering? But you've seen too many movies. In this seven-year-old memory, Professor William Hayden Calder is thirty-nine, looks younger. He's wearing faded jeans, red flip-flops, a T-shirt that reads "Contains Human Organs." Ray-Bans are perched in his glossy black hair. He looks like a much younger, leading-man kind of movie star.

Has the ego to match too. He made a name for himself early. Still a grad student, supposedly writing a thesis on the languages of pre-biblical Mesopotamia, when he took a "vacation" from his real research, made a bet with a pal, and in three weeks of all-nighters deciphered Rongorongo, the bizarre puzzle-script of Rapa Nui. Didn't win him a lot of friends among all the Polynesia specialists who had thrown their whole careers at the problem. Did net him a first job at Harvard; did result in a famous paper suggesting that most of the population of that isolated island disappeared mysteriously just before the Europeans showed up. Soon afterward he was the subject—I'd say victim, only he loved it—of a fannish profile in *National Geographic*:

> *Professor William Calder is perhaps the best known of the extremely rare "Babblers." Hyperpolyglots (to use the technical term) can speak perhaps eight to ten languages fluently, but Calder is a rarity even among them. He is said to be master of nearly twenty modern languages, and moving seamlessly from Finnish to Flemish to Farsi on demand is something of a professional party trick. But he is, more importantly, the world's leading authority on the languages of the ancient Near East.*

Ooh.

So yeah, unquestionably a freak. Unquestionably the go-to guy if you have an itch to scratch about the past tense in Old Elamite. But truly famous? Nah. He's head of linguistics at the University of Washington now (that's *the you-dub*, by the way, if you don't want to sound like a tourist next time you're in Seattle). A bit of a wheeler-dealer, an organizer of international conferences on the origin and extinction of languages, a man who's followed around campus by a flock of influence-horny junior profs and research assistants. Definitely an alpha chimp in his small patch of the academic jungle. But it'll be years yet—with his own research going nowhere—before he's infected, almost accidentally, by the terrible virus called fame.

We're in Heraklion, on the island of Crete, the dead center of the eastern Mediterranean. And this morning we have one of the world's great archaeology museums all to ourselves. No tourists yet, no fat pink people dragging their sticky, whining ankle-biters, because on Mondays the doors don't open to the point-and-shoot crowd until noon. *You would like us to make the collection available to you on Monday morning, Professor? Certainly. A pleasure! An honor and a pleasure to assist you in any way.* Bow, scrape, grovel. All we have for company is a young, prematurely bald custodian in an ill-fitting khaki uniform, who lurks discreetly in the farthest corner of the room.

Dad shifts, rubs his ear, looks at me again. He's trying to be patient, thinks I'm a bit slow. He thinks most of the human race is a bit slow. He's waiting for my reaction to one particular object, which stands upright in its U-shaped metal frame, separated from the end of my nose by an inch of bulletproof glass.

Ought to say something—but hey, this is the first week of my first trip to Crete, and I'm only ten, so a reddish circle of clay that looks like a bad attempt at a salad plate can't compete with a bare-breasted goddess. And even she can't compete with the thought that maybe, when we're done here, we'll stroll down to the waterfront for ice cream.

I look at him, look back at the salad plate, savor the coolness I feel as the tip of my nose brushes the glass. The sign says, Δίσκος της Φαιστού. He's already force-fed me enough Greek for that to spell itself out, letter by letter, in my mind.

Diskos tēs Phaistou.

The Phaistos Disk.

"It's been here for more than a hundred years, Daniel. All alone. Attracting crackpot theories the way a windshield attracts bugs."

"Why d'you say alone?"

"Because it's an orphan. Because nobody knows what it is, or where it's from. And because nothing else remotely like it has ever been found."

He kneels down, traces with his fingertip the swirl of little symbols on its surface: a human head with a kind of spiky headdress, a forked stick, a standing woman, an ambiguous shape that reminds me of an animal skin or a snow-angel.

Supposed to feel excited here. Trying.

"See? Thirty groups of symbols on this side. Thirty-one on the other. In a spiral, like I said."

"Found right here?"

"A site on the south side of the island. The Greeks showed up here around three thousand years ago, but before that Crete was run by the Minoans—a whole civilization that we didn't even know existed until 1900, when a guy called Arthur Evans dug them up. Then a few years later an Italian archaeologist, Luigi Pernier, found this at one of their palaces. Judging from the earth layer, it's thirty-six centuries old."

"That's like, as old as Tutankhamun. Isn't it?"

"Earlier." He kneels down and peers at me, assessing the effect of this knowledge. "No big deal, though. Just a chunk of old pottery."

"No big deal," I agree helpfully, my mind on chocolate versus vanilla.

"Except for that damned inscription, which is nothing even remotely like Minoan."

"What is it then?"

"I'd love to answer that question. Possibly early Greek. Or some other language the Minoans used. Or a form of Hittite."

"Hittite? The guys from central Turkey?"

"Well done," he says smugly.

The theory here is that I know about the Hittites because I've been a good boy and read his surprise archaeo-detective best seller, *The Great Vanishing*. There's a copy on the shelf in my bedroom at home. *For Daniel. An enigma about the past, to carry with you into the enigma of the future.* Groan. It describes the Bronze Age Collapse, a few years right around 1200 BCE when, to quote his intro, "something mysterious, swift, and extraordinarily violent visited the eastern Mediterranean."

I'm feeling a bit of a fraud. Truth is, I only ever speed-browsed the maps and the first twenty pages. But I know the stuff backward and forward anyway: I've endured hours of free lectures on the subject at the family dinner table. Fifty cities and half a dozen civilizations burned to the ground in a single human lifetime. Mass religious hysteria. Big, unexplained population declines across the region. About fifty theories about what happened too, but Dad says not one of them passes the smell test. It's kind of funny: I'm getting Bs and Cs, which troubles my overachieving mother and horrifies the alpha chimp, but at this point I've already absorbed so much talk about the nuked cities of the Bronze Age apocalypse that I can walk around their ruins in my head. An enigma, sure—but as familiar to me as my own Seattle neighborhoods.

Ice cream would be great right now. "So do you think it's Hittite? Or Minoan?"

"For all I know, it's the lost language of Atlantis. Or a code that unlocks the fairy kingdom at the center of the earth. Or graffiti left behind by five-eyed aliens from the planet Thark, which is the one just to the left of Betelgeuse. I'd like to come up with something better than that. Undeciphered languages to me are like a padlocked candy store."

"Maybe the symbols aren't a language at all," I suggest.

"Oh yes, people have tried to argue that too. It's a star chart! It's a game board! Everyone has a theory."

"Hieroglyphs?" The compulsory third-grade project on the Rosetta Stone is still fresh in my mind.

"Yes. If it's a language, then yes, certainly hieroglyphs. Too many different symbols for it to be an alphabet, and way too few for a language where each symbol is a separate concept, like Chinese. The third option is that most of the signs stand for syllables, like in Maya."

"Or Egyptian."

"Exactly."

"But you don't have a Rosetta Stone for this."

"No. Nothing to decode it with."

△

We thank the custodian, step out through the main door onto the steps, where the midday light is like a welder's torch. A family sags impatiently under the thin shade of a tree. That's when thinking about ice cream causes me to make my only contribution to unlocking the Phaistos enigma.

For me, reading is like balancing between two trees on a slackline: lots of concentration, lots of effort, never lasts long. But dyslexia has a silver lining. It forces you to think hard about patterns. To be precise, what I'm thinking about—I don't tell Dad this—are the spirals of alternating color that you get in a chocolate-vanilla soft serve.

"Course, the pattern on the Disk's not really a spiral."

"What do you mean?" he says sharply.

"Well, part of it's a spiral. But there's a mistake on one side, isn't there? And if you—"

I try to explain by drawing loops in the air with my hands. At first he tries to dismiss it: as usual, I've not been listening; as usual, I have it all wrong; why can't I concentrate? But something makes me insist. "There are two separate shapes, one inside the other."

He frowns, entertains perhaps a tiny suspicion that in my half-assed way I might be on to something, drags me back inside. "Sorry," he says in Greek. "Five more minutes?"

The young man in the uniform, who's probably doing overtime on his morning off so that they can accommodate the important visitor, looks at his watch, smoothes his nonexistent hair, offers a thin, polite smile. It cracks into a real one when Dad throws a second comment at him.

"What did you say?"

"I told him never to have children, because they're an unbelievable pain in the butt. Now show me what you mean."

Back at the Disk, I point to a place near the bottom edge where one line has a row of dots on it.

"Like beads on a string," he says. "There's one on the other side too."

"Yes, but the spiral starts at the beads. If you count from there, it's just eighteen groups. The other twelve, round the outside, they're a separate ring."

He nods as I talk. And then says something I carry around with me for years, like a lucky charm or an emergency food ration. Something to get me through the day when I feel, as I mostly do feel, like a dumb jock crash-landed among the supernerds.

"That's clever, Daniel. Very observant. Could be significant."

That's clever, Daniel.

Very observant.

Could be significant.

I want to stop and write it down, so there's no chance of forgetting it. Instead, I make an effort to stay focused, to keep sounding as interested as I'm supposed to be. "What about translating it then?"

"Not a chance, with just this one Disk—the sample's too short. Your mother wrote some clever software, we fed five hundred known languages through one of her company's supercomputers, and it spat out a neat formula that predicts how much text you need, in an unknown language, before you can decipher it. Also tells you how many symbols to expect in total. According to her formula, forty-five symbols here, on this Disk, means that the language has fifty-five to seventy symbols total. And I'd have to find two, maybe three *thousand* characters, to have a chance of translating it. That's the equivalent of a dozen Phaistos Disks."

"Perhaps there aren't any more of them."

"Oh yes there are."

The custodian is looking at his watch, looking at us, his impatience no longer concealed. Dad ignores him, crouches down, and points to one particular sign: a walking man. "Want to know the absolutely coolest and best thing about the Disk? Look closely at the repeated signs. What do you see?"

"All look the same to me."

"Not just the same, though. Identical."

"I suppose so."

"That's because the Disk wasn't written, wasn't drawn. Someone carved each of these forty-five signs as a stamp, probably in wood or bone, then pressed the stamps into the wet clay. Know what that means?"

"They were in a hurry?"

"It means we're looking at movable-type printing, invented by some forgotten mastermind three thousand years before our old friend Herr Gutenberg rediscovered the idea in Germany. Why did movable type transform early modern Europe? Because printing is mass production."

"So there have to be more Disks."

"Yes." He smiles. He loves it when other people reach his conclusions.

Δ

Yes, but.

Down at the waterfront, we find a place with a table, an umbrella, a view out across the sail-littered harbor to the old Venetian fortress. He buys us both extra large strawberry ice creams—my least favorite flavor, but the only one they have left. And describes a little technical problem.

"I'm a linguist, right? A well-known scholar, lots of friends in the Greek academic community, so the director of the museum says he would be *delighted* to assist me, oh, in *any* way! But the Greek authorities have spent decades stonewalling about one thing. I said thirty-six centuries for the Disk. But that's based solely on the archaeology, on where it was found. The fact is, we have no hard scientific evidence, because they've never allowed a laboratory to get near it."

"Why's that such a deal?"

"If I'm going to dig up half the Mediterranean looking for more of those things, I'd like to put a rumor to rest. Some people say that old Luigi Pernier, who supposedly found the Disk at Phaistos, actually just faked it. You know, drank too much *tsikoudia* one night, decided to have a little practical joke. So I need to know: Is the Disk a lone messenger from an unknown civilization, three and a half thousand years ago? Or is it just an Italian pot-digger's century-old hoax?"

"Surely they want to find out too? At the museum?"

"No, they don't. The glazing is wrong, for a Minoan artifact, so there's always been something fishy about it. I think they secretly believe the rumor. And if it's a fake, bad for the tourist industry. They'd rather have an enigma."

Mom's on a business trip—she usually is—but she manages to join us for a few days. Join me, anyway. The two of us retreat to the beach while Dad spends the time schmoozing the local politicians, making calls, filling people's wineglasses, being irritable because for once his influence is not getting him what he wants. "Dammit," he says, joining us briefly for some snorkeling. "I *will* find out how old that Disk is."

△

Over the weekend he flies to Athens, hoping to bend the ear of some bigger-league pol in the Ministry of Culture. Mom takes the opportunity to drag me to church. Dad thinks religion's a communicable mental illness, says so as often as possible, claims church services bring him out in hives, and refuses on principle to attend any, ever. Mom's not a believer either, or not in a formal way, but her attitude is completely different. Especially in a foreign country—Greece, Indonesia, Utah—she likes to act the benign, clipboard-carrying anthro. *If you're going to travel, Daniel, travel deep. Tourists want to experience the buildings, the food, the music. Why not experience what matters most to people? Why not experience how they worship?*

As always with her, there's more to it than she lets on. She's already told me about her migration from the Church of Scotland to Catholicism and back again. Tasting little chunks of Hinduism in India, Islam in Morocco, Judaism in New Jersey. A serious Buddhist phase too—staring into space for three months over a bowl of cold rice on a mountaintop in Bhutan. She accepts with good humor Dad's sarcastic take on her spirituality: *Iona, you're a shopper.* Still shopping now—so, under the disguise of Deep Travel, we walk the half mile from our hotel to the Ekklisia Agios Minas and join several hundred people in the colorful, hypnotic ritual of a Greek Orthodox service.

The smell of stone and sweat and incense.
The chanted liturgy.
The strange vestments and tall black hats of the priests.
The murmuring of the congregation, like bees.

Mom's whisper breaks in on my thoughts. "Something powerful going on here. Don't you think? A kind of performance. A kind of willing the world into existence. You know what your Uncle Jimmy would say—it's like they're carrying on the same tradition that human beings first performed around their first fires, in Africa, ten thousand centuries ago."

"Jimmy's an archaeologist, Mom. He doesn't believe any of it either."

"Don't focus on whether you believe it. Focus on how powerful it is. People think you have to believe in order to worship. Blaise Pascal said it was the other way around: you worship in order to believe."

"That's silly."

"On the contrary, it's brilliant. And"—her eyes are twinkling with humor—"he was a mathematician, so he must have been right. What your father and Jimmy don't see is that it doesn't matter whether it's true—it feeds a hunger to have the world make sense."

With my parents, random bursts of philosophizing are situation normal. I'm many steps down the intelligence scale from either of them, but smart enough to worry that I'll sound stupid if I reply, and stupid if I don't. The temptation is to say, That's what Dad wants too. A world that makes sense. Instead, I go for maximum bland: "Maybe people just. You know. Like getting together."

Mom surprises me: nods approvingly, echoes me right back. "'Maybe people just like getting together.' Yes. Could be just that. Striking, though, isn't it? That religion is so appealing to people. So *successful*?"

It's like she's peering into the future at that moment. Dad has not yet encountered a peculiarly intense, handsome, charismatic grad student named Julius Quinn. Nobody has heard of a movement called the Seraphim. And Quinn's book, *Anabasis*—not really a book, exactly, but a religious "revelation text" with an oddly cheerful, oddly appealing spin on *We'll all be dead soon*—has not yet been written.

Religion?

Successful?

Oh ye Architects, as a follower of Julius Quinn might say. She has no idea.

Δ

Dad gets back from Athens grinding his teeth, won't say what he's going to do next. What he does, is immediately visit the museum again several more times, alone. Then grinds his teeth a whole lot more when Mom admits to the church episode.

"Jesus Christ, Iona."

"I think he was part of the point, darling, yes."

"Why do you want to fill the kid's head with half-remembered Bronze Age myths?"

"I want Daniel to understand how other people think, and live. Come to that, you seem rather fond of Bronze Age myths yourself."

"I study why *other* people believed them, back in a time when it made some kind of sense to believe them. Back when religions were plausible theories, instead of exploded ones. *I* don't believe them."

He says it with a hint of real anger. My first glimpse of a small, deep crack in their relationship. They don't argue over money, over politics, over me, but they have this strangely abstract difference. He sees himself as a scientist, believes that only the physical is real. *Evidence, evidence, evidence.* She's a mathematician by training: *And you see, Daniel, like all mathematicians, I think there must be something else, powerful and ghostly and unseen, that lies beneath the surface of the physical world. Numbers are just one of several things that don't make sense otherwise. Your father studies the painting. And that's fine. But I'm interested in the canvas under the paint.*

Mom's not a mathematician now. One Friday afternoon in grad school, she worked out how you could encrypt data a million times more efficiently by using the structure of our own DNA as a matrix. (Dad's version: one Friday afternoon in grad school, *she and Dad* had the idea.) She wrote the underlying code in a weekend, trash-canned a half-finished PhD thesis ("Minds, Machines, and the Information Density Limit"—don't ask), and is now busy building "What if?" into a global monopoly.

Part of that, she's always on her way to a string of meetings, so she's headed back to Seattle via Amsterdam, London, Dallas,

Wherever. So, her last day on the island, the three of us hit a remote beach on the south coast. For several hours in a row, she manages to put Funding Criteria and Staffing Projections out of her head. Dad even manages to put the Disks out of his head. When we picnic right on the sand, they go all European on me and let me drink half a plastic mugful of wine. Between bites, Dad does normal-dad things: arm-wrestles me, does a pretty good imitation of the president, tells the sort of dirty joke that makes Mom go *Bill, really*—and teaches me to wink one eyelid without moving the other.

After that, for the whole afternoon, we're almost like a real family on a real vacation, swimming together in the crushed sapphires of the Libyan sea. At ten, I'm stronger in the water than either of them.

△

The morning after she leaves, a package arrives at our hotel by courier.

"Come take a look, Daniel. A new toy from your Uncle Jimmy and Auntie Lorna in Shanghai."

"What is it?"

"Plan B."

Slowly and carefully, he unpacks what looks like a cross between a pocket calculator and a low-budget ray gun.

"But what *is* it?"

Dad has a glint in his eye. "Archaeological dating tech has been changing fast. This was bound to happen, but Jimmy and Lorna are good with gadgets, and we've been talking about it for years. Actually lots of people have been talking about it—we just got here first." He mimes firing it at me. "*Zap.* Ten years and three months. Instant age verification."

I'm just young and stupid enough to take him seriously. "You can tell how old I am, just by pointing that?"

He cracks a smile and I know I've been had—which isn't funny, because it just confirms that he thinks I'm a lost cause. "Flesh and blood, no. This works only on old ceramics that contain radioactive impurities. But Lorna tested it on everything from a Ming dynasty vase to her own coffee mug, and it looks like she's nailed the technical issues. The tricky thing was when some yahoo tried to steal the Disk recently, and the museum put it behind that armored glass. I had to figure out exactly what kind of glass they used, get a perfect profile of its optical qualities, email Jimmy the deets."

When he slows down enough to explain what he's planning to do—when he gives me the Plan B deets—it sounds like a practical joke. A scheme, a scam, a bit of fun. I'm too naive to be horrified by the risk he's about to take. Too immature not to just enjoy being included.

Δ

He positions me in a cool spot across the street from the museum, puts a rewired TV remote in my sweating palm. Then he goes in with the crowd, disguised under stubble and a sun hat. He's even holding a guidebook, and wearing shorts, which he never does. The ray gun, or whatever, is hidden in plain sight in a camera case around his neck. Definitely Mr. Tourist this time: the sandals with white socks are a nice touch. My role, wingman in the jewelry heist, is to hang out across the street from our open-topped rental car, be inconspicuous, wait for the text that says *Go*.

Simple, in theory. The button in my hand will send an infrared signal across the street. The signal will cause an electrical spark. The spark will start a small, extremely hot fire in the front passenger footwell of the car, which is parked right outside the museum's front door. A few magnesium granules burning at over three thousand degrees on a rubber floor mat will produce a lot of thick, dark smoke, but the fire will be put out easily, after a brief fuss, and Dad will be able to emerge—after taking his measurements—and say, *So sorry, so foolish of me, must have been that leaky camping stove, I am a total idiot.*

That's in theory. In reality, let's face it, this is amateur hour: he doesn't have a clue what he's doing. I press the button on cue. Five seconds of nothing is followed by a pathetic wisp of smoke nobody except me even notices. Then there's more nothing—and I wait, eyes fixed on the front seat, not daring to blink.

More nothing.

I count to thirty, or try to. But the suspense is killer, and I'm worried that Dad's not getting his planned distraction. Trying to keep an eye on the car, I begin to cross the street. A motorcycle, honking wildly, nearly takes me out, and if my attention weren't on the car I'd probably learn the Greek for *moron*. I leap out of the way, only to be slapped sideways by the wing mirror of a swerving truck. I get my balance back, dive for safety, and arrive at the side of the car just as a second, bigger wisp of smoke turns into a small fireball. I take a step back, but then stand there, horrified, unsure what to do next. A couple of other people have stopped too, next to me.

We watch as the passenger seat catches fire. We watch as the dashboard catches fire. We watch too, slack-jawed, as smoke starts to billow out from around the wheels. I finally get my act together and take another step back just as the entire front end of the car goes up in a rush of flame like a marshmallow at a campout.

On my left, a woman with grocery bags has shuffled even closer than me to peer into the car. She's blown backward, clear off her feet, probably loses her eyebrows. I stay on my feet and rush to help her, hands outstretched. Just then, a wide strip of molten dashboard comes fluttering out of the sky and drapes itself neatly across my bare left forearm.

Cream-colored. Looks a bit like a waiter's napkin. Except that a waiter's napkin doesn't bubble and hiss.

A police officer came to school once, told us that being stabbed was not a "sharp" sensation, was more like being hit with a blunt object. The pain from the burning skin on my arm is a bit like that. Way more extreme than I could ever have imagined, but it doesn't feel like burning at all. Doesn't even feel hot. It feels as if there's an invisible major-league slugger standing next to me, in the grip of a blind rage, using all his strength to smash at my arm again and again with an invisible baseball bat.

I'd like to howl. Howling would help. But I'm distracted by the woman on the ground, who's letting out an earsplitting, machinelike squeal that reminds me of speaker feedback at a rock concert. Ought to get her out of harm's way. Given she's five foot nothing and fat as a sparrow, how hard can it be? I try to be all adult and just pick her up, but to my shame I can't do it. So without thinking, I grab her under the arms and pull. A big sticky chunk of skin rips off me like banana peel and attaches itself backward to her dress.

The pain, which is already hovering around nine out of ten, goes off the scale. Vomit, says one part of my brain, as I look down at the raw, exposed flesh. Forget everything else: just hurl. And I do. But somehow, first, just a split second before a ten-foot petal of orange flame unfurls itself across the sidewalk, I manage to get hold of her by the wrists. My whole face crinkling in the heat, I drag her into the relative safety of a doorway.

The next few minutes are chaos. Shouts. Panic. Multiple fire trucks, police cars, ambulances. An old Greek woman in a black peasant dress and headscarf, wailing and cursing about the upended concession cart that someone has just backed a truck into. The column of smoke is straight and thick, like the trunk of an old-growth Douglas fir back home. Must be visible miles away.

Inside, everyone has rushed to the windows to see what's going on. Even for adults, it turns out, the world's greatest collection of Minoan art can't compete with a burning car. Dad, who hears the initial commotion and thinks everything is going according to plan, has just enough time to whip out the ray gun gizmo and do his special bit of scientific vandalism. Three laser pulses, right through the glass case, vaporize three nearly invisible pits into the edge of the Disk itself.

Nearly invisible: I'm talking thirty microns each. Way less than the width of a human hair. A second, parallel beam sniffs like a wine connoisseur at the ancient traces in the smoke.

By the time he's done, the police are evacuating the building. Then they get zealous, and start interviewing everyone at the front door. Dad has to double back from the exit and sling his precious gadget out of a bathroom window. He comes outside to find that the car's a smoking, foam-drenched ruin, there are twenty-foot scorch marks on the outside of the museum itself, and I, along with several other people, am being tended by a medic on the sidewalk.

He has no choice but to go to the clinic with me, which takes hours. After that, he has no choice but to spend another hour telling tall stories to the police. TV cops would smell something funky right away, but this is the real world, and they swallow his lame tale with barely a murmur. Lucky that they've never heard of him, and nobody's looking for someone who just used a virtually unknown technology to commit an act of vandalism too small for the human eye to detect.

"Sorry about the arm," he remembers to say at last, as we're leaving the police station.

Yeah, really sorry.

I aim for a reply that suggests the right kind of casual toughness: "I'm fine. It's nothing." Which is stupid—I have a serious injury that hurts like hell, and I'm not fine, and it's not nothing. But he seems to feel I've let him off the hook, so he turns to more practical things. Like:

"If your mother finds out I involved you in this, she'll kill me. We'll have to make something up."

"We already did, for the police."

△

Early that evening, as the sun goes down, we walk around the museum twice, to make sure we're not being watched. Then find our way back to the little courtyard outside the bathroom window.

There's an open trash can immediately under the window. It's a charmer: underneath a hurricane of flies, there's a foot of greasy water, some plastic grocery bags, the festering remains of half a melon, and the even more festering remains of a foot-long, bloated, spectacularly dead *Rattus norvegicus*. We tip the can over, try not to breathe as the rancid slurry pours out. The rat lands on its back, as if deliberately displaying for us its burst-open guts, which sit between its cute little paws like a serving of pink scrambled egg. Next to it, nestled in a pool of gray-green slime, is the home-cobbled imager.

Ten minutes later we're sitting under a tree in Georgiadis Park, only steps from the scene of the crime. My arm throbs and itches. I try to scratch it through the bandage, which doesn't work, then try to resist scratching it, which doesn't work either. A souvenir is forming there, a scar that in the coming weeks will fade from brown to red to pink, then stubbornly remain. A permanent ghost-white line, hairless and shiny. A reminder of the day when I made my own small contribution to understanding the Minoans.

And the Architects.

And the deep, ugly truth about human civilization.

△

"That was a fiasco," Dad says, mopping at his gizmo with a beach towel. "I would have felt seriously bad if you had burned down the museum."

"If *I* had burned it down?"

"Hey, it was you who pushed the button." For a moment, until I see the infinitesimal curl of his lip, I think he's seriously planning to pin it on me. Had me again; not funny, again.

"Well? Did you get anything?"

"Working on it." He extracts a memory card, dumps the data into an app on his phone, shades the screen with one hand. Mutters to himself, grunts, then adjusts his position and leans closer.

Despite myself, I'm excited. My Uncle Jimmy and Auntie Lorna are way cooler than Dad, because they actually dig stuff up for a living, instead of just writing dull articles based on translated scribble. And now their clever device is going to reveal to us a secret about the past. What will it be? I try to wait patiently, finally can't stand it any longer. "So? Which is it—three and a half thousand years? Or only a hundred?"

He shakes his head, taps on the screen some more, frowning and looking closer.

"Didn't work?"

"Oh yes, it worked." His voice is a whisper.

"A fake, then? Bummer."

He shakes his head a bit more: "No."

"No what?"

"It's too old, Daniel."

"Too old to be a fake?"

"No."

"I don't understand."

"Me neither."

He looks up, peers into the middle distance, looks at the phone again as if unsure of what he's seen. Then he turns the screen toward me and points at a small graph. There are two bell-shaped curves, one red and one green, cut by a thin, vertical blue line. "These numbers are the uranium and thorium concentrations in the clay. We've been assuming that this thing is either a hoax by Pernier, from a hundred years ago, or else it's Minoan, from maybe 1600 BCE. These readings say, *None of the above*. It's too old to be Bronze Age at all."

"But it was found in a Minoan ruin, and you know the age of the, the uh—"

"Strata. Yes, but being able to date the different strata at the site only means we know when it was left there. These numbers say the Disk was manufactured over two thousand years before it was buried." He points to the graphs, puts his thumbnail against the blue line. "Absolute minimum age, six thousand years. And the average of these data sets is closer to seven thousand. That's not older than Tutankhamun. That's older than—"

"Stonehenge?"

"Yes." He looks at me with an expression I can't read and swipes to a screen filled with bunches of dots—a scatter graph. "More to the point, it's older than Sumerian, which is supposed to be the oldest written language. And there's another thing too. It's not Minoan. Can't be—the minerals in the clay are all wrong. It's not even from Crete."

A thrill passes through me. Or a chill. There's something new and strange about the Man Who Knows Everything being so obviously out of his comfort zone.

"What does it mean?"

A long pause before he replies. When he does, his voice is low, papery. "It means that when I woke up this morning I was an expert on the origins of language. On the origins of civilization itself. And now—" He looks at the graph on the phone again. "And now I don't know anything about anything."

He gets up and starts walking toward the park entrance, as if I'm not even there. I have to jump up and scurry to catch him.

"Where are we going now?"

Doesn't even look at me. Replies as if he's talking to himself—a habit I'll be getting used to.

"I need a beer."

Δ

We come back to Crete every year after that, for a couple of weeks or a couple of months. In the second year, we actually dig up three more Disks at a peak sanctuary (a kind of temple in a cave) in central Crete, but they only deepen the mystery, proving their age beyond doubt while making the language itself even more of an enigma.

Dad studies the hell out of the new Disks, spends a lot of late nights muttering *Why oh why oh bugger and damn won't you make sense?* then hands them over to the Greek authorities, who put them in the museum right next to the original. The following season, he hires a young, distractingly gorgeous marine archaeologist, Pandora Kallas. He wants her to search sites off the north coast, because significant chunks of Minoan civilization were swept underwater by a giant tsunami when the island of Thera, just seventy miles away, erupted in 1628 BCE. Pandora finds nothing. But she's nice to be around—except that being around her can interfere with normal breathing—and I get free diving lessons.

Increasingly, Dad shifts back to establishing a reputation in his other work, on the Mesopotamian languages of ancient Iraq. He publishes as much as ten ordinary scholars—partly with the help of his brilliant new grad student, the African American Julius Quinn. (Tall. Handsome. An actor's deep, resonant voice. Shockingly improbable blue eyes.) But there's a perception that in some deeper way, Dad's become a failure.

Doesn't exactly help that he gets ten messages a day from beady-eyed basement-dwellers who've dedicated their lives to the connection between the Phaistos Disks, the Nazca Lines, and the CIA's attempts to cover up the truth about Bigfoot. Helps even less when a snarky journalist describes him as *a once-promising scholar, whose obsession with the Phaistos Disks has left him increasingly isolated.*

Quinn's an enigma. Shows up out of nowhere, talks his way in by knowing a lot about a lot. It takes months for him to reveal even the most basic things: that he's from Chicago, that he once wanted to be a priest but gave it up, that he's a Babbler like Dad—a dozen languages or more, picked up as casually as pieces of litter.

Quinn encourages Dad to take Phaistos seriously, to keep up the fight to unlock its secrets, floats the odd and politically incorrect idea that the accelerating extinction of human languages, one of Dad's pet themes, is a *good* thing—and then goes AWOL. Dad has mixed feelings. *Disturbing guy, Julius. Clever, driven, obsessive. I liked him a lot, at first. But he's one of those people who always seems to be standing too close.*

When Quinn does show up again, it's not back at the UW but in the news. He has been hiking in Mexico. His companions have disappeared in circumstances he can't quite explain. Shortly afterward, he publishes *Anabasis* (pronounced, in his slow, beautiful drawl, *Ana-BAY-AY-siss*), which he describes as *a record of my encounter with the Architects*; announces his foundation of the Seraphim; mentions breezily that all of human culture, and human history itself, will soon, thank goodness, come to an end.

When Quinn has ten, maybe twenty thousand followers, people start calling the Seraphim "a spiritual movement." Then the numbers double. And double. And double again. Soon it's "a major new cult," and Quinn is compared to the founder of Scientology, L. Ron Hubbard. At maybe the half-million mark, the existing faiths wake up to how bad it really is: years of declining enthusiasm among the faithful seem like a small problem in the face of what has become, let's be clear, a wildly successful *new religion*. As if rubbing salt into the wound, the new casually dismisses the old: Quinn speaks of *the traditional faiths in all their muddle and weakness—above all, their sheer wrongness about our history and our destiny.* In the churches of Africa, the mosques of Indonesia, the smoky gilded temples of Myanmar and Laos—all across the globe, an exodus from the established religions turns from a trickle into a flood. And there is violence, inevitably, especially when the Seraphim exhibit a taste, a passion even, for burning other people's books. Whole libraries of books, on the grounds that *all human language is a distraction from the language that is rightfully our own, the language of the Architects.*

Quinn's followers adopt a simple uniform: the thin white scarf, like a priest's stole, with an enigmatic golden shape at one end—a sort of hollow triangle with the tip cut off. Critics try calling Quinn a huckster, a liar, a charlatan, but it's too late for that: when the Seraphim number a couple of million, worldwide, the mainstream media starts to adopt some striking phrases from his most goggle-eyed followers. He is the Savior, the Way, the Guide on the Stairway. The New Messiah.

And he says:

The Architects have returned.
We must prepare our minds for ascent.
We must not repeat the errors of the past.
The time of our greatness, the time of our freedom, the time of our immortality is at hand.

"Amazing how ignorant we were."

One of Dad's favorite lines. In his History of Science course, in front of five hundred new students, he'd intone it beneath a grainy black-and-white image of his great-great-great-grandfather, Dr. Hayden C. Calder. Greasy, badly cut nineteenth-century hair; sensible dark suit; severe expression. Graduated top of his class at the University of Pennsylvania's renowned med school in 1837. Already had a successful medical practice in 1842, when he sat motionless for fifteen minutes at a photographer's studio in Philly so that this image could be recorded on a silvered copper plate. Best education of his day—*and yet*, Dad would take great pleasure in pointing out: *This man was too early for Darwin. Too early for the idea that disease is caused by germs. Too early, even, for the idea that doctors should wash their hands. And what was ancient culture, for him? What was our deep history? The Greeks and the Romans. Before that, a vague era of cave men. Before that, Adam and Eve in the Garden. Look at him, ladies and gentlemen, look at him. A modern American! But from our point of view, he knows almost nothing!*

It was supposed to be a warning. Don't be arrogant. Don't assume the big surprises are all behind us.

Wise advice—such a pity the giver failed to take it. But I guess the innocence of childhood must come to an end, sooner or later.

For each of us.

Even for the species.

PART I:

PATAGONIA

CHAPTER 1

GIFTS

I kill the alarm, turn the bezel two clicks, shift onto my back. Above me, where my wrist should be, bright-green bioluminescent sea creatures blur and dance on the ink-black surface of the darkness. As I swim up toward them, toward full consciousness, they shimmer, sharpen, and clothe themselves in meaning.

ALT 6,900 FT / 2,103 M

Ah. Right.

A shudder runs through me as my mind breaks surface into the day. I'm not in bed. I'm not safe in bed, at home. On this, my seventeenth birthday, I'm waking up an hour before sunrise in a thousand-dollar sleeping bag that's rated to minus forty—and still isn't warm enough. The bag is strapped into an orange nylon portaledge, which is basically a tiny A-shaped tent with a metal ring at the top. And the metal ring is attached, by way of some wires and chocks, to a small crack in a giant rock face.

Beneath my bag, there's a thin sleeping mat.

Beneath that, a millimeter of ripstop nylon.

Beneath that, a big fat mile of nothing.

We're near the top of the South Tower, the jewel ... crown of Patagonia's Torres del Paine National Park. It's only 8,204 feet, so on the side of Everest it would look like a hangnail; even Mount Rainier, the fat white tent that dominates the skyline at home, is nearly twice this height. So no big deal! Except that the Torres del Paine are not mountains. They're mad, impossible-looking, finger-straight vertical screams of rock. Plus, they get blasted by hundred-mile-per-hour winds all year long. Plus, right now, they're wearing frozen armor.

Madness, some people would say. We're climbing the Torre Sur, by a new route, at the end of April—the beginning of the southern winter. It's one of the most beautiful, most thrilling, most crap-your-pants frightening challenges a climber can find, anywhere on the planet. Quite a gift!

"Daniel. Oh Daniel. Happy birthday, darling. And move it move it move it. No cake unless we make it to the top."

"Uh-huh. Wake me up again in an hour, Mom." I fluff up the bag, squirm deeper.

"No can do, sunshine. Up, now. You too, Rosko."

⚐

Giving the orders, from the next portaledge over, Iona Maclean. My mother. Your average middle-aged suburban mom, except for being glamorous, smart, and a superb Alpine climber who can now indulge her passion full time because she's done with all those business meetings, having retired (at the grand old age of thirty-six) insanely rich.

The name of her genetic encryption company is IONA. Dad insisted, because the Scottish island for which *she* was named was *also beautiful, and also a preserver of knowledge in dark times.* Within a couple of years of our first trip to Crete, IONA was backing up half the world's secure databases—zettabytes of the stuff, yottabytes, whatever. After that it became one of the hottest properties in the history of tech. Mom played coy with the big boys just long enough to give the stock price a major boner, then cashed in on a headline-making offer from Intel and gave up the eighteen-hour office days to start spending like a true professional.

But what does an *interesting* person do, with half a billion green? Bling was never Mom's style. Not sure she even owned a pair of earrings, and "glamorous" means she made the cover of some magazine (as Businesswoman of the Year) looking tousled and chic while free soloing her way up a giant redwood. She and Dad never collected other rich people. They also never bought fancy stuff just to impress the neighbors, and they never moved out of the Capitol Hill fixer that was a major budget stretch back when the main breadwinner was a specialist in stone-dead languages.

No. Indulgence for Mom meant two things. First, deciding to pull the plug at the end of my eighth grade, clear her schedule, and homeschool me. (*Good idea*, says one of my teachers. *You'll have the chance to get a real grip on those learning disabilities.* As if I drool or something.) Dad supported the idea from the start, even contributed here and there, and enjoyed taking the opportunity to say loudly and often that the American homeschool movement was *religious fundamentalism's great gift to the open-minded*.

Mom's second indulgence was adventure. For her own sake, sure, but it became an excellent excuse to make strange projects in exotic locations part of my curriculum. When she wasn't teaching me the chemistry of egg proteins in the kitchen, celestial navigation from a kayak on Puget Sound, or the physics of glaciation down a crevasse on Mount Rainier, she was dragging me around the world. She competed in the world's toughest off-road race, the Dakar rally (apprentice mechanic and chuck-wagon crew, aged thirteen: Daniel Calder). Designed and built a carbon fiber trimaran—*Maiandros*, "The Wanderer"—then used it to shred the world speed record for a sail-powered transatlantic crossing (CAD-monkey, logistics grunt, and then deckhand, aged fourteen: Daniel Calder). Bought a plane, a helicopter, and a couple of microlights to study dune formation in the Sahel (airsick student pilot, aged fifteen: Daniel Calder). In between, she created three different charitable foundations (coffee maker, web designer, spreadsheet jockey, and freelance ideas guy, right up to the present: Daniel Calder).

This Patagonia thing, in contrast, is supposed to be a combo Family Vacation and Birthday Gift. But a special email, from Jimmy Chen in Iraq, comes perfectly timed to rescue Dad from the obligation to join us:

Need you out here ASAP, Bill. It's a bloody goldmine.

The gold mine isn't literally gold, but it's a discovery so momentous that Mom knows Patagonia can't compete. She compensates for Dad's absence by turning our vacation into its own mini-expedition. Two French videographers, Édouard and Sophie Colbert, have been working for her company on another project since they moved to Seattle. When they get wind of the plan, they insist on coming too, and filming the whole thing. *Fabulous idea*, said Mom, *fabulous*—after which they seemed to be at the house every day. At first they chatter enthusiastically about climbing and adventure travel. Then they start chattering enthusiastically about Julius Quinn and the Seraphim. Sophie admits to Mom that they are "trying out" some of his "spiritual routines"—fasting, meditation, that kind of thing. And they've "unburdened" themselves by throwing away all their books. Except *Anabasis* of course.

This stuff annoys me almost as much as it would annoy Dad. I'm not like him—not an *atheist* atheist. Fact, I don't really know what I believe; kind of like it that way. So I don't have much patience for his endless arguing, but I don't have any more patience for smiley types selling New Age spiritual chewing gum. (*We're all going to be saved, saved!* I want to ask: From what?) Not sure why the Colberts are quite so stoked about Patagonia, either: it's not like they're being paid. Free travel, I guess. Anyway, they and their cameras and their irritating inner shine are here with us. Later today, there's supposed to be great footage of me grinning in hi-def color as I clamber hero-ically onto the top.

△

"I said rise and shine, boys. Now."

"Keep your hair on. We're moving."

"You've not moved an inch, Daniel Calder. Neither have you, Rosko."

"How can you tell?"

"Intuition. Common sense. Long experience."

I loosen the top cord and stick my head out. The down-shrouded pupa next to me shifts and groans.

"Scheisse! I mean shit! Ich bin so ein Idiot. Alles gut zum Geburtstag, Daniel! And why are you persuading me to come on this trip with this insane woman who says she is your mother? Good thing she is beautiful, heh? Or I would do nothing she tells me."

An impressive performance. My new best friend is even less awake than I am, but he's swearing in a mixture of German and English, wishing me a happy birthday in German, and somehow managing, in English, to be rude to my mother while simultaneously flirting with her.

Rosko Eisler: nice guy, blond Teutonic athlete-god, code geek. Also, like Dad and Quinn, a Babbler, drawn to Seattle by a pro-gram at the UW that's designed to solve what its founder modestly describes as *the deepest puzzle in the universe*.

ISOC, it's called: the Institute for the Study of the Origins of Consciousness. On the polished concrete wall in the main entrance, in expensive brushed-steel letters, there's a quotation from its founder, a reclusive Indian billionaire named Charlie Balakrishnan:

Bacteria are not conscious. But we are, and we evolved from them. So when did consciousness show up? Where did it come from? What is it? And how is it possible?

Charlie B is the founder and CEO of BalakInd, one of the biggest industrial conglomerates in the world. He has three private planes and houses by the dozen from Seattle to the Maldives. But at heart he's a thinker, a man with deep questions to answer, and instead of answering them by buying an armchair and a pile of books, his way of getting things done is to take the president of the UW to dinner, offer a vision in which the university puts all the world's best intellectual muscle into one building, and then write a check that ends in eight zeros.

Charlie, a Babbler himself, is especially interested in language. Why do we have it at all? Why so many, when most of us can speak only one? And why are some of us so good at picking up many? The pitch that goes out to others of his kind is roughly this:

Hi, linguistic overachievers! We have world-class people in computational linguistics, brain imaging, genetics, behavioral and cognitive psych, you name it. We're especially curious to know how three pounds of jellied oatmeal pulls off the trick of language, and how some people's oatmeal is so much better at it than others'. So could we pay you a lot, and give your whole family lavish relocation expenses, and put your very unusual oatmeal through our fancy new muon scanner? Give us a call.

Not many do. There aren't many out there. But ISOC has made Seattle the Babbler capital of the world. Dad. David Maynard Jones, the star Aussie philosopher/neurologist/cognitive scientist they hired to run the place. Charlie Balakrishnan himself, though almost no one's ever seen him. And a handful of imports like Rosko.

△

I zip off the rain fly and look around. To the west, over the Pacific, nothing but darkness. To the east, over the South Atlantic, a sky the color of dirty concrete. Still no telling if it's going to be a clear day or not. Somewhere off to my right, though I can't see it, there's another portaledge, surrounded by extra heavy gear bags: Édouard and Sophie with their cameras.

The only other evidence that we're not alone on the planet is a smudge of red in a narrow cleft between steep scree slopes. Two Hilleberg tents. Rosko's parents, Stefan and Gabi Eisler, will be down there now, squinting up through binoculars to see that we get the day started on schedule.

They're climbers too. Semiretired because of injuries and crumbly joints, but they jumped at the chance to come with us. "We'll be base camp," Gabi said. "Anything, to be in Patagonia, even if it does mean hanging around for days with a radio and a pot of freeze-dried chili while you have all the fun."

Stefan has a way of being so deadpan that you can't tell when he's joking: "Let me see if I understand. Two weeks in South America, after flying there first class at your mother's expense?" Long pause, furrowed brow, doesn't even crack a smile. "I can get some time off."

There's a small light hanging from a lanyard above me. I reach up, switch it on, rummage in a bag for my favorite climbing food, a cold hunk of greasy buffalo mozzarella. Fat, fat, fat: burning seven thousand calories a day in subzero air makes you crave it like a drug. As I sink my teeth in, the VHF crackles into life.

"Good morning, Daniel, can you hear me?"

Gabi Eisler's voice comes out of the handset tinny, bright, like she's imprisoned right next to the batteries inside the orange plastic casing.

"Mmm. Uh-huh. Loud and clear, Gabi."

"Happy birthday!"

"Thank you."

"I have messages. You ready?"

This is the morning ritual. For the duration of the climb, our only contact with the outside world is through Gabi, the radio, and Gabi's access to an email account run through a satellite link.

"Go ahead."

"Here is the latest from your father: 'Greetings from London, monkeys. On my way home from Iraq and glad to be breathing damp air again. Stopping off for an interview in Boston. Daniel, I'm bringing home a special surprise for you. Be safe.'"

Been with him in Iraq. Given Islam's attitude to representing the human form, I can guess at least that the "special surprise" isn't going to be a plastic figurine of some Babylonian god sitting cross-legged on top of a ziggurat. More likely, Dad has quietly pocketed an actual ancient artifact. A shard of pottery maybe. Something that he'll think is cool, and won't understand my total lack of interest in. Not clear if the surprise is supposed to be a birthday gift, either—his message, natch, omits that detail. Which I'm probably supposed to feel all neglected and upset about; it's so typical, it scarcely registers.

My friends do better. From pale, twitchy Aaron Wolff:

"'You're insane. Mostly in a good way, but right now I get vertigo and an urge to puke every time I think of you. I don't want to offer technical advice, but maybe, I dunno, use a rope? Hi to Spidermensch.'"

Spidermensch—that's a nod to Rosko's climbing skill by way of a reference to the Übermensch, or "superman," who shows up in the writings of Rosko's current Famous Philosopher I'd Most Like to Share a Bong With, nineteenth-century German bad boy Freddy Nietzsche.

There's a simple happy birthday from loud, sarcastic semi-Goth Ella Hardy. Another from shy, elegant cello whiz Julia Shubin. From Kit Cerenkov, who I just had an extremely hot dream about, and feel guilty for wanting to hear from most—nothing.

"One from Alex Bolyai," Gabi says. "I'm not sure I can pronounce it. '*Sok szerencset kivanok es boldog szulinapot*'?"

Figures. Sandor "Alex" Bolyai is a redheaded Hungarian whose clothes never quite fit. Like Julia and Ella, he's not a Babbler, but he seems to like dropping into his native language so that no one has a clue what he's talking about.

"I'm guessing that's either 'Happy birthday' or 'Bring back illegal drugs,'" Rosko mutters.

"There's also a message from David Maynard Jones," Gabi says.

"Really?"

"'Happy birthday, Daniel. Best of luck, and say hi to your mom.'"

"'Say hi to your mom'?" I say over my shoulder, by way of conveying both the message and a question.

"We've known each other for years, darling."

Mental note: it's kind of odd that I didn't know this. David Maynard Jones, known to all as Mayo, came to the UW a year or two ago to run ISOC. Nice guy, far as I can tell from a couple of three-minute conversations. But *known each other for years, darling*? Odd.

"I have one more, Daniel."

Of course you do. "From Morag."

It's not even a question. My "twin sister" would never forget the birthday we share.

Morag and I are *so* not related. She looks Chinese, because of her dad; sounds Scottish, because she learned her beautiful, musical English in Inverness; and has a brain like a supernova. But our moms were best friends, and we were born on the same day. Twin sister: that's how I think of her. I shift into a more comfortable position, reach into the food bag for a bagel, and settle down to find out what M has to say.

Gabi's voice comes over the radio again, teasing. "Sure you're ready?"

"Oh yes."

But I'm not ready for her message. Not at all.

Chapter 2

Rockfall

I have such a strong connection to Morag, such a sense of her presence and her voice, my mind translates Gabi's German accent directly into Morag's soft northeast-Scotland burr.

"'Safe safe safe D, and happy birthday.'"

(What I hear: *BURRUTH-deh*.)

"'The dig is fantastic.'"

(What I hear: *f'n-TUHH-stek*.)

"'Amazing what you can find, thirty feet under a desert. But get this: I persuaded the 'rental units that I should do my senior year with you and Iona. So they're sending me back to moss country with Bill, and I'm going to live with you guys! Aye, that's right: plane to Boston later today, and I'll be back in Seattle before you are. A conspiracy to make me normal before it's too late, but don't worry, little brother: it's already too late. Is this brilliant, or is it brilliant? See you soon. I miss you miss you miss you, xoxoxo.'"

Oh wow. Miss you miss you miss you too.

"Little brother?" Rosko says.

"Joke." (I'm six foot four. Morag's five two.) "Gabi, this is for real?"

"For real, Daniel. Lorna worked it out with your mother weeks ago, but I was sworn to silence until today. I hope you don't mind."

Mind? A slide show is already playing in my head of all the places Morag and I will go, all the things we'll do together, all the people I'll proudly introduce her to. Rosko looks at me, raises his voice so that Gabi can hear him over the radio, and speaks in English for my benefit: "Does he mind? Mutti, I'm telling you, if he grins any more his ears will fall off."

Mom has taken down her rain fly, so I can see her now in the glow of our light. She's looking pleased with herself. "Your father and I have been working on Lorna for a long time," she says. "I told her, it's getting too scary in Iraq now, with the Shia authorities taking the threat from the Seraphim so seriously. Being Jimmy and Lorna, they refused to leave, because their dig is going to put them in the history books and all that, but they did agree that Morag deserves to spend a year in a normal city, around kids her own age. And there's the Babbler program too—your father's been dropping hints about that. You are OK with it, yes? Maybe I should have discussed it with you?"

I shake my head, smile at her. Truth is, there's a mustard seed of doubt in my mind, but I keep it to myself. All my life, a week with Morag here and a month there; so rarely anything like ordinary life to share. After wanting that for so long, it's amazing to face the fact that my picture of how this will work is vague as a dream. My mind's racing. My heart's racing. What will you want to do, when you get to Seattle? Who will you like best? What will you think of Rosko? Kit? The rain? Will my life be good enough for you?

"So," Rosko says, "I get to meet the famous sister."

"We're not related," I remind him. "Not really."

Mom breaks in. "Lorna and I thought of ourselves as sisters. Then, you know, when we both managed to produce a sprog on the same day, it always seemed Daniel and Morag were bound to each other in some way. And now she'll get to experience a bit of normal life for once."

Normal life. Ha! That's what I want, yeah. But being home-schooled by Mom isn't exactly normal to start with, and with Morag, normal is just not on the radar anyway. Nobody could be normal after seventeen years with Jimmy and Lorna in Scotland, Shanghai, the Amazon, Papua, some mountains no one has heard of in the middle of the Sahara, and the Iraqi desert.

And then there's the additional fact, the big dash of hot sauce in the recipe. Morag's not just smart. Not even "just" a Babbler. She's an all-out twelve-cylinder prodigy.

"How good is she?" Rosko asks, unable to keep the competitive edge out of his voice. "At languages, I mean?"

"Grew up fluent in English, Shanghai Wu, Mandarin, and Cantonese. But that's kind of what you'd expect, in the circumstances. I don't think Jimmy and Lorna even twigged she was a Babbler until they moved to Papua."

"I don't even know what they speak there."

"About three hundred different languages. But officially, Bahasa Indonesia and Bahasa Jawa. Lorna says it took her just a couple of months to master them both. Then they discovered a previously uncontacted indigenous group in the western highlands. Extremely strange language structure. Jimmy told me he never got beyond a few phrases, but Morag was chatting away with them almost imme-diately. Since then she's learned—I don't know, honestly. I lose track. Half a dozen major European languages, couple of African ones, Arabic. Naturally I make a big deal out of the fact I know some Greek, because that's one she's embarrassed not to have picked up yet. If you dig, though, she'll admit she can get by in Basque."

"Basque?"

"It's a language isolate. Completely unrelated to any other—"

"I know what a language isolate is, Daniel."

"Yeah, well. She's interested in that. Just like Dad. Hey, if it makes you feel better, she said her Russian is crap. How did she put it? *Never do peas* or something?"

"*Ni v pizdu?*"

"Right."

Rosko puts back his head and laughs. "Ni v pizdu! That does not make me feel any better at all."

"Why?"

"Because only someone with excellent Russian would think of claiming their Russian is bad *that* way. It's an obscene slang-dialect called *mat*."

"Yo, boys!" Mom interrupts. "You have to yak and pack at the same time, or we'll get behind schedule."

"Roger that, Mom." I start lacing on my boots. Rosko puts some more effort into squeezing air out of a sleeping mat.

"What about school? I mean her academic ability?"

"You don't want to know."

"I do."

"OK. Two years old: arithmetic. Seven years old: college-level reading comprehension. Fifteen years old, published a research paper in the *Journal of Linguistic Anthropology* about tribal greeting rituals. Oh yeah, and she reads a hundred and fifty pages an hour, and never forgets anything. Jimmy and Lorna got out of China partly because she was becoming a celebrity. Just before they left, a shrink on Hong Kong TV went all drooly about her, said her brain ought to be mapped for the sake of science, and described her IQ as not measurable."

"Competition for your father."

"Oh yeah, and she knows it. She admires him like crazy, but he brings out her most ambitious side. She's already itching to make the next big discovery."

"So how does a regular dimwit like you manage to get on with her so well?"

Anyone else calls me a dimwit, I get angry—maybe because being around my family has taught me to think it's true. But Rosko can say it and I don't mind. Because he's a charmer? Because we're interested in the same stuff? Not sure. Before I have a chance to answer—before I have a chance to say, 'We both like tree climbing,' or 'I like to cook and she likes to eat what I cook,' or 'She likes bad romance novels and I like teasing her about them'—Mom hands me a loop of carabiners and interrupts.

"Morag has total intellectual self-confidence, Rosko. And not much confidence about anything else. A bit—jumpy. Daniel makes her feel safe. Apart from her parents, he's the one person she completely trusts."

Trees, food, and romance novels would have sounded better. But the light's growing stronger every minute, so I shrug and focus on closing up some Ziplocs. I'm so preoccupied with the thought of Morag being in Seattle that it shocks me to turn again, just a minute later, and see Mom staring into space. It's not the first or even the third time, this climb, that she's been distracted, not quite on form. She's hunched over a gear bag in her yellow all-in-one climbing suit, supposedly checking rope. On the surface, her bright, cheerful self, but something's off-kilter.

"Mom? You all right?"

She forces a smile. "I'm fine."

"No, you're not."

"It sounds silly, but I can't get those Bolivian women out of my head. Just a news story, nothing to do with me. But I feel this terrible, personal sense of loss. As if I knew them all." She frowns, shakes herself, passes a hand over her face like someone trying to get rid of a cobweb.

"You make it sound like they're dead. We don't know that."

"That's part of what I find so hard. I *know* they're dead. I'm certain of it. But how can I be?"

"You can't."

"I suppose you're right," she says, in a way that means, *You're wrong*.

"They were Seraphim, that's the rumor, isn't it? You and the Colberts seem drawn to that."

"Not drawn to it, Daniel. Maybe Édouard and Sophie are. I'm just curious about why it's so powerful. I spent some time talking to Julius Quinn when he was working with your father. He's a truly special individual, you know. Hypnotic. Talks a lot of nonsense, I suppose, but it doesn't surprise me in the least that—"

She stops. "As for the Bolivian thing, I truly don't know. These disappearances have bugged me in the strangest way, that's all."

Disappearances: something she's been mentioning off and on for months now, as if shyly trying to get me or Dad or anyone else interested. One day, looking for the car keys, I went into her home office and found she had devoted a small corkboard to it. A collection of notes and clippings about barely noticed stories from Japan, India, Tasmania, Iceland.

Reading the clippings was like intruding on her private space. Like snooping in a diary. But when I did ask her about it, all she would say was, *Nobody except me is connecting the dots*.

Then in March, just before we left for Patagonia, there were *those Bolivian women*. A story that left Mom visibly rattled and actually caught the rest of the world's attention for about half a minute.

Uyuni. A small, remote town on the wind-scoured Bolivian altiplano. One Sunday evening, a big group of friends meet as usual before walking to church together. But they don't arrive at the church, they're not at home when their neighbors go looking, and they don't come home.

Never mind, everyone says. *They'll show up!*

Alive and well?

Dead, in some grisly way?

No. They don't show up. Twenty-five women have just disappeared.

And there are the rumors now. About refusing confession, chanting among themselves, copies of a certain book.

△

Mom finishes cinching down a strap, looks around to see if she has forgotten anything, shakes herself. "It just feels so personal," she says. Then she glances at her watch. "Enough of that. Let's focus on the climb."

"Where are the Colberts?" I ask. "Can't see them."

She leans out on one of the ropes, craning her neck, and points. "They should be a little higher up, hidden behind that spine." She picks up the radio. "Édouard. Sophie. This is Iona. You still asleep?"

A gravelly French accent comes over the radio. "No, Iona, all packed and ready to go. We were just waiting for you to fire the starting gun. Everything good with you?"

"On our way in one minute, Édouard."

"Right behind you, then. Take it easy, give us some nice photo ops, and we'll see you at the top. May the Architects be with us."

"Yes, Édouard. May the Architects be with us. I'll take any help we can get." She says it in a way perfectly balanced between polite gratitude and skepticism.

"Oh, and I nearly forgot. Bon anniversaire to Daniel."

I try to empty my mind of everything except the climb now. Briefly we lapse into silence, taking one last look around. These giant pinnacles in their white robes are so beautiful they don't seem real— they look more like a digitized mock-up of an alien planet. To the south, the sky is wrapped in long ribbons of what might be more ice, but in fact it's high cirrus. As we watch, pale pink light soaks into it, like watery blood—and then a great orange blister erupts out of the world's east cheek and the pink-white world is turned to gold.

"OK," Mom says. "Enough sightseeing. Let's go."

Δ

For half an hour we climb fast and sure, in almost total silence.

We're good at this. Very good. Rosko's been climbing since he was six, with parents who consider the Bavarian Alps their personal jungle gym. Mom trained me on some of the nastiest rock in Scotland. Then Norway. Then most of the major peaks in the Wrangell–Saint Elias ranges, followed by a winter ascent of Denali. As for her— you don't summit Everest twice, then Kanchenjunga, and then do record-breaking solo ascents of both Nanga Parbat and Cho Oyu, without knowing which way is up. But still, the Torre Sur in winter is a huge challenge, especially when the wind starts to pick up.

It rises steadily at first, then comes at us in more irregular gusts. I'm focused on that, on staying calm and close to the wall, when Rosko shouts.

Mom is leading the pitch, maybe ten feet above Rosko. For no reason that I can make out, she stops for a few seconds, motionless as a statue with her neck craned back, then seems to shade her eyes, point, shade her eyes again. Then she shouts something down to Rosko, who shrugs as if to say, *Don't understand*. She shouts again, and this time there's urgency in it. There's a sort of flickering, then, as if the light is going out—or a shadow is passing over us.

At first I think there's something wrong with my eyes.

"What?"

Rosko looks down to me and shakes his head, puzzled. Maybe I imagined the shadow after all, or it's just the result of staring at too much sunlit ice.

I'm peering up past him, trying to figure out what she's saying.

That's when it happens.

Δ

Climbers rest. For instance, they get a good hold with one hand, adjust their bodies into a more relaxed stance, and hang one arm down. Lower the head too, a body-and-mind mini-chill before attempting the next move. Mom does something a bit like that, but it's not quite right. She's still holding on with both hands, but her whole body seems to go limp for a second, as if she's fainted. The thought flashes across my mind: She's about to fall. Then the opposite happens. She reaches up, almost lunges up, and starts climbing like a spider monkey. Brilliantly, deftly, inhumanly fast even for her—*without stopping to place any protection on the rope.*

On a wall like this, the lead climber is supposed to do only a meter or two before using a little device, usually a hex nut or a cam, to secure the rope to a crack in the rock face. That way, a couple of meters is as far as you can fall. Attach some protection, clip in the rope, only then look up and find a new hold. But Mom is ten feet up, then fifteen, twenty, far too fast for safety in any case, with free rope spooling out behind her as if she has forgotten rope exists.

It's as if she's desperately trying to get to something she's seen above her. Rosko and I both shout. She doesn't even slow down.

When she runs out of rope, forty feet above Rosko with nothing to arrest a fall, a projection in the rock face means that I can only just see her, but in the wind's intermittent lulls I can still hear that she is shouting, or calling out to someone, or something.

Then the shadow comes again, as if the air itself has darkened, and I see, for a second or two, something wholly impossible.

Above her, as if congealing out of smoke, there is a shape, which becomes a recognizably human figure. It's not on the rock, but floating above her. The image is so strange that my brain wants to dismiss it as an apparition, a hallucination, a trick of the brain or a trick of the light. But it's stubbornly there. Reaching down to her now. Coming almost into focus, as if it's about to be someone or something I can identify. And then as it touches her there's a noise like colliding freight trains.

Rockfalls happen all the time when you're climbing. You learn to read the surface for the marks they leave, and use other signs and bits of knowledge to pick a route where the danger from above is less. But you can't avoid it; that's why we wear helmets. In Alaska once, a piece came at me out of nowhere, made a noise like a gunshot as it was deflected by a small overhang, and just missed me. But this? This is like nothing within my experience.

For perhaps one full second the surface under my fingers twitches and bucks, like a machine being turned on, or an animal dreaming. *Earthquake* is the first word in my head. Cascades of ice start to come down. The figure in the smoke has gone, but the sense of a shadow persists on my retina, and my eyes hurt. Then, just as the movement stops, the top of the tower shrugs its shoulders.

It's not a rock that moves, not a boulder, even. Shaped like a wedge, it's *a piece of the mountain*. I'm still having trouble seeing clearly, but it's as if a giant with a sharp knife has cut a neat slice, just a couple of yards thick by a hundred long, from a block of cheese. The thin sheathing of white comes away and disintegrates like old tissue paper. Underneath, a thousand-ton blade of rock is in motion—enough to bisect an office building.

Δ

Does that much mass accelerate in slow motion? Or do your perceptions work in slow motion when you're confused and terrified? Not sure. But it takes forever to pick up speed. It rotates lazily. As it does so, a projecting part on the extreme edge, a knuckle the size of a couch, extends out toward us. It seems to catch her in the shoulder. Flicks her sideways off the rock with tremendous force, the way a boy might flick a plastic soldier.

I know she's dead before she begins to fall.

CHAPTER 3
BABILANI

At that moment, Dad and Morag are six and a half thousand miles due north of us. Just off a plane from London, they're hurrying through the big glass doors at a Boston TV station, where they're about to engage in half an hour of televised banter about God's anger management issues.

After years of getting nowhere with the Phaistos Disks, Dad's thrilled to be part of a real find again—even when the find's not his. Also, he's totally unable to resist a bit of publicity, and it's almost charmingly typical of him to show up for a TV interview with a teenage girl in tow, and simply bully them into including her on the program. Still knows how to hustle people. Still knows how to pull rank. Loves to pieces the idea that he's the guardian of fascinating secrets.

Δ

To understand what Dad and Morag are doing, being interviewed in Boston, you have to fly to Fallujah in Iraq, float down the Euphrates, and set your watch back thirty, thirty-five centuries.

A sophisticated irrigation system is already in place. Farms line the river. Boats loaded with dates, grains, and cattle go with you downstream. Seventy miles later, trailing your hand in the water, you look up and see the heart of ancient Babylon. Rising from the center of the largest city in the world, a huge stepped pyramid, or ziggurat—a stack of seven boxes in descending order of size. But the top smokes and glows and flashes with reflected sunlight: it looks like a volcano with a lit fuse.

A mile away, you hear drums. Then you catch the first whiff of roasting goat carcass from ritual fires that are kept burning day and night at the four corners. Now the angle shifts, and the light from the summit no longer blinds you. Grand diagonal stairways become visible, connecting each level with the next. At last, perhaps half a mile away, you pick out figures climbing one of these diagonals. That's when you get your first shocking sense of the scale.

The ziggurat is exactly ninety meters on a side, and ninety meters tall. Not big by our standards, but unequaled in its time: a man-made mountain. A structure you could model out of three or four hundred Lego blocks, if each block was a midsized suburban house.

Now the crowds at the base come into focus, people swarming like insects. At the same time you make sense of that earlier smoke and light. On the summit, there's a golden structure, a temple maybe, reflecting the sun's rays. And on the temple roof, in a deep stone bowl the size of a truck, a great smoky fire is burning.

What's going on?

There are three different stories about this place. Three approved versions of the truth. A modern, dull, scientific, sensible one, and two others that are old, exciting, religious, and crazy. But as Dad-the-scientist likes to say, *Weird stories don't come from nowhere.*

The earliest story belongs to the people who built this place. Babilani, they call it—"the gateway of the gods." The priests, with their shaved heads and hidden bronze daggers and robes the color of oxblood, will explain that in terms any sci-fi nerd can understand. It's the place for the local god Marduk to occupy, when visiting his puny creations; it's the portal—the transporter room, if you like— through which he steps out from heaven, and through which in turn the favored few, those who are acceptable to him, ascend into the heavenly, immaterial dimension, escaping forever the world of meat and mud.

A thousand years later, Jewish writers in exile here will come up with an even grander theory, the book of Genesis. According to them, the original structure on the site, already destroyed in their time, was literally *where civilization began*. We were seminomadic herders, careless wanderers in the East, when God (they believed in only one) dropped by and favored us with the gift of Divine Language. At last we could communicate with all people, and with Him. But we were not satisfied with divine face time. We settled down permanently, built our first ever city, and instead of worshipping or thanking God, we decided to rival Him, by building a tower that would reach right up to heaven. God became angry: he destroyed the tower, scattered us over the face of the earth, and *confused our tongues* so that we could never do it again. Then the ziggurat was rebuilt—not to challenge the heavens, or transport worthy souls cloudside, but to beg for God's forgiveness.

The Genesis version explains a lot, or it's intended to: everything from the existence of nations, religions, and racial hatred to the lists of French irregular verbs lurking in my homework. Six thousand languages: no wonder we don't make sense to each other. And hey, here's a joke to lighten up the slaughter: those Jewish writers noticed that the placename *Babilani* is close to the Hebrew verb *bal-al*, which means "to confuse." So over time it became Babel, "the place of confusion." Funny funny funny—except that it turns out the joke is on us.

OK, but I digress: here's the modern, sensible story. According to the scientific historians, the linguists and archaeologists—Dad, Jimmy, and Lorna, for starters—both the heavenly gateway and the outraged God are, to use a technical term, a crock of shit. Myths. Bedtime stories for the ignorant. *Of course* there was no such thing as ascent into heaven from some theological launchpad. *Of course* there was no Divine Language, and *of course* the staggering diversity of human languages isn't to be explained by a heavenly act of tongue-shredding. Get a grip, people! The great ziggurat was, like the dozens of other ziggurats in the region, simply a place of worship. A church, if you like. It was made from mud bricks, so eventually it collapsed. It was repaired, and collapsed again. It was even destroyed by invaders more than once, rebuilt from scratch more than once. In the end, a ruin; in the end, not rebuilt.

Whichever story you favor, there's not much left. Mud. Weeds. Brick dust. With not a shred of evidence for what truly happened. Or so several generations of archaeologists believed.

Jimmy and Lorna do love their gadgets!

We visited the Chens last year, when they decided to take a fresh look at Babylon. I remember my ruddy-faced, sandy-haired Scots auntie explaining it all. They had found nothing, at that point. It was just an idea, just a technique they were testing on some known features:

D'ye see, no? The substructures are less dense than the mud, by just a wee hair mind, because of the air pockets, and they draw down the surface moisture at a different rate. Right about dawn, even here in the desert, there's dew. A smidgin o' dampness. So I sets a camera to maximum contrast, couple it to the side-impact radar and the GPS. Jimmy attaches the whole gubbins to a tethered balloon, and a thousand feet up we go clickety-click-click! There's not much for the eyes, mind. But ye run the data through this software, which by the way

some of Iona's boys in Seattle put together for us, and bingo! See that
square? It's a storeroom. Ten meters down, completely invisible, but on
this enhanced image it sticks out like pee in the snow.

△

Ten days before we're due to leave for Patagonia, Dad gets the big
message from Jimmy. "Listen to this," Dad says. "'We've found the
library, and it's incredible. Buried much deeper than we expected,
and most of the tablets aren't in Babylonian even, but older languages like Akkadian. Superbly preserved too—like Nineveh, only
better. We need you out here ASAP, Bill. It's a bloody goldmine.'"

That night I make my special pasta carbonara. You fry fresh
rosemary in olive oil, with a pinch of salt and insane amounts of
finely chopped garlic. Add a little chopped pancetta, then make the
sauce by adding a pint of whole milk and curdling it with a table-
spoon of vinegar. Boil it down for ten minutes, and mix in a couple
of beaten eggs right at the end. Sprinkle on some finely shaved fresh
parmesan—never the pre-grated stuff—and coarsely ground black
pepper. Good stuff. When I ask Dad the significance of Nineveh, he's
so excited that he can't stop talking even with long thin worms of
sauce-flecked spaghettini burrowing greedily into his mouth.

"Ashurbanipal. Assyrian king, bit of a scholar. Had a big library
in his palace at Nineveh, in what's now northern Iraq. The whole city
was sacked and burned in 612 BCE, might as well have disappeared
forever. Fast-forward a couple of dozen centuries. In the 1840s, a Brit
called Austen Henry Layard dug it up. What you'd expect is rubble,
right? Dust? But the library preserved itself by burning. Luckily for
us, the Mesopotamians never invented paper—they wrote only on
clay tablets. Even clay would have crumbled over centuries, but the
heat acted like a kiln, baked the stuff rock hard. It's an effect I've seen
in several places. Anyway, Layard was able to send shiploads of them
back to the British Museum in London."

"Where they sat gathering cobwebs until you found them?"

"No no. Layard knew this brilliant young language specialist, George Smith—"

Mom's turn to tease. "Surely not as brilliant as you, darling?"

Dad doesn't break stride. "Obviously not as brilliant as me, no. But close. Smith started translating this stuff, and one afternoon he found himself reading the story of Noah and the Flood. Only it wasn't Noah. In the Nineveh tablets, the dude with the epic storm forecast and the floating zoo was named Utnapishtim. And the Flood was being threatened not by just one angry god in a genocidal rage, but a whole committee of them."

By this point in the conversation, I'm waving my hands back and forth like an air traffic controller. "Wait. Slow down. You're saying this story was sort of an early draft of Noah and the Flood?"

"Centuries early. But even that wasn't the *first* draft. Turned out there were half a dozen even older sources, each one with its own watery apocalypse and its own reluctant ferry captain. The version Smith discovered was part of the Epic of Gilgamesh. It totally appalled the Victorians. Forced them to consider the idea that the book of Genesis, the supposed Word of God and all that, was just, you know, a yarn. Cobbled together from a whole tradition of much earlier yarns."

Dad and the Chens are all familiar with this stuff. Mom is the odd one out, and she likes to tease them by talking as if ancient history is just a cute hobby—the sort of thing smart people do to entertain themselves if they don't have real work, such as running a global corporation. "So," she says, smiling indulgently, "you think the Chens have just found you a new Epic of Gilgamesh, lying there in the desert? And since your work on Crete is still going nowhere, this will be your next big thing. Naturally you have to drop everything, in the service of knowledge, ignore your family, and go to Iraq."

He takes a swig from his glass, lobs a fragment of my special crusty Italian loaf into his mouth. He knows she's only teasing, but still he spends a few half sentences stumbling around trying to defend himself. "If the tablets are as well preserved, and even older than Nineveh—I mean, if this *is* the library of Babel—I mean, there's no telling what we might find."

He chews, swallows, falls silent. Then he gestures through the doorway at the obstacle course of tents, crates, boots, and climbing gear in the living room. Tries, and completely fails, to disguise a smirk. "Sorry I won't be able to come with you. No Patagonia for the wicked."

Truth is, I'm jealous about him going to Iraq. Not that I'd miss Patagonia for anything. And not that I'm under any illusions about archaeological digs in Iraq, either. A hundred and twenty in the shade, dust like glass powder everywhere, camel spiders the size of rats. But I want to share in Jimmy and Lorna's glory, see history being uncovered, see Morag again.

"My love, your disappointment is heartrending," Mom says drily over the top of her wineglass. "Let's face it: you don't climb, you hate the cold, and you'd sooner have a root canal than sit in a tent making polite conversation with the Eislers about the current state of the medical-database industry. Go to Iraq. Give Lorna and Jimmy big hugs from me. And dig up your Akkadian tablets. I hope they don't all turn out to be tax records or Little League scores."

He's on the next plane.

⚠

As we pack up and leave for Chile, I get a clear picture of life at the Chens' desert camp by way of cheerful daily texts from Morag, who has so much more in common with Dad than I do:

> *Bill's taken over the largest tent. Sleeps all morning, when it's cool and he should be working. Then works all afternoon, when everyone else is trying to nap.*

Already brought several hundred tablets to the surface. Yesterday he was grumbling about the way we cataloged them. The way I cataloged them, actually. So I took him for a walk in the moonlight and spent an hour explaining to him why my cataloging system is just fine.

The tablets are in every language ever committed to writing in Mesopotamia—plus a few scripts even Bill can't identify, which means no one on the planet has ever seen them before.

We've established a rule: we talk to each other in a different language every day. Spanish yesterday, German today, Russian tomorrow.

Having admitted defeat on the cataloging, Bill is now saying Lorna's all wrong about the site stratigraphy. Er, hello? Who is the archaeologist here?

Deeply impressed. Never seen a human being drink this much coffee before.

Most of the tablets are in Old Akkadian. We think this thing was written continuously from 2500 to around 1600 BCE.

Every day I force him to answer at least one question about Akkadian grammar. I'm beginning to get the hang of the cuneiform writing system. Complicated as hell. Looks more like a carpet pattern than anything you could read. But it's logical, and you know I have a soft spot for logical.

Now he's taken to sitting up all night, scribbling in longhand while having these long, angry arguments with himself out loud. Like a cute version of Gollum. Progress? Despair? Impending madness?

I feel sorry for the Chens: dealing with him during a work binge is even worse than she makes it sound. At times like this he's capable of neither small talk nor large talk, he's demanding and rude, he doesn't tell anyone anything. I saw it in Greece, when we found the three additional Disks. A kind of frenzy: bad enough when fueled by hope, worse when our discovery only made the Phaistos puzzle even more maddeningly intractable. But each of Morag's messages brings a twinge of jealousy too, and I don't even know whether it's because she has abilities that make her close to him, or the other way around.

I ask her how Jimmy and Lorna are taking it.

I don't think it's any big surprise. Just ignoring it, getting on with their stuff. Measuring, surveying, dumping data into spreadsheets. What we archaeologists do.

I tell her I don't know why they put up with him.

Because we adore him, D.

No, M: Jimmy and Lorna admire him, love him even—as you love an annoying family member who has the redeeming quality of never being dull. It's you who adores him. It's you who wants to *be* him. Maybe, M, you should take a closer look at what happens when a brilliant person with loads of ideas and enthusiasm sprints into a brick wall.

I don't actually say any of this.

Finally, just as we finish our long drive from Punta Arenas to the foot of the Torres del Paine, all eager for the climb, the patience of the Chens is rewarded. Morag again:

Scene of triumph, D. Imagine this. Bill hasn't smiled in days, but this afternoon he pops up in the middle of camp, scruffy as hell, eyes twinkling like a Christmas tree in a storm.

Lorna: Is it good news then?
Bill: Oh I think so.
Lorna: What do we have then? Not just dates and names I hope.
Bill: What we have, Lorna, is one of the most important archaeo-
logical discoveries of all time.

And he hands her something that we, the archaeologists,
completely missed. Something impossible, D. It's a fragment only,
curved at one side, looks like a chunk ripped off a pizza. But there's
no question at all. It's part of a Disk.

WTF?

Excuse me, but *W? T? F?*

Even coming from Morag, I don't believe it. Even when I see she's
attached three photos, I don't believe it. When Dad lets his university
contacts know, they believe it even less—and yet they do believe, sort
of, because there it is in front of their eyes, and a slice of pizza it's
not. They're so shocked—*gob-smacked*, Lorna would say—that even
though they can't say anything coherent, they can't resist making the
whole thing public anyway. Suddenly everyone wants an interview.
Dad, who loves the sound of his own voice around the dinner table
but loves it a whole lot more on the idiot box, can't resist.

And thus, Boston.

"So, Professor, correct me if I have this wrong, but I understood
from our phone conversation that you have found the library at the
Tower of Babel? And in this library you discovered"—he ruffles his
notes—"an artifact that simply should not be there?"

Chapter 4
A Body Is a Body

The rock punches Mom sideways into space, then her body drops like a sack, accelerating down into the gap between us. One outflung arm smacks so hard into my shoulder and neck that for a moment I think the impact has broken my collarbone.

There are two metal cams in a thin crack just above Rosko—the last piece of safety she placed before that final, sprinting climb. When she has fallen another forty feet, and runs out of rope, they should stop her. But the fall is too long, the force too great: they rip out of the wall, one after the other, like corks from a bottle.

I expect Rosko to scream, or cling to the rock. *Nein!*—the same futile response in every language, when death jumps up out of nowhere, and stares you in the face, and you hope to frighten it away. Perhaps there's just no time to react, but it's eerie, the way he says and does nothing. The rope falls over his right shoulder, sits there harmless for a split second, and then wrenches him backward. As he pivots sideways, feet still against the rock, I get a clear view of his face. He looks perfectly relaxed. And then I can't see his face anymore, and he is falling past me too, headfirst.

I'm last in line. I've been working my way along a row of narrow bumps—*footholds* seems like an exaggeration. As if from a great distance, I see Mom still falling, Rosko falling, and the rope arcing down beside me. Then the arc passes me, lengthens, and goes as tight as a violin string.

I look down, straight past my left heel, just in time to see Rosko stopped, whiplashed backward, and slammed into the rock. He bounces off, twirls crazily for a few seconds like a plastic doll, then is picked up by the wind and smacked into the wall again.

Just above me, the last anchor holds firm. And a vicious gust of air seems to come from above, hot, like opening the door to an oven, stinging my eyes.

△

That's what I remember, anyway. I don't remember much, because I enter a sort of dream-state after that.

I shout. I shout until I'm hoarse, but I can't even tell if Rosko is alive. So instead I look up, again: hands up in front of my face, knuckles white around the rope, as if in prayer. My whole attention is focused on the small, spring-loaded metal device that's wedged into the rock above me.

It's a standard offset cam, just like the ones that failed. A mass-produced chunk of basic climbing gear that sets you back seventy, eighty bucks at the climbing supply store. I look lovingly at each tiny detail of its construction, its shape, the slight texturing of the aluminum. Something in me wants to just stare and stare at it. As if maybe staring will hold it in place. It's the only thing between me and a long vertical good-bye.

I'm beginning to shake—shock wanting to take me over. So I tear my eyes away from the cam, try not to think, and start moving.

Fast. It takes only a minute or two to get down to a position just above Rosko. He's dangling at the top of a slight overhang, so the rock slopes outward below him and his body is resting against it. It's obvious he has severe injuries: apart from anything else, his right leg is at an impossible angle.

Working my way down a couple more feet, I look over the edge. Because of the overhang, Mom's body is turning lazily in space, like a mobile above a baby's crib. She's three, four feet out from the wall. While I'm looking down at her, Rosko regains consciousness. Delirious with pain, he starts to utter a high, blood-freezing wail that sounds less like a human being asking for help than a horribly damaged animal asking to be put out of its misery.

"Rosko? It's OK. You're OK. I'm going to move you in just a minute, OK? Just hang in there. Hang in there."

Doubt he even hears me—and anyway it's for my benefit, not his. I'm trying to work something out. Should be able to make a series of loops, create a sort of sling, and slowly hoist him to a marginally safer place. OK, let's try that.

I tie it wrong, twice, before getting it right.

Good. Progress. But the rope he's on is bearing three hundred pounds—the weight of two bodies. And although I strain and strain, it's impossible to shift him.

Is there another way? Is there something I've missed?

Think now.

Think.

I must move him soon, in case I run out of strength or the last cam fails. I can't move him without first moving Mom. But there's no way to do that. So there is only one way to save him.

"You're doing good, OK? You're doing fine. With you in a sec." I curse when I hear how unconvincing I sound. Looking down, I hesitate.

Surely, surely this can't be right? There must be another way.

But there is no other way.

I am going to have to cut the rope.

△

Then I hear her. I hear her voice.

It doesn't sound like her voice coming up from below, where her body is. It doesn't sound like her voice inside my head. It's not a voice from a dream, or a memory of the way she sounded, or a freak effect of the wind. No. It's her voice. Right next to me. Speaking to me:

Not complicated, this one, is it Daniel? The issue here is Rosko, who you can still save. A body is a body. Without consciousness, we are pieces of meat. Nothing to discuss.

OK.

A body is a body. Without consciousness—

If this is a hallucination, it's totally convincing and wonderfully comforting and terrifying, all at the same time. I stare in puzzled silence at the empty air next to me, where the words came from, repeating the sound of them over and over in my head, waiting for more. But there's nothing. With an effort I tear myself away, steel myself, shift down another foot, reach down with the knife.

I try to slice through the rope, but the angle is bad. I'm bent sideways, have to use my left hand, am terrified of slipping, or dropping the knife, can't get good leverage. There's a vicious ache in my side, somewhere between my kidney and the top of my hip. Plus I'm looking down at Mom, and at the pretty, sugar-dusted gravel just beneath her, and part of my brain knows that the pretty, sugary gravel is in fact a field of snow-covered boulders a mile away.

A body is a body.

Not complicated.

Without consciousness—

I hack and saw for two, three minutes, gasping. I badly rip a thumbnail when it catches on the rock. Three-quarters of the way through now, but obstinate strands refuse to give.

"Come on, you bastard," I shout. It doesn't help that I can't see clearly because scalding salt tears are erupting out of my eyes. I wipe at them with the back of my hand, then reach down again.

At last, with one last pull on the knife, I feel the tension go. And hang there, mesmerized.

She's not facing me—that would be worse; her head is canted over to one side, as if she's lazily admiring the view. And it doesn't look like she's falling. Instead she appears to shrink, faster and faster: to the size of a child, a doll, an insect.

It's only seconds from there to the vanishing point. When my eyes are no longer sure whether they can pick out the evaporating dot of yellow from the background, I turn away, pressing my face into the cold surface of the rock, willing my mind to empty. Even if I can't see the moment of impact, I don't want to be looking.

$$\triangle$$

There's a pathetically narrow ledge not far from our night's bivouac. It takes most of a precarious, exhausting hour to get Rosko back to it, and he screams every time I move him. At one point I slip, and it scares me so badly that I have to stop for perhaps a full minute, hanging on and breathing deep, just to avoid throwing up all over both of us. A few moves later it happens again; this time I fall, and for a split second I know for certain that we're both going to die. Instead, somehow, I whirl my left wrist around the slithering rope and jam my scrabbling right foot onto a small protruding knob. I jar my knee so badly that it feels like someone has driven a chisel into the joint, and at first I think I've torn the ligaments beyond use. Once I get a foothold on the other side, I tell myself to stop again, hold still, and take five deep breaths—but at breath number three my left leg, taking all the weight, begins to jackhammer and fail.

Out of the corner of my eye I see, like a half glass of water in the desert, an old metal piton sticking out of the rock, evidence that some long-gone climber did at least cross this route. Hail Mary—last chance. I lunge wildly at it, not expecting that I can even reach, but I manage to wrap my index and middle fingers around it. As I haul upward, the corroded metal slices through my glove and takes my middle finger down to the bone. Funny, almost: *this* pain feels like fire, like my whole arm is ablaze. A second later, blood starts to leak out of the glove at the wrist and splatter down into my eyes.

The sensation is like a dentist ramming a high-speed drill into raw nerve. But I know that if I think about it, give in to it, I'll fall. Somehow I clamber back up. When I secure myself enough to ease off the glove, I'm shaking so much that the sticky mass of fabric jumps from my grip like an injured crab and tumbles away into space.

Slow, agonizing progress after that. I talk, shout, yell to all the parts of my body that are variously in pain, or going numb, telling them to just *shut up and work goddammit work and I'll look after you later.* I'm breathing so hard, sucking in so hungrily, that the freezing air feels like a blowtorch in my throat. When we get to the ledge, I work at an intense, feverish pace to secure Rosko to the rock, and despite the cold, there's sweat pouring off me.

At last I hoist myself up next to his side, remove and secure my pack. We're safe—sort of. I'm carrying a lightweight emergency sleeping bag, but there's no way I can get him into it, and who knows how much more damage I'll do to him if I try. So I secure him some more, bunch the bag around him, and stuff him with as much oxycodone as I dare. Then I find some gauze in the first aid bag, wrap it around my frozen, gore-encrusted hand.

My mind is so full—so empty? I don't even know which it is— that I almost don't notice the VHF radio on his belt. Then it dawns on me: Mom had one, and he had the spare, but the spare is switched off to save batteries. I turn it on, and nearly drop it when it immediately crackles in my hand.

"Daniel? Are you all right?"

"Yes."

"Why didn't you answer?" Stefan's voice seems to come from far away, as if English is a language that I once knew but have forgotten. It's difficult to construct a reply.

"I did answer. I didn't. Not. It was a. It was because. Because—"

I stop talking, take those two neglected deep breaths, decide not to explain that I've been too busy for the concept of a radio to even occur to me.

"What's your status?"

"Mom's dead. Rosko's badly injured."

"What about you?"

A moment seven years ago in Crete comes back to me.

"I'm fine."

"OK, good. You've got to hang on. The rock just missed Édouard and Sophie, and they're heading across to you now, but it's going to take a long time. The rockfall opened up a big fissure between their position and yours, with lots of loose stuff. They may have to go down a long way and then back up."

△

The cold is savage and terrible, won't leave me alone. The pain in my damaged knee and hand is like an earsplitting two-tone siren that I can't turn off. I think: How will I endure this? And yet I don't have to. Mercifully, after a period of time that might be five minutes or an hour, these bodily sensations begin to recede, my mind begins to empty. There's a change in the quality of my fear too, or at least my attitude to the fear: it's like I'm moving outside of it, holding it in my hands, examining it instead of experiencing it.

Is this what death feels like? If so, it's not so bad.

I let the fear go. What's left inside my head is a kind of miniature theater, all white, with random experiences passing across it like moths:

It's summer. I'm five years old, and Mom is lifting a bucket of blackberries toward me at an old farm on the Skagit River.

On that first trip to Crete, we're sitting outside at a village restaurant, and Dad is showing off his Greek for the benefit of the owner. The exact flavor and texture of a chunk of oily white fish are inextricably linked with the sound of a motorcycle in the distance and the sight of the golden oil as it slides and glistens on a pale blue plate.

Mom is at the wheel of Maiandros, in orange storm gear, somewhere in the mid-Atlantic. She catches my eye, flashes her brilliant smile, and as we crash through a wave she hoots—Wooh!—framed by a rainbow of spray.

Kit Cerenkov is lying on the floor of my room, in running gear, doing leg lifts and complaining about her math homework. I'm sitting in the window seat, trying not to look at her, because seeing her thigh muscles flex completely short-circuits my ability to focus on what she's saying, which probably means I'm just a testosterone-driven Neanderthal who doesn't deserve her anyway.

I'm brought back to the present by the fizzing squawk of the radio. Stefan checking in. My hands are almost completely numb from the wrists down, might as well be fakes made from rubber; it takes me a minute to figure out how to press the "Talk" button on the VHF.

"Sorry, Stefan, cold making me clumsy."

"Are you well secured?"

By any ordinary standard, Stefan, you bet your ass.

I have no recollection of doing it, none, but a brief inspection shows that I tied us into four separate support points and doubled all the knots. It still doesn't feel like enough. I've never felt so exposed on a climb as I do now, so aware of the yawning empty space below us, so aware of gravity's insatiable appetite.

I try to reassure him about Rosko, but I keep it short, both because I'm having trouble with words and because basically I'm lying. Rosko is completely unresponsive again, breathing raggedly, icy to the touch, and his helmet is cracked down the middle like an egg. I don't need medical training to see that he should be in a hospital operating theater, right now.

"I think he'll be OK," I say feebly. "I think he'll be OK."

Reluctantly, and with great difficulty, I take off my own climbing jacket and wrap that around him too. Then I stuff my useless hands into my armpits, huddle into a ball to preserve some warmth, and although the wind is like knives in my back, I'm soon drifting again.

It's like I'm the one who's been drugged. It's like my own body is flooding itself with some powerful homemade narcotic. I get to a point where it's obvious, and just a dull matter of fact, that Rosko is within minutes of dying, and that I will quickly follow.

"Daniel! Rosko! Can you hear me?"

When Sophie Colbert reaches us, the sun is still well up in the sky. But we've been on the ledge for six or seven hours, we're in shadow, and I'm so hypothermic that when they reach us a few minutes later I can neither talk nor move. Someone gets a jacket onto me and feeds me lukewarm liquid through a straw, then asks a lot of questions that I may or may not be answering intelligibly. At one point I think that they've dropped me, that I'm falling. I don't even care.

Somehow they get us both off the mountain. A chopper arrives and is unbearably noisy. After an airlift to the hospital in Punta Arenas, I see four people rushing a gurney down a corridor. They look like an Olympic bobsled team, about to jump aboard. There's something comical about it until I realize that Rosko is already on the bobsled. I'm just conscious enough to think: They're hurrying. So he's not dead.

Two nurses poke me, examine me, feed me more hot liquids, lower me into a cocoon of heated blankets. No idea what time it is, but it's dark outside by the time they hook me up to an IV full of drugs. I'm so exhausted that I would be asleep in minutes even without any chemical assistance, but I must be alert enough to know that something's in my system, because I can feel the way—quite different from ordinary tiredness—that the edges of my attention start to blur and fray. I'm also alert enough, despite the blurring, to hear what the nurses say to each other as they leave the room.

"¿Viste el noticiero vespertino? Dicen que más de treinta."

"¿Dónde?"

"En unas montañas de Nueva Zelanda."

"¿Treinta personas?"

"Sí. Así nomás, ¡desaparecieron!"

Never studied Spanish, but I must have gotten a few shreds of it from somewhere: *News. More than thirty. Mountains in New Zealand.* As I slip down into nothingness, the word *desaparecieron* sends an adrenaline chill through my veins.

Disappeared.

Right after that, like a fall through thin ice on a lake, I crash through the membrane of unconsciousness and carry on down, down, down into nightmare.

CHAPTER 5
INTO THE PLAIN OF SHINAR

A dark shape that seems tireless and fast is chasing me over moonlit dunes. A predator. It has been closing on me for miles. The landscape would be beautiful, but there's no end to it, no exit, and I am nearing the point of collapse. When I'm forced to stop and gasp for air, I glance back, gauging how much the distance has closed, trying to work out who or what it is.

The quality of the dream turns from stress and panic to a deeper kind of terror when eventually I get it: what's chasing me is like the smoky figure I saw hovering above Mom. Still can't identify it though. It's tall, and menacing, with a dark glow, if that makes any sense.

We're on a sharp ridge now. On my left, the steep face of the dune is silvered with light. On my right, dark gray fades rapidly to black. I plunge onward, and my chest feels as if a giant's hands are wringing it like a sponge. The figure closes to perhaps only fifty feet behind me. In a last, desperate bid for freedom, I launch myself down the silvery side of the dune, glancing back to see if it follows. It stops on the ridge, and the moon catches its face.

The thing looks down on me with the cold hostility of a hunter watching its prey.

I can identify it now. Oh yes.

It's my own double.

My *self*.

I turn again and fling my body farther down the slope. But the soft sand grabs at my shins, trapping me. As I fight the sand, looking frantically around, the figure comes down behind me, more leisurely now because more certain, and its motion causes the sand to avalanche. The soft flow imprisons me, burying me to my waist, then my chest, then my neck. I'm swimming, struggling, twisted around enough to see the dark silhouette immediately above and behind me. It takes another step, deliberately kicking up sand. Then, in a voice that's surprisingly mild, friendly even, it speaks to me in lilting warm words I cannot understand. And smiles. I have time for one last gulp of air before the warm rush of grains cascades against my cheek, flows up over my face and eyes, buries me.

As I begin the final helpless struggle against the instinct to breathe again, as I try to come to terms with the idea that seconds from now my *self* will be extinguished forever, I perceive in my mind's eye what I had not noticed before. The figure above me on the dune is not quite my double after all. Not a mirror image or a clone. Hard to describe, but it's kind of a perfected version of me; taller, better looking, a kind of original from which I might be the photocopy.

That face puts me back on the mountain, at the extremity of my cold, my fear, my conviction that I am about to die. And then Mom's voice is with me again. Fuzzed with static now, weaker, farther away. And not comforting, but crying out.

Help me Daniel help me Daniel help me.

△

I wake up in the dark, clammy and breathless, heart hammering. After the initial shock, I sit for a long time in the unfamiliar hospital room, listening to the traffic. I feel like an insomniac, like sleep will never happen again, like I will sit here, with the dream and the climb looping around in my mind, forever. But as gray predawn light starts to soak in through the blinds, a wave of tiredness surprises me. I lie back down, pull the blankets tight around me, fall back into real sleep. And, as if in compensation for the nightmare, I have a second dream that's not really a dream because it's almost pure memory.

It's four months ago, the Sunday after last Thanksgiving, and I'm in serious pain two-thirds of the way around my first-ever marathon. Headed up Lake Washington Boulevard, wind-driven rain in my face, I feel as if it's totally plausible that my legs will simply break off. The eighteenth mile alone is ten miles long. When I see the new Russian girl handing out Gatorade at mile nineteen, I'm intrigued—and flooded with relief by the excuse to stop. So I glance at my watch, decide to allow my legs a full sixty-second vacation, and take the cup of Gatorade she's holding out.

"Yekaterina Cerenkov? I get that right?"

Her eyebrows arch. "Everyone call me Kit. Is easier."

"My name's Daniel. I don't go to a regular school, but Julia Shubin's a friend and she sent me a picture of her with you and Ella Hardy. So, uh, I recognized you."

"Yes," she drawls. "Julia mentions you last week also, first day I am at school. Mentions you about three time I think. 'Such nice guy,' she says. 'Travels all the time.' Maybe she fancy you?"

"Oh no," I say, too quickly. "We're just friends. I'm homeschooled, so, uh—"

"Your mother teach you at home, yes, she explain that. Interesting crazy American idea. Son of big languages professor, yes? William Calder? See my mother over there? Natazscha Cerenkov. She is working also at university."

She gestures to a knot of people huddled under an awning twenty or thirty feet away. One is a middle-aged version of Kit—shorter, broader, with exactly the same mouth, the hair in a sensible knot.

"Another linguist?"

"Genetics. This program on brain. Where language comes from, what is consciousness. Australian guy, yes? David something?"

"David Maynard Jones. But everyone calls him Mayo. Your mother's studying the Babblers too, huh?"

"That too. But my mother is interested in more way back. You know, hominids. Neanderthals. Different shape the voice box in gorilla, blah blah. She say her main researches are"—she slows down, half-closes her eyes, and reads the words off from some inner image, wrapping her lips mockingly around the unfamiliar syllables—"epigenetics, paleolinguistics, and the mammalian box proteins."

She lets her eyes go wide for a second, as if to say, *I hope you're impressed.* But that's not the message. "Don't worry," she says. "I have no idea what it means also."

"You a Babbler too?"

"I speak only the Russian and the not good English."

"That's OK. I speak only English, and about ten sentences in French, and the not good Greek."

"Greek, yes. My mother tells me about your father's work. The famous Disk."

"Disks," I say, mock-importantly. "The first one was found in 1908. Few years ago, Dad and I found more. We just spent another summer vacation out there."

She reaches out and almost-but-not-quite brushes my cheek with her curled index finger. I register a little electric shock of anticipation, and disappointment, when the expected touch doesn't happen.

"Is still nice tan."

"Thanks. Worked on it every day. You just moved here from Russia?"

"Saint Petersburg."

I gesture at the conga line of wet, grimacing masochists. "Not a runner?"

She shrugs. "Five kilometer I do sometime, yes," she says. "Ten maybe."

I truly look at her then. Tall, yes. Straight hair so pale it's almost white. Spooky green eyes. But it's the lopsided smile that hooks me.

"So what made you volunteer at the water station?"

"One of my mother's students running today, asked us to come. Carl Yates?"

"Bates. Tall guy with a beard. I've met him."

"Seems nice."

I nod. Carl Bates: big, rangy, shaggy-headed parody of a science postdoc, complete with Minnesota accent, round steel glasses, work boots, and a red plaid lumberjack's shirt. According to Dad he crunches data for the "Australian guy" Kit mentioned—who, to quote Dad, is digging around in people's skulls, trying to find out where consciousness is located. Glancing at my watch, I see that the minute's rest I allowed myself is long gone. But who cares—I just acquired, from a lopsided smile, a whole new level of energy and purpose.

"Better keep moving," I say casually. "Promised myself I'd do it in under four hours. But hey, I just had an idea. We should run together in next year's race."

"Whole marathon? Me?" Her eyebrows arch again.

"Why not? The oldest competitor today is eighty-two. You can do it, no problem. It's just a matter of putting in the training—and I need someone to train with."

She holds my gaze for a long, appraising moment, her face perfectly still, her hair flexing like metal in the wind.

"Well? You interested?"

She can tell I'm flirting with her. I can tell she doesn't mind. That smile again. Oh God.

"Could be, Daniel Calder. Could be." She points north. "But under four hours you are saying? So go. I want to be able congratulate you."

△

Even in reality, I spent the rest of the race imagining in great detail all the ways I wanted Kit Cerenkov to congratulate me. And even though the final mile felt like an invitation to a heart attack, I finished in three hours, fifty-nine minutes, and forty-four seconds.

In the dream, though—

What can I say? It's a dream.

In the dream, I don't leave the water station quite so quickly. Instead I look her in the eye and say to her, *Hey, fifteen more seconds won't hurt.* I reach out and echo her gesture, touching her gently on the cheek with my fingertips. And then I lean in slowly, giving her plenty of time to step away if she wants to. But she doesn't want to. And we don't care that we're surrounded by people, including her mother. And our lips brush together like feathers in the most delicate suggestion of a kiss.

That would be a good final image. But dreams are strange; the last thing in it is not the touch of Kit's lips, but a vividly real image of someone I scarcely know at all and never actually saw on race day. In the dream, as I turn to rejoin the stream of runners, Natazscha begins to wave enthusiastically, and I see Carl Bates pass right in front of me, pounding along Lake Washington Boulevard in a drenched tank top, skinny legs pumping erratically, race number flapping in the wind, a look of manic determination on his face.

Should be comical. But his eyes slide over me for a moment; there's something in them, or not in them, that frightens me.

△

It's light, when I wake up the second time. My door is open, and a doctor with a clipboard is standing just outside in the corridor talking to Gabi Eisler. In educated, precise, slightly accented English, he's discussing Rosko's long list of injuries. As I listen, I think about exactly how the accident on the tower caused those injuries. It's only then that the central fact comes back to me, like a boxer's direct hit in the middle of my chest. There are three people in my mind's video of the climb. One of them is me. One of them is Rosko. And one of them, with the familiar wavy brown hair and the yellow climbing suit, is dead.

When people lose someone close to them, they're supposed to rage and weep. Or sit stone-faced, staring into the distance, grappling privately with the scale of the great absence inside them. Me, right now? I feel as if there is something wrong with my breathing. I feel a completely nameless and causeless *fear*. Also an urgency, like I must hurry, but it's not yet clear why, or for what. When I try to step outside myself and find words for this odd constellation of emotions, the first two that come to mind are *anxiety* and *panic*.

Part of it's just that the idea of Mom being dead is surreal. Not to be taken seriously—like an especially sick joke that will sooner or later be revealed as merely a sick joke. But there's no comfort in the other direction either. The religious idea, the idea that she has *survived death*, seems worse. Guess it's Dad's influence: *Nobody but a child believes Fido is sniffing the Eternal Fire Hydrant in doggie paradise. So why believe that "eternity"—whatever the hell* that *means—is waiting for us?*

I don't know.

Neither why you'd believe it, nor what it means.

I want to know, but I don't.

△

They've put me in a small, plain room, pale green with a dark-green tile floor. Out of the window I can see the snow-covered rooftops of Punta Arenas and a gun-gray surface that could be a giant empty parking lot—the Strait of Magellan. I roll my shoulders and neck, then flex my arms and legs, testing. When I tense my right leg, it feels as if someone has just hit me in the knee with a hammer.

When Gabi sees that I'm awake, she comes to sit on the side of my bed, puts her hand on mine. "How do you feel, Daniel?"

"Sore. That's all."

She gives me a long, skeptical look. Has the sense not to even mention Mom, but waits, offering me the opportunity to say more.

"OK, so I don't know how I feel. I'm too close to it. I—"

I glance around the room, searching for some words on which to hang the emotions you're supposed to have when you wake up in a hospital room to the knowledge that you just watched your mother die. But all I have is the anxiety. And the images, the endless loop of inner video like a tune I can't get rid of, in which she's falling falling falling.

"I can't imagine her not being here, Gabi. Some big part of me is sure she's still here. What about Rosko?"

"Yesterday, when we got here, I thought we would lose him. His heart almost stopped beating. Then he was in surgery for a long time. He has some bad injuries, but I think he will be OK."

"We'll have to contact my father."

"Done. I spoke to Bill myself. He knows everything. They're on their way here now."

"From Seattle?"

"They were still in Boston when I reached him."

Dad and Morag, already exhausted from too much travel: I picture them at a ticket counter, as they trade west for south. Then lining up at the gate. Then sitting in yet another airplane, too stunned to talk, as they cut a grim vertical slash down the face of the earth. Dad deals with unpleasant things by burying his head in work, and that's how he'll be dealing with the news of Mom's death: solving some obscure problem from 2000 BCE, just to get away from the present. Morag can be the same way, but I imagine her trying hard to be the adult, putting her own feelings on hold as best she can in order to coax Dad into talking.

Gabi touched my arm to get my attention. "Do you think you can eat some breakfast?"

The idea of food makes me want to gag. At the same time I'm empty, light-headed and hungry.

"Toast, maybe? Coffee?"

What I'm actually craving is tea—specifically, the British blend Mom gave me a taste for. Wickedly strong black Assam, steeped in boiling water for five full minutes and then clouded with milk. But if I ask for that they'll get it hopelessly wrong. Coffee's a safer bet.

"I'll see if I can get them to bring you something. Check this out while you're waiting." She reaches over to a chair and hands me a tablet.

"What is it?"

"A clip from Bill's Boston interview. I thought you might like to see it before they get here."

⚠

She's right, in a way. Just seeing Dad and Morag on the screen, just hearing their voices and being reminded they're real, is good for me. It's even better, somehow, knowing that I'm not seeing them in real time. This video is from just after the rockfall. Several hours before they knew. A time of innocence.

Dad has never moved an inch toward the Hollywood tweedy professor stereotype. He has on lime-green look-at-me designer glasses, a Pink Floyd concert T, skinny faded jeans, and fraying red Converse hi-tops. A handful of gel holds up the graying spikes up top. His black leather jacket is slung over the back of his chair as if he just happened to drop by. When the camera closes in you can read the lapel button: "May Cause Irritation." Next to him, Morag is dressed all in black, as usual: black canvas sneakers, black cotton cargo pants, black denim jacket over a black T. She looks neither excited nor bored, just sits there watching the two men and waiting to speak. And wait she does, because at first the interviewer doesn't much notice she's there.

He's a blond man in his thirties. Khaki chinos, blue button-down under a navy blazer, tasseled loafers: he looks like someone who wants to be a professor too, and has heard them described, but has never seen one. His opening question refers in just one sentence to Babel, the library, and the impossible Phaistos fragment. Dad knows exactly how to act the Scholarly Authority in these situations, takes the whole thing in his stride:

"What we found, beneath the ruins of an immense stepped tower, or ziggurat, is a collection of very old clay tablets. They do seem to confirm that Babylon, or Babilani, is the source of the story in Genesis. And yes, there was a strangely, uh, anomalous find."

"Perhaps you could review the story, for any of our viewers who are less than diligent in their daily Bible reading?" the interviewer chortles. "It says that God gave us one language, yes? But then we built a great tower, and were punished?"

A grin takes over Dad's face. I can tell he's just given in to the temptation to say something deliberately outrageous. I actually like him at moments like this, feel a little warmth toward him, feel his spirit hasn't been wholly destroyed by years of fruitless work on the enigma of the Disks.

"Genesis, chapter eleven. We came down, into the plain of Shinar, and said, 'Hot damn, let's show off how clever we are!' So we built ourselves a fine city, and put a *bodacious* skyscraper in the middle. And yea verily, we did the whole thing in mirrored glass, and installed high-speed elevators, and AC, and an underground garage with valet parking. And this skyscraper was so tall that it reached all the way up to heaven and"—he stabs his finger at the ceiling—"poked God in the butt."

The interviewer has his mouth open like a stranded fish. He's horrified by the casually irreverent tone, probably already fielding in his mind angry calls from the easily offended. He makes a gesture, as if about to speak, but he's too slow, and Dad cheerfully makes it worse.

"Oh yes. The Creator of Heaven and Earth, author of all things visible and et cetera, gave us a magnificent gift. The English mystic John Dee called it the Angelic Tongue, because it was supposedly what the angels spoke when they were hanging out at the water-cooler, or meeting with God in the celestial conference room. But this ultimate communications app brought out the worst in us. We became arrogant, and built this great tower, and the Creator was so cheesed off with us that he said, 'Right, that's it, I'm done. Screw you!' So he destroyed the tower and put the angelic language through the shredder. 'Confused our tongues,' as the Bible has it."

In terror for the safety of their broadcasting license, they bleep out the word *screw*. A mistake. It leaves the impression that he used a different obscenity, even more terrifying to the average broadcaster. The one that rhymes with duck.

"So," the interviewer says, pink in the cheeks and trying to get things back on track before he loses his job, "after the so-called con-fusion of tongues, we were just 'babbling,' and couldn't understand each other?"

"You've got it. One language, good—we can even communicate with God. Many languages, total bummer—we can't even communi-cate with each other."

It's almost as if they've forgotten Morag's there. But I'm watching her body language closely, see a couple of subtle shifts in the chair, know she's about to pounce. "It seems to me—" she says, and the interviewer turns to her as if surprised she can speak.

I'd be nervous on TV—probably look awkward and stupid from fear of looking awkward and stupid. That sort of worry would never occur to Morag, and she speaks exactly as she always does. With a clipped precision. Fast. And always with a kind of amusement, an ironic edge, as if the world is too crazy to quite take seriously.

"Babel's a story about parenting gone wrong, isn't it? Actually, I think religion's a story about parenting gone wrong. The gods create us, protect us, then try to keep us amused with cool toys like reason and language. But we don't want to be the gods' pets. We want to live our own lives. So we act out, and they punish our disobedience. Which doesn't work, so they go for the big guns. They leave us: that's the Babel story. Or they murder most of us: that's the Flood story. And the amazing twist is that, like all abused and abandoned children, we're convinced the whole thing's our fault!"

"I think—"

"Spooky, isn't it, the way some of those ideas keep on coming up all over the world in different forms? As if it's a *memory* of something. And in every culture, the take-home is the same. After we're punished, are we sullen and rebellious? No! On the contrary. We feel *wicked* for having been so *bad*. We go on and on and on about how unworthy we are, how absolutely right it is for us to be slaughtered, how right it is, at least, for God to pull the linguistic plug and excommunicate us."

"Excommunicate," the interviewer says uncomfortably. "I see." You can tell he's never before thought about what the word literally means. "And, uh, Professor Calder, what's so new that you have unearthed?"

Dad's itching to tell a big story. But he resists the impulse, plays it down. "The texts we have found are extremely old—they predate the city of Babylon itself by as much as a thousand years. Some of them are roughly consistent with the Genesis version of Babel—and some are not. Most of them, we've not even translated yet."

"You said *we*?"

Dad makes a melodramatic gesture in the direction of Morag. The interviewer looks mildly astonished, smiles condescendingly, addresses her in a tone so patronizing it oozes like a buttered English muffin. Even though he's seated, and not tall, he contrives to look as if he's peering down at her, actually chuckles in a disbelieving sort of way. "*You*, Ms. Chen, are actually helping to *translate* these texts?"

Morag doesn't shrug, doesn't offer up a nervous laugh or do any kind of simpery, self-deprecating routine. She's picked up on his tone; there's a little internal struggle, reflected in her expression, as she realizes that she doesn't know how to respond without either playing up to his expectations or sounding rude. She opts for saying, a bit defensively, "It's not that difficult."

N'hut THUT duffucult.

"But when did you learn—er—surely mastery of Akkadian is a rather unusual skill for a teenager?"

"Bill and I—Professor Calder and I—share an unusual ability to learn languages fast. We're both Babblers, as people say. Some people at the University of Washington are studying the possibility that it's a genetic mutation. But anyway, I've been working on Akkadian for a few months. I still only know ten percent of what he knows, but—"

"Twenty percent," Dad interrupts.

She gives an impish half smile. "Aye, twenty percent is probably about right. Anyways, enough to help speed things up a bit."

He turns back to Dad again. "From your use of the word *mythology*, I take it you don't take the details seriously? That human beings started with a single language, for instance."

"The word *mythos* is simply Greek for *story*, and some stories are true. But no, I don't take it seriously in a literal sense. My view is that there simply is no such thing as the supernatural—that the very idea of the supernatural is a confusion. But does that mean I dismiss mythology? No! The great myths and religious stories are barely legible traces of *something*. Something that was real, in the distant past. We just don't know what."

"Do we have any examples, though—I mean of myths that were based on something real?"

Morag steps in again, rubbing her hands enthusiastically. "Sure we do. For centuries, everyone said Homer's heroes were mythical. Helen of Troy, Achilles, the Trojan War, all that lovely stuff that was too romantic to believe. Then Heinrich Schliemann went to Asia Minor, figured out where Troy must have been, and stuck a spade in the ground."

"I wonder—"

"Then there's Noah's flood. Six thousand years ago, when the Mediterranean broke into the Black Sea, it delivered water into the Black Sea basin at a rate of ten, fifteen cubic miles a day, virtually overnight. Flooded thousands of square miles."

"Yes I see—"

"And my favorite example is the unicorn, which—"

The interviewer finally manages to interrupt. "So you're saying these stories are just distorted versions of real events?"

Morag has learned her lessons at Dad's knee very well: "I'm just saying they don't come out of nowhere."

"What about this fragment of material that's not in Akkadian, or Babylonian, or any of the known languages of the region? Apparently it looks exactly like something you studied in Greece? But surely it's unlikely that—"

Dad lets out a short, barking laugh. "I've been studying these objects called the Phaistos Disks on Crete for years. I already worked out that they're not originally from Crete. But finding a fragment of one in Iraq? If you'd asked me a few months ago, I'd have said, no, it's not unlikely, it's stone-cold impossible."

"That's our big incentive for translating the Akkadian tablets as soon as possible," Morag says. "Maybe the tablets will tell the story, explain it to us. Whatever we find, this is going to rewrite the early history of civilization. We don't know what's true, not yet. But what this shows us is that our current picture is hopelessly wrong."

And the way she finishes turns the tables on him: it's as if she's the one talking down to a child. She leans over, taps him on the knee, says, "Isn't that exciting!"

He draws his knee out of the way, sits up straight, and tries to look composed, serious. "All right. So you have this potentially epoch-making discovery, and for now you two are the sole guardian of its secrets. But I understand that some people are already pressuring you to publish?"

He reaches down, produces a red book from under his chair, and waves it in a vaguely threatening way. "Julius Quinn, for example."

The volume he's holding up is Quinn's *Anabasis*. Just a book—in the way that the Bible is just a book. *Anabasis* is something people don't so much read as learn, chant, pray to, stroke, venerate. Translated into over two hundred languages, it has sold in the tens of millions. It's free on the web, and you can buy copies of it dirt cheap, everywhere: from vendors on street corners, from airport stalls, from the glossy piles next to the discounted winter jackets at Costco.

"Ah yes," Dad says. "Julius Quinn. He's everywhere these days."

The interviewer flips through his notes. "He has said that any materials from Babel are 'the common heritage of mankind—'"

"I couldn't agree more."

"'—and an essential step on our common stairway to the infinite.'"

"Whatever that means," Morag drawls sarcastically.

Dad tries for a slightly more conciliatory tone: "If I understand him, he means that we can only return to our true nature as gods by forgetting our own languages and relearning the divine, original language—and hey, maybe this discovery will tell us something about it."

"Indeed, indeed. In fact he says, if I'm not mistaken"—the interviewer finds a Post-it note, opens the book to a marked passage—"'Six thousand languages are not a cultural achievement, but the symptom of a disease—and the measure of our distance from the pure minds of the Architects.'"

He shrugs, can't resist doing something with his eyebrows to convey the idea that what he's just said, on Quinn's behalf, is the equivalent of believing the earth is flat and balanced on a gerbil. Then he deploys a small, sharp weapon. "One of your own former students, I believe?"

Ouch. The personal connection is still a sore spot, and it's nothing as simple as ordinary professional rivalry. It's been clear for a long time now that Quinn has much, much bigger ambitions than a job at a university.

Dad brushes aside the personal question as best he can. "Julius Quinn came to study with me several years ago. He was an excellent student, and he has a very thorough understanding of ancient history. Also, apparently, a rather overactive imagination. At least that would be my diagnosis when someone has a personal encounter with supernatural beings during a hiking vacation."

"This book of his, *Anabasis*, has persuaded a lot of people to believe in the literal truth of, well, a kind of ancient Mesopotamian religion, is it not?"

"*Anabasis* means 'ascent.' The Greek historian Xenophon used the word to mean 'invasion,' because he was in the Army of the Ten Thousand and the Greeks had to *ascend* from the coast into the mountains in order to invade Mesopotamia. But it's Plato's meaning Quinn has in mind. Plato says we humans are half-blind cave-creatures, that everything we think of as real is just shadows on the wall, that what we need to do is get out of the cave—*ascend* from our dark ignorance into the light of knowledge."

"Sounds a lot like the Christian idea of heaven to me," the interviewer says.

"Aye," Morag cuts in. "You die. You leave your body lying on the floor like an old sweater. Then your soul walks right into the executive elevator and it's P for Paradise. Quinn's version does leave out the clouds, the harps, and the eternal boredom. Plus he doesn't believe in the soul, not in any traditional sense. He thinks that to be freed from our physical selves is to become pure intelligences. We don't get to be *with* God, or the gods, or the Architects, as he calls them. When we slip out of our bodies, we become divine."

"Quinn and I agree on one thing," Dad says. "We think all the stories that flowed out of that region, three thousand years ago, are based on real events of some kind. Quinn just takes them more literally than I do. I believe something was going on that we don't understand. He believes there really were, or are, multiple, uh, *Architects*."

Morag shakes her head. "Nutty as the inside of a squirrel."

△

When the clip ends, I'm left looking at a blurry still of the interviewer's shoulder, with Dad and Morag just visible as smudges in the background.

I look at that image for a long time.

This is my family, now: two atheist supernerds with a thing about ancient religious mythology.

Mom loved me for who I am. Even when it turned out I had problems with reading. Even when I poured extra time into math, because I was desperate to please her, and got crap grades anyway. Dad just pretends not to notice my deficiencies. Or tries to pretend, which he's not good at. He has the common weakness of fathers—he wants to feel close to me, wants to understand me, and wants the easy road to that result, which is me being more like him than I am.

He did get an excellent consolation prize: Morag. And they have a task to share that I can't help with. All I have is bad dreams.

Oh, yeah. And I'm hallucinating her voice. Which strongly suggests I'm losing it.

I don't hear my mother's voice now. But I do know what she would say.

Don't just sit there feeling sorry for yourself, Daniel.

Get up. Move.

Do something.

Might as well: the toast and coffee never showed. Maybe I should at least wash. So I drag myself into the bathroom, stand in front of the mirror, shrug off the hospital gown.

I'm a sight, naked.

CHAPTER 6

THE ANSWERING SILENCE

Hair like a toilet brush. Eyes like a pair of empty gray day packs. Both hands heavily bandaged so that just the tips of some fingers are showing. Chest mottled with bruises and scrapes. Left thigh divided by a shallow, irregular cut. Right knee—revealed only when I unwind the compression bandage—the shape and color of an eggplant that's well beyond sell-by.

There's also a bruise running from my left ear down to the inside of my collarbone. I feel all over again the whiplike impact of Mom's arm, and my hand goes unbidden to the space. In my mind's eye I manage the impossible: snatching her wrist, twisting as her body falls past, grabbing at her harness with my other hand and, by a heroic, cartoonish effort of strength and skill, saving her.

I expect—again—to feel grief. Or rather: I expect to feel a massively magnified version of something familiar, like *sad* or *upset*. Aching in my chest; bawling my eyes out; acute sense of all-over psychic pain. But, again, it's not like that. I feel terrible, but it's almost—how can I even put it? People say, *My heart has been ripped out*. A bit like that. An unendurable hollowness. Physically, I feel as if I am made of putty, and someone has used a long, thin knife to cut a hole right through my body cavity, a hole so big you could pass a suitcase through it. It's an injury so massive, so hideous, that I should be a corpse; instead, I'm standing here in front of the mirror, stubbornly breathing.

And then there's the other thing. What I saw, or thought I saw, or didn't quite see, and the shadow it left behind. Like I've lost something, and can't remember what.

Practicalities. I have a sudden and urgent need to focus on practicalities. So I clean my teeth: it's impossible with one hand, awkward and uncomfortable with the other. Then I stare at the shower, decide it's too difficult, and wipe myself over with a damp washcloth. Then the toilet: trying to bend my damaged knee makes it feel like a bag of ground glass, so I'm forced to slump down onto the seat sideways, with one leg out straight and my hand on a rail. Afterward, it's a ten-minute challenge to get into jeans, five more to do them up. I add a geriatric pair of trail shoes, one of Dad's old Ts—"This Message Brought to You by Photons"—and a frayed Seattle Sounders hoodie.

△

Rosko's in a larger room on the same floor, hidden in a maze of tubes and machines. A metal cage supports the pins in his leg. His left hand lies inert in his mother's lap like an aborted fetus.

A fizzing current of guilt goes through me, seeing him there. Irrational, sure, but it doesn't care that it's irrational, goes on fizzing anyway:

If Rosko and I had not become friends—

If I had not begged Mom to bring him and his parents to Patagonia—

If I had not agreed to be last one on the rope—

Gabi looks up in surprise, and smiles, breaking my train of thought. "Daniel! You are not even supposed to be up."

"I've got bruises, Gabi. Bruises and a couple of cuts. If Rosko had my injuries, he'd be doing wind sprints in the parking lot by now. I'm fine. I was thinking, if I sit with him a bit, maybe you and Stefan could go for a walk, get lunch or something."

"Thank you. I'm not hungry. But Stefan is downstairs talking to one of the surgeons, and it would be good to walk and stretch for a couple of minutes."

She moves Rosko's arm gently, so that it lies by his side on the bed, then gets up. Just as she's leaving the room, she turns, one hand on the door.

"Daniel?"

"Yes?"

"Rosko says you are the only person he's ever met who thinks like him. What makes you two so close?"

I look down at her son. "We worry about the same things. Most kids in high school are too worked up about their grades or their acne, or whether their shoes are uncool, to think about the big picture."

"The big picture?"

One of the machines over the bed beeps faintly then falls silent again. A red LED on an oxygen monitor shifts from 94 percent down to 92 percent, then back again.

"Abstract stuff. The kind of thing that makes even Morag impatient. Rosko and I trade unanswerable questions. Is it right to kill one innocent person to save five? Is there more happiness than suffering in the world? What if the past's an illusion? Rosko's favorite is right out of Charlie Balakrishnan's founding ISOC document: is the brain a physical object—and if it is, how can it be *conscious*?"

"Philosophers."

"Pains in the ass, Ella says. Rosko said in the lunchroom once, 'Why praise or blame anyone if they do what they do because of the way they are, and they have no control over the way they are?'"

"And you two spend a lot of time talking about these things?"

"No, not really. We're just kind of aware of them, like a hum in the background. Rosko's the only person I know, other than me, who finds it scary that our common sense makes no sense."

△

Truth is, right now I don't have any interest in chewing the cud with Rosko about some philosophical puzzle. When we're alone, I put my hand over his, listen to his breathing, focus on the climb.

"I need you back, Spidermensch. I need your memories, what you saw up there. You go die on me, I swear I'll punch your lights out."

His hand twitches, as if he's heard me, and the oxygen monitor beeps again, registers 95 percent. The pressure of his fingers causes a small, sharp pain in the line of stitches, hidden under the bandage, that's holding my injured finger together. I must have still been conscious when the stitches went in, because I remember seeing a nurse hold my hand steady as someone else, just out of my line of sight, tugged at it with a tool like a pair of thin silver pliers.

"Rosko." I start trying to describe for him the disconnect between the grief I imagined and the rattled, creepy, fogged-and-spooked feeling I actually have. When one of his eyes pops open, it's a complete surprise. Ought to call a nurse, or his parents; instead I just lean in close.

"Rosko. It's me."

He moves his head a few degrees, not quite enough to see me, gets the other lid open. The blank expression dissolves into an unmistakable hint of a smile.

"Daniel," he whispers.

"I'm here, dude, right here. We're in the hospital in Punta Arenas."

"Figured that out all by myself." His voice is just a rustle of leaves. I have to lean in to catch what he's saying.

"You been awake already?"

"Little bit. Everything blurry—feels like I smoked a kilo of weed."

"You just came out of surgery."

He glances sideways at me, turns his head just enough to see my hands. "What a fuck-up."

"You're going to be OK."

"And you?"

"I'm totally fine. Bit of rock rash is all."

"I'm not talking about your injuries. I'm talking about your mom, Daniel. I know she died. I am so sorry."

I try to come up with the right thing to say in response to this. There's no right thing, and my eyes are full of pepper, so I just squeeze his shoulder and say nothing. Then he starts jerking his head back and forth, just by an inch or so, as if there's a fly buzzing in his face. I can't tell whether he's having trouble speaking, or trouble finding the right words.

"What?"

"I need to know how bad the damage is. What I'm dealing with. What did I break? Why does my head still hurt so much? Don't sugar it, Daniel. Promise me you won't sweeten the pill. I need to hear it from someone I trust."

"OK."

I give him what I know from overhearing the doctor. "Your right leg was broken pretty bad. Also you cracked four ribs, and your kidneys are bruised. That'll all mend. What they're not so sure about are your back and your big fat swollen head."

"I got a concussion?"

"The impact destroyed your helmet. But the famous Eisler brain is intact, according to the scans. Even that freakishly enlarged Babbler hippocampus that the ISOC people are so hot to study. Still, they don't like the fact that you have intracranial swelling. They're talking right now about transferring you up to Santiago."

"What else?"

"Hairline fractures in your tailbone, something like that."

"Will I be able to climb again?"

"You've got at least one more round of surgery yet, and your Dad says they won't know how big a deal it is until after that."

"You didn't answer the question."

I take a deep breath. "At this point, they don't know anything."

"Scheisse."

With Gabi about to come back, this is either a bad moment to change the subject or the best moment I'll get. I squeeze his fingers. "Hey. I need you to tell me something too. Think back to the climb. Right before the accident—exactly what do you remember?"

He frowns, stays silent for a long minute, and my heart misses a beat as an awful thought occurs to me.

"You remember it, right? The accident and everything?"

He grimaces and shifts, then relaxes again. "Sure. I remember everything. But there's not much to tell. Iona in the lead, me in the middle. Only a hundred meters below the summit. It was windy, but nothing unusual."

"Go on."

"And then that giant rockfall. Out of nowhere."

"Go back. You're missing stuff. Give me every detail."

He tilts his head, gives me a puzzled look, stares at the ceiling in complete silence for so long that I think he's drifting, has forgotten I'm even there. "OK. I remember now that Iona paused to rest, just before it happened, and shouted something down to me. I couldn't hear her over the wind. And then, boom—and she's pushed off the wall, the aids fail, and I'm dragged with her."

My heart sinks as he carries on: "The funny thing is, I don't remember feeling fear. I knew, I absolutely knew I was going to die.

But all I felt was a kind of calm. Happiness even. Like: this is correct, this is what is supposed to happen."

"That's it?"

"It's kind of awful, now that I think about it: it was like, I *wanted* to die."

He pauses, eyes darting around as if looking for something. "So what am I missing?"

I put my hand on his shoulder again. "Relax. Take it easy."

My mind is racing over the gaps between what he remembers and what I saw. I have no idea what to say to him, and what comes out is a messy, on-the-fly compromise between nothing and the truth:

"She did something strange, just before the rockfall. Climbed ahead too far and too fast, as if she was racing to get to the top. And then it was like she saw something, and—and there was—I'm just not clear in my mind what happened."

"Sorry—I don't remember any of that."

Δ

He's about to say something else, but at that moment a nurse comes in.

"Hello, Señor Eisler. Good to see you're awake." She picks up his chart. "How do you feel?"

"Like I'm on a ship in a storm. And an elephant is sitting on me. And someone is drilling holes in my head. Fine, otherwise."

I can hear, just in the way he says those two words, that he has put our conversation aside for now and is going to switch into Charming Rogue mode.

"You have some injuries, and you are under some powerful drugs. Try to relax and not move too much. I'm going to ask you a few questions. Yes?"

"Please go ahead."

"What is your full name?"

"Wolfgang Amadeus Mozart."

"Serious, please. What is your full name?"

"Rosko Gerik Eisler."

"Where were you born?"

He pauses, as if trying to remember. "Did anyone ever tell you that you have exceptionally pretty eyes?"

She sighs, as if to indicate that she's not being paid enough. "Yes, Mr. Eisler. My husband. Where were you born?"

"München. Munich."

"Tell me something about Munich."

"It is the birthplace of many famous people. Including, unfortunately for the tourist authorities, both the Nazi Heinrich Himmler and the terrorist Andreas Baader."

"How old are you?"

"Sixteen years, seven months."

"What is twenty-four minus seven?"

"Seventeen. Which, interestingly, is the minimum number of numbers you can have in a sudoku puzzle and still guarantee a unique solution. Your husband is right about your eyes, by the way."

She puts the clipboard away, then turns to him again: "Such compliments from young men with sevoflurane in their bloodstream, unfortunately I cannot take seriously."

"I must remember to say it again later."

"One more test question," says a familiar voice from the doorway. "What is your mother's name?"

Gabi's pretending to play it cool and casual, so Rosko does the same. "Ah, hello, Mutti. Nice to see you. My mother's name is, oh, let me see. Helmut. No, wait. Gabriela. With one l."

I get out of Gabi's way so that she can lean down and plant a kiss on his forehead. As she's moving toward him, I don't give it a second thought. Until the moment when her lips touch him, I don't give it a second thought.

When I actually see the gesture, I feel like I'm being cut in half with a band saw.

△

Later, back in my room, I stare out the window and think about the fact that either Rosko has amnesia or I've become delusional. Can he not have seen what I saw? Does he really not remember? Can I have made it all up?

But no, on that last one. The bruise on my neck is there because she fell a long way before hitting me. The aids failed because she fell a long way before the rope pulled taut.

Eager for distraction, I claw around in my bag and find the paint-by-numbers thriller I was reading before the climb. My place, halfway through, is still marked by a stalk of dry Patagonian grass. *The Defenders*, it says, in embossed silver letters on the cover. A multivehicle pileup of feel-good patriotic clichés, it includes a rogue ex-Marine with big muscles, even bigger emotional issues, and a heart of gold; a gorgeous but manipulative intelligence analyst in a tight red dress; an overrated CIA director who's in bed with his own biographer. In the background, as predictable as the rising sun, there's a bearded, Hoboken-born Yemeni who has personal as well as ideological scores to settle, is also (to keep things simple) plain evil, and who has (deeply original surprise here) single-handedly buried a nuclear weapon in a tunnel under the White House.

There's a ticking clock: there always is. Muscles knows the bomb will go off in exactly This Many Minutes and That Many Seconds. Everything will depend on him racing across the city, eluding the posse of FBI second-raters who think *he's* the bomber, and cutting the blue wire (or is it the green wire this time?) with exactly three seconds left on the little red readout.

Escapist fun, a week ago, as reassuringly predictable as grass going in one end of a cow and not-grass coming out the other. But

Muscles has a couple of things going for him that I don't: he knows what the problem is, who the bad guys are, and how much time's left. All I have is the queasy certainty that something's wrong.

I read for twenty minutes, but can't even get into it when Muscles and Red Dress have the mandatory steamy hookup right in the stacks at the Library of Congress. They're still panting and readjusting their underwear when I send *The Defenders* spinning onto the floor.

Is it a sign of mental illness, or only of grief, to have half a dozen moods an hour? I look at the book, lying there abandoned in the middle of the room, and my irritation drains away like water from a sink. In place of the irritation, I feel desperately, hungrily, emptily alone. It's not the kind of thing that's going to be changed by finding something different to read, or chatting with Stefan and Gabi. Not by talking to Rosko. Not by waiting patiently for Dad and Morag's plane to land.

For a couple of minutes I've no idea what to do. Then, out of nowhere, I know exactly what I must do. So I stumble down to the nurse's station and cause a major international incident.

⚠

"Señor Calder. You are supposed to be resting."

"I don't need to rest. I'm not tired."

"What can I do for you?"

"I want to see my mother's body."

Maybe I should elaborate. Maybe I should point out that I never got the benefit of the corny movie good-bye, where she's ninety-five, and dying but completely pain-free, and I'm having Meaningful Last Words by her bedside in a sunlit bedroom on the family farm. Closer to the truth is that I simply need to believe it's true: her death is so unreal, so improbable, so impossible to believe that I might as well have read it in a news feed. I need to *know*.

The nurse looks at me with incomprehension, at first, then horror. She flusters away and comes back with one of the doctors, who repeats the performance. A second, more senior doctor offers me a lot of smooth, patronizing garbage about how it's not for the best.

"When my father asks to see her body, you will allow him to do so. Yes?"

Yes, certainly. Yes.

I try to think what Dad would say here. His swagger gets results. "You will allow him to see the body, but you have a policy, is that it, a written policy that says I cannot see her body? Because I am only her son, not her husband? Or because I am under eighteen?"

N-no, not exactly.

They are completely unsure of themselves. Nice. "So in fact you have no reason to prevent me from seeing her body?"

Well—

"She is too disfigured? And you are afraid that it will be upsetting?"

She is—The body is damaged, yes.

I'm careful to walk a fine line after that: irritated, insistent, polite, irritated, insistent. Eventually they give in, and I'm taken down to the morgue by an orderly, a middle-aged woman with a sour expression. She shows me the way with hand gestures, never offers a word, treats me like a prisoner who's been granted a special privilege that the jailers themselves disapprove of.

The morgue is in a subbasement, all concrete walls and mechanical hums, like an area that was designed as a parking garage and then taken over by the dead and their pasty-faced vampire attendants. Outside a big set of swing doors, the grim woman says a few words to another assistant, a bald man in a white lab coat, and hands me off to him. He gives me a funny look too, says nothing as he bashes through the doors. Then he flips on lights, opens a drawer, stands there. It feels awkward to ask, but I manage to make it clear that I need him to leave me alone. I don't even approach the drawer until he steps back out.

When I pull back the sheet, yeah, it's a shock. Her face is a mass of bruises, swellings, and small cuts, like she was the victim of a bad mugging. I look away, at first, but as soon as I look a second time I find it surprisingly easy to forget how she looks, treat it as a kind of static, and reach beyond it, to *her*.

"Mom."

Daniel

Thin as a whisper, the voice doesn't even surprise me this time. Once again, it doesn't come from where she is, but from right next to me, as if she's by my side looking down at her own face. I want to be able to ask someone: is this what hallucinations are even *like*?

There's a narrow cut running from her neck, up across her cheekbone, to her hairline. I reach out and touch the line of it with a fingertip, right at the cheekbone, where it's wider, then put my hand on her forehead. And wish I had not. It has the exact temperature, the exact same waxy resilience, of supermarket meat.

Find out, Daniel

"Find out what?"

Daniel

"Find out what?"

No

"Tell me what to do."

Not

"Tell me what to do."

Silence.

The fact that I hear my own voice in the echoing room, that I'm actually talking to her, is even more disturbing than hearing her voice. For a moment I feel as if I'm stepping outside myself, looking at the situation more objectively, and the obvious question—the question that would occur to anyone else—is whether I'm grieving or going insane. *Several sandwiches short of a full picnic*, Ella would say.

I wait for some revelation about this to strike me, or for the voice to come back, but there's nothing. Then I see the bald man looking in at me through the round porthole in the swing door, and I'm so angry at the intrusion that I stare him down. Seems to take forever, but eventually he gets the message and turns away.

There's nothing here to stay for, but I'm putting off the moment when I will look at her face for the last time. The tips of my fingers, poking out from their clumsy nest of bandages, go back to her, touch her hair, then, as if they have wills of their own, they trace the thin, dry wound, as gently as they can, all the way down to the point where it disappears under the sheet.

Must go now.

I'm already in the act of lifting my hand away when I feel something that's not the edge of the sheet brush against the extreme tip of one finger.

Another wound? But when I ease back the edge of the sheet, it's not a scabbed-over cut that I find, but a thin strand of brown leather, square sectioned like an old-fashioned bootlace. I glance up to check that the orderly has not returned to the doorway, then pull gently. It's a loop, around her neck. Attached to it, like a single jewel, is a tiny cylindrical vial made of blue metal.

My heart is doing one eighty a minute. I feel sure, instantly, that she has never worn this before, that I must understand what it is. I tug on the vial, but the loop passes through a hole in the metal top; no way it's coming off. Then I pull on the leather itself, harder, but clearly it's clasped or knotted at the back. Tugging some more on one side reveals a tight knot that I'll never undo, given the state my hands are in.

I sense the orderly standing beyond the door, impatient, just out of sight. Panicking, I look around for a knife, scissors, something.

Which is stupid: I'm in a sterile room of plastic and steel surfaces, all of them empty.

"Sorry." I'm not sure if the word actually escapes my lips, but I feel sure she hears it. I clench my left hand into as near as I can get to a fist, place it against the side of her head for leverage, and hook the exposed fingertips of my right hand around the loop. Then I pull with all my strength.

My fingers shriek at me. I pull again, harder. The pain is awful, and I'm worrying that my ruined fingertips will start to bleed on her. I manage to wiggle a bit more of my hand between the cord and her neck, glance again at the door.

One last chance.

I brace my legs, lock my left arm, and pull again. When the leather gives way, my right wrist jerks back painfully into the side of the morgue drawer, and at exactly that moment the orderly unceremoniously kicks the swing door open and comes back in.

He must have seen me.

But in fact, when I look up guiltily, trying to ignore the hornet sting in my wrist, his head is turned to one side because his white coat has caught on the door latch. Blushing, and hoping the blush looks like emotional anguish, I stuff the cord into the pocket of my hoodie. Then I stand there looking at her, count three long calming breaths, and replace the sheet over her face.

I leave the drawer open. As I leave, I brush past the orderly without saying a word. Out of the corner of my eye, I catch a gesture he makes with his right hand. A chill runs through me, because I don't know whether he's made the sign of the cross or the sign that the Seraphim make—a triangular gesture, sweeping four clenched fingers from the throat to each nipple and back again. Is he a devout Catholic who believes in heaven? Is he the ordinary sort of person who doesn't think too much about the Big Questions, but likes to go through the motions? Or does he believe that my mother is now— what does Quinn say?—*in the dimension of the eternal*?

And could someone please tell me what to believe?

△

Four floors back to my room, but the perverse instinct of the climb-ing addict makes me take the stairs, as if it'll be good to make my bruised body work. Can't bend the bad knee properly, so I'm forced to go up sideways. On the first floor I pass a staff break room. No one there, but just inside the open door someone has left a Spanish-language newspaper on a bench, and one word sticks out from the cover, catching at me like a thorn.

UYUNI.

It takes my conscious mind a moment to catch up—Mom had only mentioned the name of the town once. She just kept referring to *those Bolivian women.* As if something indescribably terrible had happened to them, when in fact nobody knew what had happened.

UYUNI, the headline says. Underneath: ENCONTRARON A LAS VEINTICUATRO MUERTAS. Below the fold there's a color picture that I can't make sense of at first. It looks like a giant sheet of blinding-white paper with a small hump at the far edge. The blue strip at the top edge has a single flake of cloud in it, the only clue that you're looking at a landscape.

My eyes run over the unfamiliar words below. They seem to taunt me, like a message from Mom that's been coded so I can't read it. I feel as if this story, and her interest in it, is my only real link to her—as if understanding what it's about is the only thing I can do for her. I waste some time cursing my inability to extract a meaning from the Spanish, then I drop the paper, head upstairs as fast as I can, get online.

A clip from just hours ago: a network news anchor with too much lip gloss, half a gallon of Botox, and a blonde crash helmet is mouthing earnestly into the camera:

"Uyuni lies on the edge of a giant, high-altitude salt flat," she says. "The Salar de Uyuni. The women seem to have marched more than sixty miles across it, with all these tools, in temperatures that went below zero at night, and apparently without food or water. The victims ranged in age from twenty to seventy-five."

There's an interview with a sun-wrinkled local man in a straw hat, who squints into the camera and speaks in halting English: "This volcano"—he points to the cone behind him—"name is Tunupa. Legend say Tunupa is woman. Salar de Uyuni made from her tears when her children taken away."

To one side of him there's a police Jeep parked on the salt pan, and a line of tape. Behind that, a crude pyramid of whitish blocks. The man raises his hands in a *Words fail me* gesture, and his voice goes strangely squeaky. "They walk here with shovels, saws. Build pyramid, climb on top. Then? Some kind of—"

He stops midsentence and turns away from the camera, squinting into the sun.

Another clip shows a news conference on the steps of some official building. A stocky man with a white lab coat and a comb-over, who turns out to be the Bolivian government's chief pathologist, is standing in front of a bouquet of microphones. What he says is so simple, straightforward, and honest that it's a bit shocking, coming from a medical professional. He speaks for barely thirty seconds in Spanish, and then repeats himself, first in Quechua and then more slowly in English:

"We do not know why these women came to Tunupa, or how they died. They built a structure, a kind of stepped pyramid, and stood around it in a circle. The ground immediately around has been blasted clean, as if in an explosion, but the structure itself is untouched and the bodies lack any signs of trauma. How this is possible, we have no idea. Another puzzling fact is that the three youngest women appear to have died several days after the others—as if they were not killed, initially, but simply stayed with the others until lack of water overcame them. Yet another puzzling fact is that one of the women is still missing."

△

I have the strange feeling that Mom was right—that she and the Uyuni women are linked in some way. Looking down, I see that I have been rolling the blue vial between my thumb and my blackened middle fingertip.

Can't open it with my bandaged bear paws—it's barely an inch long, with a tiny screw cap, the kind of thing people with a medical problem use to carry a couple of emergency pills. I have to get out the pliers on my multi-tool, clamp them around the vial, and use my teeth. About the tenth attempt, the top comes loose, falls on the floor. I upend the vial and nothing happens. Then I shake it a couple of times, and a square of white paper the size of a Post-it flutters onto the bed.

Neat handwriting I don't recognize. Three words. *Stairway to heaven.*

It looks like a reference to the song. Fragments of it come back to me—all soft acoustic guitar at first, mournful folk music. Then the long slow build, and a short drumroll right in the middle that announces the gear-shift into headbanger rock. Can't remember the singer's name, but I can picture him with his big blond hair, and the guy in back with big dark hair and a double-neck guitar. Bits of the lyrics hang in my mind like rags in a tree. Something about a piper, calling us to join him?

I'm tapping one hand against my thigh, hearing the exact way the instruments fade at the very end and leave the singer all alone with his last words—*stai-AIR-whey to HEH-vun*—when it strikes me that maybe the piece of paper has nothing to do with the song. A stairway to the heavens: surely that's what the ziggurats were? Surely that's what made God send in the celestial demolition crew at Babel?

I pick up the paper, intending to roll it carefully and replace it in the vial; it's only then that I see the writing, in the same hand, on the back:

"In life lies the question. The answer is eternity."

(Anabasis 11:3)

El-u-min

Kel-a-mun
Vo-ma-ga
Yir-keb-it
(Anabasis 24:8)

Those twelve syllables give me an odd feeling. They mean nothing to me; I know I've never seen them before; but they have a kind of familiarity, a resonance. A bit like the song: I can hear a voice in my head saying them. I try to speak along with it: *"El-u-min, Kel-a-mun, Vo-ma-ga, Yir-keb-it."*

For a second, just a single second, she is actually there, standing on the other side of the room in her climbing gear. Not shadowy or ghostlike, but so present and real that I scramble toward her with my arms out.

Daniel, don't let them

"Mom!"

Daniel

"What, Mom? What?"

She has gone before I make two paces. I slump to my knees in front of the spot where she was standing, lean forward on splayed fingers, hunt minutely on the floor for the tiny marks her boots must have made.

Nothing.

I see then, as if from outside, my own desperation that she be something more than an apparition. I see then, as if from outside, my fear that I'm losing my mind.

"Where are you?"

"Where are you?"—much louder this time.

"What did they do to you?"

The answering silence is deafening.

Chapter 7
Know It Is True

I'm pacing up and down just inside the glass front door of the hospital. Every time a car pulls up, I stop, look down across the entrance steps, go on pacing. Even when their taxi arrives at last, I don't quite believe it; I wait until I see her jet-black hair before hobbling out into the wind.

Morag dumps her bag on the sidewalk, sprints up the steps, and flings her arms around my neck, hanging onto me like a kid in a tree.

"Daniel. Daniel. Daniel."

"Morag."

Over her shoulder I can see Dad getting out of the back seat, paying the driver, trying to pick up four bags. A gust of wind nearly blows us off our feet, and we leave him to it, retreating inside.

She puts her head against my chest, wraps her arms around me, and goes still, as if checking that my heartbeat's there. Then, just as I expect, she pushes back to look up at me. Morag always has a kind of hunger for eye contact; it unnerves people sometimes, but I'm so used to it that I love it, experience it as a sign that she's OK. Glancing down for a split second, she finds my bandaged hands and holds them up between us, pressing the ends of our fingers together while giving me the full force of that deep, unblinking stare.

"Does that hurt? Pushing on your fingertips?"

It does, a bit, but I shake my head. She adjusts her fingers anyway, holds them so that they're barely touching mine, and looks into my eyes. It's the standard Morag greeting that I've been used to since childhood—quirky, delicate, powerful. And after this greeting it's always childhood we start with, always the shared memories. Not *How was the flight?* or *Tell me about what happened to your hands*, nothing about Mom, yet. Just childhood. Dad's still struggling through the door when she says:

"Remember hiking with Jimmy and Lorna in Northern Ireland?"

"The Mourne Mountains."

"Four-hour downpour, and then the sun breaking out right on top of Slieve Binnian. You brought the wrong map and we got lost."

"Scenic detour."

"Aye. Through a bog." She glances down at my hands again, tries to make a joke of it: "You're an accident-prone bastard." But a little tremor goes through her jaw around the word *prone*, and she bursts into tears. We lunge for each other again, hug fiercely. I'm crouching down, she's on the tips of her toes. We stand like that, soaking each other's shoulders, for what seems like a long time.

"I'm so sorry D. I'm so sorry, I'm so sorry so sorry."

It's like this is the first moment since the accident that I've been given permission to feel terrible—and it takes her crying to remind me that Mom's death is a devastating blow for her as well. We're so focused on absorbing each other's pain that it takes awhile before I become aware of the figure loitering uncomfortably behind us.

"Dad."

"Daniel."

Gray stubble. Rumpled clothes. Bags under the bloodshot eyes. He looks exactly like the man I've just seen in the Boston video, only ten years older. He steps forward now, puts his arms round us both, gets at least one other thing right. He doesn't spew platitudes. Maybe it's rehearsed, but I'm grateful anyway: instead of asking how I feel, he just says, "This is going to be hard, guys. Terribly hard. What we need to hang onto is that she would want us to get through to the other side of this. We will. I promise we will. And we'll be happy again."

What's wonderful about this: he's treating the three of us together as one unit, one family. That helps. What's terrible, and lonely and frightening about it: they both think—as Rosko thinks, as everyone thinks—that she died in an accident. So I can't say what I want to say. What it would sound crazy to say, because it sounds crazy even to me.

That we can't afford to be happy again until we find out why she was killed.

△

The three of us do descend into platitudes after that. *Got all your bags? Need something to eat?* Then Stefan comes down, and everyone's making appropriate noises—without actually saying big bad words like *accident* or *death* or *Iona*.

I want to get away from this scene. For months, ever since the Eislers showed up in Seattle, I've been itching to introduce Morag to Rosko, wondering if they'll get along. But, when I finally suggest it, Stefan explains that they just gave Rosko more painkillers. "He won't recognize his own eyelids for a couple of hours."

A nurse pokes his head around the corner, looks at me, points to his watch. "Señor Calder?"

Oh right. I'm supposed to be in a physiotherapy session. Not knowing what else to do, I tell everyone to come with me, and they sit around for half an hour, admire my X-rays, pretend to be fascinated by nine different techniques for manipulating my knee to make it even more painful than it already is.

By the end, it's not my knee that's making me want to scream. I'm just desperate to be alone with Morag, and desperate to spend an hour anywhere other than the hospital. Also ought to talk to Dad, but—

Surprisingly, he's the one who breaks the ice. "Daniel, why don't you and Morag go talk for a bit while I catch up with Gabi and Stefan?"

He probably means, go sit in the lounge, but that's not what I have in mind. "Need to be outside," I whisper to Morag. "And I need real food." I grab a jacket and my stylish rubber-tipped walking stick. While nobody's looking, we step out of a side door into the chilly blast.

When we reach street level, I take a deep lungful of the cold, damp air and make a decision. Morag is Morag: I'll just describe the whole thing, tell her exactly what happened. But something makes me hesitate. After Rosko's reaction, am I prepared to tell her? That I had to cut the rope? That I watched her fall? That, just before she fell, something happened, something I can't quite—

Maybe she's reading my mind. Maybe she's trying to give me something easier to talk about. "Look," she says, gesturing toward a flyer on a light pole. "Bill's favorite student is everywhere these days."

A familiar duotone image of Julius Quinn stares back at us, handsome and resolute, eyes piercing the future. Above his face, the favorite slogan of the Seraphim in the original English, all in caps: KNOW IT IS TRUE. Beneath, in the same typeface, is the local translation: SABED QUE ES CIERTO. And the whole thing is framed in a broken triangle with a wavy dash at the top. World's single most popular tattoo, I read somewhere: the mark of the Seraphim.

We walk north from the hospital and see that the flyer is one of dozens, papering the whole area on almost every wall, store window, light pole. I pull one of them down so that I can take a closer look, or perhaps because the Spanish gives it the feel of a souvenir. "Great slogan, yeah? Meaningless, so you get to let it mean whatever you want it to mean."

"I think he's been clear," she says. "'The gods are returning. I have spoken with them. They are ready to accept us, and humanity is about to make the great leap from the Real to the Eternal.'"

"I'm glad you think that's clear. Like, what, we're all going to be vacuumed up into the sky or something?"

"Or something. It's kind of like Internet scams—at least some people will believe anything, if it sounds good enough. In Christianity you get a cloud to sit on. In Islam you get a busload of virgins, at least if you're a guy. Quinn's deal beats the lot—with him, you actually become a god."

"What's his story? It took centuries before Hinduism and Buddhism and Christianity and Islam had any global significance. Mormonism, what, a century?"

"Aye, and fifty years for Scientology."

"But Quinn's done it in, what, two or three years? How is that possible?"

"He's good-looking?"

"I'm sure that explains everything."

"And he has that voice—how did Lorna describe it? 'Och, girl, I canna get enough of it. So smooth, aye, but with that little fiery edge. Chocolate flavored with chili peppers.'"

She's making me smile, a little: this is good.

"So big Julius gives your mother the hots. And you?"

She shudders. "He gives me the creeps. People can be too attractive."

At a hole-in-the-wall café near the cemetery, we sit at a rickety round table, order sodas and fish sandwiches. She has returned to her usual calm self; guess I have not, because when she glances down at the table, and I think she's just looking at the bandages again, I see that I've turned my paper napkin into a little pile of white shreds. I've also gone from hungry to ravenous, as if I can fill that gaping hole in myself with food, but the bandages make me too clumsy. She has to feed me. I've managed only three or four bites when a fragment of conversation comes through the noise of the kitchen behind us, catches my ear. One of the waitresses:

"Dijo que estaba rendido. Pero luego, así nomás—"

Morag has missed it. I repeat it as best I can.

"That's the accent from hell, D."

"Just tell me what it means."

She listens in to the conversation for a minute. "I think she's complaining about her boyfriend being perpetually horny. 'He said he was simply exhausted.'"

"No no. Translate the whole thing. '*Dijo que estan rendo—*'"

"'Dijo que estaba rendido. Pero luego, así nomás.' It means: 'He said he was simply exhausted. But then, just like that'—What's the matter?"

"Reminds me of something. *Así nomás—Así nomás—*"

Then I get it.

The nurses in my room, just before the nightmare. *Treinta personas* in the mountains of New Zealand. *Así nomás, desaparecieron.*

"I'm not exactly up with the news, M. What happened in New Zealand?"

"You've heard the headlines, you've heard everything. Thirty-seven people, to be exact. Some kind of multifamily camping trip on the North Island. It's like Uyuni, they're saying—probably just because it's another volcano. A place called Ruapehu. About three thousand meters, lots of glaciers and snowfields."

"And they've not found them?"

She shakes her head, obviously thinks I'm avoiding the real subject of conversation, looks me in the eye. "D, are you ready to tell me what happened up there?"

Not yet, no. But will I ever be? Probably not. I take a deep breath, fill my lungs until they hurt, then let go.

"Sure. I'm ready."

"So start at the beginning and be methodical for once. You need to tell me every detail, and I need to hear it."

△

As we walk down toward the water, I take her through the days of hiking and climbing. She interrupts, asks for detail, makes me backtrack. When I get to the "accident," I don't describe how weird it felt, or the light and heat that I only half-remember anyway, or mention Mom's voice. But I tell her everything else as I remember it. I even describe what it was like to cut the rope. To watch her fall. To have that image stuck in my head.

"I had the sense that she saw something above us, wanted to get a closer look, and was saying something about it to Rosko. But what could be up there? A group of tourists stepping out of a bus?"

"Would she have been OK, if it hadn't been for the rockfall?"

"Maybe. She put herself in an incredibly exposed position. But we were almost at the top. Knowing her, she could have done the last couple of hundred feet free."

"Free?"

"I mean without a rope or anything. The way you'd climb a fence or a pile of rubble. Just hand-over-hand scrambling."

"People do that? On, like, a vertical cliff face?"

"Good climbers, in the right conditions, yes. Mom, probably with one hand tied behind her back. She was that good."

We've done a long loop through the gray streets. I ache all over. But the wind has died and the fresh salt air feels wonderful. Should tell her about the vial, but can't—not yet. Also I can't tell her, yet, about my irrational, ridiculous, completely settled conviction that there's more to her death than falling rock.

△

Dad and Stefan are in the lobby. The words *body* and *paperwork* float over to me before they turn and see us.

"Wondered where you two had gone. Fresh air?"

I nod. He's thinking about saying, *Don't do that. Don't disappear on me,* but he manages to suppress it. "I checked in with the medevac company," he says. "I never interfered with Iona's expeditions except to insist that she carry the most expensive travel insurance money could buy. Turns out they'll fly all of us back to Seattle in our own plane, Rosko in a hospital bed and all. The doctors have confirmed they can't do the next round of surgery here. We might as well take him all the way back."

"When?"

"Nearest available plane's in Montevideo. Maybe early tomorrow."

We look at each other for a long awkward moment, then he reaches out awkwardly and hugs me. Stefan and Morag get the hint, melt from the scene, and we go over to a group of squarish institutional armchairs in an otherwise empty corner of the lobby. I'm waiting for some profundity about Mom. Instead he just points to my bandaged hands.

"Tell me about the injuries."

"Right one's worse, in the short run anyway. A cut that went through some tendon and right down to the bone. Plus superficial frost damage. Plus I ripped off the thumbnail. Only lasting damage is, I may or may not ever get back full extension in the middle finger."

"A terrible disability. You'll have to be polite to people. What else?"

I hold up the left hand. "Frostbite. All five fingernails, and apparently when they brought me in they thought I'd lose most of the fingers too, but they only had to take off the first knuckle of my pinkie."

Dad grimaces as if this is the most gruesome injury he has ever heard described. "How did you get the bruise on the side of your face?"

I don't want to go there. "A lot of things happened very fast, Dad. It's nothing. After what happened up there, all of this is nothing."

That's my attempt at, Hey, it's OK, we can talk about Mom if you want. But he bites his bottom lip, runs a hand through his hair, and changes the subject. "I was with Derek Partridge," he says. "When I got Gabi's message. Seeing Derek was why I flew to Boston in the first place, not the stupid interview."

"Partridge with the bad bow ties? Guy you knew at Harvard?"

"You remember him then."

"British historian with a thing about ancient libraries. Bit of a lunatic."

"He is a bit of a lunatic, yes. Strange ideas about all sorts of things. Highly respected scholar when I first worked with him. Excellent linguist, a dozen serious books on the culture of the Greeks and Romans. Then Harvard started to find the stuff about Atlantis embarrassing, eased him into early retirement."

"He still working?"

"Like a demon. Fat new book this year and another on the way. He commutes between Boston, London, and Rome, where he survives on a diet of red wine and cheese in the messiest office I've ever seen."

He tries to smile; his mouth makes it, but not his eyes. He's talking about Partridge for the same reason that Morag talked about Quinn—a way of not talking about what we still don't have words for. His obsession with his work, his belief that it's the most important thing in the world, has always been annoying, easy to make fun of, but I get wanting a refuge from reality right now.

"He sent me a message, wanted to see me urgently, said he had something exciting to share. Well, I had something exciting to share too—I hadn't yet told him about the Phaistos fragment at Babylon.

Morag was happy to head off and do her own thing for the day. Me and Derek—"

He lets out a big sigh. "It was so *normal*, Daniel. Not a care. Just two old friends enjoying a day out. We ate pasta puttanesca and hazelnut gelato at an Italian place in the South End. Talked about old times. Talked about work. Took a walk by the river. The best of ordinary life. While you were down here, watching your mother die."

"What did he want to talk about?"

"Several hours of getting around to the point is just Derek's way, and I wasn't in a hurry. I assumed the big reveal would be, you know, 'Bill, I have found evidence that in 200 BCE the library at Alexandria installed gender-neutral toilets.' My mind was mainly on flying home that evening, blitzing through some overdue grading, and then tackling the Akkadian material. Instead, I'm standing on Weeks Bridge with him, enjoying the sunshine, when he blurts out this amazing story about where he thinks I can find dozens of Phaistos Disks. It even sounds plausible, in a nutty, extravagant, typically Derek kind of way."

"I guess nutty is what he does best. What's he come up with now?"

He dismisses it with a wave of his hand, as if there's something wrong with dwelling on the trivia of scholarship when we should be consoling each other. But I sense the conflict between his desire to talk about Mom and his desire to avoid talking about her. I'm conflicted too: hurt, angry, resentful, and at the same time aware that I ought to be feeling as sorry for him as I feel for myself. So I press him to tell me more. And it's good, because for five or ten minutes we have something to talk to each other about that's not personal, not painful. Just a wild yarn involving a lost book called the *Geographika*.

Δ

The real world intrudes again in the form of Stefan Eisler, who's hovering at a discreet distance in the background.

"Sorry to interrupt, but Rosko is awake again. Gabi and Morag are with him now."

Two sentences. The first makes me happy; the second produces a stab of childish anger. I've imagined introducing Morag to Rosko, basked in imaginary pride, and that moment, that piece of emotional candy, has been taken away from me. Stupid. Get a grip. I cast around for a harmless, normal topic of conversation.

"Meant to ask you earlier, Stefan. Where are the Colberts?"

"I forgot to tell you, Daniel. Already gone. They left early this morning."

"Left for home? Just like that?"

"Apparently Sophie's father is ill. Édouard apologized for not waiting long enough to see Bill and Morag, but they managed to get a couple of last-minute seats on a flight to Paris. You were still asleep when the airport shuttle arrived." He looks at his watch. "They'll be almost back by now. Said to wish you luck, and they'd see us again in Seattle. Maybe in a week or so."

Strange. But Dad doesn't react, except to thank Stefan and tell him that we'll follow him upstairs in a minute. We watch him go back over to the elevators. Then Dad pulls out his phone, thumbs at it clumsily, stares at it as if seeking some crucial piece of information. Then he passes it to me.

"Derek was just getting to the meat of his story, talking at two hundred words a minute, when I got the text from Gabi. I've always hated texting."

There are two words on the screen, in all caps. *CALL NOW.*

"The instant I saw it, I knew one of you was dead."

"Just intuition? I didn't think you believed in that." I'm mocking him, can't help it, but he's completely unfazed.

"Intuition has nothing to do with it. If there had been an accident, she would have said, 'Daniel broke wrist. Summit climb abandoned. All safe.' Something like that. Not 'Call now.'"

"Then how did you know it wasn't Rosko?"

He looks round to make sure that Stefan has really gone. "Try to put yourself in my shoes. I love you, Daniel. I may not be good at showing it, but I love you. And I would have given away the world for your mother. So do you know what that does to you? What it does, the next thought in my head was, Let it be Rosko. Please, please, let it be Rosko who has died. Let it be Stefan and Gabi who have lost their only child."

He wants me to tell him that's understandable. Natural. Forgivable. Which it is. But I can't say the words, because I'm thinking how terrible it is that my own feelings so closely mirror his. Why couldn't he be the parent who died? Why couldn't I be left with the loving, engaged, competent one?

He looks out of the window. Probably reading my mind. I try to make up for it and blurt out:

"We had a good climb, Dad. A beautiful climb. There was a rock-fall, right near the summit. It was sudden. She didn't suffer."

He nods, as if thanking me. Tears are coming down his cheek, one after another, like inchworms dropping down a thread. I follow his gaze out into the slush-clotted street, and we sit there in a kind of companionable agony. Which is good, or as good as it can be. But then I ruin the moment by saying what I'm thinking.

"I can still hear her voice."

I suppose a religious person might actually be comforted by that. I'm not. And Dad looks at me as if I've just hit him.

PART II:
THE AKKADIAN VERSION

CHAPTER 8
BEYOND THE MERELY HUMAN

The house feels as if its north wall has been torn away: her absence fills every corner like a freezing wind.

And it's as if each object associated with her is speaking to me, or trying to. In the living room, under a chair, a novel she was halfway through, face down on the floor with the spine bent back. In the bathroom, her shampoo. In the kitchen, the fifty-item spice rack that I built, that we stocked together, that now I can't even use without first reorganizing the little round bottles and then reading the labels aloud, as if reminding her what we have. Their bedroom feels like trespassing, but I go in there too, pass my eyes over her clothes, her shoes, her almost nonexistent cosmetics. I even roam through the attic, where I find the picture books she once read to me, a stuffed giraffe called Lamarck she once gave to me, a third-grade school report I don't like to think of her reading. (*Daniel is trying hard.* Translation: "Nice kid. Basically a dope.")

There's only one room I don't enter, not immediately: her study. It's a cozy little finished space in the unfinished basement, wedged between table tennis and the laundry. That first day back, I go down there, open the door, look in. The picture on her desk is still there: a fading snap of us camping on Vancouver Island when I was six. I hesitate, almost step across the threshold, close the door again.

△

Every one of these reminders brings me back to what she said, an hour before she died: *It's just a news story, nothing to do with me. But I feel this terrible, personal sense of loss.*

Yes.

As if I knew them all.

Yes. Yes, Mom: me too. And I understand, I do: my job is to work out why. I'm jet-lagged, but I'm also beset by almost total insomnia. The first night home, I lie awake in the dark, my mind twitching. The second night, I get up, long after Dad and Morag are asleep, and tiptoe down to the basement in my boxers and robe. Open that door. Sit up in her chair all night, at her computer, hunting.

By early morning I've gathered thirty or forty small news stories from around the world. Each one may (or may not) be an unexplained disappearance. Names, ages, times, and coordinates. Kilimanjaro and Kamchatka. Nagaland in northeast India and Changbaishan in North Korea. Galveston. Lisbon. Tel Aviv. I even discover that survivors have allegedly been found, some of them in "an Alzheimer's-like condition," in the Mandara Mountains, an alien-planet landscape on the border between Nigeria and Cameroon.

Toward dawn I put it all in a spreadsheet and key each case to an online map, complete with color-coded digital thumbtacks. The tacks tell me which cases involve groups versus individuals, which ones still have missing adults or missing children, which ones come with reports of an explosion. There are also one or two cases I can switch to gray immediately: looked suspicious, but turned out to be an accidental drowning, a suicide, or the four fishing buddies in Nunavut who were found sleeping off a boozy seal hunt on a different island from the one they said they were headed for.

By four in the morning I have a backache, headache, eyes full of sand. I consider going to bed, but it's pointless—despite everything, I've never been so awake in my life. So I wander into the kitchen, decide that cooking will take my mind off things. Cinnamon-pecan sticky buns. From scratch: not the white-glazed garbage you buy at the grocery store but an ultrabuttery yeasted dough, drowned in a lava of nuts and caramelizing sugar. Takes an hour to put together, another for the dough to rise, but as soon as they're in the oven the smell draws Dad downstairs.

"Morning, Daniel. Sleep OK?"

He's peering at me with concern, but doesn't know what else to say.

"Fine."

Morag follows a minute later. "That smells wicked, D. Got me up at least five minutes early." She flips on the radio, sits at the place I've laid out. They're two bites in, grunting their appreciation for my culinary skills, when the announcer mentions one of the "disappearance" stories and says he's going to cut to some comments by the founder of the Seraphim—as if Julius Quinn, like the president or the pope, is an obvious choice now for some comforting wisdom in troubled times. When he's asked about the disappearances, then in the same breath about what the Christian fundamentalists call Rapture, he laughs his soft, kindly laugh, like someone appreciating a joke:

"As I foresaw, the time of our Anabasis is here. And these so-called disappearances show, I believe, that enlightened individuals are already finding the stairway, even by themselves. They have learned the language of the Architects, or learned enough of it for their minds to transition to dimensions beyond the merely human. This process is our destiny, preordained and unstoppable, and it is not to be feared but celebrated. We were once animals, and became human. In the same way, we will pass beyond the merely human. In the end, all of us will be transformed, the world left behind, the eternal opened up to us. And it will be a paradise far beyond all the petty, unimaginative daydreams to which the world's religions have attached that name. It will be infinity."

The guy on the radio clearly has no clue what to make of this, beyond the fact that he's supposed to sound all impressed and respectful. Morag seems impressed too, in her sarcastic way. "So, you explain a few people gone missing with the theory that they wore the right organic hemp, and repeated the right spells as the sun came up, and now they've become immortal! I mean, wow. What's Quinn's secret? When your average holy hoke-merchant says that kind of crap, it's because they're suffering from low blood sugar, or forgot to take their lithium, and only fools take them seriously."

"A *lot* of fools are taking Quinn seriously," I point out.

"I know, I know. And I can totally see why people drop everything and follow this guy."

"You think he's persuasive?"

"Oh aye, Daniel, totally. No, I don't. In fact I want to grab his followers by the collar, and shake them, and say, '*Where were you people, when they handed out the bullshit detectors?*' But if you're already trained from childhood to believe in God, and a personal afterlife, and then Quinn comes along and tells you it's not about being good so that you can get to heaven but about actually *becoming* a *god*, well, I can see why millions of people are buying it."

"You know he was one of my students once?" Dad says. "Charismatic. Intense and relaxed at the same time. Everyone was crazy about him, especially the women. An ordinary Chicago kid. Parents died when he was five, and he was raised by the same Irish-Catholic grandparents he got the blue eyes from."

"Wasn't he planning to become a priest?" Morag asks.

"Yes. And then he showed up here, full of sophisticated questions about the origin of language. I found him unnerving, to be honest."

I'm washing dishes by this point—offering to help has not occurred to either of them—and I can't resist throwing a comment over my shoulder from the sink: "That's because you have the atheist's stupid prejudice that religious people are stupid."

Dad lets slip a smile. Quietly admitting both the prejudice and the fact that Quinn disproved it.

"He was with you less than a year, right?" Morag says.

"Yep. Disappeared at the end of the year and never came back. He went hiking with three friends in Mexico. They all disappeared on Popocatépetl."

Morag frowns—any reference she doesn't get, she finds immensely irritating. For once, it's me who can fill the information gap. "Second-highest volcano in Mexico. Nearly eighteen thousand feet. Not exactly a hike."

"No," Dad says. "Quinn stumbled into a police station with frostbitten toes and a story so wacky they suspected him of killing the others. They held him for a month while they investigated. Found one of the bodies on the mountain, but they said it looked like a big avalanche, so they let him go. He wrote *Anabasis* as soon as he returned. The whole book in one day, allegedly. He claims it was *dictated* to him."

He makes a little spiral with his finger next to his head, indicating his opinion that Quinn is not playing with a full deck. Then gets up, eager to be starting his day. In a second he'll want to say, *You going to be all right today, then?* and expect me to neutralize his guilt by saying, *Sure, no problem, I'm doing just great.* Then he'll take Morag with him to their oh-so-urgent Akkadian translation work.

To stall them, I ask how it's going.

"Difficult material," he says evasively.

"No standard reference books?"

He picks a rogue pecan off the counter, pops it into his mouth. "Sure there are standard reference books. I wrote them. No use for this material. It's old. Unusual. And then there's the whole thing about the Phaistos fragment."

"No other clues on that?"

Dad has started absentmindedly peeling the label off last night's beer bottle. "We keep finding references to 'the round objects,' or at least that's what we think they're saying. Round something, anyway. It seems to be Disks they're talking about."

"That reminds me—you never told me why you stopped in Boston in the first place. What was Derek Partridge wetting his pants about?"

I aim this at Dad, but it's Morag who answers—which kind of emphasizes that I'm way outside their loop.

"He's spent decades trying to track down a complete copy of one particular book. *Geographika*—it was written around 230 BCE by a Greek mathematician, Eratosthenes. A kind of compendium of all knowledge about the world and its history."

Dad puts down the bottle and looks at me. "Derek's the one who taught me that myths don't just come from nowhere. And he thinks the *Geographika* could finally tell us what the historical truth is behind the idea of Atlantis. Supposedly no complete copy survived, but he thinks he knows where to find one. And not just any copy— the one that was owned by Cicero."

I've heard of Cicero, but some perverse instinct makes me want to play dumb. Maybe because it will help drag them both back to a normal level.

"Scissor who?"

"Cicero," Morag says. "Marcus Tullius Cicero. Major Roman statesman, but don't sweat the details. He went into a kind of voluntary exile from Rome for a couple of years, and in 79 BCE he ended up on the island of Rhodes."

Dad butts in: "It was like Princeton or something. A colony of Greek philosophers arguing about, well, everything. Is the soul immortal? Do numbers exist, or are they just in your head? How do volcanoes work?"

"So Cicero was, like, a rich tourist?"

"He was exactly a rich tourist. Romans were suckers for Greek art. He wrote to a friend back in Rome, bragging about buying up all the best stuff from a guy named Posidonius, who among other things had a copy of the *Geographika*. Now here's where it really gets interesting. He also mentioned that Posidonius had a collection of *diskoi* for sale."

"Phaistos *diskoi*? You're kidding."

"Derek thinks that's exactly what he's talking about," Dad says. "It's why he contacted me."

"We spent years scrabbling in the dirt in Greece, and all this time there's a whole pile of Disks gathering dust in a basement in Rome?"

"That's where the trail goes cold. Partridge found the letter in the Biblioteca Angelica. One of the oldest libraries in Rome. He's convinced the book is there too, and maybe more information about the Disks."

They glance at each other. It could be just impatience—time to go—but I sense something more; plus, he's never really answered my question about the Akkadian texts.

"You've found something out already, haven't you? Something in the translation?"

Dad looks at Morag, then at the table. Morag winces, bites her lower lip. "Aye."

"Jesus, M. Spit it out."

"The tablets, at least what we've translated so far. They, uh. We're not sure, but—"

She looks at Dad again, as if hoping he'll intervene. No chance: still examining the table.

"The thing of it is—they agree with Quinn."

"What do you mean?"

"It's his story. The one he tells in *Anabasis*. What the Akkadian scribes say is: the 'gods' were beings who visited us because they considered us ready, in some way—ready to become immortal."

She twists her lips apologetically. "I know, I know. I'm just telling you what the cuneiform says."

"Go on."

"The Akkadians say the gods taught them the divine language in order to foster their development. 'In order to make us,' it says at one point. Or maybe 'in order to complete us.' And then it says: 'But we were wicked, so we defied the gods, and invented languages of our own. Instead of reaching closer to the divine, we got further and further away from it.'"

"They say the gods punished them," Dad adds. "And one day, when humanity is ready again, they'll return. 'For their purpose is to raise us up to be with them, among them, immortal.' Sounds just like *Anabasis*."

"But what you're saying is impossible. Isn't it? This was written thousands of years ago, and nobody knew about it until now—or until Jimmy and Lorna found the library at Babel. And Quinn had already written *Anabasis* before that. So how could he have known this story ahead of time. Or am I missing something?"

Morag gets up. "You're not missing anything, D. Or, more likely, we're all missing something. Yummy breakfast by the way. Thanks."

△

Dad gets up too, and finds his jacket. They both head out, on their way to the university. I'm left alone in the house again.

Amazing, above all, how *ordinary* things are. Outside, the buses keep running on Fifteenth Avenue. The planes keep roaring too low overhead as they lumber into Sea-Tac. The joggers keep jogging in the park. People leave the same old flyers on the doorstep, offering yard service, house painting, salvation.

Even when the news comes in from New Zealand, it's like everyone's too busy to spare it more than a worried glance.

Mount Ruapehu is right in the center of the North Island. A dozen kids, mostly in their teens and tweens, straggle out of the forest at the point of collapse. When I switch on the TV, one of the people right there in the frame is a teenage girl carrying a baby. Her face is hollow, mud-smeared. "We lost track of the adults near Mangawhero Falls?" she says. "They were marching uphill really quick, and wouldn't listen to us, and we couldn't keep up?" A grim-looking man with a microphone is interviewing her at what looks like a ranger's station. Later he confides to the camera, "Twenty-three bodies have been recovered so far, in circumstances very similar to the Uyuni incident."

They switch to sports news after that. When I go online it's the same, mainly: *What a terrible thing*, people are saying—and then they get right back to the latest stock market story or celebrity puppy adoption. Sure, the CDC is onto it, or claims to be. Sure, some minor office in the depths of the World Health Organization has epidemiologists and demographers test-driving their latest computer models to no effect. Otherwise, it's like the first indications of civil war in a distant country. It's there in the news, but mostly people are ignoring it.

Me, I don't get why people aren't more *frightened*. I hunker down at Mom's desk again, listen to loud music. Out on the Wild Wild Web, I soon find myself some company, even if it's not the best for my self-esteem. Right now, the only people who agree with me that there's something to worry about are conspiracy theorists, mouth-breathers, trolls. A blogger named Epocalyps—who probably has five assault rifles, a big investment in canned goods, a network of spider-holes in north Idaho—thinks it's all mass kidnappings. Two or three others are feeding each other's desire for a new pandemic, as if the prospect of a third of the world population dying horribly is kind of sexy. (*It's a virus mutated from bats, or maybe cats. Invades the brain, drives you nuts, makes you wander off. Kind of like Ebola. Or do we mean Marburg?*) From there it's all downhill: the mass hypnosis theory, the secret government program theory, the alien abduction theory, the good ol' possessed-by-demons theory.

Can't swallow either the fanged-demons-from-hell theory or the fanged-greenbloods-from-another-planet theory? Then Julius Quinn is about the only game in town.

CHAPTER 9
GRIEVING IS A PROCESS

Over the next few days I get an hour's sleep here, twenty minutes there: I'd love to do ten hours, but seem to have lost the knack. Nobody tells me how haggard and ill I look, because I don't: some hidden reserve of adrenaline is keeping me in a state that's like the reverse of hibernation. During the night, I piece together tiny filaments of evidence for a connection between the disappearances and the Seraphim; during the day I see my friends, hang out, put on a show of *normal* that most people swallow.

I figure out right away that people think they know what grief is, even if they've never really experienced it. What they expect is a kind of dull, wounded sadness, a faraway look, tension and distraction mixed with just the occasional ability to laugh at something briefly. So that's what I give them—it keeps the questions at bay. But the fact is, none of them can relate to my experience on the Torre Sur, much less to the bizarre way I truly feel, so no one knows what to say. People I actually like, people I feel a little bit close to, end awkward silences by saying half-assed things like *Wow, I'm so sorry, Daniel*, or *It really sucks about the accident*. Adults, God help them, say even dorkier, more clueless things, like *Grieving is a process*—then give me awkward, one-armed hugs. As if they want to do the right thing, but without risking infection.

I introduce everyone to Morag. She gets on with them way better than I'd expected. With Kit especially: they jabber at each other in Russian, make each other laugh, seem compatible in a way I hadn't thought possible. But Morag herself has taken such a deep plunge into the Akkadian translations that she doesn't need any of us really—doesn't even want me to play tour guide. She goes with me for coffee a couple of mornings; because I'm eager to show off the real Seattle, I take her to the serious independent cafés—Espresso Vivace, Victrola. She likes it; in fact, it's obvious from the way she interrogates the baristas about the structure of a good crema, or the acidity balance in Sumatran Mandheling, that given more time she'll become a full-bore Seattle coffee snob. But more time is something she doesn't have now. Hike tomorrow? *Maybe next week.* Take the kayaks out? *You know I hate water.*

Even when I drag her down to Pike Place, show her troll-caught sockeye flying through the air like ingots of wet steel, she's only half there. I buy her cinnamon mini-donuts to eat while enjoying the view of Puget Sound. "It's beautiful," she says vaguely, pointing across the water to the mountains, then falls silent again, looks at her phone. She's running late. She has arranged, again, to spend the day with Dad at the ISOC library.

△

At least I can find some comfort in the Eisler miracle. First thing off the plane, highly paid butchers in blue hospital scrubs split Rosko open like a hog on a slab and spend eighteen hours using laser-guided diamond drills to do fancy stuff to his spine; he now has, in addition to the bolts in his right leg, half a dozen custom-fabricated slivers of titanium holding his lower sacrum together.

The surgery's supposed to be followed by weeks in the hospital and months of physical therapy. But Rosko is Rosko. He confounds the surgeons, astonishes the doctors, amazes the physical therapists. A couple of days after they stitch him up—by way of what's supposed to be a brief experiment—two orderlies pick him up like he's antique glass and deposit him gently in a wheelchair. A short test-drive, that's all they have in mind, then back to bed. One of them pushes him around the corridors, asks him every three yards whether he's OK, then leaves him in his room while she goes to find a different pillow. Five minutes later, the therapist comes by and discovers him doing reversed-hand chin-ups on the door frame.

"How did you even get up there?" I ask him. I'm sitting in a sunny corner window, with a view out over Elliott Bay to the jagged white underbite of the Olympics.

"Not really a problem. Left leg holds my weight. So I wheeled myself over, balanced on it, and jumped. A good workout too—the frame's only an inch thick, so you're forced to use your fingertips."

He looks at mine a bit guiltily. They've been unwrapped at last—a mass of blisters and scars.

"What did the PT say?"

"'*Get down from there immediately, Mr. Eisler. What on earth do you think you are doing?*' Like I'm eight years old and risking a major time-out. I said to her: Hey, sorry, but the parts of my body that still work are getting seriously bored."

He's already had visits from carloads of people, mostly adoring girls. He could try for sympathy by going on about how he nearly died. But he lacks even a shred of self-pity, so instead he's been spinning pretty yarns about how Mr. Daniel "Superhero" Calder, through feats of incredible skill and bravery, saved his life. I plan my visits solo. That way it's less embarrassing. That way, I'm free to talk to him about what's bugging me.

"The disappearances, Rosko."

"What really happened on the climb, Rosko."

"What really happened to the Colberts."

He tries to be nice about it but won't take it seriously. Says I'm just showing how stressed I am.

"It's weird, though, the way they left like that, without waiting to see Dad and Morag, or leaving a message or anything. I've tried to contact them. They don't answer emails or texts, and they're not updating anything online."

"Your dad say anything about them?"

"Clueless. Doesn't know them. Says Mom's company hired them once for advertising work. Which I already knew."

He shrugs. "They're videographers. Probably went straight from Paris to shooting a documentary in Svalbard, or Madagascar. I'm sure they fall off the map for weeks. Why do you want to contact them anyway?"

I can't keep the irritation out of my voice. "To ask them what they *saw*. But when I call their studio, I just get Sophie sounding all perky—'Please leave a message, back to you as soon as possible'—like she just stepped out to the grocery store. I don't believe it. I got their address in Seattle, down in the south end halfway to the airport. I managed to get into the building, just walked in after someone else."

"Nobody there?"

"Nobody. And a fat layer of dust on the door handle."

"Wait a second. You said, 'When I call their studio.' How many times have you called?"

"Two or three times."

This is a small lie that just kind of slips out. The truth: five or six or seven times.

"So you actually rode halfway to the airport just to play detective at their studio?"

"Something's not right—I needed to find out what. You think I'm being ridiculous, don't you?"

"I don't know what to think, Daniel. But you're taking this way too seriously. You tell me all this vague spooky stuff about the climb, none of which I remember, and you seem, uh, a little obsessed."

"I have to understand what happened, that's all. I'd be doing better if you could come up with any more memories."

He looks exasperated. "The shrinks have been in, Daniel, given me the full workout, and there's no evidence I'm suffering from amnesia, PTSD, or anything else except broken bones. I simply don't *have* any more memories."

"Something—something *happened* up there that you've forgotten. I swear."

"What happened up there is your mother died, and then you nearly died at least twice yourself. What you're experiencing is shock."

"You're saying I'm inventing this stuff?"

"I don't know. But you need to stop worrying about everything so much. I think your emotions are playing tricks on you."

"Do me a favor?"

"Sure."

"Just—just dig. Start with the Colberts. Find out whatever you can about them."

"All they have online is a website made from a freebie template and a couple of half-dead social media pages. Nothing else there."

"I'm only asking you to look harder, that's all."

He looks around the room. "Nothing else to do while I'm here in prison. But you have to do me a favor in return."

"What?"

"Worry less. Get out more. Go get some, you know, serious aerobic exercise." He arches one eyebrow. "With Kit."

"You're a bad influence."

"What friends are for."

△

I am getting exercise with Kit, though not what Rosko has in mind. Theory was, she'd keep running while I was in Patagonia, I'd get a workout from the climbing, we'd be doing twelve-milers together by now. But my knee's still puffy and sore. First couple of sessions, when Kit comes out of afternoon classes we go for a slow, painful jog, which turns into a fast walk, which turns into me enjoying three ibuprofen and an ice wrap while her beautiful long legs carry her up and down the Howe Street steps.

Lying in the park afterward, grass tickling my neck, I find myself trying to count bright-white Styrofoam clouds as they float in a swimming-pool sky, because it's a good way to avoid looking at Kit's damp hair, tight black running shorts, spray-on white tank top. Suddenly she rolls over on one elbow and looks at me. "I liked meeting your sister," she says. "She is maybe not easiest person in world. Ambitious, like wow yes. And so smart. A bit awkward. But I can see she is wearing mask. Something hard, for protection. Underneath, I think her real face is not so sure of everything."

This is the best description of Morag I've ever heard. Something that none of my other friends, not even Rosko, has noticed.

"Also, Daniel, I am sorry about your mother. Actually, I know what this is like."

"Nobody knows what it's like."

"You are wrong. You watch your mother fall from mountain. I watch my father drown."

"I'm sorry—I had no idea. How did it happen?"

"Slowly. It take a whole year."

I roll over and face her. "He took a year to drown?"

She holds my look for a long moment, then says in a flat, deadpan voice: "Traditional Russian story. He fall into bottle of vodka. Bottle has narrow neck. Cannot get out."

It's a kind of grim joke—permission for us both to see a flash of humor shining through the darkest imaginable material. It loosens something in me, makes me feel she's the one person I can be frank with.

"At least you were left with the functional parent."

"Your father is difficult? Yes. I see that. Containered?"

"Self-contained. That's a polite way to put it."

She nods, then pushes me to talk more about Mom, Morag, Rosko, the climb. I do—and then, because I like her, because I need to spill, also probably because I'm deeply in lust, I go on. I describe the nagging sense that Rosko and I are both missing something that happened. I even mention hearing Mom's voice. And the insomniac nights I've spent researching the disappearances. Everything.

Too desperate to hear someone say *I believe you*, I guess. But Kit doesn't say she believes me, any more than Rosko did. Instead she says:

"Daniel, I think you are basket cake."

"I'm what?"

"Basket cake—going crazy."

"No. It's, 'You are a basket case.'"

"Is so? *You are basket case*? I thought it was from being, I don't know, a kind of funny cake, like a small cake, and that a cake is not intelligent and makes the bad personal decisions. No?"

"No."

"Listen. You say everyone you are fine, everything OK. But cannot sleep, have anxieties, then you are saying me you cannot stop thinking about some news stories, maybe have memory loss, hallucinations, whatever. So this 'fine fine fine' is like, total bullshit, Daniel. Stop being the machismo guy, yes? You need help."

Does Kit's way of speaking make her seem more special than she is? Or more vulnerable than she is? Dunno. But my irritation that she too has reduced everything to a set of symptoms liquefies and dissolves in the heat of my desire for her.

Wouldn't everything else just go away, if I pulled her toward me and gave her a serious, in-depth, twenty-minute kiss?

Trust your instincts—that's what Mom always said. Fairly sure she wasn't talking about sucking face with beautiful Russian girls in the park, but still. I lean across, put one hand on the back of her neck, look into her eyes, and draw her toward me.

She doesn't look shocked or surprised. She just laughs, pushes me off, jumps up.

"Will you go see doctor, at least? For me?"

The smell of her skin lingers on the air like fine, sweet smoke. I breathe in deep, feeling dizzy.

"Will you? Daniel? You are not even listening."

"Sure."

"Not 'sure,'" she says sternly. 'Sure' is like, pathetic. Is American way of say yes when you mean no. You have to promise."

The word catches in my throat. "I promise."

"And knee is feeling a little better now, yes?"

"Eighty, ninety percent," I say, exaggerating wildly.

"Good! Race you to top of water tower, basket cake."

Chapter 10
May You Join Them

A promise.

For exactly no other reason, I go to the family doctor. We talk about Mom. We talk about The Nature of Loss. In an attempt to be at least halfway honest, I even mention both the nightmares and being saved from them by insomnia. But I leave out half of what I said to Kit; I leave out the fact that this pure thing called *grief* feels more like a dirty mix of anxiety, acute loneliness, and a crawling nameless dread.

Dr. Lovecraft has a gray buzz cut, round steel glasses, an open shirt, one diamond earring; considers himself a dude. His whole attitude of lazy, I-was-once-a-pothead good cheer makes it obvious he'll never understand what I'm experiencing. Still, apparently I "need some help," and his prescription for my continued sanity, or stability, or faked-up happiness is that each morning for the next three months—or six, or possibly the rest of my life—I should spike my morning espresso with 500 mg of Zampodex, a hot new billion-dollar molecule from one of our own biotechs.

△

On the way back to the house I text Rosko, yet again.

Anything?

Not on the Colberts. Something on me, though: freedom, tomorrow afternoon.

When I get back, Dad's off at a faculty meeting and Morag's in the kitchen, reading a paperback while doing serious damage to a pecan pie. She puts the book down; the cover features a long-haired beefcake not-quite-wearing a ruffled shirt—Cynthia Bland's deathless classic *He Stole My Heart.*

"Let me guess. The sequel's called *Then He Came Back and Stole My Pancreas.*"

"Hilarious, D."

"Those things can destroy your brain."

"You've never read one."

I drag her out for a walk. In the park she gravitates toward a giant sequoia that stands at the back of the Asian Art Museum. It's one of the biggest trees in the city; the space around its trunk, a circle of fallen material, is muffled, private. You can't be seen easily, but there's a view out to where people are biking, jogging, being walked by their dogs.

Morag looks at me, seems about to speak, breathes in deep. "I think I can get used to it here, D."

"You don't like cities."

"No. But big trees are good. You can pretend the city's just a temporary clearing in the forest. I missed trees so much in Iraq. Nowhere to climb, nowhere to hide."

"I keep trying to take you hiking in the real forest. Out at Lake Quinault I could show you the biggest spruce in the world. But you're too busy."

She looks at me apologetically, but doesn't apologize. Instead she bends down, picks up a chunk of bark the size of a brick, starts stripping the salmon-colored fibers from the underside and examining them minutely. Then, with an agility that surprises me, she jumps up, grabs a low branch. A second later, she's standing on a higher one, directly over my head. She balances there on one leg, her arms at her side, looking down at me.

"Be patient," she says. "The Akkadian materials are a big deal, but once we're done—"

I'm about to interrupt, about to tell her that the desperate impatience I feel is mainly not about her, when we hear chanting.

I can tell where it's coming from—a grass slope on the other side of the museum that's a popular spot for concerts, rallies, guys in tights declaiming that *To be, or not to be* is definitely the question. Morag jumps down from her perch, landing neatly next to me like an acrobat.

"Let's go check it out."

I feel my phone buzz, glance down at it: *Correction. Think I've found something. Later.*

"Rosko?"

"Yeah. He's—he says they may be letting him go as early as tomorrow."

"That's great."

⚠

A crowd of people is milling around under a line of chestnut trees, along a roadway in front of the museum. And it's clear now that the voice coming up from the other side of the park is no amateur Hamlet. The tone's too hectoring, too motivational for that. We're in among the crowd before I notice that some of them are holding banners. Then I get the point.

A Seraphim rally.

"Jesus, they're everywhere," Morag says, like someone who has just discovered an infestation of bugs. She immediately turns to leave. We walk north toward the Victorian white-and-glass wedding cake that's the plant conservatory. At the edge of the crowd, under the statue of William Henry Seward, we run into a smiling, moon-faced young man with a "Know It Is True" button and a stack of leaflets. Morag jumps away from him as if she's been bitten, but I'm impressed by the guy's calm, his sincerity:

"Learn the truth, ma'am. Reverend Quinn is leading us toward the light. Showing us the stairway. Leading us to our fullest potential as ascended beings."

I take the leaflet. "Thanks. We'll look at it."

He offers me a slight bow. "May you learn the language of the Architects, and in their language forget your own. May they hear you, and may you join them. *Dir-pan-uk, Ek-lim-u, Lim-go-qa, Yi-che-rin.*"

Listening to his chant, I feel as if my whole body has pins and needles. Morag is tugging at my arm before he even turns away. "Let's get out of here."

I'm fascinated and frightened at the same time, but I don't want her to see either emotion. So I try to act casual. "You're worse than Dad. Religion's not contagious." And I walk back a few paces, until I can see the speaker.

He's a prominent Lutheran pastor who has switched allegiance to the new faith. Behind him there's a white banner, big enough to carpet half a tennis court, with a twenty-foot image of Quinn's face on it. We check out the crowd as best we can, but we're at the back. I'm not looking for anyone in particular, just want to stay a bit longer. Morag tugs my sleeve again, uncomfortable as always with what she calls *public displays of religion.*

"OK, OK. Let's go, before you lose your lunch or break out in a rash." We turn and walk right into Dad's Aussie philosopher colleague.

I'd naturally say something like, 'Professor Maynard Jones—nice to see you.' Morag, who has already met him on campus, beats me to it, waves enthusiastically, gives a little skip.

"Hey, Mayo! What the hell are you doing here?"

"Daniel, Morag. An unexpected pleasure." And he deadpans: "To answer your question, Morag, I'm here because I woke up this morning and decided I wanted to find out about becoming immortal."

I like the way he takes Morag's greeting totally in his stride. It strikes me again: Aussie men are supposed to be big, loud, sunburned, casually dressed, and interested mainly in beer. Mayo so utterly fails the stereotype. Slight, pale, soft-spoken. Talks like a diplomat and dresses like a high-end banker. Despite the warm afternoon, he's wearing a crisp white shirt under a suit. As usual, despite the suit, he looks comfortable, casually stylish, relaxed.

Morag's on his wavelength: "Just for insurance, Daniel and I decided to join all the religions."

I nod earnestly and we all have a good laugh.

"Actually," Mayo says, switching to more or less serious mode, "I do find religion fascinating, the Seraphim especially. We philosophers love to dismiss other people's beliefs as irrational, and we always assume it would be better to have rational beliefs—by which we mean our own. But these people seem happy, wouldn't you say? They have a profound sense of community. They have hope. Energy. Purpose."

He's making a serious point, while also teasing. I can see Morag is going to let this go, so I put an oar in: "Even if they're happy, you still think they're wrong."

His eyes twinkle; he likes to be challenged a bit. "I do, I do. My views are even more extreme than your father's. It's taken us more than a hundred and fifty years to get comfortable with Darwin—who replaced the lovely but false idea that we are God's handiwork with the unlovely truth that we're primordial slime plus mutations. It's going to take even longer for the general public to swallow the implications of modern physics."

"Which are?"

"That the universe is a computer, and we're subroutines within it."

"Great," Morag says drily. "It's going to suck if we're badly coded."

"Oh, but we are! Total screw-up. An entire Creation that's like an early version of Windows. And yet—" He spreads his hands approvingly over the crowd. "And yet Quinn is definitely onto something. Every religion's a theory, you see. A big, ambitious, overweight theory. It wants to explain what the gods are. And how they created us. And what they plan to do with us. Past. Nature. Destiny. Quinn's offering a seductive alternate to all those traditional destinies, and people love it."

We all turn to contemplate the scene, so I'm not actually looking at him when he says the next thing. It reaches my ears like an echo. I'm hurled back seven years, into that church in Heraklion. I hear his words in Mom's voice, almost as if she's speaking to me again: "Striking, isn't it? That religion is so appealing. So *successful*?"

Morag gets into a discussion with him about the accelerating extinction of languages—how Quinn thinks it's just fine, because it's bringing us closer to Unity or something. While they're talking I check my phone again. About a dozen messages have come in. They're summed up by the one from Julia Shubin:

Rosko out THIS AFTERNOON!! Pizza at my house.

△

Julia hosting a pizza party means a guy at the front door with a credit card reader and a stack of greasy cardboard. So I let Morag get back to Dad, try unsuccessfully to get hold of Rosko again, then tell Julia

I'll handle the food. After biking to three different stores, I show up at her house with a backpack full of groceries.

Julia plays Bach for me on her expensive cello while I make tomato sauce and slap pizza dough around. Alex shows up with Aaron; Ella and Kit are right behind them. Ella has lime-green hair today—she gets it recolored once a week at a place called Scream—but mainly she's wearing all-black Goth, including a long coat, platform boots, half a pound of eyeliner. Kit, flute case in hand, is wearing the usual too: zero make-up, old jeans, a neon-yellow running jacket over a T-shirt for her favorite hometown punk band, Leningrad.

"God, Daniel," Ella says. "That smell is making me ravenous. Is it ready? Or do I have to lick the tomato sauce off your jeans?"

She's flirting because she always flirts, but also to cover for what she's actually thinking, which is that she ought to have found a way to ask how I'm feeling, ought to have actually said something about Mom, and just doesn't know how to bring it up.

Can't blame her. Nobody does.

She comes over and kisses me on the cheek, in a way that's also flirty but leaves me stone cold. Then Kit comes over and does likewise, except that her kiss is merely friendly, and feels like someone just ran a hundred volts through my boxers.

"Morag not here?" Ella asks.

"Woman on a mission. Working with Dad on the Babel tablets sixteen, eighteen hours a day."

"Guess they do have the secrets of the universe in their hands," Ella says, a distinct edge of sarcasm in her voice. "Babel Babel Babel."

I wince at this, but try to act as if I've not noticed. Then she shifts her attention to Aaron, draping an arm around his neck because she knows it will make him self-conscious. "What do you think of my nails, snuggle-buns?"

"Uh, they're, uh, nice. Kind of, uh, peach-colored?" Aaron says, vaguely aware that anything ever asked him by any girl is probably a trick question.

"Safe bet, gorgeous. But wrong. This is an all-new shade. See the way there's orange and yellow streaking in the red? Comes right out of the bottle like that. It's called Welcome to Hell."

⚠

While I'm assembling the pizzas, Stefan shows up as promised to deliver Rosko, who receives a prince's welcome. I can tell from his eyes that he wants to talk privately, but everyone's crowded into the kitchen, wanting a piece of his attention. When Aaron starts eating anchovies three at a time, I shoo them all out.

"Go. Everyone. Go now, or no food."

Rosko lags behind and for a second it looks like we'll get a minute to ourselves, but then Ella comes back in and stands in the doorway, ostentatiously lighting a joint.

"How long, Daniel?"

"No wonder you're hungry, Ella. Keep your munchies under control for another five."

I make a face at Rosko—*Later*. Not long after that, I'm slicing fresh pie amid oohs and aahs of appreciation. Margherita with extra basil for the veggies. Pepperoni for the people with only a limited allocation of taste buds—Julia, Aaron. And, for the sophisticated people, my own riff on a pizza Niçoise, piled brightly with goodies: red onion, anchovies, arugula, capers, whole cloves of roasted garlic, two kinds of olives.

"This is awesome," Ella says, snitching a hunk of loose topping from the Niçoise. "Is that lemon zest?"

"Yes."

"Weird. But good."

"Thanks."

I'm turned the other way when Kit responds to this by saying, "Daniel is genius for cook." Hearing her speak about me this way makes my ego inflate like a party balloon—until I turn round, and see that she's saying it to Rosko while leaning in close with a little giggle to brush a crumb off his chin.

Shrugging it off, telling myself it's nothing, I grab a root beer. We all gather around the TV, where Aaron is saying we should watch "something really bad, like 1970s *Dr. Who.*"

The chance to escape into another dimension for a while sounds good to me. "'Brain of Morbius'?" I suggest. "That's extremely bad. In a good way."

Julia picks up the remote to start searching. But we never do get our dose of the Time Lord.

CHAPTER 11
GOAT ROCKS

Breaking news, breaking news. From a place in the middle of nowhere that I know like the back of my hand.

A guy in a studio, pale and stunned as if his doctor has just given him three months, is saying, *Strange story, but they seem hysterical, and we don't yet have any clear account of what happened.* Then they cut to an overdressed woman in the back of a news helicopter, shouting into a mic over the noise: "We're about a hundred miles southeast of Seattle, approaching Mount Gilbert in the Goat Rocks Wilderness. Reports came in late this morning of an explosion that rattled windows as far afield as Longview and Yakima. At about the same time, a group of teens from a multifamily camping trip found their way to a campground near here and reported that the adults in their group—"

Someone cuts her off and points. As she turns, the camera follows her eyes out the open door. A mile away you can see a sawtoothed ridge that seems to grow dramatically as the helicopter loses altitude.

"You can see Mount Gilbert now. We've been told—"

But someone off-camera interrupts her again—*down there, down there to the right of the ridge*—and a hand comes into the frame, pointing urgently. In the scrubby vegetation a perfect ring is visible, perhaps twenty yards in diameter, like the raked dirt on a baseball field, except that everything is swept outward from the central circle. Inside the circle, a ring of human figures is visible.

The chopper dips forward, like a dragonfly hunting, then swoops in through a litter of cloud and settles in a whirl of dust. Then the frame veers away. The next shot—wobbly, handheld—shows three or four of the people from the helicopter, backs to the camera, hiking and scrambling across a ravine. You can hear the camera operator wheezing and cursing as he slips and tries to balance. Then a girl's voice: "This way." The lens glances in her direction. Reddish ponytail, freckles, maybe fifteen—obviously she's one of the survivors.

They come out onto less difficult ground. The wind against the mic makes a sound like someone moving furniture in an old house.

The circle is thirty feet across and has a perfectly sharp boundary, as if cut by a knife. Outside, the vegetation has been gouged away in a ring twenty yards wide; inside, the grass looks untouched. The camera examines this border, then comes up behind the motionless back of a woman, who stands with one hiking boot right on it. She's wearing a puffy green hiking jacket. The cameraman lingers, as if hesitating, taking in the sheer stillness of her body—nothing moving, except the loose end of a red scarf that twitches in the wind. Then he steps around her, keeps the lens pointed at the ground. Twenty paces later, on the other side, he raises it again.

Four people standing, the woman and three men. The other eight are lying in the snow, and there's no question from the postures: they're all dead. Spilled among the bodies, at all angles in the mud, several copies of a small red book.

Now you see that within the ring of grass, beneath the dead, there's something else—a pile of rocks. It's just rubble: a pitiful mound as wide as a small room and maybe three feet high at the center. But it has the look of something constructed. The cameraman lingers on it, then sweeps dramatically upward to reveal one of the standing figures. A young man, midtwenties, with thick, dark eyebrows sprouting from under a cloth cap. He looks skinny and frail, but his hands are holding out, like an offering, an angular chunk of rock as big as his own head.

The camera moves in to examine the rock, the hands, then pans sideways to his face. And the world gets its first close-up of that look.

That look.

The almost-blank eyes: they move about, a little, even follow you as you move, but then they drift away and never quite seem to settle on anything. The almost-blank mouth: motionless, held half an inch open with the tongue moving almost imperceptibly between the teeth as if saying *Th—, Th—, Th—*.

As if arrested midword. As if just moments ago robbed of words.

The four figures just stand there, facing the summit, almost but not quite smiling. Unbearably docile. Waiting.

There's a new sound now. The camera turns toward it, seeking it out. The girl they have brought with them, the one who said, *This way*, is on her knees among the rocks at the center of the circle, with her arms flung across one of the fallen figures, wailing. The camera goes to her face, then the man's, her dirty fingers moving against his cheek.

Same hair, same nose, same chin. The girl looks up into the camera, half-talking, half-crying. Behind her, her father's eyes are still visible, staring blankly.

"They were doing this chanting thing, and they didn't reply when we said hello, and then they went off up this track, miles and miles, and we kept saying, 'Hello, hello, where are you going,' and I said, 'Daddy, Daddy, stop,' but they wouldn't listen, and we couldn't keep up because we were trying to look after the little ones and we got lost—"

Now the anchorwoman fills the frame again. She's struggling to hold it together. "It's hard to describe what has happened here," she says, faltering. "Hard to understand what has been done to these people. We seem to be at the center of an explosion, yet the people who are, who are still standing seem to be physically unharmed. Mentally—"

She waves her hands. "And the others—"

An Asian guy with spiky hair and latex gloves, some sort of paramedic, indicates the ones on the ground. "They've been dead for approximately eight, ten hours. Ten hours ago is when the explosion was reported in Yakima."

The woman's lips tremble and she looks away into the green mountain distances, her professional composure shredded. Someone not in the frame, perhaps the cameraman, finishes the thought for her. "Shit, man. The way they look at you. As if they're expecting something. Like they're *dogs*."

The truth is, it's worse than that. The camera goes from face to face, lingering on the eyes. And looking into those eyes is as uncanny, as deeply and unspeakably wrong, as going to your bathroom mirror to look at your own face and seeing nothing there but the reflection of the wall behind you.

The paramedic is kneeling next to the girl. "Are they all here? Didn't you say thirteen people?"

She nods, trying to compose herself enough to speak, then picks up one of the fallen books and holds it tight to her chest, rocking slightly. A comfort object. Finally she says through her tears: "Reverend Hollar. He's our leader. He's the one who taught us the chanting. But he's not here."

The TV people have lost the thread, gone off-script, as if they've forgotten or don't realize that the camera is still live. The frame jumps from the paramedic to the anchor, to the girl, then to each of the victims in turn, as if the camera operator is desperately trying to take it all in. Someone says, "What's happened to them? What's happened to them?" And by chance the anchorwoman is caught, half in frame, crying openly, just as she says, "Mystery, a complete mystery."

It's a strange moment. Nobody who sees it forgets it. And something about her choice of that word instantly guarantees its status as a label. She has captured something: it's not just that the situation is a mystery, not just that the facts are a mystery. So are the victims, the silent standing people that the camera now lingers on. All over the world, that is what these people will become.

Misteri. Misterier. Mysteerit.

Rätsel. Gizemleri. Verborgenheden.

Blank faces. Parted lips with the tongue just visible, as if halted in the act of speaking. An air of expectation, combined with a profound, inexplicable absence.

The Mysteries.

People talk about them a lot. Not so much about the ones lying in the mud, who they assume are merely dead.

⟁

On the pretext of clearing up, I pick up a pile of stuff for the kitchen, nudging Rosko in the ankle on the way past. When he joins me, leaning against the fridge, I check behind him to make sure that no one has followed.

"What the hell do you make of that?" I say, piling dishes into the sink.

He shakes his head—and I'm so wrapped up in what I've just seen on TV that at first I don't even understand that he's ignoring the Goat Rocks thing, is already on another subject.

"I looked again at their website. Figured out who hosts it. They keep an archive of business files on the same server."

"You what? You—oh, the Colberts? That's good. Anything interesting?"

"I can't hack it. Not yet anyway."

"Password protected?"

He looks at me as if I'm even stupider than he thought. "Of course it's password protected, yes. That's not the problem. I have a piece of freeware called Hacksaw that can crack your average password in three seconds. Criminals helping criminals, you know. The Colberts, their password took ten minutes. That was my first little surprise. But the thing is, the files inside it use fucking 128-bit Rijndael."

"English, Rosko. *Speaka da eenglish*. I have no clue what you're talking about."

"Rijndael is a high-level symmetric-key encryption standard."

"*English*, Rosko."

"OK, let me put it this way. The labs at Los Alamos design a new type of nuclear warhead, and want to email the blueprints to the Pentagon? They'll use 256-bit Rijndael as the wrapping paper. Nobody knows how to crack that. The 128-bit version is faster and easier to use. It takes us all the way down from impossible to—well. Still impossible."

"You're telling me that's what the Colberts use to hide their movie clips?"

"Who knows what they're hiding—that's the whole point. But I have to say, Daniel, I take everything back. What the Colberts using military-grade encryption has to do with *that*"—he gestures toward the TV—"I have no idea. But you're totally right. Something we don't understand is going on, and the Colberts are just not who they say they are."

I feel a strange emotion. It's a relief that Rosko believes me. It's also worse, because he's confirming that this whole thing is not going away.

"Something else, Daniel."

"What?"

"Remember what my father said in Patagonia? That the Colberts left in a hurry because Sophie's father was sick?"

"Sure."

"After I found the archive, I asked him to remember Sophie's exact words. He did a nice parody of her." His voice goes all squeaky. "*Stefan, wir haben, wir gehen, wir müssen nach, eh, Paree zurück. Meine Vater hat der, den, uh, krankenheits.*"

"Which means?"

"It means 'My German is crap, and I'm trying to tell you that we have to get back to Paris because my father is sick.'"

"So? Her *Vater* wasn't sick?"

"Not in any way he would have noticed, no. He died in a car accident. Ten years ago."

"Rosko, get into those files, OK?"

"You have to understand: me and my laptop against that, it's like getting into Fort Knox with a bent paper clip."

"Get Aaron to help."

"I will. He's so twisted, he'll think this is fun."

⚠

There will be a lot of insomniacs tonight: all over the city, all over the world, people staring into the dark, haunted by the faces at Goat Rocks. I don't even bother with bed, just sneak back down to Mom's office, try to work again, sift through the news chatter. But at some point everything catches up with me. Eyes blurring, yawning till my jaw hurts, I put my head down for a break. And I wake up two hours later, stiff and chilled, thinking I've just heard her voice again.

My forehead has been resting on her desk. There's a taste of stale pizza in my mouth and a big crease across my cheekbone where it was resting against the side of the keyboard. Four in the morning. It takes a minute to get a grip on the fact that what really woke me up was my phone buzzing. A series of messages:

Progress maybe.

Five minutes later: *Yes. They set this up wrong. Won't help me get into the files themselves, but I might have a backdoor into the folder lists.*

Ten minutes later: *You there?*

And five more after that: *Bingo. Wake up. Just retrieved a partial list of plaintext filenames.*

△

When I call, Rosko explains that there are actually two lists, and they're all folders. The first are place names or tribal names—dozens of them:

Strongyle

Babylon
Hattusa
Troy
Mohenjo-daro
Rapa Nui
Mycenae
Angkor
Akkad
Nineveh
Cahokia
Peruvian Amazon Kulamiru
Chogha Zanbil
Mount Kailash
Mogollon Rim Sinagua
Chaco Canyon Anasazi
Göbekli Tepe
Greenland Western Settlement

I don't recognize every name, but I've heard enough over the years to know what I'm looking at—a list, stretching across the globe, and across thousands of years, of events that particularly bug Dad. Or Jimmy and Lorna. Or Derek Partridge. Cultures, cities, whole civilizations associated with sudden disappearances.

The second list is names of people. Dozens, again, a few of which I recognize:

ABalakrishnan

DMJones
CBates
IMaclean
WCalder
JChen
LChen
MChen

The first one on the list, ABalakrishnan, is the Indian dude who funded ISOC. A big fan of Mom's in the international business community, apparently—that's how he met Dad and discovered a mutual interest in, as he put it, *what a brain really is.* He's Charlie to everyone now, has been for years: according to a much-quoted interview, he took the nickname because *my name is Akshay, and Westerners kept calling me Ashkay, which sounds like ashtray, and I don't smoke.*

"Rosko, what's Balakrishnan doing on this list? What's anyone doing on it?"

"I have not even the faintest ghost of an idea."

After I've hung up, I go to the kitchen, wash my face, boil water for a cup of peppermint tea. I want to put on music, because there's something about the silence of the house that's doubly bad in the predawn dark. Looking out the window, I get the creepy sensation that someone or something is moving around in the alley behind the house, decide it's better to look away. Halfway down the mug of tea it occurs to me that I have still not really *searched* the office in which I've spent so much time.

I start with her corkboard. It's covered with the same old clippings, some of them beginning to curl slightly at the edges like dying leaves. I have already looked at them again and again, but without touching. Now I take them all down, one by one. Immediately I discover that tucked behind the largest sheet, attached to the board by the same pin, is a small envelope with three more clippings and a note. The handwriting jumps out at me like a spider, even before I see the name.

Chère Iona,

We thought you might find these interesting too.
À bientôt! Sophie

I hold the note in one hand, staring blankly ahead of me. I've seen this handwriting exactly once before. On a slip of paper on the hospital bed in Punta Arenas.

I turn in Mom's chair, stare into space for a minute or ten while I rethink that scene yet again. Finally, when my eyes come back into focus, I go to her bookshelves and take every volume down, one at a time.

Mathematics and physics. Business and finance. Philosophy and religion. A collection of papers, edited by Maynard Jones, under the title *Transhumanism*. I dip into that one, can't understand a word of it. He has dedicated it to her: *For Iona, always—DMJ.*

Always?

Finally, on the bottom shelf nearest the wall, almost hidden behind a fat textbook on *Advanced Information Theory*, there's a slim, well-thumbed hardback. That hard, grainy red cover, with the cut golden triangle and wavy line, is instantly familiar to everyone. According to Quinn it represents *our transmigration from the temporal to the eternal; from the physical to the spiritual; from the illusory to the real; from the fallible to the infallible; from the merely human to the divine.*

Anabasis. The disturbing thing isn't that Mom has read it, but that she has studied it, hard and long: every single margin, on every single page, is shaded gray with the neat tiny letters of her own handwriting.

I think at once of what Dad would say, with a little edge to his voice. *Still shopping, Iona?* But this isn't mere shopping. I desperately want to ask her about this. I can't ask her. So instead I cradle the book in my arms, sit back in her chair, rock back and forth as if I'm hugging her. Exactly like the girl at Ruapehu.

Later I notice that this book too has been dedicated to her. No signature, but it's Sophie Colbert's writing again:

Iona: Join us. You won't be sorry—not ever.

△

Time for breakfast. But first I tiptoe back upstairs to take a shower. It's only when I'm standing in the bathroom that I remember Dr. Lovecraft's little bottle of pills.

Zampodex: it sounds like the name of a bloodthirsty Mayan deity. I rip off the multifolded information sheet that's wrapped around the bottle and stand there reading the six-point type that nobody ever reads. It explains how the molecular structure interferes with a particular protein, PKMz; describes the evidence that this works just peachy in caged rodents. Then, right at the end, it mentions the more common side effects: disorientation, dizziness, dry mouth, bowel irritation, ringing in the ears, short-term memory loss, long-term memory loss, acne, visual auras, bad breath, mood changes, multiple personality disorder, bad grades in Social Studies, permanent irreversible sexual dysfunction, death.

Only a Mayan deity could do you that much damage. No thanks, mighty Zampo. I feel a need to be alert right now, to be my full self, to avoid anything that will, you know, dull the blade.

I wash my face in cold water, take a long look in the mirror—yes, my reflection is still there—and make a promise to myself.

I *will* know what happened on the Torre Sur.

I *will* know why she died.

I *will* know why the women of Uyuni mattered.

For a long minute I just stand there, listening. A shiver runs through me, bringing out my arms in fine goose bumps. The house feels like a living thing, something that already has me in its mouth and at any provocation might swallow.

Ninety Mayan gods, yellow in their brown bottle: I pour them into the toilet bowl. Most of them sit on the surface of the water for a few seconds, then one by one they tumble and sink. I push the lever, find a crumb of cruel satisfaction in watching them drown.

CHAPTER 12

ARCHITECTS

I sleep late, and when I come downstairs I assume the house is going to be empty. But both Dad and Morag are in the kitchen. Morag's sitting with her elbows on the table and a glum look on her face. Dad's pacing up and down like a caged tiger, waving his arms, saying, *How the hell?*

There's a humming noise outside. And a *Seattle Times* on the table, with a blaring headline about Goat Rocks.

"Morning," I say, attempting to be cheerful. "Talking about this?"

He doesn't even say no, never mind good morning. Twitches a blind to one side and looks out onto the street.

"No," Morag says. "Bill's campus account was hacked."

He turns around, distracted, runs a hand through his hair. "Someone found everything we've translated so far. They tweaked it a bit, to suit their own purposes, faked a couple of emails from me to Morag about keeping it all quiet, and put it up on the web. Along with a froth-at-the-mouth screed about how the evil atheist Calder has been hiding the truth from the world."

"You're pretty close to frothing at the mouth yourself, Dad. Any idea who?"

"The Seraphim—who else?"

"You have a bit of a reputation. Could be a regular hacker. Student prank. Something like that."

He shakes his head. "No. The way this was done, it just suits the Seraphim's purposes too neatly."

I stare into the fridge, decide to eat leftover mashed potato for breakfast, toss a bowl in the microwave. Dad finally stops pacing and parks his butt on the edge of the sink.

"Everything so far is from the earliest sets of Babel tablets," Morag says. "Like I told you, it's Quinn's story, totally. Not just the multiple gods, but the need to forget or destroy their own languages and learn the language of the gods, so that their minds can be—whatever."

"'Attuned to the eternal,'" Dad throws in.

"Aye. So that the Akkadians who are good enough at spiritual acrobatics can escape the merely physical world and be, you know, vacuumed up into heaven. Hundreds of other details too—they match perfectly with what Quinn wrote."

"Which," I point out again through a mouthful of potato, "is impossible. Unless Quinn saw the Babel tablets before you did."

"Slow down, D. There are three options. Number one: the similarity between what Quinn says in *Anabasis* and what we found at Babel is total coincidence."

"That's about as believable as the starship *Enterprise* discovering yet another planet where the aliens speak English and look exactly like us except for weird plastic foreheads."

"Agree, totally. Option two, then. Option two, like you say, is that he saw the Akkadian tablets before we did. Which is even more impossible, because we were the first people into that library in about three thousand years."

"He could have found something similar at a different site?"

"Congratulations—that's number three. The least crazy option."

"So there you go."

Dad gets up, looks outside again; the buzzing is still there. He turns back to me. "I want to believe that, Daniel. I keep repeating to myself the line from Sherlock Holmes about how you eliminate the impossible and what's left is the truth."

"What's wrong with that?"

"Sometimes you eliminate the impossible and what's left is impossible too. Quinn's not an archaeologist. And suppose he was. Suppose he found another manuscript with the same story—why not advertise the fact? His critics have already scoffed at *Anabasis* enough, they've already demanded evidence, and all he could say so far was 'Wait, have faith, you will see.'"

The strangeness of it is beginning to sink in. Quinn comes up with a wacky "revelation" about what he was told personally in an encounter with the gods, then someone else comes along and finds ancient texts in which the gods say exactly the same thing.

"But," I offer, "you still don't know exactly what the Akkadian documents say. You're having trouble with them?"

He and Morag look at each other oddly, and I feel, or think I feel, a strong spark of tension between them—it's like being in the room with a married couple who don't get along.

"Morag and I agree completely on the broad outline. There are just some details to clean up." And then I'm distracted by him motioning for me to look out of the window.

The buzzing: in fact it's a combination of chanting and singing. Two separate groups of people have collected right across the street from our house. One set, the singers, are swaying from side to side, waving banners; one reads, *Psalm 14:1. The fool has said in his heart, there is no God.* The other set, twenty feet farther down the sidewalk, are still as statues, like they're meditating or something. Their banners carry the *Know It Is True* slogan, or a sort of icon of a burning book, or the familiar, endlessly reproduced image of Quinn's face. Some are wearing the white scarf with its broken golden triangle.

"Shit. How long have they been there?"

"Since dawn."

As I look out, someone in the crowd sees me—sees a face anyway—and a rock hits the side of the house. A police officer, who must have been out of my line of sight, strides across the street wagging his finger.

"There's a fourth option," I say quietly, putting my empty bowl in the sink.

"What?" Morag asks.

"You don't want to hear it. Neither of you do. The fourth option is the one that's obvious to those people outside, and ten million Seraphim around the world."

"I don't follow."

"Quinn says *Anabasis* was a direct personal revelation. From the gods, Architects, whatever. Maybe he's simply telling the truth."

"Daniel," Dad says, as if I've just admitted to being a meth addict. "Give me a break. You don't believe that."

"I don't know what to believe. And Sherlock Holmes would say it's no more impossible than your other options."

Dad shakes his head, looks at his watch, heads upstairs: I'm a lost cause, as usual. Then he pauses and calls back over his shoulder:

"Morag, ten minutes OK? We'll drive out the alley and avoid these jokers." And, as an afterthought: "Do you want to come with us, Daniel?"

"I'll be fine here."

Morag is quiet for a minute, examining her nails. Then she looks through the doorway, as if checking that he's out of earshot. Softly she says, "Bill and I spend a lot of time on little debates about how to translate certain words. I'll say, 'This word is *stone*.' He'll say, 'No, it just means heavy.' That's normal stuff. But I feel as if he's trying to minimize the similarities to Quinn and *Anabasis*. Like he can't face it. There's this one word in Akkadian that keeps on coming up. Right where you expect them to say *gods*. Bill keeps saying, 'Yeah, gods, close enough.' Right from the start I thought the word they were using was more like *builders*, or *originators*. It took me awhile to make the connection, but it's Quinn's word. *Architects*."

"You're sure?"

"The more I learn, the less I'm sure of anything. But whoever hacked the files is sure. They not only changed every sentence with *gods* to *architects*—they put the word in capital letters all the way through."

△

Nobody in the wider world cares about these details. All they care about is that it's a great story—especially since Dad's supposed to despise religion in general and Quinn in particular:

DOES ANCIENT EVIDENCE PROVE SERAPHIM ARE RIGHT?

ATHEIST PROF TRIED TO HIDE EVIDENCE

ANCIENT MANUSCRIPT SHOWS GODS WERE REAL

Then the traditional faiths weigh in. One of the louder California megachurches stages a big demonstration in which people burn images of Quinn and Dad together, as if they were secret collaborators. A pastor with a shiny blue suit and the IQ of a light switch generates unintentional laughs by saying that God's purpose cannot be known by "atheists and apostates"—it can be understood only by people like him, who "study God's Word in the original English." Separately, the bishop of Johannesburg joins forces with a Chicago rabbi and a London imam to denounce both as part of a "conspiracy against faith."

In other parts of the world, life is even simpler. Neither the Saudis nor the Iranians even mention Dad, or Quinn—and besides, they can afford to dismiss atheism as ridiculous. But they recognize the Seraphim for the threat they are, and, as Dad puts it to Morag

and me, "They understand, even more than our so-called democ-
racies, the political value of terror." So dozens of people in Riyadh,
Jeddah, Tehran, and Isfahan, who might or might not have anything
to do with the Seraphim, are rounded up and beheaded in front of
their own families on live television.

The Vatican takes longer to respond than some, but then it flexes
its intellectual muscle by wheeling the formidable Cardinal Gerhard
Kirkmünde onto the talk shows. Kirkmünde, who has PhDs by the
handful, is rumored to speak almost as many languages as Dad. He
denounces "Dr. Culver"—you can tell he's getting it wrong on purpose—for "insulting all genuine faith." By *genuine faith* he means
monotheism, a group of faiths that includes Judaism, Islam, and the
Protestant denominations, all of which he has in other circumstances
dismissed haughtily as erroneous.

"This Canadian scholar," Kirkmünde concludes—*Canadian*, he
actually says that, trying (badly) to make Dad sound as irrelevant as
possible—"is meddling in matters he does not understand." And he
speaks like he expects an apology.

NPR wants to interview Dad, maybe wants to hear that apology.
He must be tempted: loudly failing to apologize for anything, in fact
laying into Kirkmünde with both fists flying, would be a nice recre-
ational break. But he resists, goes back to work. All he says—privately,
to us: "You know, sometimes evidence is puzzling. But being puzzled
is a bad reason to run around shrieking with your hands in the air,
like frightened children. It's also a bad reason for surrendering your
judgment to someone whose main claim to expertise is that he wears
funny clothes and stares out of the window a lot."

△

The protesters are there all day now, dawn to dusk, in their two
groups: on the north corner of the block, the *traditionals*, as someone has recently dubbed them; a house-width further down, their

opponents the Seraphim. They leave each other alone, mostly, but not everyone leaves us alone. After the third or fourth creepy call on our landline, we change the number. Then a visibly deranged guy shows up at the back door, tries to set light to it with the bottle of grain alcohol he's drinking, only manages to set light to himself. ("I'b doin it fuh Jesus," he shouts, through a column of greasy smoke, waving the bottle as small blue flames dance up his arm, across his shoulder, into his hair. I put him out with the first thing that comes to hand, a gallon of two-percent milk that's sitting in a grocery bag in the hallway. When a fire truck shows up, he actually complains to the paramedic about how the milk has ruined his shirt.) After that I persuade Dad to call a security company. I spend an entire afternoon supervising them as they change all the locks and upgrade the alarm system.

Everyone's expecting a statement from Quinn by now, but several days go by: he seems to be waiting for the airwaves to clear. When he does react, it's with a kind of icy, Olympian disdain. Doesn't mention Dad, the translations, the demonstrations. He just issues a media release to every news outlet on the planet.

No doubt it's inspiring, if you're either Seraphim or Seraphim-curious. If not, it's just terrifying:

The time for doubt is over. At the exact hour of the rising of the next full moon, the Seraphim will be ready for a transformation greater than any before seen in our time. At the third home of the Architects, we confidently expect many thousands will follow in the footsteps of the Maya, the Anasazi, the Babylonians, and so many others, ascending to their immortal reward. Know it is true: as they ascend, as the power of their minds is released from the prison of their bodies, the roar will be heard around the world.

Quinn loves drama, you can tell that. Everyone goes on about what he can possibly mean, what the "third home" could possibly be. Nobody knows; he's not saying. But a lot of people, me included, mark the next full moon on their calendars.

CHAPTER 13
I HAVE FOUND IT

On the day of Quinn's enigmatic announcement, there are at least ten more reports of disappearances, three more stories about Mysteries being recovered, and three news stories about arsons at major libraries. Also, I invite the Eislers and the Cerenkovs over to dinner.

I don't even bother to ask Dad and Morag if it's OK, which turns out to be the right call: when I do mention it—by email, because that's the only reliable way to get Dad's attention—they both say, *Yeah, sure; sounds good; whatever.* Gabi Eisler gets back to me right away and says they'll all be there. Nothing from Kit's mom, Natazscha, and it's only when Dad and Morag get home late in the afternoon that I receive a thirdhand reply.

"I bumped into Kit with her mom on campus," Morag says. "Natazscha was hurrying off, so Kit and I ended up hanging out. She said they can't make it tonight."

"Just like that?"

"Reading between the lines, Kit really wanted to come, but Natazscha's freaked out by the idea of her hanging around with either of us here. Pity. I really like her."

I've not discussed my feelings about Kit with Morag because, well, because my feelings are too *animal*. It's embarrassing. So I change the subject to shopping for fish.

Hours later, we're both watching from the kitchen window when the Eislers arrive. No protesters now, all gone home for the evening. But, as the Eislers get out of their car, a guy with a breezy grin approaches Stefan with his hand held out.

Journalist, I'd guess—he even has a notebook and pen in his other hand, as if to identify himself. I open the front door to greet Gabi and Rosko. Stefan is stuck at the bottom of the steps, answering the notebook guy:

"Make a statement? Ja, sure I'll make a statement. Ready? OK, here it is: You, yes you, should leave this family alone. Professor Calder has already done interviews. If you want to arrange another one, call his department at the university. This, however"—he gestures to the house—"is private."

"Sir, after these extraordinary revelations, don't you think the public has a right—"

"I think Professor Calder and his family have a right not to be harassed at their own front door."

"Excuse me, sir." He's trying for the Mr. Offended tone now. "This is my job."

"I am sorry to hear that. Couldn't get a real one? A personal tragedy in a tough economy."

"But—"

"See the lake down there?"

"Lake Washington? Yes."

"It's big, and cold, and two hundred feet deep. But you should go jump in it, because otherwise I swear to God I'll pick you up, carry you down the hill, and throw you in."

Not a plausible threat—the guy has thirty, forty pounds on Stefan. But he looks suitably alarmed, throws a wan smile in our direction, and beats a retreat to the safety of his battered white Civic, which is parked across the street.

Morag has already gone in with Gabi and Rosko. Ten seconds later, as I hold the door for Stefan, I've almost forgotten the guy. And yet—

Something in the body language?

His face, his posture. It's like, all the anxiety about being sent for a swim has just switched off. Or was never there. He's standing by the car with a phone to his ear, looking around as if scoping the area. Something not right about it.

I shut the door but glue my eye to the little brass security viewer. It's old, has a scratched lens, but I can see well enough. He saunters to the front end of his car. Peers at something out of my sight line. Slouches against the hood. And makes a series of low, quick hand gestures, like a baseball catcher.

Mumbling an excuse, I run down the corridor past the kitchen, duck into the downstairs bathroom. Without turning the light on, I close the door behind me and move slowly, inch by inch, until the view of an ornamental Japanese maple becomes a view of the street. I'm just in time to see the Civic's brake lights brighten and then disappear as the car pauses and turns at the end of the street.

So he was leaving after all. But there's only one place anyone could park, in the direction of those odd, quick gestures. It's occupied by a black Range Rover with three antennae.

◬

Morag chats with Rosko. Stefan stands around awkwardly with a glass of wine in his hand until Dad shows up from his study and condescends to be social. Gabi actually helps. I've had nothing to do all day but think about this meal, so I've gone a bit overboard: tiny salads of butter lettuce and red onion; a platter of big, pepper-crusted wild salmon fillets served with black kale and roasted sweet potato; slivers of Manchego cheese topped with fig butter; a real heart attack of a cardamom-scented crème brûlée.

While we eat, nobody talks about Quinn, the Babel documents, or the Mysteries. Gabi especially is good at small talk that doesn't seem small—she even manages to draw Dad into a lighthearted debate about parenting, then slide invisibly from there to the question of what's going to happen with Morag's and my schooling now. Rosko takes up the theme: isn't it time for us to show up to class and be regular kids?

Afterward, when the Eislers have driven home, Dad disappears back to his study without even thinking to make an excuse; Morag and I clean up. I'm scrubbing a pot, soapy water up to my elbows, when I think again of the Range Rover.

"M, do me a favor?"

"Go up and pour dishwater down the back of Bill's neck? Sure."

"No. That'll only make him worse. Just go to the downstairs bathroom. Shut the door behind you, don't turn the light on, look out into the street. I want to know what you see."

No questions. She just raises one eyebrow a couple of millimeters and vanishes. Meanwhile I head for the front door, wiping my hands on a dish towel that has all fourteen 8,000-meter peaks on it—another reminder of Mom. I look out through the security viewer again. Nothing.

Morag meets me back at the sink. "One medium-sized gray raccoon. One large black SUV."

"Still there. Range Rover, yes?"

"I make it a matter of principle not to know those things. And what do you mean, *still*?"

"Did you see anything else?"

"The raccoon was cute. I love the way their hands—"

"M."

"OK. The Global Warmer has darkened glass, but I could tell there was at least one person inside."

"It was there when the Eislers arrived. What do you remember about the journalist?"

"Guy on the front step?" She closes her eyes for a moment, no more than a lazy blink. "Dark-green jacket with an REI logo on the sleeve. Squarish glasses with blue frames, trying too hard to be stylish. Short dark hair with those gray bits at the sides. Would have looked cute if he hadn't looked terrified. I thought Stefan was a bit harsh."

"I don't think he was terrified. And I don't think he was a journalist. He made out like Stefan frightened him off, but he strolled over to his car, sat on the hood, did some kind of hand signal to those guys in the Range Rover."

"That's odd."

"Local news outlet hires 24/7 surveillance goons who drive an upmarket go-kart with three different antennae? Definitely it's odd."

"Who else, though? It's not exactly the right style for a bunch of Seraphim, either."

"Guess the people who stole the translation are more sophisticated than we thought."

Whatever the truth, it makes me angry to be inside my own house hiding and speculating. I put down the last pot and wipe my hands again. "I'm going to talk to them."

"Are you crazy? You can't do that!"

But Morag is wrong: I can. It feels good too—especially good, knowing they won't be expecting it.

I open the front door, hop down the steps as if I'm going for a stroll. The driver is peering out at me through the side window; I go right over, smile, tap on the glass. Three sharp taps, I guess that's what I'm intending, but I only manage two before the smoked barrier melts silently into the door. As it does so, the driver puts on sunglasses, a gesture so ridiculous I almost laugh.

"Can I help you?" he asks.

He looks like a parody of Secret Service. Dark suit, dark tie, square jaw, neck like a tree stump. Everything except the plastic earpiece.

Then I look over at the guy in the passenger seat.

Plastic earpiece.

"I was thinking maybe I could help you. See, I live here. But maybe you knew that already. Thing is, this is not a legal parking space. I thought you ought to know that the meter maniacs around here are, well, you know. Maniacs. Stalinists. Spawn of Satan. I'm not kidding."

They're dressed identically, like Mormons. The one in the passenger seat won't even turn to look at me—his hands are upturned in his lap, as if he'd been about to rip out the earpiece as I knocked on the window but didn't have time.

"Thanks," the driver says. "Appreciate your concern. We were just on our way as a matter of fact."

"I'm sure you were. Nice earbud, by the way. You have a simply wonderful evening now."

⚠

As I walk back into the house, Dad shouts down from his study.

"Guys. Can you come up here a minute?"

He's sitting in the fancy executive chair at his desk. Along the wall to his right there's a big trestle table covered in papers. Above it, a neat row of eight black-and-white photographs: they show each side of the first Phaistos Disk and each side of the three others we found. Looming in the semidarkness behind him are framed prints of Gustav Doré's *The Confusion of Tongues*, Bruegel's *The Tower of Babel*, and a couple of other images starring wild-eyed biblical types in front of wrecked towers.

He has a wild look in his eye too.

"I feel bad about abandoning you, but I'm going to have to go see Partridge again. In Rome."

"When?"

Now he just looks embarrassed. "Immediately. I have a flight already—it leaves in a couple of hours."

I just worked out that a couple of Bond villains are watching our house, and he's taking off on an academic vacation. I look at him but can't think of anything to say.

"Look," he says, "I'm really sorry about this. The timing sucks, I know. But I mean, whatever the Akkadian tablets say, we still don't have a clue why there was a fragment of a Disk there. If Derek knows where to find a whole collection of them—"

"You've heard from him?"

He nods. "I may need to go to Crete as well just for a few days, to see Pandora Kallas and visit the people at the museum. I'll be back in a week. Ten days, max."

"That's—"

Morag finishes the thought for me.

"That's great, Bill. Exciting. As you say, though, not exactly ideal timing, given the media circus and everything."

I'm all prepared to be annoyed with her for supporting him; instead, I love the way she manages the balancing act I can't pull off—direct and critical, without giving offense. Me, I skate closer to the edge:

"What the hell are we supposed to do while you're gone? Pull down the blinds? Turn off the phones? Live in the dark?"

He starts to say something, twice, but stops. Trying and failing to wrap his mouth around an apology? Finally: "Just refuse to answer questions. You'll be fine." He looks at me, as if seeking approval. Then he adds feebly: "I guess you could both stay with the Eislers? That might make things easier."

I almost pity him. I know he's got a lot on his mind, but how can anyone be this clumsy? It's impossible not to imagine Mom, how she would have handled a crisis, how she would have actually taken more than ten seconds to think about our point of view. I open my mouth to answer him without even knowing what I'm going to say, aware both that I'm angry and that paradoxically I don't care whether he's going to be here or not: what difference could it make?

Morag, again, beats me to the punch. "We don't need to be baby-sat by Gabi and Stefan, Bill. We'll manage. What does Partridge have to say?"

He swivels his laptop in our direction; Morag and I lean in and peer at the screen. The body of the email contains just a single word. The best-known word in the Greek language: what Archimedes allegedly said, around 260 BCE, when he leapt out of his bath and ran naked and roaring through the streets of Syracuse.

Heureka.

I translate it aloud: "'I have found it.' That's it? He didn't by any chance tell you what he's found?"

Dad reaches under his desk, pulls out a FedEx envelope. "Derek's not a stupid man. Paranoid, eccentric, probably wrong about a whole lot of things, but not stupid. I got this a couple of days ago. Apparently he's convinced that he can't tell me anything, except in person."

In the envelope there's a single piece of paper:

Bill, I'm homing in on the missing piece of the jigsaw. You won't believe me if I write it down, and anyway I can't—both of us are being watched. Come to Rome at once. I know you think I'm a fool, but speak of this to no one please. And don't delay.

P.S. If anything happens to me, look for Casaubon—remember?

"Watched," Dad says sarcastically, using his fingers to make little scare quotes in the air. "Poor Derek always wants things to be more exciting than they are. He's one step from believing the CIA has implanted a microphone in his false teeth."

I'm about to mention the guys in the Range Rover, but Morag steps gently on my foot. When I glance at her, she discreetly shakes her head.

"Casaubon?" she asks.

Dad waves his hand dismissively. "Just something I gave him once."

I take a deep breath, consciously swallowing my anger. As casually as I can: "Well then. Guess you want me to drive you to the airport?"

Δ

A few hours later, while Dad's sucking down a Scotch on his red-eye to Europe, I'm asleep and my subconscious brings me to Julius Quinn.

At least it's not a nightmare. I'm a guest at a lakeside estate. Afternoon tea, cakes on the terrace, the full English cliché. He's friendly, relaxed, plausible. Also, he's—I mean, I'm kind of a militant heterosexual, but I have to admit it: he's strangely *desirable*. And he never raises that famous voice:

It's all right to have doubts, Daniel. Preachers have been claiming since the beginning of time to have heard the voices of the gods. Ridiculous! But I'm the exception that proves the rule, you see. I really did encounter the Architects.

When I ask him whether I will ever see my mother again, he looks at me with great kindness, great compassion, but a kind of sadness too:

Think about all the priests and all the religions over the centuries, fighting each other so angrily about which of them knows the truth. The atheists say they are all wrong. But what if all the priests and all the atheists are wrong? Has it never occurred to you that the truth might simply be more strange and more magnificent than anyone has dared imagine? The truth is that the reality of the infinite lies beyond all our languages and concepts. In fact, it does not—

The scene thins and shimmers. He's laughing, throws his head back so that I can see the wet, ribbed vault of his mouth. Looks at me again with a kindly, amused smile.

Oh, Daniel, you cannot—

My picture of him is fading. Nothing is left but fragments of his voice:

It's not at all what you—

△

I'm dragged back from the infinite to the real by a single *ding* on my phone.

CHAPTER 14
THE AKKADIAN VERSION

Message from Rosko, and it's only just after seven.

Come over now. Sthing important 2 show u.

I sit up in bed, rub my eyes, can't even see straight yet. My reply reads something like *wA2 eerlgy.*

Less than ten seconds later I get: *Now.*

My pulse picks up: *What you find?*

He won't say. Only, *Parents up + headed out on bikes. Place to selves maybe 2 hrs. Urgent.*

A Saturday morning bike ride for Stefan and Gabi Eisler means eighty, a hundred miles. My thumbs are still hovering, my mind still composing an excuse to delay, when I get a third text.

NOW.

He doesn't say, *Bring Morag,* but anyway I can't bring Morag. I pad down the corridor and tap on her bedroom door only to discover, as I could have predicted, that she's not here: door ajar, bed neatly made as always, the whole room perfectly tidy except for maybe a hundred books in stacks and slews and avalanches on the floor.

Probably left for the ISOC library already. Except that when she goes out she always leaves a note on the kitchen counter, and there's nothing.

As I send her a message—*Morning. OK? Library?*—I imagine her walking over there in the gray of dawn. Then I think of the SUV again, curse myself for needing more sleep than she does, wonder why there's no reply.

What if she's not safe?

Should be with her.

I try again. This time, though, I hear a distant answering sound from right here in the house. Wandering into the living room, I find the source: her phone, right there on the couch. This is making me nervous—and when the door opens behind me, I nearly jump out of my skin.

"Morning, D."

"What the—I thought—I was trying to text you, and—"

"I was up in Bill's study."

"Oh."

"Been there all night, actually."

I breathe a sigh of relief, give my heart rate a couple of seconds to subside. She has a vacant, slightly stunned look, which I put down to lack of sleep. "So, pulling a late one. How's it going?"

"It's going brilliantly. In a way. The past two or three days, I've reached takeoff speed in Akkadian."

I give her a puzzled frown.

"A totally new level of understanding. It happens with every language: I get to a point where I'm not translating. I look at the text, and the meaning just bounces right back at me. I can *read* this stuff, D."

"That's good. Listen, I was just heading out to Rosko's. Said he's found something important. Want to come with me?"

"Did he say what it's about?"

"No."

She grabs a hunk of bread from the counter, slathers butter on it, takes her jacket from the back of a chair. "I've made my own break-through, D. Tell you as we go down?"

⚠

There are already three early arrivals on the street in front of the house. But we have a routine now—sneak through the garage, over a low fence into the neighbor's yard, then into the alley. Nobody sees us.

"Bill's methodical to a fault," Morag says. "I mean, methodical is great, but there's a limit to what I can stand. It's like we found a shelf of old books, and he decided we should find out what's in them by starting on the first page of the first book, and going page by page without even skimming ahead to read the titles. Been driving me crackers."

Crackers makes me smile: Mom used to say it.

"Dad must be in Rome by now. Not here to hold the whip over you anymore, so you can do your own thing."

"My own thing is exactly what I've been doing. At high speed, all bloody night. I'm a bit fried, tell you the truth."

It's a beautiful, warm morning. A couple of minutes after we turn out of the alley, we're passing Seattle's oldest cemetery, where the city's founders are permanently surprised to find themselves rot-ting right alongside martial arts hero Bruce Lee. We cross the street, heading for a bench that overlooks the lake, and have to jump for the curb to avoid being hit by two muscle-popping bike jocks.

They whip past us at high speed, doing their morning thing on expensive metal. I glance at them only because they come so close to us. They have the generic, aggressive look of the thirtysomething Seattle road warrior: closely buzzed hair, blue spandex, wraparound shades. Other than that, there's no time to notice anything except that one looks vaguely familiar and one is built like a cross between a stellar track athlete and a Sasquatch.

Probably a sign of paranoia that I notice them at all: I'm mainly interested in hurrying. But Morag wanders to the bench and sits, staring out at nothing. She puts her hands between her knees, hunches forward, rocks back and forth for a minute. Then she says:

"We have Quinn's story right there in the oldest of the Akkadian tablets. That's what all the fuss is about, right?"

"Ascent to the realm of the eternal. Our destiny as higher beings achieved at last. Joy unconfined. Sure."

"But there's a later set. I sneaked a peek at them when we first dug them up at Babel. Kind of caught my eye—so completely different."

"You mean a different language?"

"No no. Same language, but a totally different voice. The older tablets read like you'd expect from a religious document. Grand, poetic, repetitive. Impressive in a way, but it could have been written by a committee, you know? This later material, it's not like that at all. It's from one person, a priest named Shul-hura. And he's talking directly to the reader. It's a message in a bottle. Personal. Me to you. A cry for help."

She's fidgeting, nervous, keeps getting up and sitting down again. I can tell she hasn't finished.

"A cry for help, yes. Or a warning."

I check my phone. Another message from Rosko: *Dude. Speed it up. Drink your coffee here.* I put it back in my pocket.

"Go on."

"Shul-hura describes the arrival of the Architects. He calls them *persuasive* and *charming* and *beautiful*. He says they claim to want to raise humanity to their level, and they want to 'clarify' people's minds, so they have introduced their own language, and forbidden the use of Akkadian."

"I thought this was all *in* Akkadian?"

She nods. "Shul-hura is writing a message, in his own language, about his own language being forbidden on pain of death. He also says there are 'questions that may not be asked'—and then he goes ahead and asks them."

"Let me guess. One of them is, What do the Architects really want?"

"Close enough. Who are they? Where do they come from? Why must we give up our own languages in order to find the eternal? What is this 'eternity'?"

"So there's forbidden knowledge. Eve and the apple."

"Exactly. Another case of people being told by the gods that there is nothing more evil, nothing more corrupt, than wanting to know what's really going on."

"Anything else?"

"Oh, I've not even told you the heart of it yet. Remember the Babel story? The Genesis version?"

"God gives us the divine language, so we can communicate with each other and with him. But we offend him by getting arrogant, building skyscrapers. He doesn't like our attitude, gets his panties all in a wad, 'confuses our tongues.'"

"That's the story we've been telling ourselves for thousands of years, isn't it? But our friend Shul-hura says: 'No, no. That story is a lie. The one language of the Architects was presented as a gift, but really it was forced upon us, as the conquerors always force their language on the conquered. So that they could control us.' And then, get this, D. He says: 'The majority believed. And those with many languages became priests, and helped them believe. But some of us with many languages resisted our own belief.'"

"He spoke many languages, and all the priests did? You're saying they were all Babblers?"

"Sounds like a whole caste of priestly Babblers to me. Shul-hura lists every language he knows. The list includes every Mesopotamian language we've ever heard of, plus half a dozen more. Probably those are the other ones we dug up, that Bill's not even had a chance to look at yet."

"Holy shit, M. You realize what this dude is saying, don't you? He's saying the Babel story that has come down to us—the Bible version—is—it's—propaganda."

"Holy shit—literally." She has a glint in her eye that reminds me instantly of Dad. "A possibility that religious people and atheists both seem to miss, isn't it? That the gods were real, and really did tell us all kinds of things, but were *lying* to us. And to top it all, we're being warned about the lie by a Babbler heretic."

"Oh man. When you publish this, it's going to—Wait. Have you contacted Dad about it yet?"

"Put it all in an email a couple of hours ago. Tried not to rub his nose in the fact that I have a better grip on the verb structure than he does."

My heart sinks. "Did you encrypt it?"

"D, get a grip. You're as bad as Partridge. Those guys in the gas-guzzler weren't CIA or anything. I mean, I know this is freaky, but in the end it's just archaeology. No, I didn't encrypt it."

Her unwillingness to take the danger seriously, to take what she's just said seriously, annoys me. I want to say: M, if you've told Dad by email, you've told the world. How do you think people will react to you and Dad telling them their gods are liars? But I swallow hard and let it go.

My phone buzzes. *Daniel, where ARE you?*

"Come on. Rosko's freaking out."

I head down the hill. Morag must sense my irritation. When she catches up with me, she asks what's wrong.

"I just feel like you're still refusing to look at what's in front of your nose. Ever since we got back I've been trying to get you, and Dad, and everyone else to take seriously the idea that there was something strange about Mom's death. But nobody believes me, nobody will listen, because everyone's an expert on grief, everyone knows it's all in poor little Daniel's head. But surely at least you admit by now that there's something that doesn't add up?"

She bobbles her head, not willing to say *yes* or *no*.

"And now this. Not just evidence that Quinn knew something he could not have known by any natural means, but evidence that he and everyone else was deliberately misled, just like our heretical Akkadian blogger."

We're at the top of Interlaken, a wooded ravine that provides a convenient shortcut to the Eislers' neighborhood. As we descend into the trees she pauses, breathing fast, her eyes darting all over the place.

"I'm just trying to focus on one thing at a time, D. I know it's important to you to understand Iona's death. I know that seems to be wrapped up with other things—the message in the vial, Uyuni, and now this stuff with the Colberts. But try to understand where I'm coming from. I've spent all my life hearing people who aren't particularly brilliant say how brilliant I am. They don't get it: *Brilliant* isn't having a normal brain with a turbocharger bolted on. Mostly, it's just an abnormal capacity to concentrate. Most people can focus on a task for two minutes, then they have to pick their noses and stare into space for twenty. Me, I'm like Bill: I can think about one thing, think about it hard, for eighteen hours straight. And I've been using that ability on the Akkadian translations. Which, believe me I know, makes me a pain in the bum for everyone else."

Yeah, it does. But then I probably wouldn't love Morag, feel this deep need to protect her, if she wasn't like that. Before I have a chance to reply, she says:

"I have to admit, the Akkadian Version—Shul-hura's story— gives me the creeps. It feels so real. Like I'm reading a cry for help that I could have written myself."

"What if it is? Real, I mean."

She pauses, temporarily lost for words. I experience a kind of elation, because I can feel the sand shifting under her feet. Doubt creeping in. A willingness to at least consider the idea that we'll have to throw away all our ideas and start again.

She laughs, as if to suggest she's just thought of a joke. But then she says, in a tone as serious as can be: "If this is real, D . . . If this is real, then everything we thought we knew about human civilization—the origin of cities, religion, language itself—it's just frost on the windowpane."

△

A small, root-strewn path goes steeply downhill through the undergrowth. Soon we're in deep shade under the trees—red maple, elm, birch—and we have to tread carefully, eyes on the ground. Morag is so silent now behind me that, as the path tacks left along the top of the ravine, I turn to check that she's still there—and that's when I see handlebars poking out from a thicket of blackberry vines.

I don't think anything, really, except that it's odd. Just take an involuntary step toward it, have time to notice that it's three thousand dollars worth of exotic chromium-molybdenum alloy, the sort of machine that's hand built and weighs less than a piece of toast. Then—

Thokk.

I've missed the last six, seven karate practices in a row, through no fault of my own. Besides, How to Remain Alert While Your World Is Falling Apart has probably not been covered any time recently in the post-practice chat at the dojo. So I'm not exactly thinking through defensive techniques at the moment when that first blow sends me reeling into a patch of salal.

Luckily for me, I turn my head to glance at Morag and then flinch when I see the bike, so the chopping hand of Bike Jock Number One lands fractionally off target. My internal lights flicker dangerously, but they don't go out. Twice-luckily, I'm not the only one who's out of practice.

The guy in the blue spandex probably knows his chop is off target, but as I roll over he reaches down, casually, his body language proclaiming loudly a major wrong assumption: that I will be offering no further resistance.

Lying on your back's a pretty good position from which to kick—and being angry and afraid *concentrates the mind wonderfully*, as some English literary heavy once said. I slip my hands closer in to my sides for better leverage, roll my shoulders back, and adjust my left foot so that it's planted flat against the ground directly beneath my knee. Then I suck in a quick breath, take mental aim at a passing cloud, and launch my right heel at it with all the force of my thigh, butt, and back muscles combined.

He's still smiling as his jaw breaks. He's probably still smiling as his neck snaps backward. After that, not so much: his teeth come out in all directions at once, like the shards of an exploding tea cup.

With a backward roll I'm on my feet, standing next to the poorly concealed bike. Lost track of Morag. Never heard her shout, protest, nothing. The guy with the catastrophic dental problems is lying to my right, motionless. Should I check that he's alive? I step forward, realize that he's the "journalist" who accosted Stefan—and hear a distant, muffled cry.

"Morag!" I scream. "Morag!"

Impossible to tell what direction it's coming from. I look around, but all I can see is trees.

Oh yeah. The Sasquatch. He must have grabbed Morag from right behind me. But he didn't come past me. Going toward Capitol Hill, and downhill, farther into the ravine, there are only two paths. They both lead through the trees to an old road, but one of the paths downhill is steep, stony. Not great for a guy who is presumably carrying Morag under one arm.

I fling myself sideways and start to run, jump, slide down the slope. It's irregular, muddy, forty-five degrees. Most of the ground is obscured by plants. I get a branch in the face. Twice I end up sliding on my butt. Once, my foot comes down at a bad angle. Has to be my right foot, of course: my still-damaged knee feels as if it's been split open with an ax as I go headlong into a stand of ferns. I pick myself up, slip again, keep moving.

As I glimpse the road through a gap in the trees, there's a flash of color to my left.

The whole thing comes to me like a premonition. They've parked a car in here. Sasquatch will be dragging her toward it. But I'll come up behind him while he's bent over, struggling with her, the base of his skull unprotected. I'll drive the heel of my hand so hard into his occipital crest that both his cervical spine and my wrist will probably break, but who cares about a wrist? Morag and I will be safe in the trees, back safely at home even, before anyone even finds him.

Doesn't quite work that way.

⋀

Morag is kicking, trying to bite him, screaming at him. Stress tends to bring out her accent: "If ye dinna put me doon, ye greet fockin eejit, I'll kick yer nuts into next month." It's not making any difference. I crouch out of sight for a moment, look frantically around for a weapon. A big stick would be good just now, or maybe three feet of steel pipe. All I can find is a fist-sized rock.

I come at him from the side, think I've judged it well, aiming right for his temple, but he sees me coming and dodges at the last second; all I manage to do, maybe, is bruise his shoulder. Turning his full attention to me, he literally throws Morag away like a doll, one-handed, and comes at me fast with a vicious kick to the kidneys. Huge guy, huge kick; flailing for a block with my left hand, I reduce the power in his foot by perhaps a third, at the expense of nearly breaking all my still-healing fingers. As my bones scream, I'm thinking of whether Morag is injured while simultaneously entertaining a melodramatic image of a splintered rib piercing one of my lungs.

Meanwhile he steps fluidly through the kick, and as if from nowhere produces a vicious-looking combat knife.

This is not good.

Winded and off-balance, I manage to dodge the first thrust, barely. The second one I manage to not-quite dodge: a stinging, bone-deep cut across the chin. Not good, some part of me registers: he was aiming for my throat.

He grins at me then, I swear it, a dirty little smear of triumph he can't keep from his face. There's something both cruel and arrogant about it. Two of the things I like least in the whole world. Fury is not supposed to bring out the best of your training, but somehow, for a second, the pain and fear step out of me. I relax. I feel calm. I know instinctively that I can't beat this guy, but I stop caring about that. Time slows down, and I even notice a little triangular tattoo on his neck. *Watch the weapon*, sensei would say. *Watch the weapon, trust your training, and don't think.*

I'm as surprised as he is. I string together three moves in a blur of energy: the sudden, twisting crouch; the spin, with a rising arm block to protect against his own next kick; the whirling, low, lateral kick into the side of his kneecap.

He roars in pain, or anger anyway. The knife, released from his hand, flutters away into the bushes like a dying bird. He falls onto his other knee. And to my utter astonishment, Morag, who must have been directly behind him, comes out of nowhere, lands on his back, grabs his hair, and jackknifes forward with a savage head-butt right into the base of his skull.

"Take that, ye miserable shite," she says as he topples sideways. And to me: "Let's get the fuck out of here."

"Wait."

"No. He could wake up any minute."

"Yeah, exactly. So we have to make sure he can't follow us."

I never thought I would have to do this. It's the most unpleasant skill I've ever learned: because it's something you do to a person who's already defenseless, it's not easy, even with someone who just tried to knife you. But it's what sensei teaches. *Nobody can pursue you on a broken leg.*

He's still in bike shoes. I push one of them with my boot until it's turned flat on its outside edge against the road.

"Don't watch, M."

When she sees what I'm going to do, she doesn't actually turn away, just stares resolutely at a point somewhere over my head. I aim, jump, and come down with one heel right in the thin middle of his tibia. The sound is fainter and simpler than I expect—less like a stick breaking than the click of a latch.

I grab Morag's hand. And we run.

△

"Daniel, what—?"

After shouting Rosko's name and hammering on the door, I'm surprised to see Aaron standing there and Kit in the background talking to Rosko. Aaron's looking at me with his mouth open, stupefied.

"Aaron, let us in. And get some water, maybe Tylenol or something."

Kit looks at me and Morag with a stricken expression. With Aaron still gaping, she rushes to the bathroom.

"I got hold of them when neither of you would answer your ph—" Rosko says as he comes to the door. Then he really sees me. "What the hell happened to you? You're covered in blood."

Funny: the cut still stings, but I've almost forgotten about it. Kit comes back with a handful of medical supplies and two damp towels, one of which she hands to me. I wipe my face, feeling the coolness; sure enough, it comes away with the bottom half colored like raspberry puree. I clamp it back against my chin.

While I explain what happened, Kit fusses over Morag with another towel. Then she turns to me and starts torturing me with a Q-tip dipped in alcohol.

"Ow, that hurts."

"You almost cute when you try to be tough, Daniel Calder. Stay still and be quiet. How you managed to get mud in here?"

"Beats me. Can't you just slap in some Neosporin and tape it up?"

"Getting there."

"If someone's prepared to kill you while kidnapping Morag," Aaron says, nervously peeking out the window, "you guys will have to go into hiding or something."

Morag gets up, twists from side to side, and then touches her toes, as if testing to make sure nothing is broken, then turns to me. "Aaron's right. And I'm sorry, D. You were right too."

"About what?"

"I need to stop worrying about Akkadian long enough to work out what's going on now. I should have listened to you earlier."

I turn to Rosko. "What was the message about? What have you found?"

He looks deeply uncomfortable, doesn't say anything until everyone stops what they're doing and looks at him. Rubs at his face with his hands, as if trying to scrub off dirt. Then looks at me:

"They were filming right when the accident happened. Aaron and I found the video."

"What about that unbreakable encryption?"

As usual, Aaron has barely said a word, but he steps in now—literally steps in, standing in the middle of us like a middle schooler about to give a class presentation. He holds his hands awkwardly, taps his thighs with his fingertips, speaks quickly:

"When Rosko said he had files in Rijndael-128, I thought—well, I like a challenge, but that's a waste of time. You need supercomputers to even have a prayer with that stuff. Then he explained about the file lists. The weak link in digital security is always the implementation, because the coders know what they're doing and the end users don't. I worked out that they'd put some of the files on a backup server, and I got into that in no time. It's like, you put your key in a bank vault, and then, just in case, you leave a spare under the doormat."

"And these files weren't encrypted?"

He shakes his head. "Only a few of them were on the server at all. But one was your mom's"—he blushes, throws Rosko a *Help me* look—"and then all these pictures and videos."

"What's in my mom's file, Rosko?"

"You can read it later. Basically it shows two things. That the Colberts have been spying on her for years. Right back to when she was still a grad student. And—that she knew Mayo back then."

"Knew him? As in—?"

"They were in the same master's program. Then they were lab partners with a shared interest in the relationship between biology and information. Then, by the time your parents met, they were living together."

Mom and Mayo. I'm not exactly shocked by this. It's just like: Oh. A chapter of Mom's life I had never even imagined.

"They split because she met Dad?"

"No. Before that. Looks like they had some kind of big argument. There's an old email in there where she says she doesn't trust him."

"O-kay. What about the video?"

Rosko looks at the others. "Can you leave me and Daniel alone for a few minutes?"

They're halfway out of the room before I stop them.

"No. I want you to stay. I need you to know everything."

CHAPTER 15
HORROR MOVIE

The table in the middle of the room is invisible under a thick, unstable ice cap of books and papers. Balanced in the center of the ice cap, like the research station at the South Pole, there's an open laptop.

"Sit down," Rosko says to me, indicating the chair next to him. It's a command, not a suggestion. The others gather behind us as he drags the machine into his lap and flicks his hand over the trackpad.

An image of Mont Blanc: the website of Ciné-Colbert—except that there's a group of folder icons along the bottom edge. One of them is labeled "Patagonie." When Rosko clicks on it, the whole screen is populated with thumbnails. One, near the bottom, is a video clip—an image of rock and ice beneath a white "Play" icon.

"I would not show this to you unless I absolutely had to," he says. As if apologizing in advance for any damage it will do.

He clicks the arrow, the image expands to fill the whole screen, and there we are: three ants in a line on the ribbed trunk of a Douglas fir. The camera wavers, catches us again, then zooms in on me, but the angle is wrong and all you can see is my pack. Better luck with Rosko: his best relaxed-and-determined look; the hair coming out from under his helmet tousled just so, as if he's in an advertisement; some nice examples of excellent climbing style. Each movement precise and separate. Power perfectly controlled. It's like being in karate class and watching sensei demonstrate an advanced kata.

Then the frame shifts a little and I can see Mom. Too far away for the best resolution, but what happens next is clear enough. Looking up, pointing at something, shouting down to Rosko. Then the crazy, sudden, rushing climb.

She stops, uses a small vertical crack as a grip for her left hand, and starts tearing at the rock with her right, managing to dislodge a chunk the size of a football. It should simply fall: it must weigh twenty, thirty pounds. Yet she wields it easily, pushes it over her head, and you can see that she's straining upward, as if trying to pass it on to an invisible partner above her. She stays like that, her body and arm at full extension, for twenty seconds. The only movement is a sort of twitching in her upraised arm, like someone trying to push a heavy pot onto a high shelf.

Part of me already knows what I'm seeing; part of me won't accept it, or accept the implications. I try to shut the thought down, because at the same time I'm determined not to miss any detail.

I can see the explosion—but *explosion* is the wrong word. It's a visible pressure wave, like heat shimmer on a Texas highway, emanating directly from her body. Perfectly spherical—an expanding bubble. Then the lens vibrates, goes still again. By the time it stops moving, the wave has vanished and the rockfall has begun.

It's clear, from this new angle: the knuckle of rock, which has reached out to her in my mind's eye ten thousand times, comes within three feet of her, rotates to within a foot perhaps at the last moment, and never hits her.

She doesn't go limp all at once. For a couple of seconds after she drops the rock in her hand, it's as if the right side of her body is still

functioning; she still has a toehold with her right foot, is still gripping with her right hand, and her body swings outward, away from
the rock face. Then her head pivots down, and for just a moment
she's looking in my direction, her face fully visible.

Back then, in Patagonia, the look on her face would have puzzled me.

Not now.

△

I feel as if I'm about to be physically sick. Nobody says a word, but
Morag's hand tightens on my shoulder. The silence in the room
seems to crackle. Just as I contemplate sprinting for the bathroom,
Rosko puts his hand on my arm and says:

"There's something else."

He brings up another gallery of thumbnails, clicks on one. There
she is in the yellow climbing suit, just after the sudden rushing climb,
moments before the fall. Both feet and one hand firmly planted,
pointing to a place above and farther to her right. The next image is
a tight, fuzzy close-up of her arm and hand. And the next—

Kit gasps. "What this?"

Beyond Mom, standing not on the summit of the South Tower
but in midair, is the outline of a figure. It looks like a child's scribble
of a bat, done with a stick of charcoal. In the next image, it's silvery, more refined and definite—fuzzy still, but with a human head
and arms—and seems to have come closer. In the next, it's different
again, more abstract again: a tube made from fire. In the last shot, the
light from it almost burns out the rest of the image: just a white flash,
and the sky behind has turned the color of charred flesh.

"Go back to the second one."

It's not obvious. Not until you look closely. But the smoky, silvery
outline, floating above her—

"Engel," Rosko mutters to himself. "Das sieht aus wie ein Engel."

"Angel?"

"Engel." He repeats it dreamily, as if he hasn't heard me. "Yes, I remember now. Engel. I saw it, Daniel, you were right. And even before Iona fell I thought, just for a moment I thought, 'Now I will die, and it's OK.'"

He shudders, then snaps out of it and zooms in closer to the corner of the image, adjusts the contrast. When we see what it reveals, I feel as if every one of us is thinking the same thing. But either no one can speak, or they know that it has to be me who speaks:

"Not an angel, Rosko. Look at the face. It's *her*."

There she is, etched in the smoke: Iona Maclean. And yet it's not her, not exactly. It's more a sort of unearthly, perfected, more-than-human or not-quite-human idealization of her.

△

I spend the next several minutes hunched over the Eislers' downstairs toilet, throwing up everything I've eaten in about a month. Morag crouches beside me, a hand on my back. When I'm done, she hands me a glass of water, lets me gulp, then gives me her deepest, most concentrated stare.

"I'm sorry. OK? I'm with you now. I'm with you totally. What are we going to do?"

"Contact Dad."

She nods and hands me my phone, which I must have dropped. I walk back into the dining room, punch the speed dial, then put it on speakerphone. There's a pause, a click, but no ring at all, just an immediate transfer to the familiar friendly greeting: "You have failed to reach William Calder. If this is important, please leave a message. If it's not, please don't."

"It's important, Dad," I say to the phone even before the beep. Hang up, call again, same result. And a third time. It's only then that I notice the "Missed Call" icon.

"Wait. Check it out—two missed calls from a number in Rome. He's been trying to reach me after all." I look up brightly, seeing in my friends' faces a reflection of the relief I feel.

When I return the call, it's answered right away. But the voice is not Dad's—or not unless Dad has turned into a mad English aristocrat.

"Hello? Hello? Daniel?"

"Yes, but—Professor Partridge?"

"Yes, who else would it be? Anyway, thank you for ringing back. Just thought I should get in touch to see if everything is all right."

"Everything's fine. But—"

"Good, good. Worrying unnecessarily then. Afraid I've been a bag of nerves recently. I'm being followed, you see. Ever since I found the *Geographika* and contacted your father about it."

Given what he's saying, there's something weirdly cheerful, almost bubbly, in his delivery. I'm still wondering why he's been trying to contact me, what he's talking about, and why he's talking so oddly, but stupidly I just lead him on:

"Followed?"

"Undoubtedly. The irony, I ask you. For centuries they've been trying to destroy knowledge, and now I've got hold of the one book they need."

I think of the SUV outside the house. I think of the attack on the way to Rosko's. "I don't understand you, Professor. Who is 'they'?"

"The Seraphim, of course! The Seraphim were the highest order of angels, you know. It comes from *saráf*, which is Hebrew for 'burn.' The word's been used for centuries by people whose idea was that we needed to burn away our corrupt knowledge. Including our corrupt languages. They associated fire with God, as so many cultures have done, and they thought that burning away corrupt knowledge was a way of getting back to God. What my next book's all about. They sometimes called themselves Fire Seekers."

There's a slight, almost inaudible hiccup on the last word. *A diet of red wine and cheese*: I'm talking to a man who's pickled.

"Professor—"

"It occurred to me twenty years ago, when I was talking to my cat one morning. 'Eratosthenes,' I said—that was the name of the cat—'what if Atlantis and Babel are actually the same story?' When I shared the idea with actual *people*, they just dismissed me as a senile old coot. But then I made the mistake of including it in a course and admitting to my students that I didn't think it was really a myth. Disturbing young people into actually thinking for themselves— must be prevented at all costs! That's why the Athenians executed Socrates, d'you know? But now I have the evidence. Now I've tracked down the *Geographika* at last, and Cicero's letter about it, and it's all there, safe in my bank deposit box. I've got the key hidden—"

"Professor, please—"

"Mark my words, Daniel. Nearly all crazy theories are false. That's the easy part. The hard part is that there are no interesting theories except the crazy ones that turn out to be true."

"Professor Partridge, please listen. I need you to focus. Can you pass the phone to my dad?"

"Daniel, don't be silly. He's not here. That's the whole point."

I resist the temptation to smash the phone into the tabletop. "He's supposed to be with you by now. Isn't that right?"

"Well, yes. But you see, he never showed up. That's why I rang."

An icy wave of fear washes over me; like a drowning man, I grab for the nearest explanation even though it looks useless: "He is pretty hopeless about communicating. His flight went through London— maybe the connection was delayed? Have you tried calling him on his cell?"

"About fifteen times, I should think. I promised to pick him up at the airport as soon as he gave me the flight number. Nothing. Funny that Americans call it a cell. A small locked room from which you can't escape! We Brits call it a mobile—a colorful toy you suspend over a drooling infant's crib. But I digress again, forgive me. Bottle and a half of a really excellent old Barolo, must try to cut back a little."

I try not to think about Partridge doing airport pickup on six times the legal blood alcohol. "What do you think's going on, then?"

"With the Mysteries, and the Seraphim?"

"No. With Dad."

"Don't have a clue, my boy. But he is internationally famous after all. Or notorious anyway. Perhaps this Quinn chappie had him kidnapped when he worked out the significance of Strongyle and the third home."

Stron-GUY-li. That's what it sounds like. Rings a bell, but I have no idea what he's talking about. I'm about to ask when he hiccups again, or belches—the connection's too bad to tell—then there's a loud bang as he drops the phone. After more banging I hear him talking to himself—a muffled "Blast," then "Bloody hell," then "Clumsy old fool you are, Derek, really must get a grip, old boy"— then he's back on the line. "Daniel, I've got to go. Some other things on my desk here that I need to put into safekeeping."

I think he's about to say more when the call ends. I try to get him back on the line, but there's no connection.

△

Everyone's looking at me, or everyone except Kit, who's still dabbing minutely at Morag's face with the corner of a washcloth, like she's restoring a painting. The funny thing is, they're focused on me, expecting me to make a decision. And that seems natural. Something has changed: I'm in control.

"We need to get over there. Now. My dad's missing."

"Get over where?" Rosko asks.

"To Rome."

"Are you crazy? You mean me too? Fly to Rome, just like that? What am I going to say to my parents? They'll kill me."

Morag gently pushes Kit's hand aside. "It'll be OK. Leave them a note that you're with us. We'll call them when we get there and they'll have plenty of time to kill you when we get back."

Rosko's struggling with this when Kit has a flash of inspiration. "Wait," she says. "Maybe your father changed his mind and went straight to Crete. Morag said he maybe is visiting his diving assistant there?"

It's possible. Don't know why I've not thought to contact Pandora already. Crete seems so distant. When I text her, it amazes me that the phone rings almost immediately; when I pick up, I'm transported as if by magic to the exact spot where the background noise tells me she's standing—at the old pay phone behind the bar in her parents' restaurant in Rethymnon.

Glasses are clattering in the big steel sink. There's a loud rumble of dinner conversation. Loudest of all, the big bassoon voice of her cheerfully foul-mouthed father.

"Hello, Daniel, good to hear from you. Everything OK? No, that's right, he was supposed to be seeing Partridge and then coming from Rome tomorrow. But he sent me a text saying he'll be longer than that."

"He what?"

"Said that he was planning to stay in Rome a few days longer."

"I'm sorry, Pandora. One more time, slowly."

"Something to do with the *Geographika*. He will be here maybe Thursday."

"No. Repeat what you said before that. I thought you said he was already in Rome. And sent you a text."

"Yes. A few hours ago. It said something like, 'Change of plan. Staying with Partridge a couple of extra days. Crete probably Thursday, will let you know when I have a new flight.'"

Δ

When I put the phone down, Morag is the first to speak. "Sounds like he's already in Rome and just hasn't contacted Partridge yet. It's odd, but not all that odd. You know what he's like."

I shake my head. "He wanted to see Partridge ASAP. He hates last-minute changes of plan. If he had made changes, he would have told Partridge. And he would have left Pandora a message."

"Pandora just told you he did leave her a message."

I shake my head. "A voice message."

"So, big deal. He sent her a text instead."

"No he didn't."

"How do you know?"

"Because he hates the whole concept. He never texts."

⚠

Life's a lot easier if you're not scared out of your wits. Failing that, life's a lot easier if, despite being scared out of your wits, you have a trust fund and a titanium American Express card.

The card is black. It's called the Centurion Card, officially, but everyone who has one, or wants to have one, calls it the titanium card, because *the card itself is made of titanium*.

How sick is that?

You get a titanium card by proving ahead of time that you can cover any monthly bill it's possible for the human mind to imagine. Armed with one, you have all manner of help on the other end of your speed dial, right now.

I'm in Manhattan. I need to buy a Picasso.

Certainly, Mr. Calder. No problem at all.

I'm in Novosibirsk. I need to consult a reputable expert on the history of Japanese motorcycles.

Certainly, Mr. Calder. No problem at all.

I'm on top of a sand dune in the Mojave Desert. I need fresh sushi for ten, an electron microscope, a symphony orchestra, and a personal interview with the prime minister of Iceland.

Certainly, Mr. Calder. No problem at all.

Punch one button, and well-oiled machinery for satisfying your every whim is instantly in motion. The power of serious money!

So: "I need three first-class tickets on the next flight from Seattle to Rome."

They sound almost disappointed, as if it's too easy. "Certainly, Mr. Calder. No problem at all. One moment please. Ah yes, your quickest way is on a Lufthansa flight with a change in Frankfurt. But I'm afraid that flight leaves Seattle in only ninety minutes—"

"Ninety minutes is fine."

"Will you need a limousine to pick you up?"

Aaron shakes his head at me, waving the key of his rust-bucket nineties-era VW Rabbit.

"Thanks, that won't be necessary. Just the tickets."

There's a faint wisp of static on the line. It's the sound of thirty thousand dollars evaporating.

Part III:
Home of the Gods

CHAPTER 16
ETERNAL CITY

Distant views of Rome. Then the airport at Fiumicino. Then the stippled metal sea beyond. Again and again. For an hour we do slow circuits, and everyone's in a state of nervous tension from the moment the pilot casually explains the delay as *technical problems*—pilot-speak for "Catastrophic landing gear malfunction: prepare to die." Actually, there's nothing wrong with our bucket of Boeing bolts; we even survive a scary, spine-shortening landing, performed sideways into a strong crosswind. When we do get to the terminal, there's a sense of relief, at least until we experience the chaos inside. Crowds, shoulder to shoulder. Long lines everywhere. No official explanation. Apparently the "technical problems" have something to do with everyone shouting *bomba, stazione termini, terroristi*.

Rosko and Morag have no trouble finding out more—disaster makes people talk—but it's mostly rumor. Rosko yells a translation to me over the background noise: "Big bomb in an apartment building, they're saying. Twenty people dead, near the train station."

A television is showing pictures of a collapsed building, but you can't see much because the camera is behind a line of tape a couple of blocks from the scene. In the distance: flashing lights, guys trying to look important in fluorescent vests, a white shape on a stretcher.

"Via Cavour," Morag says, coming back from a knot of people around a policeman. "Isn't that Partridge's neighborhood?"

We muscle our way outside so that I can call him, but it's still tough to hear over the traffic noise.

"Your arrival is poorly timed, Daniel. Yes. What? What? No, it's not a bomb, don't be silly. It's all part of—"

The call gets dropped. I try him again.

"Professor, they closed the train down, so we're stuck at the airport. They're saying it's a terrorist attack."

"My dear boy, what else are they going to say? That evil flesh-eating demons have been unleashed from the pit of Hades? I don't think so. Terrorism is the only remotely plausible explanation, you see. And that frightens people less than admitting that there is no explanation."

"I'm sorry, I don't follow. You're saying it wasn't terrorists?"

"Complete nonsense. I heard the explosion from my office, and walked by only minutes after it happened. Doddery old fool like me, leaning on my cane and pretending to be deaf, people tell me everything. Even the police. Even a couple of teenagers who saw it happen. But who believes teenagers, eh?"

"They're saying a lot of people were killed."

"Only one or two—unfortunate passersby. About half the people inside the building seem to have survived. If one can call that surviving."

"Are you saying—?"

"Mysteries, Daniel, yes—right here in Rome! Which might seem a bit of a puzzler, because almost all the other ones were associated with mountains. But I do have a theory about that. Anyway, I got the whole story from a neighbor, and what you won't hear on the news is that someone bought the building months ago, quietly ripped the guts out of it, and built an elaborate four-story concrete structure inside."

"Shaped like a ziggurat."

"Clever boy, made that connection, have you? You could still see it quite clearly, even in the rubble. A neighbor said a group of people had been standing outside for days, going on and on about our dear friend Mr. Quinn, to anyone who would listen. Locked the doors, weren't seen for a couple of days, bit of chanting, and Bob's your uncle."

"Bob's what?"

"Just an expression."

"Did they—" I'm thinking of the Colberts' footage of Mom's last seconds in Patagonia. "Did anyone see anything?"

"Oh certainly. There are half a dozen witnesses jabbering hysterically about shining lights, demons, voices—all sorts of quasi-religious language that will be written off as Post-Traumatic Whatever. But the whole thing was quite obvious. You see, the building itself was totally destroyed, blown up from the inside out. And that caused damage to the buildings around it, as you'd expect. But the thing inside, the ziggurat, not a scratch. The authorities are dismantling it now. They say it's unsafe. The truth is, they don't want people to see it."

"What's happening, Professor?"

"Our friend Mr. Quinn is nurturing a power he does not understand. They're getting stronger, you see."

"Who are?"

"The Architects! My guess is that they've been picking people off in ones and twos since the beginning. But they obviously prefer to drive us in the direction of cities, organization, ritual, religion: that gives them whole groups in the right frame of mind at the same time, and they seem to thrive on that. Obviously Strongyle was the jackpot, and probably the whole Bronze Age Collapse was a sort of mopping-up operation. But then they went away, more or less. I wonder why that was, don't you? Scared off by something? And why have they come back now?"

He lets out a high giggle, like a twelve-year-old girl. I get the impression it's the noise he makes when he's excited, and also the noise he makes in states of extreme anxiety.

I don't know what to say, so I say nothing.

"Are you there, Daniel?"

"I'm here."

"Do my ideas sound crazy enough for you so far?"

"Definitely crazy enough. Have you heard from my father yet?"

"Not a word." Suddenly his voice drops, becomes more serious. "Listen to me, Daniel. They are onto us. I'm worried about your father, and I'm worried about the information I have falling into the wrong hands. Come to my office as fast as you can. You have the address? Good. I want to show you what I've found."

△

As fast as you can is always a relative term in Rome—even more so during a terrorist attack that's really something else. There's a collective groan in the terminal when they announce that the train connection has been shut down for the remainder of the day. A tsunami of people heads for the taxi ranks. When we join the wave, it only results in us waiting in line for over two hours. By that time, traffic is so epically snarled that it takes another half hour of honking and swearing just to get out of the airport.

Then our taxi's AC stops working.

Then things really slow down, and we sit motionless for fifteen minutes on the autostrada entrance ramp.

The engine's running and all the windows are open. At last the fumes get to be too much even for our driver, who bangs the dash, blurts out a stream of angry-sounding Italian, and switches the engine off.

"He thinks we should bomb Iran," Morag says, translating. "Never another traffic jam, if you did that."

"We could walk into the city faster than this," Rosko says, stating the obvious. Then, when he opens the door and gets out of the taxi, I realize he's serious.

"Rosko, it's about ten miles or something."

"Hey, we have almost zero bags, how long could it take? Three hours, tops?"

"Don't be an idiot, Rosko," Morag says. And to me, "You should call Partridge again. Tell him we're going to be late in any case. At least find out how long he'll be there."

Nothing's moving, so Morag and I get out as well. To the amazement of our driver, and a large Italian family crammed into a small Fiat in the lane next to us, Morag stands on one leg in a yoga pose, I put my foot on the hood of the car to stretch out my quads, and Rosko gets down on the roadway and hammers out a couple of dozen push-ups.

"Go on," Morag says from behind closed eyes. "Call him." I'm just about to when the traffic ahead of us lurches forward, our driver leans out the window and yells a sarcastic "Ehi, ginnasti! Saltate in macchina!" and my phone rings.

Partridge. And he's neither drunk nor cheerful now: he's hyperventilating.

"Daniel? Daniel?"

"Yes, Professor. We're still in a t—"

"You need to come now."

"We can't. The traffic is barely—"

"All right. Just be quiet and listen carefully. I don't have much time. I was followed again on my way back to the office. When I got here, I found that the place has been, well, *ransacked*. I know they didn't find what they wanted, because I've got it on me, but I—I think they—oh dear. I don't like the look of this."

I'm wondering how to calm him down and which of fifty questions to ask, when I hear a thudding noise, like a dropped box or a car door being slammed. In my still-dazed state, I think someone's banged on the back of the taxi. I've spun all the way around before I realize the noise is coming out of the phone.

"Professor? Are you there?"

There's a pause, a wheezing noise. I wonder if he's having a heart attack. Then a sound like someone rummaging around in a pile of papers, and loud banging. When his voice comes back, it's a hiss.

"Daniel, are you listening? They're *here*. In my building. Now."

"Who?"

"They're going to be looking for *The Key to All Mythologies*—have you got that? It's a book. I'm going to have to hide it, and hope that I can put them off the scent. They—"

A pause. Another, even louder bang. Then a whisper, "Got to go. Be brave and don't give up. Get the book. Behind the desk. Everything depends on you now."

"Professor. Professor Partridge—"

Nothing.

◬

"Well," Rosko says after I've repeated everything to them. "I don't know what he was talking about. But *The Key to All Mythologies* I do know. Morag?"

She looks blank and slightly annoyed—she can tell he's testing her.

"Sad that it's the German who knows his English Lit."

She rolls her eyes. "Spit it out, Eisler."

"*The Key to All Mythologies* is a famous book. Written by a Victorian expert on mythology, the Reverend Edward Casaubon. He was obsessed with the idea that all the world's mythologies are linked."

"Sounds like an early version of Dad."

"Wait," Morag says. "I've heard the name. *Casaubon*. D, remember the note from Partridge, the one Bill showed us just before he left?"

"Yeah, he mentioned Casaubon in that. Dad said it was something he gave to Partridge."

"I guess we're supposed to find Partridge's copy of the book."

Rosko's shaking his head. "He can't have a copy."

"How do you know *that*?" Morag asks.

"Because *The Key to All Mythologies* is a book that doesn't exist."

"But you just said—"

"Edward Casaubon isn't real. He's a character in a novel—and even in the novel he never finished the book."

"Oh, *fock*."

△

It takes another hour to crawl into Rome. Because I'm alternating between calling Partridge (nothing), calling Dad (nothing), and replaying the conversation with Partridge in my head, the slowness of the traffic is even more agonizing now.

At last the taxi loops around the Colosseum, passes the end of the Via Cavour, and drops us nearby, just a few hundred yards from Partridge's office. We walk past his building twice; nothing seems to be wrong, but again he's not answering the phone. So we install ourselves in a window seat at a café across the street, where an elderly waiter with a stained white shirt and a crooked smile is instantly hovering over us.

His exaggerated *bu-on gi-OOORRR-noh* could be old-fashioned politeness, or could be mild mockery. Clearly he knows we're tourists, but he's charmed by Morag when she keeps up our innocent appearance by saying something about the weather, telling him she's so delighted to be back in Rome after being away so long, and then ordering a round of *espresso ristretto* and *sfogliatelle*.

When he's safely out of the way, we have a brief argument. Really brief, as in:

"Rosko, I think you should come with me. Morag, you stay here and watch the door."

"Who are you to be giving all the orders, General Calder? And why is it the 'little sister' who gets to sit out all the fun stuff?"

"This is not going to be fun, M. It could be dangerous. And I just thought—"

"No, you didn't. You didn't think."

"Sorry. But—"

Rosko holds up his hands. "Guys, chill. Daniel's right—one of us should stay here to watch the door and make sure no one follows us in. I'll stay here, and you two go. I have no idea what this nonexistent book is going to look like anyway."

Partridge's building is more like a boardinghouse or an abandoned youth hostel than anything you'd associate with the word *office*. We reach the third floor up a long, narrow, dimly lit stairwell, then emerge onto a landing that smells of cabbage and cats. The sounds are muffled—nothing but creaky boards and the muted distant buzz of Vespa scooters and car horns. We peer at several unmarked doors before finding one down a short hallway that has a white three-by-five card, printed with the words:

DEREK PARTRIDGE, MA, MLITT, PHD
PROFESSORE DI STORIA ANTICA

"Pretty sad, aye?" Morag says in a low voice. "A professor of ancient history with a fistful of research degrees who has no college, no colleagues, no students—just wacky ideas no one will listen to, and a dingy office on a back street."

The door is hanging open by an inch. I hesitate for a moment, but she pushes right past me and swings the door open.

The blinds are closed, so it takes a minute for our eyes to adjust to the dirty-yellow light filtering through from the street. But the space that unpeels itself from the gloom is very strange: it looks as if it's been arranged by an Olympic gold medal neat-freak using white gloves, tweezers, maybe a laser level.

Messiest office I've ever seen: that's what Dad said.

Ransacked: that's what Partridge said.

Yeah, right—though I guess this could be one version of "ransacked." Everything has been carefully placed, but nothing is in the *right* place. A swivel chair and a filing cabinet are parked on top of the desk. Bookcases have been emptied and pulled away from the walls. But there's a surreal precision about everything. Files in boxes on a side table. Books on the floor—thousands of them—in piles so orderly they look like a miniature Manhattan. Someone has been here for a long time, searching.

Somewhere behind me a door slams. My heart pops like a snare drum in a marching band, and we both stand utterly motionless for a minute. Nothing. Then I walk to the street-side window. After almost falling over a box of papers, I push aside a blind and stand there looking down into the street until Rosko sees me and raises his hand.

Morag flips the switch, bathing the room in cheap workshop neon. Behind the desk, where he said the book would be, there's precisely nothing except the largest of the empty bookcases.

"Damn," Morag whispers. She's already crouched on the floor between two stacks of books, running her finger up the spines. "I'd hoped by some miracle we'd be in and out of here in ten minutes. This is going to take forever."

I take a circuit of the room, scanning the floorboards, the furniture, the ceiling even—as if staying still, just thinking and looking, will make some clue jump out to explain what happened here. The dust in the room, stirred up so recently, is making me itch: I have to stifle two big, powerful sneezes. Well, better get on with it—and I'm already kneeling down to join Morag in the search when I look at the big empty bookcase one more time.

It's an institutional-looking thing in green metal, five feet wide by six tall. It's obvious, when you bother to look, that it's not supposed to be here.

"M. Look."

Being empty, the bookcase is surprisingly easy to move. Hidden behind it there's a classroom whiteboard. Taped on the wall above, a colored paper map covering an area from Italy in the west all the way to the Persian Gulf. On the left side of the board, in black dry erase, there's a handwritten list that would look like an assignment for students, if Partridge had any students. The right side of the board is blank.

Morag's looking at the list. "Ziggurats."

"I didn't know there were so many."

"Common as goat shit in Mesopotamia. Ashur. Uruk. Sialk. Ur. Eridu. Fifty or sixty that we know about, and probably three times as many more buried under the desert. But this includes stuff from all over the world."

"Yeah, I recognized Chichén Itzá. That's Mexico, right—and Cahokia also?"

"No, Cahokia's in the US. American Mound Builder culture near Saint Louis. From about a thousand, maybe eleven hundred years ago."

I'm already looking at the right side of the board, which isn't quite blank after all. The black dot near the center, about the size of a pencil eraser, is not a dot—it's a hole, and around it, there are traces of something sticky and dark.

"Is that what I think it is?" Morag whispers.

My skin is crawling. I rip the board from the wall, heave it aside, and the answer to her question is right there, embedded between two bricks: a flattened small-caliber bullet. I try to pick it out with my fingernails. In too deep.

"Look at this," Morag says. She's kneeling on the floor beside me. There's a shape there, faint but unmistakable, drawn in blood. The broken triangle of the Seraphim.

I get down next to her, then lie on the floor, trying to imagine the scene. Around me there are floorboards. Balls of dust. The dark-green metal of the bookcase. The silvery-gray metal of an old heating vent that comes out of the wall at floor level.

And an anomalous stripe of rich blue.

The book has been tucked into the vent, with only part of the spine visible. I take off the vent cover and pull it out—an old hard-back, bound in expensive-looking silk. I hold it out to Morag with the spine forward, so she can see the one word in black lettering on the spine: CASAUBON.

I get to my feet. "Let's go."

But Morag looks puzzled, weighs the book in her hand. "Must be three or four hundred pages. But it's too light."

She flips the cover open. Inside, there's a creamy, almost card-like title page, brown and speckled at the edges just the way old books are:

THE KEY TO ALL MYTHOLOGIES

by
The Rev'd Edward Casaubon

William Blackwood and Sons

Edinburgh and London

MDCCCLXXI

In the white space between author and publisher, Dad has written in his loopy, showy handwriting:

For Derek

Maybe we'll write it for him!
With best wishes, Bill

Morag flicks the page with her thumb. We're both expecting a table of contents or something, but this is where the pretense ends. No more words. No more book. Just a shallow compartment big enough for—what else?—a key.

There's a noise from one of the lower floors. Probably just the plumbing, but we nearly jump out of our skins.
"Let's get out of here," we both say at once.

Rosko is exactly where we left him, hiding behind a magazine at the café window.

"Sorry about the long wait," Morag says. "Anyone see us?"
"Nobody came to the door. Couple of guys wandered up and down looking suspicious, but then a police car cruised by and they vanished. I asked the waiter what's been going on. All he would say is that no one in the neighborhood believes the official story."
He points to the magazine. "Showed me this. A big feature on Quinn and the Seraphim, complete with a lot of useless speculation about what the 'third home' might be. Even an interview with a Seraphim figure saying, 'It will be revealed,' and a moon-phase diagram emphasizing how close we are to—whatever. You two look terrible. What happened up there?"

I glance round to check that the waiter's not in hearing range, then describe the office: the stacks of books, the list of ziggurats, the obvious search, the bloodstains.

"You think he was *killed* up there?"

"That's my guess."

He has a blue espresso cup cradled in his big hands like a hummingbird. As he puts it down, it rattles against the saucer—it's the first time I've ever seen him unnerved.

"Das ist ja furchtbar," he mutters. "But you found the book?"

Morag puts *The Key to All Mythologies* on the table, shows him the hidden compartment with its key.

His eyes widen. "The key to all mythologies—really? OK, next step: if this is the key, where's the lock?"

"Banco Popolare," Morag says, reading the tag on the key. "Hang on a minute."

She goes over to the counter and talks rapidly with the waiter, who nods and waves his hands at the door.

"Grazie mille!" And to us: "Just a couple of streets away. Let's go."

The waiter, who is just setting out our coffee, looks horrified.

"Sorry, gotta run," I say in English. "Drink them yourself." And I throw twenty euro on the counter.

△

Inside the bank, there's a long counter with half a dozen teller windows, all but one of them empty. We walk forward, stop at a little rope barrier, and a doughy woman looks up at us the way a large, bored fish might look at something inedible. She has lots of mascara, a cheap top that's too tight, and peroxide-white hair with inky roots. Forty-five, trying for twenty: doesn't work.

She looks down, ignores us ostentatiously while she scribbles something, looks up again. Finally, in response to a query from Morag, she sighs in a theatrical way and confirms that, yes, they have a deposit box under the name of *DAY-reck Para-TREE-jeh*. But it can be accessed "solo dal proprietario e"—she peers myopically at her screen—"da *O-illium Gala-DAI-reh*."

"Only by the proprietor and who?" I whisper.

"Not proprietor, owner. And Bill."

"Oh, right. Only the owner and 'O-illium Gala-DAI-rah.' Got it."

The bored fish-woman turns away again, as if dismissing us. We're screwed. What we need is right here, and there's no way to get to it. I waste some time and energy imagining all the ways we could (but really could not) get to the box. Digging a tunnel? Having a professional makeup artist disguise me as Dad? Being equipped with a getaway Maserati and a kilo of C-4? Then I see the blue-jowled security guard eyeing us from the other side of the lobby, as if reading my thoughts. But either Morag's not getting the social cues or else she has a better feel than I do for what works. She grabs my passport, thrusts it in the woman's face, points from me to it and back again, and starts talking angrily in Italian at a mile a minute.

I've never seen anything like it. Her entire body language, her entire set of facial expressions, changes until she's not so much talking Italian as *being* Italian. I hear *Gala-DAI-rah* several times, but otherwise it's a blur. It goes on, and on, rises to a shrill crescendo, then ends as she slaps down the passport, eyebrows arched and hands flared out, drilling the teller with her eyes.

Rosko is grinning. The teller is not. After losing the staring competition, she makes a show of examining my passport minutely, then looks me up and down slowly, as if noticing I'm male for the first time and deciding whether I'm worth hitting on.

Finally she does a little sour puckering thing with her lips. Either she's disappointed I'm not more of a stud, or she's just decided she can't be bothered to get into an argument with this crazy Asian chick. Either way, seconds later she jangles a bunch of keys, stops to adjust her bra's underwire, then gestures toward a big steel door.

"I'll wait outside and keep an eye on things again," Rosko says, still smiling. "You go ahead. A-plus on the rant there, Morag."

Morag and I step inside the vault. When I hand our key to the teller, she inserts it next to hers in a steel plate, and Partridge's box slides out of the wall. It's at least eight inches deep, must weigh twenty pounds. She hands it to me, then ushers us into a private side room that's decorated with two plastic chairs, a metal table, and a mold problem. Also strip lights that sound like an approaching swarm of bees. When Morag and I sit down, the woman hangs over us for a minute, as if expecting to see the goodies, then leaves, slamming the door.

Inside the deposit box there's a plain brown envelope; inside that, a clear plastic folder; inside that, some sheets of written text, cracked and stained and full of holes—midbrown script in Greek, on a pale-brown surface. I hear Dad's voice, from any one of a dozen museums: *Look at this, Daniel! Papyrus—the hot new Egyptian technology that took over from clay tablets. What everyone wrote on, for a thousand years. See how the edges of the sheet crack along the horizontal lines? Those are the reeds it was made from.*

I hand the folder to Morag. Underneath, a thicker envelope contains what appears to be an unpublished book galley—a preprint—of Partridge's next masterpiece of quirky historical scholarship: *Burning the Books: What Really Happened at Alexandria?* There's even a photocopy of the author photo they're planning to use, in which Partridge looks like a cross between Gandalf and a chicken.

Finally, at the bottom, there's a sturdy cardboard box. The lid slides off to reveal layers of tissue paper over a cocoon of bubble wrap. Inside the bubble wrap, there are three scrolls. I gently untie some modern ribbon from around the first scroll, worried it will disintegrate if I breathe too hard.

"Can you read it?" M whispers.

Ordinary modern text is split up by the spaces between the words. But this stuff dates from before word spacing was invented—it's just a bewildering, continuous string of characters, fragmented only by the dozens and dozens of what look like moth-holes in the papyrus itself. The letters dance before me, teasing. Most of them are still legible, individually. Even a few words are familiar. But the meaning is beyond my reach.

"I know a bit of modern street Greek, M. This is a dialect of ancient Greek. Almost a different language."

"So we don't even know for sure what it is. Doesn't it have a title?"

"I think we're a few centuries early for title pages. If they put the author's name anywhere, it was—hang on a sec."

I can hear Dad, in his museum voice again: *Centuries before books, Daniel, before book spines that you could print a title on, they used a little parchment tag. The Greeks called it a* syllabos. *Attached to the end of the scroll, so that the librarian could identify it without unrolling it.*

I pick up the third scroll and hold it up like a telescope. Miracle: tucked inside, there's a small slip of material. Can't even get my fat fingers in there: Morag has to pick it out. She holds the curled fragment up to the light. It's torn, the writing almost impossibly faint. But I know what I'm looking for, and there's no question what it says:

Eratosthenes
Geographika

She puts the syllabos down on the table; reaches out and touches the scroll with her fingertips, the way a pilgrim might touch a holy relic. Then she picks up the plastic folders again. "So this must be the letter from Cicero. Damn. I assumed it would be in Latin."

"I think all those guys wrote both."

"I kinda realized that. Just hadn't thought of it." She spreads the documents out on the table. "The crafty old bastard."

"Cicero?"

"Partridge. He must have stolen all this from the Biblioteca Angelica."

"Trouble is, he could read it—and we can't."

"Aye. Seriously annoying, from my point of view. I've been meaning to tackle Greek for ages. Wasn't exactly top of the list in Iraq. Or Africa. But a script I can't read, oh, it's like being a kid looking at a big slice of cake from the wrong side of a shop window."

She touches the scroll again, adds wistfully: "I could learn it in a couple of weeks."

"We don't have that kind of time, M. And I know only three people I'd trust who could read it now."

"Partridge himself, obviously. Bill."

"And Pandora."

"Of course. Problem solved, then. We take it to Crete."

"Yeah, that simple. Take it to Crete. I'm sure the Italian government won't mind us walking off with an ancient national treasure, so long as we don't, like, get it wet or anything."

"Hey, does the *Geographika* look Italian to you? It's already been in the wrong country for more than two thousand years. We'll just be taking it home."

Ridiculous argument—but then, what choice do we have? So the scrolls go back in their box, then we load everything into a green plastic supermarket bag and manage to squeeze the whole thing into my day pack. On the way out, I slide the empty metal deposit box back into its place.

Back in the bank lobby, we thank fish-woman, who ignores us totally. We nod politely to the security guard, who dittos. And step back outside, where Rosko is nowhere to be seen.

Δ

I'm scanning the street, wondering whether to panic, when Rosko comes up behind us, head down, walking fast.

"Follow me," he hisses. "Quickly."

Just as we catch up, he turns down a small side street, then another, and another.

"What's going on?"

Another side street. "We're being watched."

"Who? Where?"

"Two men. The pair I saw outside Partridge's office. They were scoping the bank the whole time you were in it. A short one with gray hair, maybe forty-five, and a younger one with a dark ponytail."

We duck into a pharmacy, study a display of hair-care products. No other entrance that I can see—if they saw us come in here, it's a dead end. After a few uncomfortable minutes, Rosko sidles to the window and looks out.

"I think we lost them for now. What's the plan, Daniel?"

I take the opportunity to get him up to speed about the documents.

"So you're carrying something in your pack that's the whole reason Partridge thought he was being followed. And we're going to take that to Crete with us?"

"If these guys already have Dad, they could have taken him anywhere. Getting Pandora to read this is our best chance of understanding what this third home thing is all about. I don't know what else to do."

Rosko's reading the label on a tube of sunscreen, as if that might tell us. "I guess you're right. We need Pandora to read the documents—and maybe Crete's the right place to go anyway."

"So much for relaxed sightseeing in Rome," Morag says, jabbing at her phone. "Whole bunch of flights to Athens, then Heraklion. Should be no problem—assuming we can even get back to the airport."

"Come on, then."

For almost a whole minute, we're on our way.

△

The pharmacy is on a street that's little more than an alley. No one about. And the men step out of their van only three or four paces ahead of us.

Rosko coughs to warn us, but doesn't look at them, which gives us a small element of surprise: they don't think we've rumbled them. And a second mark against them is that they choose a classic pickpocket's trick, which sets off one of the little alarm bells sensei installed. The younger, taller one with the ponytail, call him Paulo, moves around to my left side. The shorter, paunchier one—call him Lucky, if you have a taste for irony—locks eyes with me and smiles, raising a folded newspaper, pushing it toward my face and jabbering something I can't follow.

The standard version goes like this: They're after my money and my passport, so Lucky's copy of *Il Fatto Quotidiano* hides his hand as it goes fishing in my pockets. He palms the contents to Paulo, who vanishes into the crowd while I'm still wondering what Lucky's rabbiting on about.

But the same two Roman street grifters, outside Partridge's place and the bank, and now here? Nah. Lucky's hand does go to my chest, as if reaching for a wallet, but I guess that he's only planning to shove me back, off balance, so that Paulo can have an easier time grab-bing—or razoring—what he really wants. The goodies in the day pack.

Your average tourist would do just what Lucky wants: step back. Thanks to hundreds of hours of cajoling by sensei—*No, Daniel, not like that, like this. No. Again. And again. OK that's better*—I do the opposite. Rising on the balls of my feet, I step sharply forward, trap-ping his wrist against my lower rib cage, and get myself a firm double grip: one hand around the back of his elbow, so that his hand can't escape, and the other around the lower forearm. Crushing his ulna and radius together is merely painful; what does the serious damage is the twisting downward dip, which forces all those imprisoned metacarpal joints to bend in impossible ways. He gasps. But before he even has a chance to convert his new lungful into a scream, I pivot sharply on one heel, spinning him over my thigh.

The theory is, he will collide with Paulo. But Paulo isn't behind me, and Lucky collides instead with a parked motorcycle, which goes over. Paulo is several steps away, wrestling with both Morag and Rosko at once. One look at the scene and I know that I guessed wrong. They were betting on Morag's bag, and Lucky was just trying to take me out of the picture. Paulo has Rosko in a headlock; his other arm is looped around the handle of Morag's bag while she hangs on to the other side and kicks out at him.

When the handle breaks, Paulo stumbles backward. I throw out a foot. Bag in hand, he goes airborne, and when he lands his head whiplashes down onto the sidewalk.

Suddenly there's too much happening to take in:

Paulo is lying on the ground, screaming, "Cazzo cazzo cazzo!" I notice for the first time the Seraphim triangle tattoo on his neck. Inexplicably, Rosko and Morag are shouting at each other in what sounds like Russian. Lucky has gotten up and looks like he's about to jump on me. I spin awkwardly, almost too late, but as he lunges forward, I take a step toward him and manage to plant my knee in the exact place already being rented out by his balls.

Lucky makes a noise like a tire with a nail in it, folds in half, drops. Then things really get strange. Rosko grabs Morag's bag from the ground, says something else to her that I don't understand, and sprints away down the street, disappearing around a corner. Paulo says *cazzo* one more time, even louder, picks himself up, and throws us a look of pure hatred before sprinting after Rosko. Lucky, completely silent in his agony, is doubled over to the point where his head's between his knees—but when he sees Paulo depart, he gets up and starts to hobble crabwise after him.

"What the hell just happened, M?"

"They thought the stuff was in my bag. Rosko's a quick thinker, I have to say. He ran away with it, so now they're chasing the wrong person."

"What did he say to you?"

"'Get out of here, now. I'll draw them away. Don't wait for me, don't try to find me. Just get to Pandora and I'll catch up with you later.'"

I start to say, We can't simply leave him: we need to go to the police or something. Then I remember that I'm carrying a bag of inconveniently stolen museum artifacts, and the police may not be our best friends right now.

Then we hear the sirens.

Instinctively, we start running away from them. Only to realize we're running toward them. Only to realize they're not exactly after us. The sirens die as we reach the corner of Partridge's street. At least five emergency vehicles are parked across from the café, where the waiter is standing outside with a rag in his hand, drawn by curiosity. A swarm of bubble lights: luckily, the carabinieri seem preoccupied mainly with shouting at each other. But the waiter turns, looks at us, and there's a flicker of recognition.

"Time to go, M." I step back, away from his line of sight, then step out into the traffic and almost literally grab one of the familiar white taxis. For some situations, even I can get by in Italian:

"All'aeroporto, per favore. Di corsa!"

At one point, on the return trip to Fiumicino, we get all the way to forty-five kilometers per hour.

Chapter 17
Antikythera

On the plane to Athens, I don't even worry much about being arrested or attacked: I can't think about anything much except Rosko. If he didn't get away from Paulo in those first couple of minutes—if the Seraphim catch up with him and discover he doesn't have the documents—then what? I have a gruesome vision of him bound, shot, and dumped alongside Partridge in a Roman ditch.

Morag puts up with me panicking about this for a few minutes, then squeezes my hand and proceeds to vacuum up the entire contents of an Italian-to-Greek phrase book, interrupting my thoughts from time to time for my input on pronunciation and idioms. Maybe my face betrays irritation. At one point, she stops and says with exaggerated patience: "I know, D. I'm worried about him too. But there's nothing we can do *now*." The usual Morag combo of right, rational, and really annoying.

Waiting for our connection in the Athens terminal, I'm certain that someone is about to stop us, demand ID, discover that my backpack contains something over which, by rights, the Italian and Greek governments should be having a medium-sized diplomatic crisis. We stand with our backs to a pillar near some bathrooms. I pretend to read a freebie newspaper while scanning the concourse for a threat I couldn't identify if I saw it. Morag's looking at online maps and muttering to herself. Then she realizes how jumpy I am.

"I've been thinking about Partridge's list of ziggurats," she says. "He's interested in a problem my parents have been chasing for years."

"How to find more of the things?"

"No. The fact that there are already so many of them. They're all over the bloody planet. Why? I mean, it makes evolutionary sense that we're hardwired as a species to like sugar, and sex. But why would evolution hardwire us to build stepped pyramids in honor of invisible beings?"

"You have a theory. I can tell."

"Maybe. Jimmy and Lorna convinced Bill they'd found the library of *Babel*. But when I translated the Akkadian Version, I started to wonder: how do we know that was the *true* Babel at all? The original?"

"Uh, because it's at Babylon?"

"That's the tail wagging the dog. It's like thinking *angels* must come from Los *Angeles*. It's like thinking Jesus was crucified in the village church because there's a cross at one end of it."

"So you think it's somewhere else."

"Could be. Could be at Uruk. Or Chogha Zanbil. But no—I don't think it's somewhere else. I think it's *something* else. What does a ziggurat *look like*, D?"

I don't answer for a minute; a cleaner is pushing a cart full of mops and supplies past us. When he's gone:

"A pyramid?"

She lets out a little sigh—I'm being slow. "Sure. A pyramid. What does a pyramid look like?"

"A mountain?"

"Top of the class, D. And at many of these ziggurats—Babel, for sure—the priests maintained fires on top. So inevitably all the scholars jump up and down bleating 'ritual religious sacrifice,' because it helps the poor bastards maintain the illusion that they have the ghost of an idea what they're talking about."

As she says this she pulls out a notebook, balances it on one knee, and starts scribbling. A crude ziggurat, stairs and all. Then she adds a single vertical wavy line, just like the symbol on the front of Quinn's *Anabasis*, and looks at me. Finally she scrabbles in her bag, finds a red ballpoint, and starts adding more wavy lines at the top.

Flames.

"What do you think, D? What if all the ziggurats in the world are *copies* of something? *Images* of something? Little models—and what they are models of is a volcano?"

"You're saying the original Babel itself was a *volcano*?"

"Remember what Partridge said to you. 'Atlantis and Babel are the same story.'"

△

After a short, uneventful hop to Crete, we're met at Chaniá by Pandora Kallas.

Far as I know, there were not many sources of friction in my parents' marriage, but Pandora was one. This is, what, her fifth year working on Dad's Greek obsession? Dive master, but also research assistant. A few summers back, a work crisis prevented Mom from joining us in Crete; somehow she got the idea that in her absence Dad and Pandora were becoming way too friendly. No idea whether it was true, but you couldn't exactly blame Mom for worrying. Pandora's closer to my age than theirs, shares a lot of Dad's interests, has a PhD in marine archaeology. She's also interesting, likable, fun. And then there's the visual factor.

Her eyes are like pools of molten milk chocolate. She has a halo of wavy golden hair, and cheekbones like cliffs I could fall to my death from. When she meets us, she's wearing blue espadrilles, white Capri pants, and a very thin bleached-pink cotton shirt that has way too few buttons. In good news, I'm used to this. I've carried around with me for years the brightly colored mental snapshot that I collected on our first day together. Climbing back onto our dive boat near Agios Nikolaos, with a gallon of Mediterranean cascading off her wet suit, Pandora looked like a stunt double for the goddess Aphrodite.

"Daniel! So good to see you again." Big hugs and kisses. Her lips brush my ear, causing an instantaneous reaction down below that I could really do without. "And this must be the famous Morag. So nice to meet you! Welcome to Crete!"

"Ya sas, Pandora," says Morag. "Harika epitelous."

"Ah, the Morag language phenomenon! I did not know you speak Greek also."

"I don't. Just three hundred and four words and seventy-eight phrases that I learned on the plane."

Pandora raises her eyebrows in appreciation, then turns back to me, her expression serious again.

"OK. I have bad news and good news. But first tell me about your visit to Rome. How is the professor, and did you catch up with Bill?"

I hold up my hand. "Rome was all bad news. But let's get on the road. I'll tell you in a minute."

She throws me a puzzled frown, but walks us over to her familiar Peugeot truck, with its rack of oxygen tanks in back. As soon as we're in, she clunks it into gear and roars out of the parking area in a shower of gravel. As we head west across the Akrotiri peninsula toward town, I tell her everything: no idea about Dad, Partridge missing and apparently shot, Rosko missing and probably kidnapped.

"This is terrible," she says. "Nothing from Bill at all? And Partridge—I got a message from him only yesterday. Such a good, good man. Who are these people?"

"We don't know. But I think we've been spied on by the Seraphim in Seattle, Dad thinks they hacked his accounts, and Partridge was convinced he was being followed by them just before we arrived. The only good part is that we have the documents he was talking about, including the *Geographika*. I'm hoping you can translate them, maybe help us figure out where this third home is."

"You have the copy of the *Geographika*? With you?" She lets out a low whistle. "OK, so we need to get it—and you—somewhere safe. The boat is probably the best place away from prying eyes."

"How far?" Morag asks.

Pandora puts her foot on the floor and glances at her watch. "Thirty minutes."

"So tell us your news."

"The bad part is, last night gunmen broke into the museum in Heraklion. They stole all four Disks."

"Seraphim?"

She shrugs, focuses on the traffic for a minute. "Good news is, Professor Partridge left me a long voice message a few days ago. A bit strange, like he was trying to tell me something without actually *saying* it—"

"He was probably drunk," Morag says. "Or worrying that he would be overheard. Or both."

"He did describe to me what he found in the Biblioteca Angelica, and gave me some clues about what he thought it meant. It sounded so crazy that nobody could have invented it. And also it was quite easy to check."

"You're telling me you already know where Cicero's Disks were stored?"

"*Stored* is the wrong word. But yes. I already found them."

In the manner of Greek drivers, she casually takes her eyes off the road and all but one finger off the wheel—just as we're negotiating an intersection—in order to root around under her seat. I never get used to this kind of thing, but the creative driving doesn't bother Morag. She's staring out of the window, deep in thought.

"Here," Pandora says, handing me an unsealed manila envelope. I extract a single, grainy photograph. It looks black-and-white at first, but then you can see it's just been taken in low light, underwater. Sand. Rocks. Wood. Several dozen small, round objects lined up in a neat row like dirty plates in a rack.

Dirty salad plates.

"Jesus."

"Beautiful, yes? Sitting under our noses all these years. Bill will be so happy!"

Morag reaches forward between us and takes the photograph. "Bill won't be happy unless he stays alive. Where are they?"

For a few minutes, as we skirt the southern edge of Chaniá, Pandora doesn't answer. Just concentrates on the traffic, her jaw set. When we leave town and start heading west along the coast road, she says:

"I still can't believe it. I still don't understand it. He leaves this, this drunk message, which says something so ridiculous I almost don't bother to check it out. But I had a free weekend, and I was curious."

She's stalling, as if she doesn't want to say something that will make me laugh at her. When she does say where the Disks are, I happen to be taking a swig from a water bottle. I nearly choke.

"*Antikythera?* You have to be kidding."

"Hard to believe, I know. His message said, 'They were Cicero's ships, and there were two of them. The other one must be close by.' And it is."

Pandora and I are so wrapped up in this—a famous wreck we thought we knew all about—that we've almost forgotten Morag.

"Are you talking about the wreck where they found the Antikythera Mechanism?"

Pandora's eyes light up. "Quite a story. You know it?"

"Homeschooled by Jimmy and Lorna Chen—aye, it came up. The first ancient shipwreck ever found, correct?"

Pandora nods enthusiastically. "In 1900. Sponge-divers from the island of Syme. Just chance, it was—they took shelter from a storm, decided to see if they could find anything while they were waiting around. Put on their big old diving helmets and dropped over the side right into the debris field. Can you imagine? Hundreds of pots, jugs, plates—and life-size bronze statues just standing there on the sand, as if waiting for them."

"And," Morag says, "a mangled chunk of metal that turned out to be the world's first analog computer."

"That's right. The Antikythera Mechanism was a complete shock. A thousand years too sophisticated. It attracts almost as many eccentric amateur theorists as the Phaistos Disk. You know how it goes—people assume the ancient Greeks were too primitive to make it, so therefore it was a gift from another planet. Anyway, we always assumed the ship was on its way to a rich Roman's villa on the Italian coast. Now we know whose."

"How did you find the second wreck?" Morag asks.

"Archaeology is not so different underwater. You need a system, and luck. I drew a circle around the original wreck and split it into ten identical segments. About a third of the water covered by the segments was too deep to dive safely. In what was left, the sonar gave me half a dozen interesting anomalies, so I checked them out. It wasn't even one of them, in fact. Just happened to be right next to one, hidden in a trench."

△

A half hour's drive turns into three. Halfway there we're nearly side-swiped by a fuel tanker that overtakes us at 120 kilometers per hour on a bend. Pandora swerves as it cuts in ahead of us, hits a razor-sharp section of broken curb near a lonely bus stop, and gets a double flat. Half a dozen calls result in a long wait for a mechanic who shows up with the wrong tires. Then there's a longer wait while he goes all the way back to Chaniá for the right ones. Afternoon stretches into evening. We end up grabbing a bag of dinner essentials at a village shop. The last shreds of light are already dissolving into the ocean when we arrive at the dock.

"Good," Pandora says when we're aboard. "Food. Then the *Geographika*. You're stuck here unless we can work out where Bill and your friend Rosko are. If we do, I'll get you out of here in the morning. If not, Daniel, you can help me catalog the Disks while Morag keeps trying to work out what the third home is."

"There's no question what Bill's first priority would be," Morag says. "Recover the Disks. It's clear someone else is after them now, and I'm not surprised. In some way they hold the key to all this. I just hope we weren't followed."

Despite all the years with Dad here, the thought of diving to retrieve Disks infuriates me. We should be finding Dad and Rosko. But she's right: our only clue, our only hope, is the third home. And our only hope of finding that lies, perhaps, in the *Geographika*.

Once we've motored a little way offshore, we feel secure on the boat. But it's a work boat, not a yacht: the "accommodation" is a pilot-house big enough for one person who doesn't mind sleeping curled up. So we sit under the canopy at the back, hunkered down amid the dive gear, and eat our picnic dinner—bread, graviera cheese, olives, taramasalata. Pandora uncorks a bottle of local wine and pours for all three of us. Morag takes a thirsty swig, and grimaces. Pandora passes her some fizzy water. I hold out my mug for a second round.

The air is the temperature of blood. The lights on the harbor church at Kissamos are twinkling prettily. Every twenty seconds or so there's a sound like fries dropping into hot oil as another wave washes across the beach. A little wine in the system, I manage to relax just a little. Only a seven-months-pregnant moon reminds me how little time we have to catch up with Quinn.

△

Pandora eats only a few bites, carefully washes her hands, then powers up a deck lantern, unpacks the bag, and starts looking at our fragile whispers from the past.

"No question," she mutters after a few minutes. "This is the *Geographika*. And the letter is from Cicero. I feel like a criminal, reading such things on the back of a boat! I should be in an air-conditioned archive, wearing white gloves, with a guard standing over me."

We leave her to it for more than an hour, even when she mutters and exclaims under her breath. Morag settles herself cross-legged on the bow and seems to be meditating. I pass the time climbing around in the pile of dive gear, obsessively checking regulators, valves, O-rings—I'm driven by the superstitious hope that if I prepare carefully enough for our dive, it won't be necessary, because Morag will have a blinding revelation about where we're going to find Dad and Rosko.

When there's no more prep to do, I sit with a little whetstone and carefully resharpen my dive knife. All that relaxation gone now: I'm acutely aware of the seconds and minutes ticking away. At last Pandora closes the book, puts it carefully aside, and takes a big, thirsty pull from the wine bottle. Then she says, as if to the darkness:

"Professor Partridge may have been drunk, and he may be a thief, but he was right."

"About what?" Morag asks.

"Everything. Cicero's ships, in the first place. The letter tells the whole story. He is visiting Rhodes, pays a lot of money for the best possible souvenirs, then ships them back ahead of him. Ships, literally: *skaphe*—the plural jumped out at me. The plan was for them to go from Rhodes to Rome by way of Crete—so they must have passed just north of here. One ship carrying mainly art, and the other his newly acquired *diskoi*."

"What about the *Geographika* itself?" Morag asks.

"Ah yes. We were lucky with that one. Cicero says that for safety he will carry home his single most prized souvenir personally. 'Beta's book,' he calls it—Beta was Eratosthenes's nickname. Bill made fun of Partridge's obsession, but it's just as he suspected. This contains the true story of Atlantis."

Morag obviously thinks Pandora's yanking her chain. "You're kidding, right? Ancient Mystery Beneath the Waves? If this turns into a two-hour mockumentary with one of those doomy voice-overs from an 'explorer' who wouldn't know real evidence from a hole in the ground, I'm going to scream. I hate that stuff."

"So do I, Morag. You forget that I'm an archaeologist too. But it's not what you think."

"What's so new?" I ask. "And are you going to tell me *Atlantis* is the third home?"

"No." She taps the *Geographika* again. "Our sole source for all those hundreds of stupid books and TV programs about Atlantis is half a dozen lines in Plato, written twenty-four centuries ago, and he was just repeating a story from the Athenian statesman Solon, who'd been playing tourist in the Nile Delta two centuries before that."

The whole idea of an ancient Greek tourist in Egypt is a little hard to swallow. "What, like with a tube of sunscreen and a *Lonely Planet* guide?"

"Something like that. No camera, unfortunately. Anyway, Solon heard the story of Atlantis from an Egyptian priest. And the priest said it all happened a thousand years before *that*."

I'm keeping tabs on the dates with my fingertips. "So we're talking 1500, 1600 BCE."

"Yes. An interesting date, in the eastern Mediterranean."

It does ring a bell. Not that I can figure out which bell—something from Dad's book about the origins of the Bronze Age Collapse?

Morag's voice is reduced to a whisper. "The Thera eruption."

Pandora points across the water to the northeast. "Exactly. In 1628 BCE, one hundred and eighty kilometers that way, Thera erupted in one of the largest explosions ever recorded. This north coast was hit by tsunamis fifty, maybe a hundred meters high. And what I just read in this book is not a few lines of half-remembered myth. It's a specific, detailed history, describing a powerful early civilization on Thera that we had no idea even existed. We always assumed it was just another outlying island. A few Minoan settlements and some goatherds. But Eratosthenes tells a wholly different story: he says it was *the* power center of the region. He says it was 'the most ancient of all civilizations.'"

She opens one of the *Geographika* scrolls, finds a passage. "Let me read you something. 'Here, they say, the divine language was lowered down from heaven for the first time. Here, they say, the idea of cities and kings, of priests and the knowledge of eternity, was lowered down from heaven for the first time. They say that the greatest of all gifts, the fragment of the infinite within us, consciousness, was lowered down at Strongyle.' And he calls it the first home of the gods."

"Wait," I say. "Stron-GUY-li—*that's* what Partridge said. When I spoke to him in Seattle. And—I didn't make the connection before, but it was one of the first names in the Colberts' folder list."

"Pandora," Morag says, "if that's a Greek word, what does it mean? Where does it come from? What's the etymology?"

"*Strongulos* means 'round.' Spelled s-t-r-o-g-g-u-l-o-s, but we slip an *en* sound in there. So, 'the round place.'"

"I knew it!" Morag says with a burst of girlish excitement. "I kept telling Bill he was wrong. Wouldn't listen. Stupid, stupid, stupid pigheaded oaf."

Gotta love Morag. This is the first time anyone has ever described my Dad, the great William Hayden Calder, as a stupid pigheaded oaf. But—"M, what are you talking about?"

"This one unfamiliar word kept coming up in the tablets. Something related to *circle*, or *curved*. It has two forms, and Bill wanted it to be a reference to the Disks, so he kept insisting it must be a singular form and a plural: 'the round thing' and 'the round things.' Disks, obviously. But one of those words just kept on not making sense to me, in context. Now it does. The round things—the Disks—come from the *round place*. And that's the real Babel."

Pandora and I are both just looking at her with our mouths open, trying and failing to formulate a question. She rolls her eyes at us.

"Remember what I said in Athens? Not a ziggurat, not originally. The *volcano* at Strongyle was what every effing ziggurat in the world is a model of."

"But I've been to Thera. It's crescent shaped, not round."

Her eyes widen fractionally. It means: *Daniel, think.* "Giant volcanic island sticking out of the sea? Cone with a bomb inside? It's not round *now*."

"Right. Blew itself to pieces. Like Krakatoa."

"Aye. Except that Krakatoa was a zit compared to Thera."

I'm still not quite seeing it, though. "Wait. If there were all these people on the island, and it was such a big deal, why no archaeological remains? And where did they all go? They're living around a great volcano—even if a lot of people were killed, wouldn't there be records at least of, I dunno, fleeing refugees or something?"

Pandora picks up the *Geographika* again. "Eratosthenes describes a civilization driven by, structured by, obsessed with religion. The religion was centered on a towerlike temple at the summit of the volcano, a place of communion with the gods. The temple kept being damaged or destroyed, over several centuries, and the whole culture was organized around constantly rebuilding it."

"But," I insist, restacking wet suits to make more space, "where were the people?"

"There's a whole chapter here on the capital city. He describes it as the largest in the world. He also says it was designed as an outer defensive ring, in twelve segments, with the main city as a spiral of eighteen segments running up to the summit temple."

A ring of twelve, and a spiral of eighteen. "You mean they designed their entire city based on a Phaistos Disk?"

"I'm sure the city came first, and then Disks. Anyway, he says the city was confined to the upper half of the mountain. If your gods are located at the top of a mountain, and they tell you to keep building, because your reward will be heaven, are you going to run away from them or go to them?"

Morag shakes her head in disgust. "Death's never the end. The gods promise a fabulous time in the next life if we just do the right thing in this one. Death is just a point of transfer to the sweet eternal. It's the ultimate come-on: be obedient, give your whole life to us, and then step through the door for your fucking *reward*."

"That's exactly what Quinn says," I point out. "And what the Akkadians believed—at least until your Shul-hura blew the whistle."

I crawl into my sleeping bag, shivering at the thought: a great city, built around the summit of a volcano, precisely where it can best be destroyed. "Wow. When the right moment comes—when the gods are ready, or the volcano's ready—boom. A civilization vaporized whole, without a trace."

"That's right," Pandora says. "No survivors, no trace—except the *diskoi*. Which were their religious texts. They mass-produced them for several centuries, and scattered them like seeds all over the region."

"Eratosthenes actually calls them *diskoi*?" Morag asks.

"That word is in here, once or twice. But the inhabitants apparently preferred another word, which he translates into Greek as 'o logos tēn demiourgon.'"

Morag frowns and concentrates, like a student faced with an exam question. "*Logos* is 'word' or 'reasoning,' yes? So *O logos tēn* means—I'm guessing here—something like 'the language of'?"

Pandora nods approvingly.

"What's the last bit?"

"The noun *demi-ourgos* is an interesting word. It can mean 'municipal worker'—like the man who's employed by the city to mend potholes. It can also mean 'designer.'"

"One kind of designer is an architect," Morag says.

Pandora nods. "Yes. And Plato used it to mean the *original* designer. The architect of the universe. God."

CHAPTER 18
DEVIL IN THE DEEP BLUE SEA

We're in the darkening blue of forty meters, near the practical safe limit for diving without a decompression chamber. Above us, brilliant afternoon sunlight is flooding across this corner of the southern Aegean Sea, and an army of long-wavelength photons—red, yellow, green—is surging down toward us. But they run out of energy and drown up there: only blue light has the buzz to swim this deep. Down here, the color and the silence give the dive site a spectral feel, like the crypt it is.

On our first dive, half an hour after sunrise, it was still dark underwater. In the glow of our headlamps, we removed a couple of two-thousand-year-old elm planks to reveal a neat line of a dozen more Disks. After all those years of searching and digging with Dad, I wanted to laugh out loud at how easy it was; wanted so much to have Dad here, share the moment with him.

The site is on the crumbling lip of an underwater cliff. Algae-crusted rocks on one side; on the other, a swift plunge into darkness.

Pandora moves methodically, her body suspended above the edge, recording the Disks with a new underwater camera. This gear uploads pictures directly to a laptop on the boat, which is anchored in shallower water a quarter mile away; it also tags the photos with time, GPS location, and both the magnetic bearing and the angle at which the camera is being held. The geospatial software will have built us a 3-D model of the whole site before we even get back on board.

Morag's in the Zodiac, directly above us, looking green. A night without sleep—a night without an answer, more to the point—and she'd do just about anything to be on land. Good thing the work is quick, and not only for Morag's sake. We've squeezed this second dive as close to the first as the chemistry of nitrogen absorption will allow, and our dive plan allows for only a few minutes of bottom time before we must begin the dull routine of returning, via timed safety stops, to the world of normal pressure and unbottled air.

At least while we're down here I don't have much to do. My job is only to be Pandora's safety buddy, keep my eyes open for anything we might have missed, keep track of the time and the pressure levels. So I'm just floating, trying to puzzle out what a man like Quinn can really want with Dad—or Morag, or Rosko. Surely he's spoken to the "Architects," or thinks he has? Surely he knows everything already?

Seems we've only been at work a couple of minutes when my dive computer starts winking at me: only five more before hitting our safe margin for ascent. I look up at the bottom of the Zodiac, a flexing shape on the surface, and follow the long sloping line that reaches down from it to the spare tanks. The hull's shadow shows up quite distinctly on a big boulder at the lip of the trench, like a throw rug drying on a wall.

A pretty scene, though the dark chasm to my right is unsettling. I rotate lazily, get myself one more look at the patterns on the surface, and take my knife from its sheath on my leg. I'm just about to tap three times on my tank with the metal handle, to get Pandora's attention. Then I turn and look at her for the first time in thirty seconds.

Something is very, very wrong.

△

At the end of basic scuba training there's a scary little rite of passage. You've shown that you can maintain depth. You've aced the test on hand signals and emergency drills. You know how to buddy-breathe from your pal's tank. You can even do those gnarly little calculations about pressure, multiple-dive nitrogen accumulation, stop time, ascent rate. (Important, getting the math right: it greatly reduces the chance that you'll pop up too quickly after a long dive, then die an agonizing death as your blood celebrates its return to normal pressure by turning into pink champagne.) So: the final ritual. After carefully explaining what's next, your instructor takes you down to twenty feet or so, checks your gear, probably sits you on the nice sandy bottom. Then rips off your mask and tosses it away.

Your job: don't panic. All you have to do is keep your eyes open— they sting less than you expect—then reach for the mask, put it back on, breathe out through your nose to expel the water. Oh, and give your instructor the thumbs up. You're a diver at last.

I'm years beyond that elementary stage, and Pandora's a senior dive master who has trained dozens of people herself. But nobody forgets that early experience with the mask. Fear. Liberation from fear. Achievement. It's what I think of immediately, as I see her mask floating gently down into the darkness.

△

She's drifting, neutrally buoyant, with her head down as if she's watching the mask disappear. Then the current, combined with the flotation in the PFD, rolls her over, so that she's on her side, as if sleeping.

By the time I reach her, the regulator has fallen from her slack mouth and is floating beside her, gently bubbling. A few more stray bubbles are coming from the side of her mouth. As I reach for the regulator I notice a kind of stain in the water behind her. Because the colors are all wrong, the first thing I think of is spilled coffee. But coffee isn't what you get when there's a harpoon sticking out of your back.

Part of my brain says the obvious: she's dead. But part of it must be running a forgotten subroutine from a CPR course, because my right fist, as if working on its own, reaches out and punches her in the stomach. The water resistance softens the blow, but it's enough: she lurches forward, mechanically expelling water, and I stuff the regulator back in her mouth.

Miraculously, she inhales, and her eyes come back to life. Then she starts throwing up. I hold on to her firmly, hold the regulator in place—gross, but they're designed for this. Eventually she's breathing properly again.

I look around frantically. There are shadows moving in the depths that might be something, and probably aren't. I can see the fear in Pandora's eyes, see too that she's trying to master it. Thank goodness we've been diving together for so long: our basic hand signals have developed into almost a complete sign language. When I convey my intentions to her, she repeats them and nods weakly: I will hold on to her as we work our way dutifully up the dive line, stopping at the correct depths but cutting the stop times in half—balancing the fear that we'll both die of the bends against the fear that she'll bleed to death first.

Δ

"Thank goodness you've come back up, D. I've been dying to tell you—I figured it out! The third home. It's so easy. I should have thought of it right away. It's—*Oh shit*."

Getting Pandora onto the Zodiac ought to be neat, swift, dignified—in some alternative world. In reality, I'm still in the water and Morag is trying to haul her on while leaning out of a pitching inflatable and asking fifty questions. It's not working.

"Don't talk, just get her in."

We waste five minutes in struggling and shoving, but we can't get her in.

"You'll have to tow us to the boat. Slowly." For five more agonizing minutes, I hang onto the Zodiac's deck line with one hand and the back of Pandora's PFD with the other. Can't even tell if she's still conscious. At the boat, we can't get her out of the water either, despite the steps at the stern—but by using them as a kind of lever I do at last get her into the Zodiac.

"Leave this to me," Morag says, jumping in beside her. "Easy job, not a problem." She's talking to Pandora, not me, trying to calm her as she takes my knife and starts to cut away the wet suit. "Look at me, Pandora. Concentrate on breathing slowly and calmly. You're going to be fine. My mother trained as a nurse, and I've handled worse than this. D, get me the first aid kit. And a cloth. A T-shirt, anything."

"Someone attacked her and stole the camera," I'm explaining, as I climb from the Zodiac onto the dive boat.

"Two guys," Pandora says weakly. "They were wearing military rebreathers—no bubbles. Came out of nowhere. But it doesn't matter about the camera. The imagery uploads in real time, remember? Already on the laptop."

She flicks her eyes in the direction of the pilothouse.

"They'll come right back for the Disks themselves, soon as they have a chance." I'm talking to myself as I watch Morag at work, but I've said it out loud and Morag must think I'm seriously proposing to go back down. With a hard edge to her voice she says, "I think we have more important things to worry about."

When she peels the neoprene off Pandora's wound, blood floods out onto the deck. It looks like dark velvet in the sunlight. Shocking, but Morag visibly relaxes. "Not as bad as I thought. I can't get the tip of this out of you without causing more damage, but that's not arterial. Once we stop the bleeding you're going to be OK."

"Time to get out of here," I say, and I head for the wheelhouse.

Things are way, way worse than I thought.

△

First of all, the laptop's gone. Second, I'm standing at a slight angle to the wheel, and a quick look in the hatch confirms my suspicion. The engine compartment is filling with water: someone has put a hole in the boat, and we're sinking.

"Can we bail it?" Morag asks when I explain the situation.

"Not fast enough. We have ten, fifteen minutes, max."

"Then we'll have to get Pandora back to Antikythera in the Zodiac."

A loud, harsh *No!* from Pandora, followed by a whisper. "Morag. You were about to say something about the third home. You found it?"

"Aye, but that doesn't—"

"Tell us. Quickly."

"It just came to me. I should have thought of it a long time ago. Thera, or Strongyle, was a volcano. Nearly all the Mysteries have been associated with volcanoes, or with mountains anyway. What's another volcano in this region, associated with gods?"

I get it at once. Almost went there with Mom, in fact, only we couldn't get the climbing permits.

"Ararat. Because of Noah."

"One out of two. Mount Ararat, yes, but not because of Noah. It shows up in Armenian mythology a thousand years before the Noah story was written down. The ancient Armenians believed, just like the Greeks believed about Olympus, that Ararat was where their gods lived."

"Great. Ararat is a seriously remote mountain in the badlands of far-eastern Turkey. If you're right, we have maybe thirty-six hours to find medical help for Pandora and then get there."

I'm already running through a long list of issues, options, problems, but Pandora beats me to it.

"Here's what you are going to do, Daniel."

I have to crouch down to hear her.

"Whoever those guys were, they'll be looking for you—for us—on Antikythera and in Crete. You don't want to run into them, so you cannot take me there."

"But—"

"Please. Shut up and listen. Best is if they believe we all drowned. Yes? So you are going to hope the boat stays afloat a little longer, and take it north, just as if we hadn't noticed anything wrong. Then get into the Zodiac, let the main boat sink, and get us to Kythera. Bigger island, bigger hospital. And a direct ferry to Athens."

It's a horrible idea, for a whole lot of reasons, but I don't have a better one. I grab a mesh dive bag, stuff it with essentials—dry clothes, passports, money, a couple of jackets—toss it down to Morag. By the time we're ready, the dive boat is listing another five degrees to starboard.

Luckily the engine catches immediately, despite all the water down there. As I come up to about half speed, the Zodiac starts to buck horribly on the wake, so that Morag has to cling on to Pandora just to prevent them both being thrown out. Nothing to be done; I press on, making another couple of miles northeast.

A quick scan with the binoculars. No other boats around, and Antikythera is fading out of sight. I give it another two, three minutes at half throttle, and it seems I'm doing fine. The engine coughs ominously. Then a larger than average swell catches the hull broadside, causes a sickening slow roll, and for a minute I think it's going to take me over.

No sign of land now. "Time's up. Coming to join you," I yell.

Morag yells something back, waves an arm, points.

"What?"

I can't make it out, and the boat's lurching on the swell like a drunk on a trampoline. Throttling back to slow, I center the wheel, untie the line, dive over the stern rail. Seconds later I'm back in the Zodiac.

The dive boat putters away without us, on a slight arc to the north, leaning over like a man with one short leg. It looks as if it could go on like that forever, but on the next big wave crest it straightens and heels over the other way. Then it heels over some more, stops almost completely on its side, and vanishes as if tugged from below.

Morag is staring after it as if she's witnessed a cold-blooded murder.

"What? What were you waving about?"

She takes about three shallow breaths before answering, then nods in the direction where the boat went down.

"Still in the wheelhouse."

"The laptop? No, I looked."

She shakes her head. "The *Geographika*."

"Oh crap. Please tell me I didn't do that."

"You didn't. We did. We just destroyed the last surviving copy of one of the greatest lost works of antiquity."

Dad would rate this right alongside burning the *Mona Lisa*. But Dad is precisely the reason we can't waste time thinking about it. Good to be with Morag at a moment like this: she blows out a long breath, as if ridding herself of the thought.

"It's gone, D. Nothing we can do. The question is, what now? What's the plan?"

I point north. "The plan is, we go that way and try to stay warm until morning."

Night's coming on. We're in an inflatable that has a mosquito for an outboard, with no lights and no compass. We need to cross a notoriously rough patch of sea that's also one of the busiest shipping lanes in the Mediterranean.

At least the flashlight shows plenty of gas in the tank. "It's twenty miles, twenty-five allowing for current. We get there by dawn, we can be in Athens tomorrow afternoon. And we'll know nobody followed us."

"We have enough time?"

I shrug. "Either we do or we don't."

As the air cools, the air currents should fade too, calming the sea. Instead, the wind veers until it's directly against the current, forcing the surface into a steep, uneven chop. We thump laboriously north, waves coming at us out of the dark at an awkward diagonal, making the boat slew and lurch. What will it be like, I wonder, for some marine archaeologist to explore the mud beneath us a couple of thousand years from now and come across a rusted motor, some fragments of rubber, a single steel harpoon point?

Thank goodness it's a clear night. Which means we're too cold, but at least I can see the Big Dipper pointing north. Just hope we have enough gas. Just hope Pandora stays alive.

CHAPTER 19
CROSSING TO KYTHERA

It's another half hour before Homer's rosy fingers of dawn are due to show up, but the darkness is already thinning. The waves have subsided into ripples at last. When the island of Kythera appears, a beached gray whale on the horizon, I throttle back to the slowest possible speed, then take us a mile closer. But the noise still sounds outrageously loud in the still air, so I cut the engine, fit the oars into the oarlocks. I've been standing in a steady breeze, wet with spray, all night. I'm exhausted, shaking with cold, desperately hungry. Wonder if my numbed arms are up to the job.

Pandora is wrapped in a tarp. Her exposed face looks ghostly, but she has all Morag's remaining pain meds in her and she's breathing more or less normally. Morag comes over from the bow to check on her, unwraps the tarp enough to look at her back with a flashlight.

"I don't think it's infected, or not yet. But she's lost a dangerous amount of blood. And there's no way she can walk."

She rubs her face, rummages in the bag, silently offers me a small square of chocolate. I'm grateful, eat it at once, immediately wish I'd resisted—I could eat five bars.

"What you thinking about?" she asks.

"I'm thinking about Eggs Benny and a side of pancakes. You?"

"No thanks on the breakfast. Thrown up more times than I can count. If you really want to know, I was thinking about Zeus's sex life."

Sometimes Morag says things so odd that there's no point in trying to formulate a response—you just wait for her to go on.

"Zeus disguises himself as a shower of gold and seduces Danaë—she gives birth to Perseus. To get into bed with Semele, he disguises himself as an eagle—she has Dionysus. For an afternoon of lakeside fun with Leda, he's a swan—she produces both Helen and Polydeuces. It goes on and on."

"Guy must have been exhausted." I start rowing.

"But it's the same story over and over, in more cultures than you can count. God meets girl. Every single time, the result is crazy sex and a child who's a half-divine miracle-worker. We tend to forget that it's the Christian story too."

"Except in Christianity they skip the sex."

"Aye."

"What's this have to do with anything?"

"I'm not sure. But I keep hearing Bill say, 'Myths don't come from nowhere.' I'm starting to wonder if the Architects messed around with us in more ways than one."

"You notice you just spoke as if you believe the Architects exist?"

Long pause.

"I do believe they exist, D. I'll give you that: I do believe they exist. I just don't believe anyone has a single effing clue what they are."

Another long pause.

"Which is kind of cool, really. Because it means we get to find out."

She smiles a hopeful smile, her eyes gleaming. I absolutely love her at that moment—for her optimism, her brains, her sheer naive refusal to let a problem go.

△

Looking over my shoulder, I can see Kythera much more clearly now, a pale streak of shoreline under dark hills. And a triangular rock appears—only in fact it's not a rock, but the accidental landmark I've been hoping is still there: the prow of a modern freighter that went aground years ago on an islet half a mile offshore. That's the good news. The bad: now that I have a landmark close by, and enough light to see detail on the shore behind it, I can compare the two and judge our drift. There's maybe a two-knot current sweeping us southwest, away from the point where I wanted to land.

Pandora groans and begins to wake up. I look again at the landmarks. Every moment is taking us farther from medical help, from the ferry dock, from any hope of catching up with Dad. Really could have used a lucky break at this point.

I take a long deep breath, savor the last aftertaste of chocolate, say a prayer to Neptune. Then I start rowing a race against the sea itself.

△

By the time we scrape up onto a pocket of rocky beach, an hour later, my shoulders and back are on fire. We manage to half-carry Pandora out of the boat and lay her down, then I take a minute to stretch. A remote piece of coast. No one around.

I have everything worked out, sort of. Load everything into a mesh dive bag, along with some rocks. Lash the bag into the boat.

Swim back out, sink the whole thing. Then get Pandora to a clinic. Then get to the ferry.

But this scenario is seriously short on detail, especially how to do those last parts in the couple of hours we have available. I'm still looking over it in my mind when I realize Pandora is awake and arguing with Morag—if *arguing* is the right word, for someone whose voice is as indistinct as a mouse in the grass.

"Morag, I cannot even stand. No way you can get help for me. Not without missing the ferry. Go."

"D, help me out here. Make this woman see reason."

I hesitate, kneel down beside her.

"I'm not dying, Daniel," she says. "You leave the boat right here, with me. People come to this beach every day. I'll get help soon enough."

That's the big question—will it be soon enough? But she's right. What can we do? I look at Morag. "It's four, five miles over that ridge behind us to the port. Steep, tough hike. I don't even know if we can make it."

"Go, now," Pandora says to Morag. "And stay alive."

I kneel over her and kiss her forehead. "You too." Then I give her an almost empty water bottle, put the clothes bag over my shoulder, and start walking.

Δ

The upward hike is even worse than I expected—dusty, pathless, steep. It's not made easier by the fact that for a long time, as we ascend, we can look back and see Pandora. She has crawled maybe fifty feet up the beach. She has stopped moving.

"Is she going to make it?" Morag asks.

"Sure she is. Someone will find her soon." But I look back again, soon after that, and the rest of the beach is ominously empty. She has been reduced by distance to a tiny fleck. Then the angle changes and we lose sight of her.

Another twenty minutes of blisters, gravity, and exhaustion bring us to a white-painted chapel on the summit of a hill. At last we change out of our salt-crusted clothes. I stuff them back into the bag, so that we have something to carry, hoping that we'll pass as totally unmemorable backpackers, then it's two or three easy miles on a gravel road that slopes down to the ferry dock. Halfway down, we see the ferry coming in and quicken our pace; we're lining up for tickets with minutes to spare. At a quayside stall I resist the temptation to draw attention to myself by ordering a whole tray of baklava.

△

We're both desperate to rest, but it's hard to do when you think you're being hunted and don't even know who to be suspicious of. Luckily the ferry's not crowded; the only people who draw our attention— and everyone else's—are an elderly couple who keep to themselves in a corner. The woman talks constantly, in a low private voice, as if to a child. For a minute I think innocently that her husband is senile. I'm looking out the window, thinking about Dad, when I hear Morag's sharp intake of breath. The man has looked up. Or maybe that's the wrong way to put it. Raised his head, anyway. The blank eyes, the mouth, the tongue: he's a Mystery. His wife gets something out of her bag, and lovingly places it around his neck. A thin white scarf with a golden Seraphim triangle.

Morag finds a Greek newspaper and I do my best to decipher it. Sure enough, more Mysteries everywhere. I can't read the details, but there are reports coming in from all sorts of wild places, and cities too. Hanoi, Accra, Chennai, Anchorage.

For a while I watch the old man, wondering what really happened to him. Then I go into a daydream about Kit—and even that refuge fails me. I miss her. I think about how painfully obvious I've been about my attraction to her, and how infuriatingly, enigmatically, blandly *nice* she's been in response. Is she clueless? Is she politely saying, *Get lost*? I think about the moment when Morag and I arrived at Rosko's house, and the image of Kit standing over him, apparently rubbing his shoulders. Amazing how quickly, how convincingly my imagination creates more. Kit leaning down. Rosko reaching up to cup her face in his hands. Her hands straying south. The way she runs the very tip of her tongue, so lightly and delicately, over his upper lip.

I'm saved from my ridiculous, baseless, hi-def jealousies by a blast from the ferry's horn. When I look up, the Mystery is looking steadily at his own hands, as if bothered by a memory of what they are. But his wife has turned to look out the front of the boat. I follow the line of her gaze. Up past the bow, a wall of white apartment buildings is crawling across the blue water toward us.

CHAPTER 20
THE ENEMY OF MY ENEMY

Greece and Turkey may hate each other, but they're right next to each other: how hard can it be?

Hard.

Our taxi driver insists on a "shortcut" through the center of Athens. Stuck in another traffic jam from hell, we spend way too long on a free view of the Parthenon veiled in smog. I try not to look at my watch every three minutes. At last we crawl into Athens International. Then the fun really begins.

"Beautiful Eastern Turkey is popular tourist destination, sir!"

The man at the Turkish Airlines counter smiles broadly and delivers his line in perfect, almost accentless English, as if he's been rehearsing for weeks. *Flying to the Kurdish city of Van, good idea, sir!* Only, there is a problem: we have to go via the capital, Ankara, and the *very next flight for you, sir*, involves a long wait, a long layover, and not getting to Van until late tonight.

I waste a lot of energy grinding my teeth; ask questions at every airline counter before going around and asking them again; even investigate whether we can fly to Ankara and drive to Ararat from there. (No. I'm too young to rent. And it's a thousand kilometers—eighteen hours on mountainous roads, if you're feeling lucky. I'm not feeling lucky.)

Morag has to virtually drag me back down into a chair. "There's nothing we can do about it, D. We'll get to Van tonight. We still have all day tomorrow."

I can see several problems with that. It's maybe a four-hour drive to Ararat even from Van—a four-hour drive into Turkey's Wild East, the rugged, politically unstable country near the Iranian border—and we have to get a car. I go back to Mr. Smiley at Turkish Airlines: he wants to sell us a bus tour from Van to Ararat—*very good, with hotel*—but the bus takes forever, and only goes three times a week. I'm about to plead with the rental people again, offer them a deposit the size of Texas, bribe them, when I remember the titanium guys at AmEx.

Bad, bad cell phone connection, but eventually I get through. Even more eventually, make myself understood. No, I don't want a van. I'm *going to* Van. But I do need a driver, yes. With a four-wheel drive vehicle. Has to be an English speaker who can find his way around eastern Turkey in the dark, yes.

A pause, during which I think I've lost the connection.

"Certainly, Mr. Calder. No problem at all."

△

Half an hour into the flight from Athens to Ankara, I'm so lost in my anger and frustration—about Mom, Pandora, Derek Partridge, Dad, Rosko—that it's a complete surprise when someone inserts a rusty chisel into the space between my top cervical vertebra and the base of my skull.

Should not be a surprise, but at first I just think, Whoa, that's a headache. A few minutes later, when the invisible assailant with the chisel sinks it in an inch further and gives a twist, the "head-ache" becomes a savage, gasp-inducing shocker. But it's only when my arms start to feel as if someone is pinching them that I put two and two together.

Time to stop thinking *shit shit shit this hurts*.

Time to start thinking, *Oh right, panic: you have the bends*.

Do I tell Morag I have decompression sickness? Do I warn her that I may be about to die, balled up in unbearable agony, right next to her? Do I mention it to the nice, harassed-looking woman in the ridiculous 1960s stewardess hat, and risk the possibility that she will tell the captain, who will say, *Ladies and gentlemen, we have an idiot on board*, and initiate an emergency landing in Albania, or what-ever godforsaken hole we are currently flying over? I close my eyes against another wave of pain, and wonder whether Albania has a single hyperbaric chamber in the entire country. A peek through one watery eye at the in-flight map gives me a small cool droplet of relief when my besieged brain catches up with the fact that, oh yeah, wrong direction: we're nowhere near Albania. Still, not getting to Ararat is something that just can't happen right now. No time for a medical crisis. So I restrict myself to clutching the back of my neck, trying not to visualize the nitrogen bubbles, trying not to scream.

Morag doesn't notice, for a while. She's hunched over a tablet, looks like she's playing a computer game; in fact she's working with a program Dad wrote that combines and recombines groupings of the Phaistos symbols. She's muttering to herself, and there's something even more intense about her than usual. But she won't say anything. Finally I give myself away with a strangled grunt.

"Headache?"

"If Jupiter's a planet, this is a headache."

She digs around in her pockets, produces a translucent brown pill bottle identical to the one that held my drowned Mayan gods.

She pours the contents into her hand. Except for the variations in size, it looks something like a pile of M&M's.

"What's all that?"

"Oh, you know."

"No, M, I don't know." (Shit shit shit.) "That's why I asked."

"I've got a little of everything. Ibuprofen. Diazepam. A couple of Ambien. The antinausea stuff that did squat for me on the boat. These are Cipro. The fat gray ones are generic multivitamins, which it turns out don't do a bloody thing for you. This is leftover amoxicillin from when I had strep throat about a year ago. Pepto—"

"You're not supposed to *do* that."

"Do what?"

"Mix them up. It's dangerous."

She gives me her most skeptical, you-have-to-be-kidding-me look. "Old antibiotics are pretty low on my Threat Assessment List right now. Thanks for the advice, though." She puts the in-flight magazine in her lap and dumps the entire load, spreading them out. "Oh look. These two here will be your special friends. Yummy, yummy Percocet. I have to tell you, these are seriously good stuff."

"You sound like an addict."

"I had a pinched sciatic nerve in Baghdad. It felt like someone was trying to remove my kidneys with a power tool. Believe me, they're good."

"Can I have them? Please?"

"How bad is it?"

"Right now, I'd kill a small defenseless animal for them."

"Hint of desperation in your voice there, D. What's wrong exactly?"

"Just give the fucking things to me, M."

"Who's sounding like an addict now?"

"It's you who's carrying a complete pharmacy in one pill bottle."

She gives me a disapproving look, followed by the pills. After I wash them down with a mouthful of bad OJ, the pain keeps spreading through my joints for ten, fifteen minutes. The sensation in my head, and the back of my neck, goes from Bad to Shockingly Bad, then hovers for a minute on the extreme edge of Unendurable. I'm clutching both armrests, trying not to cry from the combination of fear and self-pity, when the drugs start to kick in, a little. Stepping outside of the pain for a moment, I recall Rosko, hunched over a bowl of Vietnamese noodles, saying, "That's the big puzzle. Why is pain, you know, *painful*?"

A moment later the engine note changes, seat-belt signs go ping. When I feel my ears pop, I allow myself to entertain the idea that maybe I'm not going to die of the bends after all.

At least Ankara has that great, great invention called Turkish coffee. I buy two cups, but to my surprise Morag waves hers away—she's back to staring and muttering—so I drink hers too, then get a third. I'm staring at my fingernails, gratefully feeling the buzz, when Morag shakes me. The screen in her lap has Phaistos symbols marching across its surface in shifting ranks, like beetles in an old-fashioned video game.

"I'm getting somewhere with this, D. Right from the start, Bill and I have been asking all the standard questions linguists ask: What structure does this language have? Is it hieroglyphic or not? Do the verbs come after the nouns, or before? But more and more I've been thinking: what if we stop asking what kinds of structure a human language has to have? What if we ask: what kind of structure does *this thing* have?"

"What difference does it make?"

"You can classify languages into a pretty limited number of structures. This thing, it's not like any of them, not at all, so I don't think it's a *language*, in the ordinary sense. More like a digital code. Chanted syllables, sure. But I've figured out what the underlying structure is. Or, well—actually, you did."

"Excuse me?"

"Our counting system is decimal. Base 10. Computers use binary, which is base 2. But you can use any base you like: eight, sixteen, whatever. The Phaistos Disks are numerical too, but they have 'words' or groups in base 12, with a kind of digital key that's base 18. Sound familiar?"

I'm back in Heraklion again: *That's clever, Daniel. Very observant. Could be significant.*

"So I was right."

"You were right. And it's a tragedy that a great scholar like your father couldn't pay more attention to an annoying small boy with dyslexia."

"Can you crack it, make any sense of what it means?"

"What it *means* may be the wrong question. This may be something more fundamental than a language. It's like, your computer has programs, but all the programs depend on the operating system. What if this Phaistos thing is the operating system that *underlies* all language? What if it's the thing that made us capable of language?"

The Percocet must be even stronger than I thought, because this sounds unbelievably flaky, especially coming from her. "You're saying the gods—the Architects—were like, uh, computer programmers from the eleventh dimension or something? Who programmed us?"

"I'm not saying anything about the Architects. Not yet. All I'm saying is, if this thing is at the root of our ability to have language at all, then oh, I need to crack this. And I will."

"Before we get to Ararat?"

She shakes her head. "I'd need a spare month, a more complete collection of the Disks, and serious computing power—just to get started. And a complete Antikythera Mechanism might help."

"You mean—"

"Just guessing. But it fits, doesn't it? Here's what I think. Eratosthenes finds out about what happened at Thera, or Strongyle, and he sees, just as we have, that there's something seriously whacked about the Phaistos language. He wants to solve the mystery. Being one of the smartest mathematicians alive, he knows that what he really needs is *the* smartest mathematician alive. Who happens also to be a mechanical genius. His buddy Archimedes of Syracuse."

"So he invites him to Alexandria? And they come up with the Antikythera Mechanism as a decoder?"

"It would be like having your Dad and Maynard Jones in the same room, only better. Or worse. So. A century later, Posidonius reads the *Geographika*. That makes him want to start collecting the *diskoi*—obviously soon enough he's going to want the Mechanism too. And suppose those divers in 1900 brought up only a fragment of something far more complex?"

$$\triangle$$

The drug/caffeine cocktail has done its work; when we board our next plane, and climb through twenty thousand feet, my headache doesn't come back. We get treated to gorgeous views of emerald fields and cracked-leather uplands, all lit by the final rays of sunset. Then the sky goes dark and the plane is banking over the darkening vastness of Lake Van. We descend steeply, as if preparing to land on the water. Runway lights show up on shore at the last moment.

It's another hard, military-style landing. The plane bounces on its left-side wheels, threatens to take off again. We thump back down, skitter, skid to an awkward halt.

Welcome to beautiful Eastern Turkey.

$$\triangle$$

The little arrivals hall is chilly, poorly lit, has the feel of an old Midwestern bus terminal—but our driver is waiting for us. He's a big, broad guy of maybe forty, with a heavily creased face and a spiky, theatrical beard. Looks like a peasant, maybe a shepherd or something, except that he has perfect teeth and modern-looking frameless glasses. He doesn't want to talk, but his heavily accented English is flawless.

"No four-wheel drive?"

"My four-wheeler is dead. Broken axle."

"I paid for four-wheel drive."

He looks at me as if he'd really rather kill me than either talk or drive, then shrugs contemptuously, as if I'm just wasting my breath because I know, and he knows I know, that there's nothing to be done about it.

His name is—or isn't—Mack.

"Mack, yes. Do I drive you to Ararat or not?"

"You can do that? Tonight?"

"Ararat is a big mountain. I can drive you to the base at Dogubayazit, maybe."

"Why Dogubayazit only *maybe*?"

He looks away, as if embarrassed by something, then scans the arrivals hall. "Come outside."

He walks us over to his busted-up Toyota minivan. It's sitting alone under the yellow glare of a sodium light. Most of the bottom third has been blasted down to bare metal by rocks and gravel; the rest of it is caked thickly with dust. Also, the windshield has a long, diagonal crack that runs right across the driver's field of view. Also, one wiper, one headlight, and both fenders are missing.

Morag walks around it, inspects it with a skeptical eye. "You can tell this was dark blue, once," she says, pointing at a small section of the roof.

Mack ignores her and talks directly to me. "Strange things are happening there. We have heard rumors."

"Rumors about what?"

He peers closely at me, seems to want to ask a question, doesn't. "The Seraphim. People say they are doing something—I don't know."

Morag again: "Can this piece of tinfoil even get us there?"

He looks at her then as if seeing her for the first time, and gives the driver's door a vicious kick, as if to prove that the whole machine is invincible. Surprisingly, nothing comes off except dust.

"My Toyota never goes wrong," he says. "Not like your stupid American Land Rovers."

"Land Rover is a *British* brand owned by an *Indian* corporation," Morag drawls without looking at him.

He ignores this completely, or pretends to. "OK, Ararat. Four hours in daylight. Middle of the night, maybe five or six."

I resist the temptation to check my watch yet again.

"Let's do it."

△

Can't complain about Mack being slow, anyway: he drives like a suicide bomber. In the town of Van itself, he simply ignores the few red lights. Once we leave the city for the vast inky blackness of the East Anatolian countryside, he's way too fast on bends, drives with just two fingers on the wheel, always prefers the horn to the brake. Luckily there's not much traffic—when overtaking a slow truck on a blind curve, his safety technique is a muttered prayer.

I'm up front, and as we track north beyond the tip of Lake Van, I try repeatedly to draw him into conversation. Hoping to find out more about *rumors*; hoping also to understand why his English is so good and what his humorless, silent, disapproving manner is all about. Is he just a grinch? A Turk who disapproves of the rich tourists he has to serve? Or a Muslim who disapproves of American infidels? He won't say anything. When we get a six-inch nail in a tire, only an hour into the trip, and he has to put on the spare by flashlight, the answer comes to me.

"Mack?" I say, as we hit the road again, with several hours to go and no second spare.

No answer.

"Mack?"

I can tell he's heard.

"Mack, you're not Turkish, are you?"

In the glow from the dash, I can see his face crinkle as if he's bitten a lemon. But he still doesn't say anything.

"You're Armenian."

He doesn't smile, but at least the look he gives me is neutral, even surprised. "Armenian, yes." He pulls a small wooden cross out from under his shirt. "Armenian Christian."

"And you don't like us, because you think we're Seraphim, going to this, this—to whatever's happening at Ararat?"

He doesn't exactly answer the question. "The Seraphim should stay away. But they are powerful now and there's nothing we can do. Ararat has been a sacred place to Armenians for thousands of years. Since before Christianity, even."

"Home of the gods, yes? Like Olympus for the Greeks."

Mention of the Greeks produces another lemon face—then finally, as if it has been waiting for permission to come out, a big smile and even a chuckle. "I am Armenian, so I hate the Turks. I also hate the Greeks, the Iranians, the Russians, and the Kurds. If I have time, maybe at the weekend, I remember to hate the Israelis and the Americans too. But right now it's difficult to keep up, because I'm busy hating the Seraphim even more. You see, my wife and daughter both converted to the Seraphim. And then they vanished."

He pauses, fingers the cross again. "I am an Armenian, and therefore I hate everybody. I am also a Christian, and therefore I love everybody. Life is complicated."

"But Mack, we're not Seraphim. We're going to Ararat to find my father. And my best friend."

"They are Seraphim?"

"Sort of the opposite. We think the Seraphim kidnapped them. My father had information they wanted. Or they thought he did."

Now Mack wants to know everything. I start by telling him about Dad. When I've paused to let him digest the uncomfortable fact that my father is the notorious William Calder, I ask him for his real name. No particular reason; it just seems the right thing to do.

He mumbles it through his beard. At first I don't get it.

"Tarnel. Tenyal?"

He slows way down: "Tah-ni-yel."

"Ta-ni-yel? That's *my* name."

He looks at me as if I've just claimed to be the pope.

"No, really, it is. Taniel. Only we say *Daniel*."

I find my passport, point to the word. He can't read it in the poor light, peers close, and swerves into the wrong lane, narrowly missing three guys who chose that moment to roar out of the gloom on one small motorcycle.

Morag is in the back. She leans her head in between us, doesn't even mention the near-miss. "This is going to be confusing, Taniel. And you just kind of look like a Mack to me, frankly. I think we should stick to calling you Mack."

He looks over his shoulder at her, amused or offended, it's hard to say. "Where are you from? China? America also, like"—he exaggerates the unfamiliar pronunciation—"*Daniel*?"

"Me? I'm not from China or America. I'm from everywhere."

He considers this for a minute. "Call me Mack."

"I will," she says. "By the way, your English is extremely good, Mack."

"Good for an Armenian peasant who drives tourists around in an old Toyota? Is that what you mean?"

"I'm sorry, I—"

"Relax. You're right. I am an Armenian peasant. Was, anyway, before they civilized me. I grew up in a wooden hut with a grass roof. I hunted boar with my father in the Zangezur Mountains. But I did well in school, got a scholarship, and ended up teaching history at Yerevan State University."

He points to the northeast, in the direction of Armenia. "Let me tell you something about Yerevan. From there, looking south, the skyline is dominated by Ararat. Just like Rainier in your Seattle—I have seen the pictures. Except that Ararat is our national symbol—and it used to be *in* Armenia, before half our country was stolen from us by the Turks."

"So why did you become a driver for hire in Van?"

"I was kicked out of Yerevan when the Seraphim became strong there. I was angry about my wife and daughter; when they left me, I felt they had been brainwashed, and so I led a protest movement against the Seraphim. That is dangerous: I received threats, my apartment was looted, and I was beaten up. It seemed safer to get out of the country. I am an exile—just like Mount Ararat itself is an exile."

"It seems to me," Morag says, "that Taniel and Daniel are on the same side."

He reaches across without taking his eyes off the road, shakes my hand. When he laughs, it sounds like water in a long metal pipe. "The enemy of my enemy. Good enough."

CHAPTER 21
LITTLE ARARAT

Just after dawn, we stop at a tiny village in the middle of nowhere, screech to a halt, and Mack disappears without a word. "God," Morag says, stretching, "I hope he's getting us some breakfast."

He is. After twenty minutes he returns with two plastic grocery bags that seem improbably white and shiny in this remote, gray-brown place. The bags are full of paper-wrapped parcels containing steaming lavash flatbread and a single pottery bowl full of stew. I take them from him and spread the contents on a patch of grass near a stream. The smell is more dinner than breakfast, but all three of us are ravenous. And the stew—lentils, vegetables, meat—is chewy and tough, but tastes wonderful.

"Lamb?" I ask.

"In theory, lamb."

"What about in practice?"

"Times are difficult."

"Meaning?"

Mack stabs a piece of the meat with the tip of a knife, conveys it to his mouth, chews for a minute. His mouth is still full when he answers: "Times are difficult. They had a very old goat."

He takes another bite before gesturing back at the village. "Friends. They let me know what's happening. We can't go to Dogubayazit."

"Why?"

"It may be just talk, just people getting frightened. But they say the Seraphim have taken over the whole area in the past few days. Either Quinn is the world's best liar, or thousands of people are about to ascend into the dimension of the eternal. We could try to blend in, but it may be better to avoid them."

"How long?"

"There's a side road. It means longer in the car, a couple more hours maybe. But it will get us higher up the mountain."

Morag takes the front seat next to Mack after that. At some point, despite everything, I fall asleep. In a fragment of a dream, Dad and Quinn are having an angry argument in a supermarket. I'm trying to pretend I'm not there; Rosko is trying to pull them apart.

When we hit a large bump, I crack my head painfully against the window frame and wake up. Still fifty miles to go, but Ararat already dominates the land in every direction. A conical, five-thousand-meter volcano. It does remind me of Rainier—only it's even more isolated, and looks more elegant, more magnificent, more deadly.

Morag turns round to make sure I've seen it. "Impressive, aye?"

"A home fit for the gods."

Soon we can see two peaks: Ararat itself, and a secondary peak, Little Ararat, a few miles farther southeast. The traffic thickens around Dogubayazit. Groups of people are standing by buses, clutching their little red books. Mack hits the gas and speeds on. Ten miles later, he pulls a sharp left onto a rutted gravel road, and for several more miles, as it gets steeper, we hang on to any available surface as the minivan bucks and groans its way upward. For the last half mile, we're grinding forward in the lowest gear at such a steep angle that I wonder if we'll just flip over backward. When we do stop and pile out, Ararat lies to the north, partly hidden from us behind the lesser peak. There's barely a goat track in front of us.

"I guess you have to leave us here," I say to Mack. "Thank you anyway. It was a pleasure—*Taniel*."

"*Daniel*." He offers a little bow. "What the Seraphim are doing here, I have a bad feeling about it. If I leave you, I have a bad feeling about that as well. And feeling guilty is something that annoys me."

Reaching into the back, under the rear seats, he pulls out an old woolen blanket. Underneath there's a small backpack, a couple of water bottles, and a large hunting rifle. He points the rifle up the goat path.

"Someone has to fight these people. Follow me."

⚠

For three or four miles we do just that, silently picking our way across stony fields, through gullies and deeper ravines, past stubby little birch trees. The day is hazy. The great mountain, with its cap of snow, appears and disappears among the nearer ridges of Little Ararat. The air smells of juniper bushes and damp sheep.

Nearing the saddle between the two mountains, we find our-selves in a narrow valley filled with fog. Mack holds up a hand to stop us. There's a sound like wind passing through autumn leaves. And the Seraphim emerge out of the fog as if congealing from it, like a platoon of ghost soldiers.

Thirty of them, in single file, each with the thin white scarf—a group of eighteen, followed by a group of twelve. Each one is chant-ing softly, each one carrying the little red book. The chant has a simple musicality to it, with the stress on the second syllable in each set, a deliberate breath between each group of four lines.

Or-DA-na
Mi-CHE-fa
Kul-DE-nu
Qu-QA-lan
Rem-XU-xi
Kol-BA-kol
Ip-DA-hin
Ul-GE-mun

"Mysteries?" Mack asks.

"No," Morag says. "Not yet, anyway." She steps right up to one of them—an older woman in a long brown skirt, heavy pleated jacket, and head scarf.

"Excuse me. Where are you going?"

The woman smiles pleasantly and replies in what I guess is Turkish, but then a man behind her, also dressed as if he's local, addresses Morag in English.

"We are going home," he says. "To the Architects." He talks normally, casually—like someone who might say, *We're on our way to the game.* And another man hands Morag his book. "Here, take it. Perhaps you will follow us. When you are ready."

"Thank you," Morag says, accepting the book. And to Mack: "No. Not Mysteries. Quinn would say these people are still on their way to the light. Just try not to listen to the chanting, or you'll end up following them."

I understand what she means. There's something overwhelmingly *comforting* about the sound, something elemental, magnetic.

"Shouldn't we stop them?" Mack says, but Morag shakes her head. It's odd to see how easily she asserts her authority. "We're here to find Daniel's dad, and our friend Rosko," she says. "Above all, we're here to work out what's happening and see if we can stop it. No purpose getting into a fight down here."

By the time Mack puts his head to one side, then straightens it again—an eloquent gesture of grudging assent—the last figures in the column are already dissolving into the fog. They leave behind only the warm inviting rustle of their voices. I don't want to stop them; I want to follow them. Morag seems to sense it and grabs me by the elbow. "D, don't listen. You're tuned to this. Vulnerable to it. Just like Iona was. *Don't listen.*"

△

Several hours later we're at least two thousand feet higher up on Little Ararat. We come to an abandoned monastery, just a couple of stone walls. "Big earthquake," Mack says laconically, pointing at a pile of rubble. "In 1840. A couple of villages on the north slope just disappeared."

"Did Ararat erupt then?" I ask him.

"Ararat is about as extinct as you can get."

"Don't tell me—there's evidence it was a major population center until an eruption during the Bronze Age."

"Yes—how did you know?"

"Lucky guess."

Five-thousand-year-old bodies, entombed in the ash beneath our feet: I wonder what they could tell us. I'm also hungry, thirsty, sore—and Morag's in worse shape than me. We slump down amid the broken stones, finish the water, contemplate the misery of having no food.

There's a rotted, lethal-looking stone stairway up the side of one wall. Mack trots up it like a mountain goat; on a precarious fragment of turret, he produces a pair of binoculars from his bag.

"Daniel. Morag." He pronounces it *Morek*, but at least he's pronouncing it. "Look: you can see them now."

We peel ourselves off the ground and claw our way up to his perch. Stupid for all three of us to die because a bit of old masonry collapsed. But the structure is three feet thick. Could probably support a bus.

The main peak is a lonely giant with a cape of ice, six or seven miles away. Mack's binoculars bring great lines of ants on its upper slopes into view: people, hundreds of them, converging from almost every direction. But Morag takes the binoculars from me, pans them over the whole landscape, and points to something up to our left. "Look."

Hard to know how we missed what's visible even with the naked eye. Not much further up Little Ararat itself, there's a leveled area the size of a soccer pitch. The bulldozers that made it are still there. It looks like a small military encampment, with tents, a helicopter. At one edge there's a low concrete building, obviously new, like a bunker.

"Some kind of headquarters?" Mack says. "See how it's positioned behind that ridge, like it's protected from view? Let's take a look."

"We don't have time," Morag protests. "How are we ever going to get to the main peak before moonrise?"

"We're probably already too late for that," I point out. "Anyway, Dad and Rosko might be up here."

We hurry up the loose, dusty scree in single file. It's so steep now that we have to lean forward, dig our toes in, constantly use our hands. But Mack has good hunter's instincts. He takes us in a curve that brings us up behind a big yellow backhoe, right next to the back of the building, and we're not observed. In fact it looks as if the place is deserted, until we see a man at the front, sitting casually on an upturned crate with his back to us. He's smoking a cigarette, but there's a gun across his lap.

The building is smaller than it looked. When I scoot along the back wall, under a row of high windows, I have no trouble seeing in, and there are just three rooms in a row. The first is a sort of mess hall, with long tables and an open kitchen running down one side. The second is a bathroom. But when I heave myself up and look in the third window, what I see is so improbable that it's hard to take in.

A bare concrete cell, maybe twelve by twelve. There's a single door on the other side, and a small window through which I can just see the head of the man seated outside. Inside, the only furniture is two metal chairs, back-to-back. Chained to the chairs with their arms behind them—chained to each other in fact, and held by a single big padlock—are two prisoners in stained clothes.

The one on the left, wearing a bloodstained Seraphim scarf, is Julius Quinn—which makes no sense. The other one I have trouble even identifying at first, partly because I'm looking for Dad and partly because his face is a purple mass of bruises.

Rosko.

Yes, Rosko.

Things happen fast after that.

CHAPTER 22
HOME OF THE GODS

The guard has heard something. I see him look up and move away to my left. No time to warn Mack and Morag—a few seconds later, he comes around the end of the building, sees them, and raises his weapon with a shout. Thank goodness I'm on a grit-free concrete walkway: as they raise their arms, Mack still holding his rifle in one hand, I'm able to take six long, silent strides that put me right behind him. Several methods of disarming him run through my mind, all of them useless, because I can't risk him getting off a shot. As I hesitate, and he screams at Mack to drop the rifle, Morag's eyes dart toward me. He senses I'm there, steps slightly forward as he turns. I jump, have to overreach, the angle's not right. His gun is already aimed at me, I'm already tensing for the explosion in my chest, when the butt of Mack's rifle slashes down across his temple.

He goes limp, drops the gun with what sounds like a groan of disappointment, and sinks to the ground.

Édouard Colbert.

I'm so shocked that I stand over him motionless. It's Morag who collects the gun, Mack who snatches some discarded electrical cord from a pile of builder's rubble and expertly ties Édouard to the backhoe, pulling his arms up hard behind him.

At last I find my voice. "Why the hell do you have Quinn in there, Édouard? You and Sophie taken over the Seraphim or something? And where's my father?"

Quinn?—Morag mouths the word and throws a questioning glance at me. Édouard looks at her with a sort of leering interest for a moment, then at me with undisguised contempt. "Your father is where he is needed, on Ararat. Those two are here"—he gestures toward the cell—"because they will be needed later."

"I don't understand."

"Of course you don't. Dumb little rich boy."

"Give me the keys to the cell."

He spits and looks away. In response, to my astonishment, Morag walks over, crouches between his outstretched feet, and places the muzzle of his own gun directly against his crotch. In an icy voice I have never heard before, she says:

"We're not exactly flush for time here, soldier-boy. Give Daniel what he wants. Now. Or I'm going to shoot your two best friends."

Sounds like a bluff to me. Édouard too: "You don't even know how to fire it," he says in a defiant tone—but the words aren't even fully out of his mouth when the gun goes off. He gasps, like a man in the first moment of terrible pain, and looks down in horror. But the only sign of injury is the dark spreading stain of his own urine. It takes him, and me, a second to process the fact that Morag has deliberately put a bullet into the ground half an inch from his body.

"I spent a year in Iraq, Édouard. Amazing what skills a girl can pick up. I'll give you another three seconds. One—"

He doesn't need three seconds. "Keys," he breathes. "Top left pocket."

I scoop them out and run to unlock the cell door. Mack's right behind me. Morag lingers long enough to point the gun back at Édouard. Stress brings out her accent again—so much so, this time, that apart from the content she sounds exactly like her mother: "Steh right therr. And if ye so much as blink withoot permussion, Cohlbehrt, I swear to God I'll blow yer fockin' heid off."

As soon as I swing the door open her whole attitude changes. She drops the gun, rushes to Rosko's side, and starts examining his mangled face.

"Roh-skoh? Wha' the fock did they do to you?"

"Nice to see you too, Morag."

"Noo noo, it's great." *Greet.* "It's amazing. It's—but—how—"

"Those two Italian guys. Seraphim who turned out not to be Seraphim—just like the Colberts. The one with the ponytail tried to beat some information out of me."

"Like, where's the *Geographika*? What did you tell him?"

"I told him the truth. I said, 'Your breath smells like rotting meat mixed with gasoline.'"

"He could have killed you."

As if from all around us, Quinn's rich voice fills the room. "Rosko is a Babbler, like me. He was probably safe. Whoever these people are, I get the sense that they need Babblers."

Rosko smiles. "Meet my famous cellmate, Julius Quinn. We've had a lot to talk about."

"A pleasure to meet you at last," Quinn says. "Though the circumstances are less than ideal. I have planned today for a long time, but my arrangements have been"—he looks down at the chains—"interfered with. We have about twenty minutes to prevent a catastrophe."

"Could one of you two explain what the hell is going on? And start by telling me whether my father is dead or alive?"

Rosko drops his gaze, as if embarrassed. For a moment I think the worst—and then I discover that if possible it's worse than the worst.

"Daniel," Quinn says, "I'm going to make an educated guess, based on what your friend has told me. You think that I—or the Seraphim—kidnapped your father, killed Derek Partridge, and have been stealing Phaistos Disks. I assure you, I do want to see those Disks, because in a sense that you still do not appreciate, they are quite literally the word of the gods—of the Architects, as they in fact call themselves. But you have been chasing the wrong villain. I am the leader of a spiritual movement—a religion, if you must. I don't like the term, because I am leading people toward the truth, toward their actual destiny, whereas all the other religions in history have the terrible disadvantage of being wrong about everything. Be that as it may, I am not in the business of murdering elderly professors. As for your father—"

For a moment even he seems lost for words. "I do not know who these people are, or what exactly it is they want. But they are powerful, and well-organized, and they infiltrated our organization months ago. Unfortunately, they have no idea what they are dealing with. They're on Ararat right now, interfering with the Anabasis, and your father is one of them."

"That's ridiculous. He was *kidnapped*."

He holds my gaze for a moment. "Was he, Daniel? Was he really? And what is your evidence for that?"

While Morag and I stare at each other open-mouthed, Quinn continues. "I understand from Mr. Eisler here that he left Seattle in a great hurry, having received a message from Derek Partridge, and then disappeared. Right after that, you found evidence that Partridge had been killed. At about the same time, the Phaistos Disks were stolen from the Heraklion museum, a place with which—yes, he told me—you and your father have a previous criminal connection. And right now he is alive and well on Ararat, with others, no doubt."

"But why would he—Why would anyone—?"

"It sounds as if you have tried commendably hard to make sense of what's going on. Lists of Mysteries, maps, spreadsheets. Good. You inherited from your mother one great intellectual advantage over your father, which is not assuming too readily that you can understand everything by holding up the right scanner."

"What I overheard," Rosko says, "it sounds like they're planning to, I don't know, measure the Anabasis or something. You know, get the Architects on infrared, figure out what's really going on."

"They don't believe any of what I have said," Quinn continues, "because it is too far outside their current understanding of the world. But, unlike most people, they have grasped that something involving great power is going on, and I suspect that appeals to them. They are children in a dry forest with a box of matches. When the Architects help a trapped consciousness make the transition from the physical, you see, there is an immense transfer—"

"The explosions."

"*Explosions*, yes. For want of a better word, since no scientist on earth has come even close to making sense of them."

Mack, who has been standing at the doorway, interrupts. "I'm sure this is fascinating. But if the ceremony is due to begin at moonrise—"

"Your friend is right," Quinn says. "Ten thousand people have gathered here to participate in a delicate, difficult ritual. They knew the risks—and the rewards. But they also understood that I would be leading them in the preparation, guiding their minds with the Architects' language. Any interference with that—" He shakes his head. "It *must* be stopped now."

"So," Rosko says, shaking the chain behind him, "maybe get us out of the heavy jewelry?"

He heaves his chair up with an effort and scoots it round so that we can see where the two sets of chains are padlocked together. I hesitate, then look at Édouard's keys for one that might fit. While

I'm doing that, Mack seems to come to a decision. He strides across from the doorway.

"You wanted to set up a vast Anabasis," he says flatly, to Quinn. "Ten thousand people going to their immortal reward. And you all knew that some would appear to die, but they would be the successes, and others would fail—they would become Mysteries."

"We prefer to call them Partials," Quinn says. "We don't know exactly what happens to them. But yes. This is what we have been planning. Success depends on exactly the right sequences, exactly the right words, and I am still feeling my way toward that. Everyone up there knows this, but they trusted me to help them ascend. And any interference in the language of the ritual will guarantee its failure. I tried to explain this. Of course, they don't believe me."

"My wife and daughter went to the Seraphim," Mack says. "Or were taken by them. Even if I believed what you say—even if I believed they had been shown the *stairway*, and were now *Architects*—I would still want to kill you."

He raises his rifle, aims it directly at Quinn's chest.

"And if you don't help us stop this, I will."

Without moving his eyes from Quinn's, he shifts the barrel sideways, in an almost casual gesture, and blows the padlock to pieces.

△

The helicopter is a squat old Soviet-era military transport. The paneling is dented, a logo on the side has been made illegible in a hurry with gray spray paint, and the tires I wouldn't trust on a wheelbarrow. It's a big beast—I could park Mom's Westland Wasp, rotors folded, in the cargo bay.

"Édouard Colbert came back from the main peak in this thing a few hours ago," Rosko says. "Can you fly it?"

Briefly, I allow myself to wonder if I'll even be able to identify the essential controls. But if I don't fly it, then what?

"Sure. No problem."

Simple to start, anyway, but a complicated, unfamiliar layout. The *thok thok thok* of the big rotors feels as if it will shake the machine to pieces. While I try to orient myself, Mack bags the co-pilot's seat and grins, pointing and flipping switches.

"Armenian! It's Armenian!"

I don't know what he's talking about. I'm too busy struggling with the fact that half the controls have labels in a language—a script, in fact—that I've never even seen.

"Armenian!" he says again, bashing me in the shoulder. At last I get it. "That's—that writing is really—?"

"This is an Armenian Air Force machine," Mack says, slapping the control panel as if this is the best joke in the world. "At last, my country's military doing something useful!"

Not a textbook takeoff, but my passengers don't seem to notice, and at first the power of the thing surprises me. As we rise to a hundred feet and start moving away across the roof of the cell building, I catch sight of Édouard Colbert, still tied to the backhoe, straining to one side to protect his face from the gray storm of ash and rock dust that's being kicked up by the rotor wash. Then he melts into the haze, we clear the ridge, and the great peak of Ararat rises before us like a giant.

"What the hell am I looking for?" I shout to Quinn, who's sitting behind me.

"Head directly for the peak, aim just below the snow line, then veer west around the slope. There's a glacier on the north side. We built a landing pad near there."

"What's going to happen?"

"Moonrise is a psychological trigger, that's all. This is supposed to be the largest single Anabasis in, well, we don't know how long. Probably centuries. Anabasis is detachment of the mind from its physical basis—exactly what all those cognitive scientists, who think they understand consciousness, say is impossible. We can achieve it only by hitting exactly the right note, so to speak, and we don't yet fully understand why that sometimes happens and sometimes does not. There's a powerful PA system covering the whole top of the mountain. I was supposed to direct the event, to maximize the chances of success."

"And without that?"

"Anabasis releases vast amounts of energy. There's no scientific accounting for what that energy is, but it's why the Mysteries are associated with explosions—and it's why these people your father is with, whoever they are, have become so interested. They think they can harness it, poor fools."

Rosko interrupts him: "The energy is proportionate to the number of people, yes?"

"No," Quinn says. "It's not proportional. It's exponential."

I'm about to admit I can't even remember what *exponential* means, when I glance back and catch sight of Morag. Her eyes have gone wide. She looks like she's just seen an oncoming train.

"M, what is it?"

"Say the power released during one person's Anabasis is the energy equivalent of a small grenade. I'm totally guessing here. A hundred grams of high explosive, maybe?"

Mack nods, as if to say, *That's reasonable.*

"If it's exponential, with ten people gathered together, you don't get ten times the power—you get a hundred times."

"Enough energy to destroy a building," Rosko says. "Like in Rome."

"Aye. And with the Anabasis of fifty people, it would be a factor of twenty-five hundred—you're going to hear it miles away."

I'm starting to catch on. "What if you have a thousand people? Or ten thousand?"

She speaks almost too softly to hear. "Ten thousand squared is a hundred million. We're in atomic weapon territory."

Quinn is nodding. "A successful Anabasis on a large scale means a massive release of energy. But the people at the center, the people undergoing Anabasis, they are protected. All the destructive force is released outward from where they are."

I glance at Morag and catch her eye. We're both thinking of the same image: Mom on the Torre Sur, and that strange pressure wave like a bubble around her.

"So," Rosko says, "if everyone succeeds—if everyone ascends or whatever—the explosion doesn't matter."

"Anabasis is what the traditional religions say will happen to our so-called 'souls,'" Quinn says. "But there is no soul. Only the mind, and it can survive death only in particular circumstances. Any interference will cause most of these aspirants to fail, and become Mysteries. Or perhaps half will succeed, and everyone else will be killed in the explosion."

△

I've just managed to take on board that I'm flying us into a potential nuclear test zone when the helicopter drops, recovers all on its own, drops again. For a second I think we've run out of fuel, but it's just that we've climbed to over twelve thousand feet—too close to this death trap's operational ceiling. My whole body is trembling, my palms slick with sweat. "It's OK," I tell everyone, trying to sound confident and flipping some irrelevant landing light switches. It's not OK. I feel like I'm pushing a loaded supermarket cart, with one funky wheel, across an ice rink in a hurricane. In good news, or bad, I'll be landing it in a few minutes.

As we begin to circle the peak, we're close enough now to see that the fundamental pattern has already formed. On the top three or four thousand feet, inside the snow line, a great Phaistos Disk, made entirely from people, circles the ice-capped top of the mountain. You can even see the ring of twelve "words" around the bottom, and the spiral of eighteen circling upward to the summit.

"How do they know what to spell out?" Rosko says. "They can't know what the right combination is supposed to be."

"They don't," Morag says. "What they're doing is guesswork."

Quinn speaks up, his voice so much richer and more persuasive, so much more arresting than anyone else's: "What they are doing is not guesswork," he says. "It is faith."

I'm not sure whether his tone is meant to be intimidating, or just authoritative, but it works for me—I feel physically drawn to him as he says it, can feel why people follow him, as if his confidence has the power to make things true. But Morag's not intimidated, not impressed. I see in my little pilot's mirror the withering look she throws at him.

"Faith is just the problem, isn't it? You've been taken in by the Architects, Quinn. Lied to. Just like the Babbler-priests at Strongyle were. And then the Babbler-priests in Mesopotamia, and the Yucatán, the Indus Valley, ancient Elam, Rapa Nui. They had buckets of faith, and what did it give them? Just a heightened capacity not to ask questions until it was too late. Rosko, did you tell him about the Akkadian Version?"

"Wasn't exactly top of the priority list the last couple of days, Morag."

"None of this matters now," Quinn says decisively. "For today, whatever you believe and I believe, we are on the same side. This has to stop. If we can disconnect all the amplification in time, then perhaps—"

△

A sudden turbulence has me wrestling frantically with the cyclic— the helicopter's equivalent of a steering wheel. We slew sideways and fall more than two thousand feet. The lower altitude is probably good, but what saves us from zero altitude is Mack's swift, unexpected reaction in adjusting the antitorque pedals. I shoot a questioning look at him and he grins again, obviously both fearless and pleased with himself:

"I flew shotgun in these when I was in the Army. Kept my eyes open, that's all. But I could get the hang of this."

More than five thousand feet of mountain towers above us now, and nearly all the Seraphim are there. Rosko shades his eyes, squinting out at the vast crowd. "We're never going to pick out Bill in all this."

But dyslexia comes to my aid again. Can't do letters, can do patterns. I knew, as soon as I saw the mass of people, that all I had to do was get within range and then not try too hard: like looking at an acre of grass, and just *seeing* the four-leaf clovers pop out at you. Can't even say what exactly catches my eye, but—

"There they are. Just upslope to the right from the helicopter pad."

"Aye," Morag says. "And someone's already taken your parking space."

She's right. There's a big shiny new Sikorsky on the pad, glinting expensively.

"Do you have room to put down behind it?"

I'm about to need a thousand percent of my available skill, so I don't reply. I come in from above, slow us to a crawl, hover, rotate left a little. Double-check the altitude. Triple-check the angles. Yes, there is room for both machines. Just.

And I get so close to the right spot, I really do.

So close.

△

We're sinking gently from twenty feet above the pad when a gust drifts us backward, off target. I correct it, kind of: the machine moves back across the pad in the right direction, but at the same time yaws left. Partially correcting that makes the nose pitch down. Worrying that I'll clip the Sikorsky, I fix the pitch, only at the expense of making the yaw worse.

Then we're forced backward again, we're sinking again, and there seems to be nothing I can do this time. When the tip of a rotor hits the edge of the pad itself, the whole airframe twitches, like an animal that's touched a live fence.

There's a pause. Just long enough for me to think maybe everything's OK. Then the cyclic comes alive and kicks my hand away.

No control.

△

When you dump a large helicopter on a steep mountainside, there's a standard, simple procedure: everyone dies. In our case, the engine stalls and one rotor blade sheers off with a sound like a cat being strangled. Then the landing gear catches in the steel underside of the platform. Mack and I are wearing three-point seat belts, but when we go over sideways, everyone in the back is hurled against the left side of the cabin.

We hang motionless over the long, icy drop. For a few heartbeats we all hold our breaths, waiting for the fall. When it doesn't happen, Mack is amazing:

"One at a time," he says, already out of his belt and scrambling for the right-side (now the upper) door. "Morag first. Move, now." He levers the door open, calls each name in turn, takes each person by the arm, hauls them out. One by one we climb up over the lip and clamber out to safety. But he calls Quinn's name last, and Quinn hasn't moved. He's lying oddly twisted against the left-side door, a pool of blood on the glass next to his head.

"Hang on," Mack says. He's already moving to climb back in when Quinn's voice comes up from below, ragged and weak now but still commanding: "No. You can't get me out—my neck is broken. I must speak to Morag."

He means he wants her to listen, but she bends down, grabs the sill, and before I can stop her she's swung herself down beside him. She kneels, puts a hand on his forehead, talks to him. I can see by the way his eyes strain to look at her that he can't move even an inch, but his lips are moving rapidly. Then there's a noise exactly like someone popping the tab on a giant soda can—a loud crunch followed by a kind of scraping note that goes up in pitch at the end—and the helicopter settles a foot lower.

"The undercarriage is separating," Rosko yells. "Morag, get out now!"

Quinn's blue eyes go perfectly still. In one movement, she brushes her fingers across his face to close them, leaps up onto the sideways backrest of the pilot's seat, and jumps, a bloody arm outstretched. In the hole formed by the right-side doorway, I get a one-handed grip on her, then Rosko manages to grab her other hand just as a single loud pop announces that the metal strut holding the undercarriage in place has failed.

The helicopter falls away from her body like a discarded prom dress—except that there's no floor for it to fall to. It plunges, hits the snow, begins to roll over and over. As I haul her to safety, we watch it reach a band of rock, where it spins hard, shreds itself prettily like something made from tissue paper, and drops out of sight.

△

The shock of the moment has immobilized us—it's a few seconds before we become fully aware again of where we are. I'm still gripping Morag in a bear hug when Mack looks up, leans his head to one side like a swimmer with water in his ear. Then I notice it too: a noise that reminds me at once of the Seraphim rally in the park.

"Listen," he says. "They're broadcasting his voice."

Yes, that's what it is: Quinn. A recording of one of his speeches, sermons, whatever you want to call them. I can hear fragments only, but it's as if he's speaking in the language out of which the chants are made:

Ok-DE-chol-chol. Chol-BAN-qi-jat. Ul-fet, ul-fet. Ul-ROX-vo, ix-ep, ep-WO-dze.

"M, what did Quinn say to you just now?"

She struggles out of my arms and looks up the slope toward the crowds. "I didn't even understand most of it. His last words were, 'You will have to give them back their own voices.'"

I grab her by the shoulders, try to give her back her own hardest, most penetrating stare. "I don't know what he meant, but we're out of time for giving them anything. We need to find out why the hell Dad is here, and get him out—and then get you out. If Quinn is right— if your Shul-hura is right—we need to know what happened to the Disks and have you working on them. Otherwise we're finished."

She shakes her head. "There are ten thousand people on this mountain. I have to try to save them."

"You can't. Quinn's talking about the Phaistos language—you've not cracked it, and there are seven billion other people who need you to stay alive until you do."

"I have an idea. And fortune favors the brave, doesn't it?"

"No," Mack says. "In my experience, fortune only favors the fortunate."

Morag looks at me and Rosko. "Ten thousand people, who have probably spent months training to speak only the chants from *Anabasis*."

"Returning to the language of the gods," Rosko says. "Returning to the time before Babel."

"Aye. That's what Quinn taught them to believe."

"Quinn's gone," I insist. "And you don't have the Phaistos language."

"There's another possibility, though. I'll need you to help me get to the PA system. Come on."

And she starts sprinting upslope across the snow.

△

I'm fast, but her athleticism always takes me by surprise: by the time I catch up with her, she's already reached a point just below a kind of speaker's platform, with a podium, an electrical generator, microphones. Sophie is there, barring the way, and with her is Dad. They're both dressed in down parkas like scientists on a field trip—which is, I guess, what they are. Off to one side, as if spaced evenly along the edge of the crowd, I can see other figures who are clearly not Seraphim, clearly observing, not participating. And there's a third figure near us, on the platform, a man who gives off an aura of being in charge even though his back is turned to us as he surveys the great sea of the Seraphim faithful.

"Morag! Daniel!" Dad says. "You should not have come here."

"Where is Édouard?" Sophie says.

I'm looking forward to saying, *Your husband got tied up*, but I don't get the chance, because the man behind them calmly looks at his wristwatch, puts his hands together behind his back, turns around.

Unbelievable.

I'm lost for words.

Morag, on the other hand, is never lost for words. "You?" she says. "*You?* Cognitive science. Computational models of the mind. Consciousness. So interested in both Bill's and Iona's research; so interested in me and all the other Babblers. But I jus' dinna put two and two together. Well *fock*."

He smiles and gives her a formal little bow, polite as always. Even here, on a snowfield on the summit of a volcano, David Maynard Jones is wearing an expensive wool coat and a silk tie.

CHAPTER 23
IN THE ARMY OF THE TEN THOUSAND

"Morag. An honor, as always. And delighted that your idiot brother didn't kill you just now. I've been trying to catch up with you for some time."

I take a step forward. "I think the word you're looking for is *kidnap*."

He raises one eyebrow about a millimeter—like he has no idea what I'm talking about, or anyway the distinction's not important—then gestures to the crowd farther up the slope and continues to address Morag, as if I've not spoken. "Let's cut to the chase, shall we? Julius Quinn has managed to create a global wave of religious hysteria. Quite aside from all the people who have died, and will die, in the resulting sectarian conflicts, he has helped turn hundreds of people around the world into Mysteries, and those numbers are accelerating rapidly. Because sometimes Anabasis works, and sometimes it does not. For a while, a lot of us in the science community buried our heads in the sand, pretty much pretended it wasn't happening.

Didn't we, Bill? All that blather about the *Architects*—ha! It played so well to the gullible that we became gullible in our own way: we just dismissed the whole thing."

"Until Patagonia," Sophie breathes, in her silky Paris accent.

"Yes. I'd been keeping tabs on Iona Maclean for years. A dangerously intelligent woman, for a non-Babbler. She and I had what you might call a *philosophical* disagreement, a long way back, after I told her a little too much about my own research. I wanted to be sure she didn't dig too deep. That's why the Colberts were in Patagonia—just part of a procedure to find out what she knew, what she suspected. Her dying that way was—well, I don't want to appear heartless, but from the point of view of getting at the truth, it was a piece of luck."

He flashes a look of insincere apology at me, then can't prevent himself from smiling. I can't really take in what he's said—I'm just reduced to a raw sense that I once mistakenly liked him and now I want to kill him.

Rosko puts a hand on my arm, as if sensing that he might need to restrain me.

"What happened in Patagonia persuaded us to take Quinn's religious mumbo jumbo more seriously. Persuaded us that it might have some direct connection to the work on the nature of the mind that we were already doing. As your father likes to say, myths don't come from nowhere."

He checks his watch again. "And now we are simply gathering more evidence, in this picturesque laboratory the Seraphim have provided."

"It doesn't add up though, does it?" Rosko says. "You're supposed to be a professor. Just a professor—someone who works in a Seattle lab studying how the brain works. But somehow you're up a mountain in eastern Turkey with a million-dollar helicopter."

Mayo laughs heartily. "It all adds up perfectly, according to Charlie Balakrishnan's accountants. He pays for everything, and for the same reason that he set up the Institute for the Study of the

Origin of Consciousness. He wants answers to a deep question, perhaps the deepest question of all. Why do we humans have this inner world of concepts, of feelings, of hopes and fears that we can express and manipulate through language? Ten million species on the planet, but only we are like this—why? *What is this thing?* Then the Mysteries came along, and turned the question on its head: where is their consciousness *going*? The Seraphim have an answer to that—a new version of the old, old answer: the faithful are taken up into heaven! When the old religions talked about immortality, you could dismiss it, of course—no evidence. But in the case of the Mysteries, obviously *something* was going on. But what? Charlie B is not young, he's afraid of dying, and he will pay any amount to find out."

"He's not going to find out anything," I tell him. "By taking Quinn out of the picture, you've interfered with the Anabasis. All you're going to get is—"

But I don't know the ending to my own sentence. Sophie turns to address me—which is good, because she's turning her back on Morag, who is inching closer to the amplifiers.

"Quinn's fairground performance is not essential in any way," Sophie says. "What's essential is that this is a measurable physical process, and measuring is exactly what we intend to do. We've already made progress. At first, we thought the dead at places like Uyuni and Goat Rocks were the failures, and the Mysteries were the successes. Now we know it's the opposite—whatever's happening, the Mysteries are the ones who are not quite ready. We want to understand the difference, and we have everything covered. Video, audio, infrared, electromagnetism, ultrasonic shock, radiation. We're going to get some serious data today."

"Aye," Morag says, "but you underestimated Quinn's role, and without him here, you won't get what you want. If the Architects show up at all, everyone up here will either be turned into a Mystery or be killed. Doesn't that bother you at all? Didn't think so." Turning to Dad, she says: "Have you actually swallowed this crap? How naive are you, Bill Calder?"

Dad has been watching Mayo. Now he turns slowly to face us again, but he doesn't answer Morag's question. I sense that he's betrayed me in some way—betrayed Mom in some way—and I'm so angry that I can barely meet his eye. But something in him forces my attention.

"Remember those first trips to Crete, Daniel? The museum? How badly I wanted to know about the Disks? Plan A was to talk to all the important people, let them know what I wanted. Didn't work. Plan B, with Jimmy's imager, that required a bit of subterfuge, didn't it? A bit of not playing by the rules? And it was successful."

I push up my sleeve to reveal the white scar. "I remember."

"Well, this is Plan C."

I'm tossing this around in my head, wondering what the hell he's on about—Plan C? Subterfuge?—when he winks. Briefly, once, with one eyelid, just the way he taught me on the beach all those years ago. And then he turns back to the Aussie, but he's still addressing me.

"Mayo and I have been working together for a long time. Now that he has all the Disks safely housed at Charlie Balakrishnan's compound in Delhi, we can really begin to get a grip on them. Master the Phaistos code at last. With Morag's help: I have no doubt it will take Morag's help."

"Want my help, do you, Bill? After what this lot's done to me, and Partridge, and Rosko? Well ye can jus' go screw ye'self."

He turns again, winks again. Morag sees it this time, and a shadow of confusion passes over her face like a racing cloud. Then Sophie interrupts.

"Too much talk. We're set up now—anyone who's not ready for heaven, it's time to get out of here."

"Yes indeed," Dad says, but then he takes three paces toward me, sloughs off his down jacket, holds it out.

"I've been a crappy father, Daniel. Wasn't a great husband either, and I'm sorry I ever teased your mother about her spiritual shopping. One thing I never teased her about was her judgment of other people. That's the reason I listened carefully when she talked to me about my old, ha, rival, and said 'Watch him. Don't trust him.' It's the reason I'm here."

He thrusts the coat at me. "You look cold, take this."

"No, I'm fine. But I thought she—"

"*Take the damn coat*," he hisses, strangely insistent. "And get Morag safely off the mountain. I'll deal with those two."

"But—"

He touches a fingertip to his lips, then turns back toward Sophie, his voice changing back to Pompous Scientist on a Mission. "Have you double-checked the audio? That's the most important thing for me. I must have all sixteen channels on line to get a full—"

"Everything's fine," she snaps. "We have three different backup circuits. We're also behind schedule now. Come on."

Dad shrugs meekly. The three of them turn in the direction of the landing pad. A small gust of wind reminds me that I have Dad's parka on, but it's not zipped, so I cross my arms over the chest to keep it around me. My right palm lands over the breast pocket, where there's something hard and rectangular, like a pack of cigarettes. That's when Morag makes a dash for the microphones and starts speaking.

△

"Damn," Mayo says, and he and Sophie turn around as if to stop her. But Rosko and I are barring the way. Mayo's about to speak when Dad, standing directly behind him, says, "Game's over, Mayo." The Aussie turns again, surprise written all over his face, and Dad clouts him in the mouth. Not an expert punch, not even a good one, but

Mayo's wearing ridiculous dress shoes and loses his balance on the steep snow. Dad jumps, hands around his neck as they go down.

Dad has Mayo pinned under him, motionless and gagging, just long enough to turn and catch my eye:

"Get yourselves out of here. And save that jacket. It was hard to get."

Mayo grunts, shifts, manages to slither halfway to freedom and hack sideways with one elbow across the bridge of Dad's nose. Dad gasps in pain and loses hold.

"You stupid man, Calder," Mayo says as he gets to his feet. "I trusted that you understood what's at stake here. What's at stake here is infinite."

He aims a kick, but it misses completely.

"I know what's at stake," Dad says calmly, and launches himself headfirst at the buckle on Mayo's expensive, probably crocodile-skin belt.

They go down again, rolling.

The roll turns into an uncontrolled slide.

Below them, maybe fifty or a hundred feet away, there's a curious shadow line across the snow. Not as obvious as it sometimes is—you'd need a lot of mountain experience to recognize it.

When they get there, still accelerating, there's a little puff as the snowbridge explodes under their combined weight.

And the crevasse opens wide like a leering, blue-lipped mouth.

$$\triangle$$

Morag's alone now at the amplifier panel. Her voice comes streaming around us like the wind, carried everywhere on a thousand watts of high-end amplification. And I think, irrelevantly: That voice, that exact accent, is one of the things I love most in the whole world.

"Listen to the sound of your native language," she says. "That sound is what freed your ancestors from the Architects. Their language is not a gift. It's a curse. A lie. The road to enslavement. Listen to your own language. Listen, listen."

And she repeats herself in language after language:

Ecoutez la musique de votre langue maternelle—

Sentita la musica della vostra lingua madre—

Hören Sie den Klang Ihrer Muttersprache—

Prislushaytes' k zvuku vashego rodnogo yazyka—

"It's not going to work," Rosko yells to me. "Most of these people probably speak Turkish, Kurdish, Azerbaijani. I don't think she has a word of those languages. Neither do I."

"It's also not going to work because you are out of time," Sophie says, backing toward the helicopter as her eyes drift from us to the sky above our heads, as if searching for something.

The clouds are darkening, as if a storm is brewing in the clear blue sky. Then there's a rustling, fizzing sound, like wind coming through a forest. For a moment I think it's something wrong with the amplification, but Morag's voice continues, clear and strong—except that it's being drowned in the rising volume of the new sound:

Ol-CHI-ma

Va-MA-je

Bin-AR-bin

Qa-ROX-ret

The Seraphim on the other side of the peak must have just seen what they were anticipating all these weeks.

The moment Quinn chose for maximum effect:

Moonrise.

Sophie glances at the sky again and a look of panic passes across her face as she turns and runs for the helicopter, with Rosko close behind her. When she reaches it, Mack is standing in the doorway. He looks at the sky too. It's shimmering now, sulfurous and blotchy like an oil slick. Sophie looks up at Mack, glances over her shoulder at Rosko, stumbles away across the slope.

△

By the time I get back to Morag, the whole mountain has begun to shake. Above us, little pools of darkness in the air are beginning to thicken, come into focus. But she's still talking steadily into the microphone:

Istamti biranini lughatil thad—

"Not even Arabic, Morag," Rosko says.

I grab her arm. "The Architects. They've come."

She looks up. "That's just a word, Daniel. *Architects* is just a word, like *God*. It's just a net we throw out in the hope of catching what we don't understand. Like once we didn't understand lightning, or stars, or dreams."

Never won an argument with Morag; no time to lose one now. I rip out the microphone cable. Then I grab her, kicking and screaming, and start carrying her back to safety.

"Damn you damn you damn you, Daniel Calder. I have to do this, and I can resist them. Put me the fock doon."

I ignore her. Maybe she looks up again and sees how close to the end of things we are, because she stops resisting. When I'm halfway there, Rosko comes scrambling toward us. Behind him, the Sikorsky's rotor begins to turn. I drop Morag in the snow and look down the mountain at the point where Dad and Mayo disappeared.

"Get on board, M."

"What about Bill?"

"Going for him now."

I run, slither, fall. I scrabble back to my feet using my still-damaged fingers like hooks in the snow, then run and slither and run some more. It's much farther than it looks. My lungs are screaming, but as if in a dream, Kit is floating miraculously by my side in her running gear, smiling.

Go Daniel yes you can do this.

The chanting has spread across the whole mountain, louder and louder and unnaturally louder, as if the faithful themselves have been amplified. It's a high, keening, ecstatic sound. As I get to the lip of the crevasse, I remember the scene outside the museum in Crete. I imagine scooping Dad up, the way I couldn't scoop up that woman on the burning sidewalk. So much stronger now! I'm looking around, unsure whether I've come down to the right point, when a massive jolt makes me lose my footing, get up, lose my footing again.

And I'm falling.

△

The crevasse is thirty, forty feet deep—I've seen worse on a dozen glaciers, but I'm not roped this time. The only reason I don't die is that I land with a thud on a narrow ledge ten feet down. No injuries, but the ledge slopes away into the abyss, there are no handholds, and the entire mass of ice is shaking.

"Dad!"

No sign of him. Nothing. I lean my whole weight into the blue wall, claw at it. Inexorably, I begin to slide.

"Dad!"

"Daniel!"

For a moment in my confusion I think it's him, but when I look for the source of the voice, it's Rosko, above me. "Hang on."

"No, Rosko, no!" But it's too late. Spidermensch is climbing into the lip of the crevasse, digging in as he goes. He has an ice ax in each hand.

"These were in the other helicopter. Hoping I could put one through the back of that Australian bastard's head."

"Rosko, get out. You could kill yourself in here."

He's just above me now. "Look who's talking, Mr. Clumsy. Shut up and hold on to me."

Maybe I ought to argue some more. Maybe I ought to say, You're insane. But there's that special look in his eye: *It's OK; trust me; I'm totally comfortable with this.* And there's a natural pecking order here: he's the better climber, the natural, so I obey. I grab his hand, haul up next to him, use his leg as a step to climb out. I'm flat on the surface again, scooting round to give him my hand in turn, when the ground itself makes a noise like an injured animal. The ice beneath me ripples and bucks, just the way it did on the Torre Sur. I steady myself, then fling my right arm down for Rosko. But he's gone.

"Rosko! Rosko! Rosko!"

Nothing.

Just a blue silent rift in the mountain, fading to black.

◬

I'm on all fours, out of breath, out of hope. But now there's a different roar, and the ice begins to split and steam all around me, and I stand and raise my face to the amazing, amazing sky.

My breathing slows, my heart rate slows, all the panic and horror washes away. I feel a wave of joy washing over me too. I reach down and find at my feet a great splinter of ice-crusted rock. It's volcanic, and surprisingly light. I raise it up in offering.

For my Architect has arrived.

He is surely the most beautiful, terrible, and seductive of all. Seductive, because I am honored and happy and thrilled to surrender myself to him. Terrible, because I know that I must obey, that there is no choice but to submit utterly. And beautiful—oh! He is tall, and slender, but he has the casual power of a giant. I can't tell whether he is wearing clothes, because the body looks as if it is still an immature form, in the process of emerging from a chrysalis of light. But the arms, shoulders, and head are there, recognizably human and yet so different, so *other*, because they are the perfection of the human. Not some beautiful *thing*, this, but the ideal of beauty itself. Not a human being, but a designer. A maker. A god.

His eyes envelop me. I feel his delicate, cold, powerful fingers reaching right through the meaningless barrier of my physical body and down, down, down. Into my *self*.

Life passing before your eyes? How poorly our imaginations do justice to that idea! I feel each digital constituent, each atom, each moment of my conscious existence flooding up through me now, like a stream of iridescent butterflies, each one as unique, distinct, unrepeatable as the next. I feel as if I am examining each one of them in the minutest detail, and nothing from my whole life has been lost, but time itself must have bloated and slowed, time must have changed its nature, because though it happens quickly, there are thousands upon thousands of these moments. The trivial. The painful. The sublime.

I'm a small child, being carried by my mother in a winter land-scape by a river, and a great V of geese is flying overhead, their wings creaking in the still air.

I taste a pomegranate for the first time; the sweetness of the pulp lingering under the surprise bitterness of a single bitten seed.

We're at the Nigambodh Ghat on the banks of the Yamuna, in New Delhi, and a woman is hunched down near the small burning pyre of a child, and she looks my way, looks into my eyes, her face a picture of inconsolable grief.

In a sunlit classroom on a Wednesday, Mrs. Rosales is at the board in a blue dress, writing out for us in her loopy old-fashioned writing the word people; *I feel proud that I can spell such a big, grown-up word.*

A red barn is caught in a shaft of sunlight in the middle distance, on a lonely road between wheat fields; in the blue sky above it, flat-bottomed lozenges of cumulus fall into ranks, like fat white tanks moving into battle.

In dense jungle near the Ucayali River, in the western Amazon, Jimmy and I are breaking trail in a storm of biting flies while Morag, also swinging a machete, talks about Darwin's theory of NUT-urull sul-AKE-shunn.

At home in Seattle, Kit gives me her lopsided smile in the street outside our house, then turns without saying anything and walks away down the block under the cherry trees.

These are not memories: no one ever confused the taste of a lemon with the memory of it. What I'm having is *the experiences themselves*, for a second time. I am present again—in no order, and every order, and simultaneously it seems—at every single moment of consciousness that has made up my inner life and world.

It's as if the Architect is saying to me: *This is what you have been, Daniel Calder. What you have been is what I need. All that you have been, I now consume.*

The light intensifies until it cannot brighten more.

Then it brightens more, and still more.

But it's OK. I feel calm, and safe. And the heat is immense but all I feel is enveloping, protective warmth.

Ok-DI-ke
Qom-FU-nu
Bes-YEH-min
Gor-CHAM-xi
Tel-DZU-juk
Mul-SHU-lah
Ol-QO-hut

Kai-FI-mun

The white scar on my forearm is healing, vanishing. As if from far away, I hear-see-feel Morag, screaming for me from the door of the great metal insect whose name I no longer know or need.

She thinks something terrible is happening to me. I can see it in her face. But she's wrong. I want to tell her not to worry.

Because after all, a body is a body, Morag.

After the body, there is no more to smell or taste or touch.

No more to tell.

All language falls away, all concepts, thoughts, emotions, and there is no more to see, even, at the last. Except that everything, everywhere, is light.

And more light.

And more beautiful light.

And amazement and free fall and wonder, and then I, Daniel Calder, am taken up at last from the prison of my body into understanding. Into knowledge.

Immortality is mine.

And I welcome it, at first, because it is what I have been promised and it is perhaps where I will hear my mother's voice again.

But I do not hear her.

Instead, the sound I hear is the distant wasp swarm of a billion billion voices pleading into silence.

For I am ascending now,

disintegrating now,

evaporating

now

now

now

now

now

into the bright bright trickery of heaven

EPILOGUE

SEEING IN THE DARK

Minutes to midnight.

I'm standing alone at the top of a low gravel ridge, on the beautiful high rangeland of eastern Washington. An hour's drive farther east, the Grand Coulee Dam lies hidden like a dog's bone in an inky ditchful of night. North of us, according to the map, the vastness of the Colville Indian Reservation stretches halfway to Canada. A few miles south, the lights of a small wheat-farming town are just visible—a smear of glitter across a thumb's width of the horizon.

On the lower side of the twenty-acre field below me, near the dirt road, a dozen cars and tents are clustered. There's a slight rise at the other side, where a couple of big Dobsonian telescopes stand like wrecked filing cabinets on their simple, blocky stands. They make me think of my mother, who bought one in Scotland once, on a whim. Useless, of course. But there's no cloud here, and no light pollution either. This is one of the best places in the whole northwest for seeing in the dark.

An hour ago, I stood at this same spot with my arms around Kit, and we watched the new moon, thin as a blade, ride a blue velvet cushion down the west. As the blue faded to indigo, the sky began to swarm with its dozens, hundreds, thousands of tiny thermonuclear fireflies. And she turned around, hugged me urgently, and said yes, and I kissed her on the lips for the first time.

Maybe she just needed warmth and reassurance. But I don't want to believe that. I don't believe that: when our breath mingled and our lips touched, I felt as if I'd been hurled from a cliff only to discover I could fly.

"Morag Morag Morag," she said.

△

It's six weeks since Ararat. A thousand people died there, and five thousand more became Mysteries. Some say that all those people would have lived, if only I'd kept out of it. Others—the Seraphim, naturally—say that they would all have ascended to the Architects. Lots of confident opinion. Me, I only have the guilt, combined with the knowledge that, as usual, the loudest voices have the least bloody clue what they're talking about.

At least we had more warning than we expected. The Architects took their time doing whatever it is they do. But the main "explosion," when it came, was so powerful that nobody will ever know for sure how many were taken up and how many were simply swallowed whole, like krill in the maw of a whale, when the southern flank of the summit collapsed. Or how many more were incinerated in the lava flows when the shock waves set off Ararat's first eruption in centuries. Latest estimates of the initial "energy transfer" are in the megaton range. But that number is just a fig leaf—something behind which the physicists and seismologists can hide the embarrassing truth: an explosion with no source and no plausible cause, which can destroy everything around it without touching those within it, is not something anyone understands.

"Amazing how ignorant we were." That's what Bill used to say to his students. Even more amazing how ignorant we are now. But I'll be better prepared, next time. Among other things, Bill's hard drive—Mayo's hard drive, which Bill must have somehow gotten a hold of, and stashed in the parka he gave to Daniel—has thirty perfect images of thirty different Disks: a record of the real Babel, if I can unpick it.

△

Sophie Colbert chose exactly the wrong direction in which to run. I saw her scrambling down a rocky gully below the snowline, and wish I had not seen her as she was engulfed by the first lava flow. Up on the glacier, I saw Daniel standing there, saw the Architect shimmer and re-form above him, like it was having trouble coming into focus. I had assumed Rosko was gone, along with Bill and Mayo. Mack already had the helicopter in the air, veering away fast, when I spotted a figure emerging like a cartoon devil from the surface of the ice itself.

Rosko Eisler. Covered in sheets of his own blood.

I saw what he did then. Saw how he threw Daniel's limp body over one shoulder even as that *thing* was swirling around them, saw his stumbling uphill run, back to the landing pad. Huge chunks of shattered ice were already pouring down onto the pad as the glacier began to disintegrate.

I thought I would have to threaten Mack, but when I pointed to Rosko, he landed again without hesitation. My heroes, both of them.

△

A meteor rakes across the sky to the southwest just as a thin, high, elderly voice carries across to me from near the telescopes.

"Frankly, Julia, my dear, I've seen about as many stars as I can take, after those Roman goons shot me through the shoulder and tried to open up my head with the other end of the gun. Trussed me up like a turkey, drove me to some woods north of Rome, and dumped me in a ditch, d'you know—not at all dignified. They must have thought I was already a goner, but apparently I'm indestructible. Didn't survive an English boarding school for nothing, eh?"

"Do you think we'll survive this?" Julia asks him. "I mean, the sheer numbers, all over the world—"

"Oh yes, we'll survive it. Humanity has survived the Architects before. Someone in the distant past has always been persistent enough, and confident enough, and clever enough, to master their game and then beat them at it. We can do it again. But not unless we get enough sleep. Good night, and thank you for showing me M13— hadn't seen it since I was a boy."

Partridge is using a walking stick, and picks his way cautiously across the broken ground in the direction of a camper van. A door opens and slams. A light comes on inside. After a minute of silence, I hear heavy shuffling footsteps behind me, and two voices.

"Morag?"

"Morag."

The first voice wants to know where I am. The second—flat, distant—is just repeating the word, as if comforted but puzzled by it.

"Over here, Rosko. What's up?"

They come up the ridge slowly. "Time to say good-night," he says. "Let me take his hand. Hey, D, it's me. Morag."

"M—. M—. Morag. Dark."

I've noticed before that he seems to find the dark comforting. He moves close, so that his arm presses against mine. It's as if he can read my moods better that way. He's like an animal—intelligent still, instinctively sharp, but with a mind that's both limited and unreachable. And yet sometimes he'll snap entirely out of it and look at me with his old eyes, even say a sentence or two that sounds completely normal. It's like witnessing fragments from a dream of his former life. Every time it happens, I experience this vast surge of hope—and then his eyes go dull again.

It's easy to see now that every Mystery is a partial case—a person whose mind was taken, but not so completely as to destroy their basic functioning and cause death. Alzheimer's, that's the comparison people keep on making, though it's not the same. Most, especially the adults, are left with nothing but a functioning brain stem: a heartbeat, breath, nothing else. Some recognize a few words, more rarely still a few faces, but even they can't speak or understand or *decide*. Then there are the few like Daniel, normally younger people, who are deeply absent yet not wholly gone. Partridge has a theory about it. He always does.

"I'd better take him down again," Rosko says. "I think the Star Mafia is about to pack up for the night."

I give Daniel a hug, which he returns like a swimmer clinging to wreckage. Rosko pulls him away gently, speaking softly to him; he uses a matter-of-fact tone, without that condescending, lilting child-speak so many other people are falling into. "Hey, Daniel, long day, huh? Let's head down, do our teeth. Don't know about you, but I need some sleep."

Å

Ella and Julia—the Star Mafia—are already breaking down the telescopes, with some help from Kit. I'm not wanted for this delicate ritual, and neither are the Y-chromosomers, who are already busy spitting toothpaste into the bushes. So I stay up on the ridge and enjoy the solitude.

There's a circle of flashlights where the boys are grouped. I can see the pool of bluish light from Rosko's headlamp as it crosses to that corner of the field, see how he wipes Daniel's face with a towel, talks to him, then takes his hand to steady him over the rough, dark ground toward their tent.

Rosko Eisler, who used to be handsome. Now he has a mauled ear, bad scarring all down one side of his face, and two missing fingers that he fed to the crevasse on Ararat—and poor Ella, who doesn't have a chance, thinks he's more handsome than ever.

I look north toward the Pole Star. Putting to one side the commonsense illusion that I'm standing on a flat surface, I tilt my head and make an effort to visualize the whole earth beneath me and the imaginary axle around which it turns. The plane of our orbit appears in my mind's eye too, a translucent silvery circle that arcs out westward into space. For a minute or two, in my solitude and silence, I can feel the planet balanced there: a fat dancer, pivoting on its solitary polar heel as it spins backward, away from the sun, into darkness.

My parents got safely out of Iraq, just hours before it erupted into a full-scale religious war. Thank goodness for that. And Pandora survived. But I miss Iona. I miss Bill too, partly because nobody else seems to miss him. A high standard for me to aspire to. So much knowledge. So much *passion to know*, even if he was wrong about Phaistos and the Architects.

Above all, I miss Daniel—even though I can see him fifty yards away, his slumped shoulders and bowed head silhouetted for a moment against the side of an orange tent.

$$\triangle$$

"Morag? Morag?"

Kit. She has left Ella and Julia to finish up, and I can just make out where she's standing, near the tents. I can hear the fear in her voice. She doesn't want to be out in the dark alone. Not many people do, after everything that has happened. We live now, as our ancestors did for five thousand years, in a world haunted by demons. The sound of her fear produces a rush of tenderness in me. Daniel always tried to protect me, and that was good, I guess, but it allowed me to be selfish, narrowed me, gave me the luxury to be the cold prodigy everyone expected. I feel I have been released from that now. I have never before, not even with him, felt this intense desire that *someone else not hurt*.

Interesting emotion. Must be a name for it.

I shout down to her, trying to inject into my voice all of the warmth, and strength, that I feel. "With you in a minute!"

One last look at the Pole Star. One last look at the patch of cat-black sky where Julia's telescope revealed M13 to us—a fuzzy little star cluster that looks like a small piece of lint. *But it contains a quarter of a million suns*, she said. *So much out there*, she said. Oh yes, Julia. You have no idea.

Time to go. So I tip my head back, look straight up, and speak out loud, enunciating every word slowly and carefully as if addressing the Milky Way itself. Wouldn't want a syllable to be wasted:

"I'm onto you now, you greedy miserable bastards. And I will defeat you."

THANKS

Novels are a pack of lies. The best part of assembling this pack was discovering how many smart nonfiction writers—people actually investigating what's true—committed the foolish error of leaving all their best ideas *just lying around in books*, from where I could easily steal them. Much of what I did steal, I only partially understood; whether I understood it or not, I bent it shamelessly to my own purposes. To all of those writers: my gratitude, my admiration, my apologies.

On a more personal note, thanks to Nick Harris at the Story Foundation in Los Angeles, who is solely responsible for this whole thing ever happening in the first place; Stephen Barbara at Foundry Literary + Media in New York, who is to the common literary agent as champagne is to beer; the whole team at Amazon for their patience, warmth, hard work, high standards, and enthusiasm, but especially editor Courtney Miller and copyeditor Kyra Freestar, who each made many excellent suggestions while saving me from more of my own errors than I care to count; and Kate Egan, my wonderful editor, who among many other skills had a knack for expressing her confidence in this project at just the moments when I had none.

For various other kinds of help, knowledge, or support, I'm also grateful to Tim Ditlow, Olivier Fabris, Aidan Farr, Clarissa Farr, Declan Farr, Paula Gottlieb, Chaouky Kaboul, Fiona Kenshole, Dirk Obbink, Rosalie Wells, several anonymous translators at AOLTI, Andrea Soroko's entire fourth-period tenth-grade Language Arts class, several anonymous Teen Center Advisors at the Seattle Public Library, and the staffs of several different Seattle Public Library branches and of the Suzzallo and Allen Libraries at the University of Washington.

As usual, my greatest debt is to my wife, Kerry Fitz-Gerald. Despite holding down a real job, she spent countless hours on this book, improving it in many ways. She also put up stoically with months (OK: years) of authorial *stercore tauri*, including but not limited to moaning, whining, rationalizing, complaining, procrastinating, not earning any money even when not procrastinating, and the occasional episode of blind roaring panic. I know, love, I really do: no amount of *Thanks* is ever going to be enough.

From the Author:
Some Notes on Fact and Fiction

You probably don't want to read straight through these notes. Just browse the headers and dip into anything that looks interesting. The true nerds among you can find a much fuller version, plus additional notes and a partial list of sources, at my website. For a cautionary note on the sources, or rather, my use of them, see Thanks.

Prologue

Rongorongo and Rapa Nui
Dutch explorer Jacob Roggeveen discovered Paasch-Eyland (Easter Island) on Easter Sunday 1722—hence the name. The supposedly original Polynesian name, Rapa Nui, was probably made up more than a century after this; we don't know what the island was called before European discovery.

The strange and beautiful script found there, Rongorongo, never has been deciphered, or not convincingly, and perhaps never will be.

Old Elamite
Old Elamite is one of several languages associated with the kingdom of Elam, which existed around the northeast end of the Persian Gulf from about 2700 to 540 BCE.

The Bronze Age Collapse
The Bronze Age Collapse was a real event that saw the partial or total destruction of Ugarit, Troy, Tarsus, Knossos, Aleppo, Byblos, Ashkelon, Paphos, Carchemish, Hattusa, and Mycenae, among other cities. Theories include a massive drought (some evidence there); a storm of earthquakes (surprisingly, ditto); a mysterious invasion by so-called Sea Peoples (much-quoted but both vague and doubtful). Also climate change, defeat of charioteers by guerrilla foot soldiers, and "general systems collapse" (which sounds to me a lot like "if we give it a name, it'll sound like a theory"). Different experts are so keen to push the evidence for their favorite hunch that in reading the literature, it's hard to hang onto the essential point: *nobody knows what happened.*

Types of writing
A quick and dirty way to divide up writing systems is this: in *logographic* systems like Chinese, symbols stand for words; in *syllabic* systems, like Egyptian, symbols stand for syllables; in *alphabetic* systems, like English, symbols stand for phonemes or sounds. In reality it's a lot more complicated. Still, it's broadly true that a highly logographic system like Chinese will have thousands of distinct characters, a mainly syllabic system like Egyptian will have a hundred or more, and an alphabet will have anywhere from just over a dozen main symbols (Hawaiian) to fifty or sixty (Khmer, Sanskrit).

Making sense of the Phaistos Disk

Daniel expresses a simplified version of my own puzzlement. It is said, as if it's just obvious, that the Phaistos Disk has thirty-one groups of symbols in a spiral on one side, and thirty groups in a spiral on the other. But it seems to me this is just obviously wrong, in two ways. First: as Daniel says, the shape is really an outer horseshoe with a separate inner spiral. Second: there are two lines that look like a short string of beads (one on each side), and *on one side only* there's an extra "unbeaded" line next to the beaded line. If this third line is a mistake—a slip of the stylus—then you have a pattern that makes much more sense: thirty groups on both sides; each side divided into the twelve-group outer horseshoe and the eighteen-group inner spiral; and each spiral beginning with a single unique L-shaped group. Check it out and see what you think.

Storing data in DNA

Can we store data in DNA? Shortly after writing a draft of this book, I learned that a team at Harvard Medical School is working on how to do just that. It's in the early stages, but DNA could provide astonishing information density—and, unlike that flash drive you just put through the laundry, remain stable for ten thousand years.

Some Yahoo

Bill Calder isn't referring to Jerry Yang's Internet company, but to the disgusting apelike creatures (or disturbingly humanlike apes) in the fourth part of Jonathan Swift's *Gulliver's Travels* (1726). Apparently the company's name really is a direct reference to Gulliver, but you have to wonder whether any of the Sunnyvale geeks had actually read the book. A cursed race of unteachable, stinking, irrational, odious brutes? Really?

Uranium, thorium, and a low-budget ray gun

I've given Bill Calder a fancied-up form of optically stimulated luminescence (or thermoluminescence) dating. Can you really do it through a glass museum case, with a handheld laser and a phone app? No—not yet.

Darwin, germs, and hand-washing

The Swiss medical pioneer Ignaz Semmelweis first suggested in 1847 that doctors' own lack of hygiene might be causing the puerperal fever that was killing so many of their patients; the idea deeply offended the medical profession and was ridiculed. Darwin published *On the Origin of Species*, cracking the deep problem of how things in nature can look "perfectly designed" without having a designer, in 1859. The germ theory of disease was not widely accepted until the work of Louis Pasteur and Robert Koch in the 1870s.

PART I: PATAGONIA

The Torre Sur and "a big fat mile of nothing"

OK, a bit of an exaggeration. The Torre Sur is over a mile and a half tall, but only from sea level, and the longest vertical face on it is maybe half that. The nearest you can get to a mile-long vertical fall, anywhere in the world, is probably on Great Trango Tower in Pakistan. Look it up; if you suffer from vertigo, keep a plastic bag handy.

"Not really an atheist atheist"

Most people think they know what an atheist is, but it's not as simple as it looks.

Socrates (see the later section "Some Dates") was accused of being an atheist in 399 BCE, but what the outraged conservatives of Athens meant was that he was teaching *false or nontraditional beliefs about the gods*, not that he didn't believe the gods existed. Early Christians were described as atheists by the Romans, for the same reason.

Modern atheists like Richard Dawkins usually talk as if they think that we can prove God doesn't exist, as if "I know God doesn't exist" is the meaning of the term. But you can't prove that something doesn't exist unless you can first say what it *is*, and one frustrating thing about religious belief is that even within the same religion, different believers give widely varying and incompatible descriptions of what sort of entity God is. So it's not clear what the atheist has to disprove, or how to do it.

In my view, it's more useful to think of atheism as the claim that *theologies are fake systems of knowledge.* You shouldn't believe what any particular theology says about the nature of God, for exactly the same reason that you shouldn't believe what I say about the committee of eighty-nine invisible pink hippopotami that run the universe from a couch in my attic: there's no evidence—or nothing that in any other field of inquiry would count as evidence—either for or against them. And, since there are infinitely many things that *might* exist, though we have no evidence about them (to mention just ninety-one: any particular conception of God, the Blueberry Muffin at the Beginning of Time, and those hippos in my attic), it's hard to see how it makes sense to believe in any of them.

The island of Iona

You can find it off the west coast of Scotland, near Oban. It was an important monastic and scholarly center in the early Middle Ages— and it is beautiful. I visited it when I was fourteen, and remember the occasion all too clearly. The ferry from Mull was tiny. An exceptionally heavy swell was coming south down the sound. When my parents and I finally set foot on Iona, soaked to the skin, we were quite surprised to be alive.

Muon scanner?

Muon scanning is a cool idea dreamed up to check cargo containers for contraband and bombs. Also known as cosmic ray tomography, it doesn't quite exist yet in any practical sense, but we'll get there—and soon after we do, it will be adapted for medical scanning. Then, instead of making pictures by shooting X-rays through you, or using huge MRI magnets to pat down your atomic nuclei, a muon scanner will create images of your insides using naturally occurring muons—particles a bit like electrons that originate in deep space and are passing through your body all the time anyway.

Freddy Nietzsche

Friedrich Nietzsche lived in an age that was even more deeply impressed by the excellence of "man" (i.e., the human species) than we are today. He wasn't impressed at all—and, in *Thus Spake Zarathustra* (1885), he argued that humans as we currently understand them will be "surpassed" by Übermenschen (overmen, or supermen). These are *not* flying guys in capes; nor are they Nazi-style tyrants. Nietzsche thinks of them as exceptional people whose self-confidence, creativity, and courage will help humanity break free from what he sees as the suffocating constraints of guilt and self-loathing imposed on us by Christian morality.

Uncontacted indigenous groups

Around the world there are probably about a hundred groups of uncontacted people—those who have either totally avoided contact with the outside world or have actively resisted it. To find out more, visit www.uncontactedtribes.org and www.survivalinternational.org/tribes.

"Ni v pizdu"

I'm not going to translate this. Imagine starting with the expression "a load of crap," and then turning the crudeness dial all the way up to "Unprintable."

Pronouncing "Babel," translating babilani, and building ziggurats

I'm British, so I grew up saying *BAY-bl* (rhymes with *fable*). Most Americans are used to *BABB-l* (rhymes with *rabble*). British dictionaries go for the first pronunciation; most American dictionaries give both. Maybe we could all agree on a "correct" pronunciation if we knew how the Akkadians or Babylonians pronounced *babilani*. We don't, so pronounce it however you like.

The word *babilani* actually comes from Akkadian, the earlier language (and civilization) out of which Babylonian developed. The even earlier (Sumerian) name for the place was Etemenanki, which has a similar meaning. The usual translation of *Etemenanki* is "the house of the foundation of heaven and earth," which has the distinct disadvantage of not making sense. A better stab at the meaning might be something like "the place between heaven and earth."

The most magnificent version of the ziggurat at Babylon—the one that best fits Daniel's description—was finished around 600 BCE by King Nebuchadrezzar II. Just two centuries later, only a ruin remained. Alexander the Great pulled that down, planned to rebuild yet again, then got distracted by a sudden itch to invade India. He did get back to Babylon—but only for long enough to be poisoned by one of his own generals. The "Tower of Babel" never rose again.

The origin of the book of Genesis

Daniel gives just the one-sentence version of a complicated and controversial history. But most scholars seem to think that most of Genesis, including the Babel story, was written around 550 BCE, during the Babylonian Exile.

Noah, Utnapishtim, and all the others

The Nineveh tablets are from about 1200 BCE. The "Noah Version" of the story was first written down in roughly 600 BCE, or possibly as early as 800 BCE. So Utnapishtim precedes Noah by at least as much as Shakespeare precedes us. The oldest Sumerian flood narrative, featuring Ziusudra, goes back at least another five hundred years before that.

Akkad and Akkadian cuneiform

Cuneiform ("wedge-shaped") writing was developed by the Sumerians well before 3000 BCE, and was later adapted for many other languages, including Akkadian, Babylonian, Assyrian, Elamite, and Old Persian.

Why God destroyed the Tower

People often think the Babel story is all about the *height* of the Tower: God has a migraine because he thinks we are threatening to climb up, like Jack on his beanstalk, and invade heaven itself. This idea *is* in some versions of the story—but all we get from Genesis 11:6 is this: "And the Lord said, Behold, the people is one, and they have all one language; and this they begin to do: and now nothing will be restrained from them, which they have imagined to do." In modern English: *They've understood how powerful their unity makes them, and now they'll stop at nothing.* It's not clear from this exactly what the divine worry about Babel really is. You might ask, What's so bad about being united and building cities? But the Bible does not answer that question.

Obscenity and broadcasting

For an amusing account of our irrational attitudes to obscenity, especially as they relate to free speech, I recommend chapter 7 of Stephen Pinker's *The Stuff of Thought*, "The Seven Words You Can't Say on Television."

"The same idea comes up all over the world in different forms"
In the case of language origin myths, at least, there are many, many examples with remarkable similarities.

In *The World Until Yesterday*, Jared Diamond describes a myth from New Guinea involving a murderer who escapes into a tree with his relatives. When the relatives of his victim haul down the treetop using vines, the vines snap, and everyone in the tree is flung far and wide. When they land, they set up separate communities that have mutually unintelligible languages.

According to Andrew Dickinson White's *A History of the Warfare Between Science and Theology*, there's a Hindu story that neatly combines Babel and Eden. A tree grows too close to heaven, and the creator-god Brahma punishes it by turning it into many little trees; they are not big enough to shade all the people, who therefore divide into separate groups and come to have different languages.

The rediscovery of Troy
The Iliad, Homer's ancient epic about the siege of Troy, was widely believed to be a true story, well into the Middle Ages. It was only later that people started to get more "realistic" and dismiss it all as mythical. It took the archaeologists Charles Maclaren and Heinrich Schliemann, among others, to get us back to the more improbable, more romantic truth.

Noah's flood and the Black Sea theory
Geologists are pretty clear that a catastrophic flood, around 7,500–6,500 BCE, greatly increased the Black Sea's size: the Mediterranean broke through a narrow gap, spilling hundreds of cubic miles of seawater into what had been a lake. This may well have *something* to do with *some* flood mythology. But geologists disagree about whether this event happened suddenly or not, and anyway it's a poor source for Noah's story. Most of the flooding happened in the north, near

Odessa in modern Ukraine. Mount Ararat is two hundred miles southeast of the Black Sea, in an area that didn't flood at all.

The perhaps-not-mythical unicorn

In the interview, Morag is interrupted just as she's about to discuss the theory that the myth of the unicorn comes from actual human contact with *Elasmotherium*, a one-horned rhino that went extinct perhaps fifteen thousand years ago. It appears to be depicted in cave paintings, for instance at Rouffignac in France. *Elasmotherium* doesn't look a whole lot like a modern "unicorn," but stories do get garbled over fifteen thousand years.

Plato, mathematics, and the soul

Plato was impressed by the spooky power of mathematics, and his big philosophical idea is essentially the one that Iona, like most mathematicians, finds attractive. Maybe the world we experience through our senses isn't the real world at all, but rather a kind of illusion, or at best a mere shadow cast by the *real* real world—a realm hidden behind or beneath or beyond our experience that we can approach only through pure reason.

Part II: The Akkadian Version

"A stuffed giraffe called Lamarck"

Joke. Jean-Baptiste Lamarck (1744–1829) was responsible for the pre-Darwinian idea that animals evolve by inheriting "acquired characteristics"; thus, giraffes stretch their necks to get food, and giraffes with long necks give birth to offspring with long necks. This isn't true, but it isn't stupid either, and in fact Darwin himself didn't wholly reject Lamarck's theory. He just thought it was less important than the mechanism he proposed: natural selection.

Cicero at Rhodes

Cicero became one of the most influential writers and statesmen of all time, but he was only twenty-six in 80 BCE, and just starting out as a lawyer. When an enemy of the dictator Sulla was dragged into court and framed for the death of his own father, Cicero successfully defended him. Sulla's anger made Cicero fear for his own safety, and he went into a two-year self-imposed exile, visiting Athens, Asia Minor (Turkey), and then Rhodes. The connection I make later between his shopping habits, his return home, and an ancient shipwreck seems intriguingly plausible given the dates and the geography, but there's no other evidence for it.

The "guy named Posidonius," with whom Cicero met and studied at Rhodes, was in fact one of the most celebrated geniuses of the entire ancient world, spoken of in the same breath as Aristotle. He wrote voluminously on almost every subject and also traveled widely—so the project of collecting *diskoi* from all over the known world, which I ascribe to him here, is not so implausible. Alas, nearly all his writings are lost, so most people have never heard of him.

William Henry Seward

Seward was Lincoln's close friend and secretary of state, and in his own right a brave and persistent opponent of slavery. He also negotiated the purchase of Alaska from Russia. The statue in Seattle's Volunteer Park, which I walk past nearly every day, shows Seward with the 1867 Alaska treaty under his arm. The Wikipedia article on Seward originally claimed, plausibly, that the statue faces Alaska. My greatest contribution to human knowledge so far has been to correct this; in fact he faces south, with Alaska somewhere over his right shoulder.

Rijndael encryption

Pronounced *RIN-doll*, and also called AES (Advanced Encryption Standard), this is a widely used symmetric key algorithm for high-level encryption. But I only pretend to understand it, so please look it up and try for yourself.

Star Trek and plastic foreheads

Before you join in the scoffing—which I've been doing for years—check out Cambridge paleontologist Simon Conway Morris's book *Life's Solution*, in which he argues (contra Stephen Jay Gould and most biologists) that if complex life evolved independently on other planets, it would probably look a lot like us. Maybe the Trekkie scenario is right after all. *Live long and get this superglue off my fingers.*

Sherlock Holmes and the impossible

The famous line is, "How often have I said to you that when you have eliminated the impossible, whatever remains, however improbable, must be the truth?" (From *The Sign of Four*, 1890.) Like many things Holmes says, this seems to impress a lot of people—but then a lot of people don't stop to think.

For Holmes to "eliminate the impossible" is for him to judge that some explanations on his list cannot be true. But how can he know this, when his own knowledge is finite, and therefore the process by which he comes to such judgments must itself be fallible?

Here's an infamous example of the problem. In 1835, the French philosopher Auguste Comte announced with great confidence that "we shall never be able by any means to study the chemical composition of stars." (Savor that: *never by any means.*) Must have sounded like a safe bet, at the time, but German optical theorist Joseph Fraunhofer was *already working on* the process—stellar spectroscopy—that within a generation would allow us to do just that.

As this suggests, the "Comte problem" is really two separate problems for Sherlock. He's wrong to think he can ever be confident that an option on his list is impossible. But he's also wrong to think that what remains, after discounting the "impossible," is a complete list: what about all the options that his lack of knowledge (or imagination) has caused him to exclude from the list in the first place?

Watson may seem stupid compared to Sherlock, but he's mainly just weak-kneed. He should have fought back a bit harder against literature's most successful intellectual bully.

Archimedes, "naked and roaring"

There's no evidence for the famous story about him leaping out of the bath, but it's irresistible in any of its several forms. According to the Roman writer Vitruvius, the king asked Archimedes to determine whether the new royal crown had been adulterated with silver, or was pure gold. Archimedes puzzled for a long time over how to do this, and the "eureka moment" was realizing that because a crown of pure gold is denser, it will displace less water than an alloy crown of identical weight. Verdict: probably fiction. Galileo himself heard the story and dismissed it on the grounds that the difference in volume would have been too small for Archimedes to measure. Others think Archimedes was merely noticing that any submerged object displaces a volume of liquid equal to its own volume. A third idea, which gets my vote, is that the "eureka moment" was really Archimedes discovering his great principle of buoyancy: not just that an object displaces its own volume, but that it is buoyed upward by a *force* equal to the weight of the *liquid* it displaces.

Perhaps it doesn't matter which version is true: any way you look at it, Archimedes was so far ahead of everyone else that he was probably from another planet.

"Lowered down to us from heaven"

That kingship—and the whole notion of submitting to the authority of a ruler—was a "gift" from the gods, is an idea from a real source: the Sumerian King List, a document that survives in various forms and fragments, notably on the cuneiform Weld-Blundell Prism in Oxford's Ashmolean Museum.

The date of Atlantis
According to the version in Plato's *Critias*, it all happened nine thousand years before Solon—but it has been suggested that Solon got his Egyptian wrong, and the priest really said "nine hundred." It needs to be nine hundred to a thousand, roughly, for my purposes—but that's fine, since these dates all have pretty much the flavor of "like, dude, a really long time ago."

PART III: HOME OF THE GODS

Casaubon, "a character in a novel"
Middlemarch, by George Eliot. "MDCCCLXXI" is 1871—the year Eliot began to publish the book in a serial version.

Krakatoa, "a zit compared to Thera"
The destruction of Krakatoa in 1883 unleashed two or three cubic miles of rock and ash, triggered tsunamis that killed thirty-six thousand people, made a noise that was heard as far away as Australia and the island of Réunion, and produced a shock wave that traveled seven times around the world. Thera's eruption was thought to have been "only" three or four times that big, until a study in 2006 raised the estimated size of the ejection to around fourteen cubic miles. If that's right, Thera was the third-largest explosion in recorded history, beaten only by Tambora, Indonesia (1815) and Changbaishan, China (ca. 1000).

The Antikythera wreck(s)
While I was planning, researching, and writing this book, several coincidences occurred that you probably won't believe. The most

amazing to me was this: in the summer of 2012, I decided for fictional purposes that there would turn out to be two ships (*skaphe*) at the Antikythera site; three or four months later, a team from the Woods Hole Oceanographic Institution led a new dive investigation at the site which found evidence suggesting exactly that. For photos of the 2012 dive, use the search phrase "Return to Antikythera" and look for the photo archive of *The Guardian*.

Eratosthenes and the size of the Earth

Eratosthenes's calculation was based on reports that there was a deep well at the town of Syene (modern Aswan), in the bottom of which you could see the sun's reflection at noon on the solstice. (In other words, the sun was directly overhead.) He also knew that the sun was about seven degrees off vertical at that same time where he lived, in Alexandria. After estimating the distance from Aswan to Alexandria, he concluded that the earth must be about twenty-five thousand miles in circumference. This staggeringly good estimate was partly due to accurate measurement, and partly due to luck: some of the errors in his data cancel each other out.

The Antikythera Mechanism

Professional archaeologists brought many treasures from the Antikythera wreck to the surface, including a blue glass bowl that somehow, miraculously, spent almost two thousand years underwater without sustaining more than a few scratches. But the "mangled chunk of metal" was so mangled that for a long time after the salvage operation it sat in a warehouse without anyone noticing that it might be unusual or interesting.

When they did notice, it appeared, absurdly, to be a mechanical clock, like something that belonged on the mantelpiece in a Victorian living room. It had wheels, hands, levers, dials, and more than thirty interconnecting gears. After the archaeologists had finished with the

X-rays and reconstructions, it turned out to be the world's first—or first-known—analog computer.

EPILOGUE

Seeing in the Dark
It seemed appropriate to steal the title of this section from Timothy Ferris's excellent book on the culture of amateur astronomy. Informative, lyrically beautiful science writing—read him.

Some Dates

Most of these are accurate, at least approximately. A few are mere conjecture. One or two are unmitigated fiction.

7000–6000 BCE: A new civilization emerges in the eastern Mediterranean, at the island known as Strongyle. Strict social hierarchies emerge for the first time, along with city-building, written language, and the first organized religion. For at least a thousand years, the civilization develops in isolation; then a powerful priestly caste begins exporting its language, and its revolutionary new religious and cultural ideas, across the eastern Mediterranean and Mesopotamia.

5000 BCE (not, as previously believed, 1600 BCE): Approximate date that the so-called Phaistos Disks were made, according to William Calder's measurements.

5000–4000 BCE: First wave of city-building, combined with massive population increases, across the ancient world.

4000–3200 BCE: True writing emerges in Sumer, the Indus Valley, early Minoan Crete, and Egypt.

3000–1200 BCE: Minoan culture flourishes on Crete.

2800–2500 BCE: City of Akkad founded in Mesopotamia; Akkadian (the parent language of both Assyrian and Babylonian) emerges as a distinct language; explosive growth in the number of languages in the region, including Assyrian, Babylonian, Minoan, Proto-Elamite, and possibly many others that are now lost.

2700 BCE: Gilgamesh is king of Uruk, in Mesopotamia; the Elamite civilization and language emerge on the northeast coast of the Persian Gulf.

2560 BCE: Great Pyramid of Khufu built at Giza in Egypt.

2300 BCE: Akkadian Empire under Sargon the Great controls most of central Mesopotamia.

1770 BCE: Babylon is at the height of its power under Hammurabi; a massive influx of people to Strongyle begins, from Greece, Crete, North Africa, and as far away as Mesopotamia.

1628 BCE: Destruction of Strongyle.

1327 BCE: Death of Tutankhamun; approximate date of the original ziggurat at Babylon.

1250–1150 BCE: The Bronze Age Collapse, which includes the destruction of Troy and about fifty other cities, causes a massive drop in population throughout the eastern Mediterranean; the Nineveh "Deluge Tablets" from the Epic of Gilgamesh are dated from this time; the Harappan civilization of the Indus Valley also suffers massive population loss at this time, and then collapses.

600 BCE: The great ziggurat at Babylon is rebuilt for the last time.

560–550 BCE: Authorship of the book of Genesis by Jewish scholars during their exile in Babylon; the Roman statesman Solon visits Egypt and hears the story of Atlantis.

399 BCE: The Athenian soldier, historian, and philosopher Xenophon takes part in the epic retreat from Mesopotamia of the Army of the Ten Thousand and describes his experiences in the original *Anabasis*; back in Athens, the philosopher Socrates, a relentless critic of Athenian society, is executed for "corrupting the youth" and "teaching false gods."

360 BCE: Socrates's student, Plato, mentions Solon's story about Atlantis in his dialogues *Timaeus* and *Critias*; meanwhile he is developing his massively influential idea that the "real" world is in fact an illusion, or at best a mere shadow of something else.

285 BCE: Eratosthenes is born at Kyrene, on the coast of modern Libya.

260 BCE: Greek mathematician and inventor Archimedes is living at Syracuse, in Sicily.

240 BCE: While serving as the librarian of the great library at Alexandria, the Greek polymath Eratosthenes is visited by his friend Archimedes; the Antikythera Mechanism is created at about this date.

230 BCE: Eratosthenes writes the *Geographika*; only a few copies are ever made.

79 BCE: The great Roman lawyer, orator, and statesman Marcus Tullius Cicero visits the island of Rhodes and meets the Greek philosopher, educator, and collector Posidonius, who owns probably the last surviving copy of Eratosthenes's *Geographika*.

78 BCE: On their way from Rhodes to Rome, two little elm-planked merchant ships sink in a storm, just a stone's throw from Point Glyphadia, off the island of Antikythera; two thousand years later, in 1900, one of them will become the first shipwreck from the ancient world ever found.

250–300 CE: Neoplatonism puts an explicitly religious spin on Plato's idea that the soul, spirit, or mind has to be released from the corrupt prison of the body in order to find its way to the truth/the realm of Forms/enlightenment/heaven.

900–1000 CE: Collapse of the Maya Empire in Central America and the Aksumite Empire in northeast Africa; building of Monk's Mound, Cahokia, Illinois.

1200–1400 CE: Collapse of Khmer and Angkor Empires; collapse or disappearance of the Sinagua, Anasazi, and Fremont cultures in North America; end of the Mound Builder cultures in the American Midwest.

1400–1800 CE: The cultures of the central Amazon Basin build sophisticated urban civilizations and are able to sustain a population of over ten million people; by the mid-nineteenth century, nearly all of them have vanished, and Europeans will discover what they believe to be virgin jungle.

1500 CE: Extinction of the Greenland Vikings.

1872 CE (December 3): George Smith presents his translation of the "Deluge Tablets"—part of the Epic of Gilgamesh—to the Society of Biblical Archaeology in London.

1874 CE: Heinrich Schliemann publishes his claim to have rediscovered Homer's "mythical" Troy at Hisarlik in Turkey.

1900 CE: Sir Arthur Evans begins to uncover a great building at Knossos on Crete, identifies it as the palace of King Minos, and names as Minoan the previously unknown civilization that built it.

1908 CE: Luigi Pernier discovers the original Phaistos Disk at a Minoan palace in southern Crete.

1952 CE: After decades of work by Michael Ventris, Alice Kober, and others, the riddle of the Minoan Linear B script is solved. Despite the strange script, it is not an unknown language, but a very early form of Greek. The other famous Minoan script, Linear A, remains a mystery—along with Rongorongo, Proto-Elamite, the Indus Valley script, and several other scripts known only from fragments.

ABOUT THE AUTHOR

© David Hiller

Richard Farr is a recovering philosopher.

His first book, *Emperors of the Ice: A True Story of Disaster and Survival in the Antarctic, 1910–13*, describes the legendary 1911 Winter Journey on Ross Island. It won both a Washington State Book Award and a starred Outstanding Book listing from the National Science Teachers Association. Reviewers have described it as "spellbinding," "enthralling," and "so gripping you will not want to put it down."

Richard has also published a short introduction to science, *You Are Here: A User's Guide to the Universe*, and a novel about obsession, art forgery, murder, and madness, *The Truth about Constance Weaver*. He is currently working on three new projects: Book Two of the Babel Trilogy; a middle-grade novel set in the thirteenth-most-boring place in the world (*A Plague of Frogs*); and a memoir (*What I Expected: A Love Letter Written During a Panic Attack*).

Like some of the characters in this book, he lives in Seattle's Capitol Hill neighborhood, enjoys the coffee at Espresso Vivace and Victrola, and gets his hair cut at Scream. More at www.richardfarr.net.